kop

TOR BOOKS BY WARREN HAMMOND

KOP
EX-KOP (forthcoming)

"kop"

WARREN HAMMOND

TOR®

A Tom Doherty Associates Book
New York

KOP

Edited by James Frenkel

A Tor Book
Published by Tom Doherty Associates, LLC
175 Fifth Avenue
New York, NY 10010

www.tor.com

Tor® is a registered trademark of Tom Doherty Associates, LLC.

Library of Congress Cataloging-in-Publication Data

Hammond, Warren.
    Kop / Warren Hammond.—1st ed.
      p.   cm.
    "A Tom Doherty Associates Book."
    ISBN-13: 978-0-7653-1272-3
    ISBN-10: 0-7653-1272-7
    I. Title.
    PS3608.A69585K67   2007
    813'.6—dc22

2007009544

First Edition: July 2007

Printed in the United States of America

0 9 8 7 6 5 4 3 2 1

With love and respect,
I dedicate this first novel to the first novelist in the family,
my uncle, Clyde Farnsworth.

acknowledgments

I HONESTLY have no idea how many hours it took to complete this story, but I can safely say that it's a big, big number. Day after day, month after month, I toiled away in solitude, lost in a world of my own making, wondering if there was any chance that the novel I was writing would ever get published. On the rare occasion that I came up for air, I shared whatever I'd written up to that point with friends, family, and eventually professionals in the publishing industry. Without exception, I was received warmly and encouraged to continue, a kindness I'm not likely to forget. I'd like to recognize some of these people now. Without them, this book simply wouldn't exist. Richard Curtis, Suzanne Czech, Clyde Farnsworth, Jim Frenkel, Kathy Gansemer, Rachel Hutson, Lisa Ledet, Jean Monforton, Elisavietta Ritchie, Jim Sailer, Shawn Stugart, Jamie Sudler, Julie Wahlstrom, George Whelpley, John Whelpley, and Ruth Whelpley, I sincerely thank each and every one of you. Your feedback and support are evident on every page.

kop

one

THE place was almost empty. There were two boozers split-ting a bottle at the far end of the bar and a gray-haired woman with her head on a table, out cold with an empty glass in her hand. The windows were closed up tight. The aircon was blow-ing full.

Bensaid and I were standing face to face, the bar standing between us. Bensaid was the owner of this rat hole. He ripped off his patrons by cutting his brandy with water. He kept a bot-tle capper in the back room that he'd use to seal the bottles back up so you couldn't tell.

"You better not be holding out on me," I said as I pocketed the thin wad of bills, too thin.

"You don't trust me? You know I wouldn't short you." Ben-said tried to look offended.

"Bullshit. Where is the rest of my money?"

"Son of a bitch!" He slammed his drink glass on the bar, splashing brandy up onto his bushy arm. "I'm sick of your bitchin', comin' in here every month 'cusin' me of this shit. It's all there. Count the fuckin' money yourself you don't believe me!"

The pair at the far end of the bar looked our way. Gray-hair didn't flinch.

I should've smashed the glass into the side of his face. Forced him to count aloud as I laid out one bill at a time—prick thought he could cheat me! When I was younger, I wouldn't have hesitated. I used to be KOP's ass-stomper supreme, but that was a young man's game. These days, I'd just make my collections and try to stay out of trouble. Besides, I wasn't as quick as I used to be.

I patted his cheek, all cool. "Why didn't you just tell me it was all there? That's all I need to hear."

Bensaid glared at me, pissed times ten. First I'd accused him of cheating, and now I was pulling this fake nicey-nice shit on him, saying, "Why didn't you just tell me it was all there?" If I wasn't a cop, he would've jumped me already or pulled out that shockstick he kept back there for bouncing rowdies out of his dive when they got carried away.

"See ya next month," I said, grinning in his face . . . extra long . . . then I turned my back on him and walked out of the bar snail-slow. *I dare you to jump me, you fuck.*

The truth was I wanted to count the money as soon as he forked it over. My right hand shook, and all I needed was for a bastard like that to see and start thinking I was old and weak. I'd first noticed that I couldn't hold it steady a few years ago. When I'd gotten it checked out, I learned it was a degenerative thing, caused by a twenty-five-year-old injury. Nowadays, I'd keep my right in my pocket most of the time. People around here would walk all over you if they saw you had a weak spot.

The heat hammered me when I hit the street. Lagarto's sun had been up for a couple hours. The thin cloud cover didn't do much to minimize the late morning sun scorch. I could feel the prickle of sweat breaking out on my forehead as I headed down the block. I should've started my rounds earlier. I was getting too old to be out in this shit. One of these days, I'd have to face facts and hang it up, turn in my shield, and take Niki out of the city. She'd been after me to quit. We had all the money we'd ever need, but I just couldn't get the job out of my system. What else would I do?

I crossed the street, weaving between the puddles and piles of rotting garbage. Geckos scattered out of my way, running for cover under green weeds that had pushed up through the rippled pavement. Every few months, the city would come through on a slash-and-burn. They used to poison the encroaching jungle growth until people started to notice tumor-ridden fish belly-up in the Koba River. Citizens' groups got worked up over their health and forced the city to change methods. Now, they blasted the streets with flamethrowers, crisping anything green, leaving only the smoldering stench of burned trash and vegetation in their wake.

I rounded the corner and strode into Li's Parlor to hit up Li for my cut. The entryway was done up in Asian silks, reds and golds. The aircon was blowing in my face. I fanned my shirt to get some of the cool inside. One of Li's women led me back to the lounge. On the left was a bar where the johns would knock back a couple before heading upstairs; on the right, velvet sofas were backed against the wall. They were used to display the merchandise.

Li's Parlor was one of a thousand snatch houses on this planet. We were experts at drawing tourists down to Lagarto from the Orbital and the mines, feeding them some hot tail, and relieving them of their offworld dollars.

Li was counting pesos at the bar. Rouge and caked-on lipstick both feminized and anglicized his Asian features. His hair was in a net, too early for the wig.

"Juno!" He singsonged my name.

"Hello, Li."

"It's so nice to see you. Would you like to join me for some tea?"

"Not today, I'm running behind schedule."

"Why are you always in such a rush?"

I shrugged a response.

"You must come back this evening. I have two new girls. One is just your type . . . tall and quiet with a real wild streak. You have to let me earn back some of the money I give you every month."

"Sounds interesting, but I don't think the wife would let me."

"Oh, stop it!" He mock slapped me. "Mr. Tough Cop turns into a little kitten at night? I don't believe that. My mother used to tell me stories about you."

Li's mother used to run the joint before she'd died.

"That was a long time ago," I said.

"That wife of yours won't mind if you get your main course at home and get your dessert at Li's." His eyelids fluttered. "Are you still worried she'll be upset? I'll tell you what, if she feels left out, you can bring her along. You can still handle two women at a time, can't you, Juno?"

Smiling, I said, "I'll have to ask her, Li."

"You tell her first-timers are free."

"How's business?" That was my usual signal; it said I was done with the small talk.

"You know how it is." He passed me an envelope. No need to count, Li always played it straight . . . so to speak. "I have to let Ramona go. You know how offworlders are. They keep wanting them younger and younger."

I shook my head in that what-can-you-do way.

"I just can't make sense of it, Juno. Those mines are booming, and I still have to let her go. I'm telling you, the market for mature women is dying. More than half my girls are in their teens now. You know how old Ramona is? She's twenty-seven. She started here when she was nineteen. That's only eight years, Juno. How's a girl supposed to earn enough money to set herself up after only eight years? It used to be, a girl could have a fifteen- or even twenty-year run."

I nodded my head in agreement.

"It's not fair," he said like a spoiled kid. "I don't know how Ramona's going to make it."

Christ, here we go. Li wants me to lower his rate. "So slip her a bonus before you kick her out."

"If I had the money, I would, but I'm just barely making it as it is." Li leaned in close. "Ben Bandur is squeezing me dry, Juno." Benazir Bandur was Koba's kingpin, the top dog in this town. The Bandur cartel took a piece of all the rackets . . . just like us cops.

I grinned at him. "So it sounds like you need to talk to Bandur, get him to cut you some slack."

He knew I was screwing with him. The Bandur outfit had never been known to show mercy. He put his hands on his hips. "Be serious."

"Just raise your prices," I said.

Li poo-pooed. "I've already tried that, but I started losing customers. You don't understand how fierce the competition is. Heck, you know what they always say about this planet?"

"What's that?"

" 'Come to Lagarto, where you'll be welcomed with open legs.' "

I smiled as if it were the first time I'd ever heard it.

Li said, "It's so true, Juno. You've seen it. You know how bad things have gotten. Shoot, these days, an offworlder can go into just about any bar and get a roll with the owner's daughter or some skank runaway for a cut rate. Sure, the service isn't anywhere near as good, but you know how offworlders are. They've spent five or ten years flying in from some star or another. They're already popping erections when they get off the shuttles."

"C'mon, Li. It's not that bad."

"Oh, yes it is! After five years, they'd bang a beehive."

"But you said yourself that the mines are booming. Those

guys come down from the asteroid belts every year. *Every year.*
And there's more of them all the time. You can't expect me to
believe you can't make your payments. We both know you've
got plenty saved up. You could set Ramona up for life if you
wanted to."

"It's not like that, Juno. Do you see this place? It's falling
apart." Li lifted one of the silks, showing the molded-over wall
that stood behind it. As he poked at the soggy parts, crumbling
clumps of plaster fell to the floor. "I'm telling you, I'm flat
broke. You've always been fair to me and my mother. Just tell
me you can help my girls. It's them I'm worried about. You
can make an exception for Li's girls, can't you? I won't ask for
much." He batted his lashes.

"When are you letting Ramona go?"

"Today."

"Let me talk to her."

Li stepped out, coming back ten minutes later with Ramona
on his elbow. "I just told her the news and helped her pack her
things," he said. He sat her down next to him, his arm around
her shoulder. Ramona was looking scared and teary-eyed, and
she had a sloppily packed carpetbag resting on her lap. She was
rubbing the back of her arm where Li had probably pinched
her to get those tears flowing.

"Do you have a place to stay?" I asked her.

"I have a sister," she said.

"See what you're making me do to her?" Li said. "This kind
of thing is going to keep happening if I don't get some financial relief."

I pulled the money from the envelope Li had given me. "Go
find your sister," I said as I handed Ramona the cash. To Li, I
said, "I'll see *you* next month."

✣

I was back on the street. The heat hung heavy on my shoulders. Sweat dribbled down my back. I cut down an alley. Geckos ran rampant on jungle-crept walls. Some street kids spotted me and scrambled to hide their glue jars—huffers. I didn't pay them any mind. They were too poor to afford the good stuff.

Next stop: Fusco's. He ran a gambling den on the roof of his apartment building. I'd heard he put up some tarps so he could stay open rain or shine. Sounded like more profit to me. We'd have to hash out a new rate.

Phone rang. The display told me it was Paul Chang, chief of the Koba Office of Police. Officially, he had been running the show for more than ten years; unofficially, he had for over twice that long. Twenty-five years ago, we were partners.

"Yeah," I said.

Paul's smiling hologram appeared alongside and kept step with me. It didn't move its legs. It just skimmed along like some freaky ghost. "I need you to work a case."

"What kind of case?"

"Homicide."

No good. There was no money in homicide. Sure, sometimes you could land a big payoff when somebody wanted you to lose some evidence, but emotions ran high on homicides. You could never tell what was going to happen. A lot of cops would look at the big payoffs and buck for spots in homicide, but they wouldn't think about the risks. Murders were mostly poor-on-poor anyway, no money to be made from either side. The real money was in vice, where I'd been for almost my whole career. No major scores, but low risk and steady income.

"Send Josephs and Kim," I said.

"They're already at the crime scene. I don't want them working this one. I need *you*."

"Why?"

"Quit jerkin' me, Juno. You taking the case or what?" The expression on Holo-Paul didn't match Real-Paul's clearly annoyed tone. Instead, it smiled personably. That was why I hated this holographic shit. They'd scan your looks into the system so they could construct an image that looked like you and beam it from the Orbital to anywhere on the planet. Sounded good until you found out that they didn't adjust the image to your emotional state. They'd just give your holo this canned, perpetually pleasant attitude. Somewhere in Paul's office was a happy-go-lucky me, smiling and acting all cheery instead of showing my actual sweaty and out-of-breath mug.

Paul wanted me to take a case. Reasons to say no ticked through my mind . . . I'm behind on my collections . . . I made lunch plans with Niki . . . I don't enforce for you anymore. Instead, I asked, "Who's the vic?"

"He's an Army guy."

"Where?"

"The alley outside the Lotus."

I knew the place, a snatch house a few klicks from here. "Be there in twenty."

"I'm partnering you up on this one."

"You've got to be kidding me. No way, Paul."

"She's new. She needs to learn the ropes."

"Are you nuts? No way I'm taking on a green."

"Listen, there's nothing I can do. She has family pulling strings."

I started to cave. "How green?" I asked.

"This is her first case."

"First homicide?"

"No, first case."

"First case! Holy shit, Paul. I don't care who her family is. I'm out." I accelerated my pace, but Holo-Paul stayed right on my hip.

"I know how it sounds, but she's tough, and she has a good head on her shoulders. Without her family greasing things, she'd still make detective as fast as anybody. You have to do this one for me, Juno."

"I work alone, Paul."

"Listen, we can talk about this later. I'll send her out to meet you at the Lotus. Her name's Maggie Orzo. You check her out, scope out the crime scene, then come by my office, and we'll talk it out."

"No."

"Juno?"

two

I COULDN'T say no to Paul. I'd do anything for him, and he'd do the same for me. That was the way we were. The reason that it was usually Paul who was doing the asking, and me doing the doing was simply because he had far more ambition than I did. He was the one that had set out to change the world all those years ago. I'd just gone along for the ride.

It was too hot to walk, and I'd left my car at home, so I hopped into a taxi that smelled like the inside of a brandy bottle. Jiggling tassels hung down with decorative panache from the top of the windshield. The dash was covered by shiny decals of the Virgin Mary in various poses, all with bigger than normal eyes and a smaller than normal nose—supposed to make her look noble and compassionate at the same time . . . hard to look noble on a shiny decal.

I was bounced about as the driver jerked the car down Koba's traffic-choked streets. He followed a ribbon of flood-warped pavement that ran flush with the river. I looked out the window. The garbage-littered riverbanks were peppered with adults napping under makeshift lean-tos while their kids panhandled on the road. On the river, fishermen in docked boats gutted their morning catch and tossed entrails into the water, setting off the splashing frenzies of monitors fighting for the free meal. The gator-sized reptiles thrashed in the black water, creating a roiling mass of whipping tails and snapping jaws.

The Lotus Club was on the other side of the river. We hit a

jam-up just before the bridge intersection. It looked like a car accident. Two drivers were out of their cars, screaming at each other, their faces red with the strain. The fading aircon threatened to suffocate us until the driver dropped the windows. Children immediately reached into the cab with their palms up. I looked straight ahead.

I called Niki. Her happy-to-see-me hologram sat next to me as I told her I wouldn't make lunch. I hung up without telling her why. I'd try to finesse that one later. She didn't want me taking any risks. She was always telling me I was getting too old for it.

The car accident cleared, and the driver gunned it over one of the half dozen riblike bridges that arced up over the city's backbone, the Koba River. Rejuvenated aircon pumped out the chill as I took in the city, a haphazard sprawl that sat buried under a wavy brown cloud of polluted jungle haze. Koba was Lagarto's capital city, its one and only political, cultural, and economic center. My eyes scanned from neighborhood to neighborhood, each one bordered by canals that spiderwebbed through the city, evidence of our once proud agricultural history.

An offworld vehicle suddenly screamed by, putting a lump in my throat. Sons of bitches thought they owned the road with their accident-proof cars. Only the most filthy rich could afford an offworld vehicle. Lagarto was the victim of a galactic-sized trade imbalance that made the purchase of offworld products next to impossible. Almost everybody on this backwater planet was forced to live a life absent of offworld tech.

Shit, when I was a kid, the only ways to get around were boats, bikes, and feet. It wasn't until some enterprising businessmen began manufacturing these antique cars that we finally had an almost affordable mode of transportation. These things were practically medieval, fossil-fuel powered and human navigated. And they came in only three accident-prone models: car, truck, and bus. If you smashed one up, they'd just hammer out the dents and hose off your blood to get it ready for the next owner. Not many people owned one, but cabs and buses were now accessible to all but the severely poor, of whom we had plenty.

Arriving at the Lotus, I used my left to drop a five-hundred on the driver, keep the change. The morgue boys had already arrived and were waiting in the shade. A couple beat cops blocked the public from the alley. They stepped aside when I flashed my badge.

The Lotus Club kept a low profile. You entered from the alley, not the street. There was no sign over the door and no ground-level windows. They catered to a higher-class crowd than most whorehouses. Their customers liked discretion. I went past the entrance then back behind the cooling unit. Homicide dicks Josephs and Kim were chatting in the shade.

Detective Mark Josephs was a thirty-year man. He had worked with me in vice for many years before moving to homicide. Back then, he wouldn't take his payoffs in cash. Instead, he'd take his cut in the form of drugs and hookers.

Josephs got in serious trouble back in '83. It started when he hit a dealer up for some pills. The dumb-shit dealer got confused and gave Josephs a flat from the wrong stash. Dealers would keep two stashes. The good stuff was for the regulars, and they'd unload the cheap shit on offworlders. What were the chances of meeting an offworlder twice? They were all just passing through.

A few days later, some street cops got called in on reports of a drug-crazed freak at the Royal Hotel. They found a naked Detective Mark Josephs face down on the lobby sofa, humping away at the cushions. The cops tried but couldn't talk him down from his bad-trip high. Finally, they dragged his naked ass out across the lobby floor. They brought him down to the station, sedated him, then slapped a prison jumpsuit on him and tossed him into the padded room.

Come morning, he woke up puzzled to find himself locked up with cuff-bruised wrists and rug burn raspberries dotting his face. Cops crammed around his cell. "Nice jumper." "Hey, Josephs. When did you start headlining at the Royal!" "You go queer yet?"

When they cut him loose, he came up to vice on the third, grabbed a cup of coffee, and sat down at his desk like always. His partner asked, "You okay, Mark?"

"Yeah. It just stings when I pee. Rug burn."

We all broke up. Then back to business as usual.

That night, Josephs caught up with the pusher that dealt him the bad pills. He beat him with a copper pipe and put him in a coma. It turned out the dealer was a minor. The public threw a fit. You know, police brutality. Had the dealer been an adult, nobody would have cared—one less drug-dealing lowlife on the streets.

As chief of the Koba Office of Police, Paul Chang had to move fast. He'd always said we couldn't have the public losing faith in KOP. There was always an anticorruption faction in the city government, and if they got hold of this, it could threaten the police empire the two of us had built two decades earlier. He hurried to put a story together: Josephs saw the dealer making a score. He didn't know he was a minor. It was too dark. The kid resisted arrest and fell during the struggle, hitting his head on the pavement. Josephs was only too happy to play along.

Paul sent me to the hospital to do some intimidation— medical style. After a five-minute scare session with a doctor and a defibrillator, the docs rewrote the charts to match Paul's cover story. That was my last rough-up job before I went to

Paul and told him I didn't have the heart for it anymore. At first, he fought me on it, saying I was betraying him. I told him he owed me. For twenty years, I'd done the dirty work. The blood was always on my hands. He tried to tell me to get over myself. He said he was the one who made all the tough calls. All that blood was on his hands, not mine. Fuck that, I told him. I had to *face* them. He was just the general giving orders. I was the soldier, the executioner. There was no comparison. When I finally made him understand the toll it was taking on me, he relented and recruited some new heavies for himself, categorizing me as "ass-stomping inactive." He still sent the occasional bagman job or frame job my way, but other than that I was strictly a collections man.

As for the Josephs situation, Paul sent the news station some KOP-approved vids of the kid. The vids showed concerned-looking doctors hovering over the hospital bed. Tubes ran from the kid's mouth to a ventilator that pumped his chest up and down. White blankets covered him from the neck down. One bandage was strategically placed on his head to match the fake single-head-trauma story. The pictures didn't show the broken ribs, legs, or arm. You couldn't see the punctured lung, ruptured liver, or internal bleeding.

To make it look good, Josephs was suspended for thirty days and transferred from vice to homicide. Paul told the press how they put every officer through a two-hour refresher course on proper restraint techniques to "prevent further unfortunate accidents like this one." Paul's out-and-out mastery of public manipulation never ceased to amaze me.

Paul put Josephs in rehab, out of the public eye. He told him he had thirty days to clean up his act or else. . . .

As for the kid, he died before the suspension was up.

These days Mark Josephs partnered with Detective Yuan Kim. I didn't know Kim that well. What I did know was this: Kim was second-generation police. His father and uncle were both cops. His pop did twenty in homicide. He and I crossed paths a few times over the years. Good cop. His uncle was a beat cop for his whole career. When Kim joined the force, Daddy pulled strings to get him a stint as a beat cop in the Northwest Quarter. We're talking seriously soft duty, rich neighborhoods with nothing but burglaries and domestic disputes. He made detective in record time and was assigned to homicide just like his father. Cops didn't respect him. They said he never did shit to get that job. They thought he was living off his father's name.

Josephs shook my hand. I pulled it out of my pocket fast, quick shake, back in. Josephs looked wired, eyes on fire. He was probably back on stims. "Juno, how ya doin'? Haven't seen you in a while."

"Okay." Straight to business. "What do we have so far?"

Yuan Kim's face was soaked in sweat. His glasses slipped down his nose. "What the hell's goin' on, Juno? Why are you taking over our case? You haven't worked a hommy in ten years."

"Take it up with the chief."

Josephs said, "The chief put you on this? Does he know the vic or what?"

"Beats me. He just said he wanted me to work this stiff."

"You still takin' care of his dirty laundry, Juno? I know you two are still buds, but enough is enough. I'd tell him to fuck off and take care of his own shit."

Kim wiped his forehead with his index finger and flicked the sweat to the ground. "This is bullshit. Chang can't just take our case and give it to a vice cop. No offense, Juno, but this is our case."

Josephs scoffed at his partner. "Get over it, Kim. We got three missing-persons cases to work. If the chief wants Juno to work this one, fine by me. I just don't see what Juno gets out of workin' a homicide after all this time."

I was getting irritated. "Leave that to me, okay? What I do is my business. I don't need you humps telling me this is fucked up. I already know that."

Josephs said, "That's cool, Juno. No need to get pissy. We're all on the same side. Isn't that right, Kim?"

"Yeah, that's right." He said it in an unconvincing mumble.

I asked, "You guys know a detective named Maggie Orzo?"

Yuan Kim replied, "Yeah, but she's no detective. She's fresh out of the academy."

"She's a detective now. The chief's partnering me up with her on this one."

Josephs started chuckling. "Holy shit. Hooking you up with a rookie on a murder case? First, I thought Chang was using you as his errand boy. Now, I think he must be punishing you. That or he's gone fucking ape shit. I never heard of anything so crazy in my life."

"What's she like, Kim?"

He pushed his glasses up his nose. They just slid back down. "She's solid. Smart and tough. Still, I think she's a little green for a job like this."

"A little?" Josephs was winding up. "She's a *rookie*. Juno's gonna have to work twice as hard just to keep her from screwing things up. Hell, she's gonna start puking the minute she sees that body."

Kim shook his head, "She's not like that, Mark. You don't even know her. I'm telling you, she's solid."

"What the hell you talkin' about? You got a crush on her or what?"

"No." Kim said it too fast. It came off defensive. "I'm just saying she's not your typical rookie. She's got a way about her."

"Shit, you're in love with her, aren't you? You believe this shit, Juno?"

Kim was getting flushed. "Fuck you, Mark. I am *not* in love with her. She's just not what you think. She's not the type to lose her shit just because she sees a corpse, okay?"

"She's comin' here, right, Juno? This is gonna be good. I can't wait to see her on her knees heaving her guts out. Hey, Kim, you gonna hold her hair back?"

"She's not going to puke."

"You wanna put some money on that?"

"I told you she's not going to puke."

"I got five thousand says your girlfriend is going to blow her breakfast all over this alley. You want in on this, Juno?"

I said, "No way, I don't want any part of this. I have to work with her."

Josephs prodded. "C'mon, Kim. You in or not?"

"Five thou?"

"Yeah five . . . whatever you want. I don't give a shit."

"You're on. Five thousand."

"Yes! You sure you don't want in on this, Juno?"

"I'm sure. Now, can we move on? Fill me in."

Kim pushed up his glasses and held them in place for a few seconds. "We don't know much yet. You know Rose?"

She ran the Lotus. "Yeah."

"She called it in two hours ago. One of her whores came out here bringing out the trash. She spotted the body and tossed the trash—" He paused to point to a bag on the ground. "—then ran back in, literally screaming bloody murder."

I wiped my brow. "The chief told me he's Army."

"Yeah, we bagged the vic's wallet. He's an officer." Kim checked his pad. "Lieutenant Dmitri Vlotsky. No cash in the wallet. Could have been a robbery, but I doubt it. Whoever it was butchered him pretty bad."

A female voice came up behind me. "Excuse me, I'm looking for Detective Mozambe."

"I'm Juno Mozambe."

"Hello, I'm Maggie Orzo." She put her hand out for a shake. I shook hands with her. I made it a quick shake, and I made sure to say something at the same time so she wouldn't notice my quaky hand. "Nice to meet you, Detective Orzo."

"You better call me Maggie if we're going to be partners."

Partners. We'll see about that. "Maggie it is," I said.

I could see right away why Yuan Kim had eyes for her. She was young with a confident smile and her hair was done up in the latest style. She was wearing a stylish outfit that made her look far too nice to be a cop. Cops didn't wear "outfits." Her most striking feature was her eyes, which were a stunning sky blue. Her dark hair and olive complexion told me those eyes couldn't have been her birth eyes. Surely, she'd been born with brown eyes. She had to be rich. How else could she afford replacement eyes? Knowing her eyes weren't original, I wondered what else wasn't . . . maybe that perfect little nose, or maybe those round lips, or how about those nice ample breasts. After taking in the complete package of Maggie Orzo, I decided that I really didn't care what was original and what wasn't.

She said, "Must've been quite a surprise to find out you had a new partner."

"Yep," I said without trying to hide my unhappiness. Pretty or not, I didn't need a partner slowing me down. "We're just getting started."

Maggie Orzo looked at a smitten Yuan Kim. "Hi, Kim."

Kim was looking stupid as he pushed his glasses back up. "H-hey, Maggie, this is my partner."

"Nice to meet you, Maggie. I'm Mark Josephs. Kim here has been telling me all about you. I think he likes you."

Kim looked stupid-angry.

Maggie Orzo changed the subject. "What have we been able to determine so far?"

Josephs said, "The coroner is still working the body. Why don't you come check it out?" He gave me a look as if to say, "Watch this," then he talked to Maggie, real patronizing. "Now, are you sure you're ready for this?"

She was emphatic. "I'm sure."

She walked deeper into the alley. We all followed her past some garbage cans and around the corner. Sweat streamed down my face and back. My shirt was soaked through. The ripe smell of the corpse was overpowering in the heat. Blood was pooled on the pavement. Lizards chattered in small groups, waiting for an opportunity to scavenge while flies buzzed around our heads.

Koba's head coroner, Abdul Salaam, was hunched over the body. How did he still do it at his age? Down on his knees, with the heat kicking off the pavement like that. Abdul was one of the few guys around who was older than me, in years, that is. In attitude, he must have been half my age. Abdul and I went way back, old friends. "Hey, Abdul."

He looked up, squinting through his too-thick glasses. "That you, Juno?"

"Yeah, it's me."

"What are you doing here?"

"I'm working this case, with Officer Orzo here."

He tried to wave the flies away, his bloodied gloves acting more like a magnet than a repellant. "I don't get it," he said.

"Paul sent me."

"Doesn't he know that you're too old for this kind of work?" he said with his poker face.

"Fuck you, old man." Poker face right back at him. I couldn't hold it. I broke out in a wide smile that Abdul mirrored back.

I studied the vic. He was dressed in blood-soaked white linens with good shoes. He couldn't be poor. Poor people went barefoot or wore jellies, not shoes. And there was no way a poor person could afford to get laid at the Lotus. Rich, then? No. His watch had a plastic band. He was strictly middle class.

His fingertips were gnawed off—lizards. Abdul had the vic's shirt open. Maybe a dozen wounds, all festering, overflowing with maggots. Abdul was bagging some maggot samples, cleaning out the rest. Lagartan flies were nastier than flies from any other planet. They would drop eggs from the air. Living or dead, an open wound would get infested in less than five minutes. Abdul would use the maggots to nail down the time of attack—very accurate.

The corpse's throat was cut deep and wide. His face was already cleaned and had yellow gel laid on thick—the gel would kill flies and eggs. The mutilations were still visible under the gel mask. The stiff 's teeth and gums were showing—lips gone, cheeks gone. The rest of his face was pocked and chewed upon—lizards again.

I looked up to find Josephs and Kim watching my *temporary* partner. She was focused on Abdul's ME work. Her face was pale . . . very pale, but holding together.

Yuan Kim was looking stupid-satisfied now, imagining how he was going to spend the five g's.

Josephs decided to push things. "The killer must've used a knife on the face. He trimmed away the lips and cheeks real careful. Notice there's no cuts on the gums. My father was a butcher. I used to watch him work. He would trim the fat off beef the same way. Grab a hold of the fat and pull. Run a knife along nice and slow. Sometimes the fat would slip through his fingers. He'd have to grab on tight."

Maggie Orzo turned green; Kim turned red, ticked to the nth. Josephs's father was never a butcher. Maggie closed her eyes and breathed deep, concentrating hard. She opened her eyes and eyeballed the gore with determination. Color started to return to her cheeks. She was a strong woman. Josephs saw her pull herself together and stormed off. Kim was beaming, five thou richer.

Abdul finished cleaning out the maggots and started applying gel to the body wounds.

I leaned in close; the blood stench just about knocked me over. "Stab wounds."

The old coroner stopped and wiped his face off with a rag. The top of his bald head was still speckled with perspiration. Some drops broke loose and ran down his face, reminding me of a windshield the second after the wipers sweep it dry. "I count fourteen to the torso. Three slash wounds to the throat. Killer grabbed him from behind, dragged the blade across the throat right, left, right. Nobody would have heard a thing."

"Makes the killer right-handed?"

"That's right, blade in the right hand . . . pull to the right, push left, then pull right again. Like a saw. Here's the first incision. Notice how the skin is torn here, not sliced. The blade was dull." He pulled the edges of the wound open. "See the windpipe, there? Barely scratched on the first swipe. The second and third slices cut deeper. It was a long blade, maybe thirty centimeters. Our vic must've been dead inside a minute or two. Then the killer stabbed him repeatedly and cut up his face."

Maggie Orzo asked, "Can you determine what kind of knife was used?"

"I can't tell you for sure, but when I get him to the morgue, I'll be able to measure the wounds precisely and compare them against every kind of knife I can find. There are no burns, so he didn't use a lase-blade. My guess is a plain ol' butcher knife."

Josephs returned with a bowl of soup from the stand down the street. We all turned to look at him. He was up to something. It was way too hot for soup.

Kim looked stupid-suspicious. "What you got there?"

"Menudo."

Oh shit. Here we go.

Josephs stood over the body and started to dig in, sweat dripping off his nose into the bowl. Maggie the rook seemed wobbly.

Josephs carried on, acting superfriendly. "Where are my manners? Anybody want some? You have to like tripe. Some people don't like it. It's stomach, you know. I love it. Let me see if I can find some." He fished with his spoon. "Ah, there's a big chunk. Anybody want it? No? Okay, suit yourselves." He slurped it in then talked with his mouth full. "Mm, not the best tripe I've ever had. A little on the chewy side. You have to prepare it just right."

That did it. She took off, hurrying for the door to the Lotus. She didn't make it far before she bent over and groaned up her breakfast.

Yuan Kim was livid—just lost five thou, and that wasn't even the worst of it. Mark Josephs was not the type to let you forget it. Josephs laid a shit-eating grin on Kim . . . only the beginning.

Maggie Orzo finished barfing and wiped her chin. She looked back at us. I tried to quit smiling, too late. Her sky eyes burned into me. She headed into the Lotus to find a bathroom.

I didn't know what the hell Paul was thinking teaming me up with her. I didn't care who the rich girl's parents were. I wanted her out.

three

I SCOPED the area. The blood trail started by the door with just a few drops. I thought it through: The killer must've hidden behind the cooling unit and waited for Lieutenant Dmitri Vlotsky to come out of the Lotus. Then he snatched him from behind and sliced his throat straightaway. There wasn't much blood at the door—too easy for somebody to spot. The perp dragged Vlotsky down the alley, quick, before he was seen. Then he stuck him fourteen times and cut his lips off. Next, he took Vlotsky's money and split.

It didn't play as a robbery. Muggers killed out of necessity. They usually didn't use knives, and when they did, they used lase-blades, not butcher knives. It wasn't that lase-blades cut that much better—a sharp knife could kill you just as well—but lase-blades were so much more intimidating. Imagine your vic was watching you swing the tight beam of a lase-blade through the air. He'd hear the crackle of humidity flash-frying as it came in contact with the blade. Flies attracted to the light would pop off the blade's edge like black popcorn. Your vic would be feeling mighty compliant by now. There was no way a mugger was going to use a regular old knife. The vic might've started thinking he had a chance if he fought back. Definitely not a robbery. Besides, muggers didn't take their victim's lips with them. What would a pair of lips bring on the black market anyway?

Conclusion: Our killer was either a hit man trying to throw

us off course with the mutilations or a genuine psycho . . . or both.

Maggie Orzo came back out to the alley wearing a clean shirt. She looked less sick but no less steamed. She was working up to saying something.

I cut her off before she could give me some shit about how I needed to respect her as a cop. I didn't want to hear it. "We have to canvass the area. You ready?"

She answered with an off-guard, "Yeah, I guess so."

A welcome gust of cool greeted us upon entering the Lotus. Rose had dry shirts at the ready—classy place. I dipped behind a screen, stripped my shirt off, and dropped it into a hamper. I washed my face in a basin of fragrant water that had flower petals floating on top. I toweled and made a rare check in the mirror. My hair was low-tide receding and frothing white at the edges. My slightly darker than average skin and barely kinked hair were the last remnants of my diluted African blood. I looked more Latin than African. Most everybody on Lagarto looked Latin, though many had a little Asian or a little European mixed in. We were all mutts of one sort or another.

I slipped one of Rose's white short-sleeves over the sturdy shoulders I'd inherited from my wife-beating coward of a father. I labored over the buttons with one hand—fucking ridiculous. Niki had taken all of my own shirts to my tailor and had the buttons replaced with snaps.

A houseboy grabbed the hamper when I came out from behind the screen. From experience, I knew he'd have my shirt laundered and ready for pickup in thirty minutes.

Rose wore a wrinkled sarong, and her lipstick was uneven. I'd never seen her look so scattered. She was usually done up nice, if a bit overdone. "Oh, Juno. I am so glad to see you."

"Hi, Rose. You've met Detective Orzo?"

"Yes, of course. You're looking much better, dear. Would you like some tea?"

"Yes, we'd like that," I answered.

Another houseboy bolted off.

She led us into her staging area, where she would serve her clients tea and sweets. The room was decked out in rugs and antiques. The Lotus was only for the refined palate. The air in the room choked with the smell of soaked-in perfume. My new partner and I sat on wooden chairs with embroidered cushions, the johns' seats. We were sitting opposite a floor-to-ceiling two-way mirror looking into the empty showroom. Its chairs, sofas, and game tables all faced this way.

Rose flopped into her seat with an uncharacteristic lack of grace. "Are you going to handle this, Juno?"

"Yes, I am." I didn't say, "Yes we are." This was a one-man show, and the sooner Maggie Orzo realized that the better.

"Thank god! I did not like those other two officers one bit. They came in here like they owned the place and started asking questions of the help. The *help*. I especially don't like that young one with the glasses, not at all." She directed herself to my new partner and said, "Now you stay away from him, dear—nice girl like you. He told me to hand over my books! Who does he think he is?"

I soothed with my voice. "It's okay, Rose. I took over the case. They left a few minutes ago."

"Oh, that is such a relief. Those two, they have no business sense. You know what I mean? They're not like you, Juno. You always know how to handle things—isn't that right?" She was scared to death that word would get around that one of her customers was murdered right outside her door—bad for business.

I said, "I'll get Jessie to take care of it. We have an arrangement. She'll know how to play it."

Jessie Khalil was the top reporter for Lagarto Libre. The Libre was the only media company on Lagarto. It ran the newspaper and the vid station. They had a fifteen-minute news program that aired four times a day; it was their only show. They filled in the rest of the day with decade-old offworld programming. Jessie could handle the story and leave the Lotus out of it. She'd bend stories in my favor. In exchange, I'd pass her juicy tidbits on offworlders—drug possession, sex with prostitutes—the usual shit. The public would eat it up. It brought the high and mighty down to our level.

Rose let out a sigh of relief. "Thanks, Juno. I was really worried, but as soon as I saw you come through the door I thought, 'It'll be all right, Rose. Juno is going to take care of you. He always knows what's best.'" To Maggie she said, "You can learn a lot from him, dear."

Maggie Orzo was confused, not sure what just went down. "I'm sure I will."

The houseboy arrived with tea. He served us Arab style. He poured the tea from a metal teapot into glasses instead of cups.

"Can you tell me anything about the victim, Rose?" I asked.

"Sure, Juno. Anything for you. I wasn't going to tell those other two a damn thing; I simply don't trust them. Your victim is named Dmitri Vlotsky. He was a nice boy. I don't understand why somebody would do such a thing. Just horrible."

I kept my right hand in my lap and drank with the left. That was strong tea, mint with lots of sugar. "He a regular?"

"Not so regular recently. He was in the Army, you know. But he came by whenever he was on leave."

"How long has he been coming here?"

Rose set her tea down. The glass was full. She hadn't touched it. "He first came when he was still in school. He couldn't have been more than fifteen or sixteen years old. His father brought him in. Peter had been a loyal customer for years. He told me his boy Dmitri was dating a girl, and Peter had asked him if they were using condoms. Peter had high hopes for his son. You know how it is. He didn't want Dmitri to knock this girl up. Based on the way Peter talked about her, I got the feeling that both he and the missus weren't too impressed with her.

"Dmitri told his dad they weren't having sex yet. Now, Peter figured she was a prude and said so, but Dmitri told him no, that she'd been with other guys. So Peter asked why she didn't want to be with him, and Dmitri said she did want to be with him, but he kept putting her off. He told his father he'd never been with a girl before, and he was afraid he wouldn't measure up to her exes. So then Peter asked him if she knew he was a virgin, and Dmitri said he'd lied to her, told her he'd been with lots of girls. He wanted her to think he was some kind of stud.

"Peter didn't want his son to look like a novice, so he brought Dmitri down to Rose for some lessons. You should have seen Dmitri then . . . he was terrified, poor kid. His dad brought him in, introduced us, and left. I told him to pick a girl out. He went up to the window, and his eyes went straight for Lucy. She was lounging on that love seat, the pink one. You remember Lucy, Juno?"

"No."

"No? Come on, Juno, gorgeous eyes, nice figure? Anyway, I asked him who he wanted, knowing all along he wanted Lucy. He wouldn't answer; he was so scared. I sent Lucy up to one of the rooms, told her to be gentle, then sent the kid up. Peter brought him back three days straight. After a couple years, Dmitri started coming back on his own."

"Was he alone last night?"

A lock of Rose's hair fell onto her shoulder. She tucked it back into her disorganized mop. "Yes. He said his unit was on leave for a week and this was his second night back. He spent the first night with family. He told me all about how his father was doing. How he bought a car and a new house, as if I didn't already know. Peter was just in here last week. Peter had told him he'd stopped coming here when he married Dmitri's mother. He didn't want to ruin the kid's picture of a happy home. It's a good thing Dmitri went into the Army and wasn't around so much. I was worried that someday they would bump into each other in the hallway. Can you imagine that? Father and son. What a scene that would be."

"What time did he leave?"

"Dmitri went for the works. He'd been out in the jungle for eight months. He must have left just after midnight."

"Did your staff see anything strange?"

"I've talked to all of them. Nobody saw anything."

"Who did you set Dmitri up with?"

"Kimi. Mohamed, go get Kimi." Houseboy Mohamed took off on a run. Rose continued, "Dmitri was into the mature types like Lucy when he was a boy; now he likes them young. You know how men are."

"Rose, I know you won't like this, but I need a list of your johns from last night. I have to find out if any of them saw anything. I'll be discreet."

"I know you will, Juno. I'm not unreasonable. I want you to catch this monster. My girls and I are scared silly. It could have been any one of us out there."

"Thanks, Rose."

Kimi came in and sat next to Rose. Without any hooker rouge or hair spray, she looked the schoolgirl. Her skin was honey-brown, a lighter shade than most.

Rose stroked Kimi's dyed-blonde hair. "Now, these officers are going to ask you some questions. Just tell them the truth, sweetie."

Kimi nodded.

"You were with Dmitri last night?"

"Yes."

"Was he acting strange?"

"No."

"Afraid?"

"No."

"Anything out of the ordinary?"

"No."

"Did he talk to you?"

"A little."

"What did he say?"

"He just talked about being glad to be back in Koba. He is a . . . was a captain in the Army."

"He told you he was a *captain*?"

"Yeah. He's been fighting the revolutionaries, and he told me how hard it is out there in the jungle, never knowing when the enemy is going to jump out at you. He killed thirty-three men on this tour alone."

Lieutenant Dmitri Vlotsky was a big-time liar.

I took another sip of tea. "You were impressed?"

"Yeah, sure. I mean, with a guy like that I don't really mind doing . . . you know . . . what I do."

"Why's that?"

"I don't know. I guess it makes me feel . . . sort of . . . patriotic. You know, like I am, in my own way, helping them fight the war. You know, keeping Lagarto unified."

"Did he talk about anything else?"

"No, just that he had a good time."

"I'm sure he did. Can we look at the room, Rose?"

"Of course. Mohamed, show them the way, will you?"

Mohamed left us alone in Kimi's room. The bed was in the center, encircled by candles on pedestals. Wax-drip stalagmites grew up from the floor beneath. Sunlight poured through wide windows that opened onto neighboring rooftops. The walls and ceiling were solid mirror all around. Blinding sunspots reflected around the room.

"What was all that about?" Maggie's tone was accusatory.

I turned to look at her. She stood with her hands on her hips. Her eyes were squinted almost shut, and her jaw was clenched in defiance.

"All what?" I knew what she meant but asked anyway.

"Who's Jessie?"

"She's a friend of my wife's."

"What kind of friend? Who is she?"

I thought about it and decided to come clean. I must've felt guilty about laughing at her in the alley. "Jessie Khalil."

"The reporter? You're going to cover this up?"

"Who said anything about a cover-up? I'll just get Jessie to make sure the news reports leave the Lotus out of it. They'll say, 'Lieutenant Dmitri Vlotsky murdered in an alley on the West Side.' No mention of the Lotus."

"Why would you want to protect that woman? It's disgusting what she does here. Did you see Kimi? She's just a kid."

"We're here for one reason only: to work a homicide. That's it. Rose is a businesswoman. She wasn't going to talk to us without getting something for it. It's a business transaction—nothing more, nothing less."

"And you think that's okay? She exploits those girls' bodies for money."

"What would you have done?"

"I would have arrested Rose and seized her books to get the list of johns. Then I would have talked to Kimi."

"You think Kimi would talk to you without Rose's say-so?"

"Hey, I know she'd be scared, but separate her from that witch, and I think she'd be thankful."

"You don't know that. The Lotus is first-rate. Rose takes

good care of her girls. They're all very loyal to her. Not every-body grows up rich like you. These girls have limited options."

"That's bullshit, Juno. The fact that they're poor makes what Rose does to them worse. She takes advantage of their vulnera-bility."

"Of course she takes advantage of them. What you don't understand is that being taken advantage of and eating is bet-ter than going hungry with your virginity intact. And what about the vic's family? You think they want people to know their son frequented whorehouses?" With that I climbed out the window, onto the roof.

Maggie followed, "What are you looking for?"

"I don't know. The fire escape on the other side goes down to the alley. Our killer could have climbed up here to watch through the window." I crossed the roof, swimming through the sticky-wet air. Insects dashed over the roof's sunny spots, eating mold out of cracks and crevices while geckos sat still, clinging to the shaded portions of the walls, too hot to chase potential prey.

My scalp itched sweat; my skin itched mosquito bites. I wan-dered around, looking for the primo peeping position. This was it. It had a view of four windows and the alley, but more impor-tant, the eaves of a neighboring roof hung overhead—perfect for keeping in the night shadows.

I noticed a block of wood plugging a hole in the wall. I pulled the block out, exposing a rumpled magazine cover. Skin mags. I took one out and flipped through the pages—hard-core bondage. The edges were mildewed, and half the pages were spotted with fuzzy mold. When my hand started shaking, I gave the mag to Maggie.

Rookie Detective Maggie Orzo tried to put it together. "The killer hangs out here. He reads his magazines and watches through the windows. He sees Kimi with Lieutenant Vlotsky and something snaps. He goes down to the alley, waits for Vlotsky, and kills him. Maybe he's fixated on Kimi. He wants to protect her."

Not bad. It fitted.

I went to the fire escape and looked down at the alley. Med-techs were bagging Vlotsky's corpse.

Maggie called me over. "Hey, isn't this a strange place for a puddle?" She stood where I had left her and pointed to a puddle at her feet. I noticed her chic shoes.

"What's so strange about that?"

She pointed to the overhang above. "Can't be rainwater."

Good call, I thought to myself. She was smart—just didn't know shit.

When I came over, she moved out of the way. I got down on my hands and knees, careful not to burn my hands on the tarred roof. Even in the shade, it'd get plenty hot in the middle of the day. I took a long whiff. "Urine."

"Urine?"

"Yeah, urine." Didn't fit. Not right, not right. The heat dizzied me.

Maggie thought aloud. "Our killer had to go, so he did it on the wall. It pooled up here and the wall dried."

I was shaking my head. "No. He comes here a lot. This is his spot. I don't care how crazy he is; nobody soils their own nest."

"He was afraid of being seen. He didn't want to come out of the shadows."

Perspiration stung my eyes. No. He could've pissed over the wall, down to the alley—check first, nobody there, let it rip. Not right, no, no. It clicked. Yes? Yes! "We have a witness," I said.

four

I GOT Maggie to tear a page out of one of the mags—carefully. We didn't want him to know there was a page missing. I would have done it myself if I could have kept my hand steady. We bagged the page, returned the mags to the wall, and shoved the block of wood back in place.

I explained my witness theory to her: The killer stayed in the alley the whole time, never going up to the roof. The killer didn't realize that there was a peeper up there who got off on watching. The peeper probably hung out on the roof all the time, flipping through his stroke books and catching the action through the windows. The peeper heard a commotion in the alley when Lieutenant Vlotsky came out and started getting sliced. He looked down to the alley and saw the killer stabbing away at Vlotsky. The peeper watched as the killer carved up Vlotsky's face and pocketed the lips. The peeper was scared. So scared he peed himself. When the killer took off, the peeper waited to make sure the killer was gone, then soggy-pants split.

We shared a cab to the station. The driver had put some work into this car. It was white, not one of the manufacturer's three colors. The thing was tricked out from fender to fender, chrome hubs, flaming racing stripes, and neon-trimmed windows. The overall effect was trashy. Cab by day, cruiser by night. Lagartan car owners would spend tons of time personalizing their vehicles. It was the only way to get some status out of owning a car. Who would want a car that looked exactly like every other car?

Maggie held the baggie with the skin mag page in her hand. She set it on her lap, three leather-hooded individuals looking up at her from the page. She self-consciously turned the page over to a pic of a hog-tied woman at the feet of a man armed with a whip and a hard-on. Maggie tucked the page between her leg and the car door, safely out of sight.

I looked out the window. Shanty homes rolled by in a ramshackle blur. Opium-ravaged hopheads slept on the sidewalks, looking like piles of dirty laundry.

I saw an offworlder on a corner trying to flag down our cab. She was fair skinned with flowing blonde locks that morphed into her dress. I couldn't tell where one ended and the other began. I would've mistaken her for a goddess if it wasn't for the sweat stains. Our driver started to pull over. Cabbies were known to kick locals out of their car for a chance at an offworld fare. A flash of my badge talked him out of it.

Even though the Koba Spaceport was kilometers away, I could feel the rumble of a launching ship over the car's normal vibration. I looked up but couldn't see the vessel. It always sounded like it was right on top of you.

We crossed a narrow canal and entered Cap Square, the government district. There was a crowd gathering by City Hall, peaceniks waving homemade placards denouncing violence. They were worked up over the most recent victim in Lagarto's latest organized-crime war, a young girl who caught lase-fire from a street skirmish. Every time an innocent died, the peaceniks would take to the streets in an ineffectual attempt to get city leaders to crack down. The dumb-shits didn't get it—where there was poverty, there was crime, and where there was organized crime, there was always going to be a battle for supremacy. You couldn't stop the violence.

Koba was run by the Bandur cartel. It was started by Ram Bandur, aka the Kingpin of Koba, aka the Nepali Svengali. Ram Bandur was a crime lord the likes of which Lagarto had never seen. He seized control of Koba's illegal activity more than twenty years ago. He was the first to consolidate every one of Koba's neighborhoods under one criminal house. Bandur would take a piece of all the city's action—prostitution, bookmaking, loan-sharking, extortion, pornography, cloning, protection rackets, gunrunning, con games, fraud, drugs, bootlegging, DNA smuggling . . . He stood unopposed for two decades.

Ram passed away three years ago and willed his criminal empire to his son Benazir—a weaker version of his father. The criminal kingdom had since been under attack from Carlos Simba, Loja's crime lord. Loja was the planet's second largest city, two hours upriver. Simba declared all-out war against Ben Bandur's organization and launched the two cartels into an ever-escalating bloodbath. I hoped the Bandur cartel would quell the Simba uprising soon. Paul and I had a vested interest in seeing the Bandur cartel victorious. KOP had a secret and unholy alliance with the Bandur outfit. Hell, it was Paul and me that put them in power.

The driver dropped us curbside. KOP station loomed over us, its stone steps and columns streaked with lizard excrement. I marched straight to Paul's office, Maggie trailing a half step behind. Out came Diego Banks, KOP's chief of detectives and Paul's number two. His jet black hair was slicked back into a duck's ass hairstyle. The tension crackled between us. I didn't take kindly to traitors. The latest lowdown was that he'd become chummy with Mayor Omar Samir. It sounded like the number two had his eyes on the number one job, angling for a post-Paul appointment as chief.

Banks wrung the tension out of his voice and spoke in an

easygoing tone. "Thanks for coming by, Juno. The chief says go on in. Maggie, why don't you come with me?"

I went in, leaving her behind . . . hopefully for good.

Chief Paul Chang sat at his desk. His hair was streaked gray, and his familiar Asian eyes had started wrinkling in the corners. His trademark smile took ten years off his age. He sprang from his seat when I entered. He was wearing a spare-no-expense hand-tailored suit with diamond-studded cuff links and tie tack. His badge sparkled, shined to diamond intensity. "It's good to see you, Juno."

My eyes went straight to Karl Gilkyson who was sitting to the right. I immediately wondered what that asshole from the mayor's office was doing here. "Isn't this a police matter?" I asked.

"Don't mind Karl. He's just doing his job, Juno. I told the mayor we had nothing to hide, so he suggested Karl tag along and see how we conduct business. You know how tense things have been between the police and the mayor's office. I thought this might promote cooperation between us. He's been a fly on the wall for a couple weeks now."

Shit. Things were worse than I thought. Clearly I had lost track of what'd been going down since I'd stopped enforcing for Paul. Mayor Samir took office almost three years ago promising to clean up the city's government with KOP as his first target. He launched an investigation into police corruption that had been slowly gaining momentum. Paul must've been feeling the heat to be letting that bastard Karl Gilkyson in here. I thought that investigation was pure get-the-vote-out posturing. I had no idea it had legs.

Gilkyson was a typical lawyer: tight suit, tight lips. He leaned forward in his chair. "That's right, 'fly on the wall.' Don't mind me. Just pretend I'm not here."

I was happy to oblige by pretending he wasn't there. I said to

Paul. "Why do you want me on this case? Josephs and Kim can handle it."

"Because you're a better detective than both of them put together. The victim's father is a bureaucrat who works for the city. I told the mayor we'd put our best man on the case. That's you, Juno. Besides, Josephs and Kim are swamped with missing-persons cases."

Gilkyson broke from his supposed fly-on-the-wall persona. "Don't feel pressured to take the case. The mayor made his wishes very clear to me and Chief Chang. He doesn't want any special treatment just because the victim is the son of a city employee."

"Nonsense," Paul dismissed him. "We're all city employees here. When one of our sons is brutally murdered, we all take it personally. I know the mayor understands that. So what do you think of Officer Orzo, Juno?"

"I haven't had a partner since you, Paul. I don't see the point of having one now."

"I know this is hard for you, but I'm in a bind here. She's descended from plantation owners. You know what that means."

Yeah. It meant she was rich. Very rich.

Paul said, "Her mother keeps calling me, wondering when she's going to get a big case. I really want to call her now and let her know her daughter is working a homicide before she calls me again. As long as I have to give her a case, she may as well learn from the best."

"I don't care how rich she is. She's not ready for this."

"She doesn't have to be ready. You don't have to give her any responsibility. Just let her look over your shoulder."

I turned to Gilkyson, hoping the bastard could bail me out. "Isn't this unethical?"

He turned his palms up. "We don't have a problem with it. The mayor often has to grant favors. It's the way the system

works." His left palm caught my attention. It was glassed over—
no, not glass; it was flexible but clear like glass. I could see the
circuitry behind it. It was a scanner. He could swipe his hand
over documents, uploading them through the phone system to
the computers on Lagarto's orbital station. They must've sent
him up to the Orbital to get that thing installed. I couldn't imagine how big a dent it must've put in the mayoral budget.

Paul put his unaugmented hands flat on his desk. "What do
you say, Juno?"

He always could talk me into anything. I said, "I think Officer Orzo is going to need some convincing. I don't think she's
very enthusiastic about working with me."

"I've got Banks talking to her right now. He'll smooth things
with her. You'll report direct to me on this one." He laid one of
his toothy smiles on me. "Thanks for coming by. I'll see you
and Niki at the banquet tonight, won't I?"

"Yep, we'll be there," I said reflexively as I walked out, though
we both knew I hadn't had any plans to attend the mayor's banquet. I hated that hobnobbing bullshit. I didn't fit in. So why did
he say he'd see me there? He wanted me to come so he could
talk to me without that prick Gilkyson listening in. I knew right
then that this case was bigger than he'd been letting on.

five

I LEFT Paul's office, right hand in my pocket, my shoes crunching weeds that sprouted from floor cracks. The ceiling lights were penny-saving bulbless. The dim passages were lit by misty sunlight beaming through sparsely placed windows. The building was half abandoned. Lagarto was perpetually entrenched in rough times.

I headed up to the third, taking the stairs slow. Their sharp edges were now rounded from a hundred years of wear. I'd lost my footing more than once, so I held the rail tight in my left, my fingers running over the crusted mold of the underside.

I called home. "We're going to the banquet tonight."

Niki's hologram was all smiles, matching her mood. "That's great! What made you change your mind?"

I smiled back at Holo-Niki. "Paul. He's got me on a case, and he wants to talk to me tonight."

"What kind of case?"

"A homicide."

"But you work vice."

"I know, but Paul asked me to take this one."

"Why?"

"I don't know yet. That's why he wants me to come to the banquet."

"I don't believe this. I've been trying to get you to go for weeks, and Paul just snaps his fingers."

"I know, I know. I gotta go. I'll check in later, okay?"

"But—"

"I have to go, Niki."

I clicked off. Niki's hologram vanished. That was easier than I thought. She must've been too excited about the banquet to give me a serious tongue-lashing. I thought she'd go wild when I mentioned Paul. I wasn't supposed to do jobs for him anymore.

I went into vice to find my new partner. A plantation owner! What was Paul doing, putting me on a homicide and partnering me up with a fucking plantation owner? The plantation owners had developed this planet, setting up a booming brandy trade that made Lagarto the talk of the Unified Worlds. Lagartan fruit tasted like shit, but let it rot with some sugar for a couple years, and you've got gold. The plantation owners made a killing exporting their brandy to the stars. Even after the crash, plantation owners still occupied the highest seats in Lagartan society.

Vice was almost empty. It didn't get buzzing until after sundown. The floor was molded over like a pale green carpet. Wooden desks were topped by computer terminals that had quit working decades ago.

Maggie Orzo was sitting at my desk. She ran her fingers through her hair, pulling it up off the back of her neck the way women do when they're trying to cool off. Her hair looked nice up like that. I noticed she was on hold with an Army logo hologram floating over my desk.

I marched up to her. "Have you talked to them?"

"Not yet. They're trying to find an officer to talk to me."

"Hang up."

"Why? I want to inform them of Lieutenant Vlotsky's death."

"Hang up."

She pulled her hands out of her hair and severed the connection.

I said, "Once they hear about Vlotsky, they'll recall his unit. They'll call it a military matter and clamp everything down tight. We won't get to talk to anybody in his unit. I'll call Jessie Khalil at the station and have her delay the story as long as she can, so we can get to some of them first."

Maggie had no objections. She looked pensive, then said, "Why do you think the killer took the lips?"

I shrugged. I didn't know. Who knew what was in the mind of a serial? "Why don't you bring the skin mag page downstairs and have it checked for prints."

She sensed the brush-off but didn't say anything about it. C of D Banks must've done a job on her. He must've told her to do what I said. Maybe this could work out after all.

I called Jessie and set her to tracking down a roster of Vlotsky's unit. She had contacts everywhere. I told her the angle I wanted her to play on the Vlotsky story—keep the Lotus out of it. I asked her to shelve the story as long as she could, but there was nothing she could do about that. Her editor already had it scheduled for the next broadcast. That wouldn't leave us much time.

Maggie was back. "What next?" she asked.

"I hear you're a plantation owner."

Her face tightened up. "That's right, but don't think that's how I got here. I'm here because I deserve to be."

"So the fact that you're filthy rich is just a coincidence?"

"I make my own way. Chief Chang assured me that my family had nothing to do with this posting. If they had, I would have refused it."

"You really believe that?"

Maggie was pissed, more pissed than she had been in the alley. "I don't care what you think. I earned it. You're just going to have to get used to it."

I let it go, wondering why a plantation owner would choose to be a cop. Our collars were way too blue for their tastes. Even after they'd lost the bulk of their wealth in the brandy market crash, they were still the richest of the rich, at least on a Lagartan scale. On an offworld scale, the crash had dropped them down a few rungs to upper middle class at best. It was their own fault. What do you expect when you try to build an entire economy on a single product?

I split Rose's list of johns with Maggie. I took seventeen, gave her sixteen. After a half hour's work, I scored seven left-messages, six didn't-see-anythings, and four can't-talk-to-you-right-nows. Maggie scored about the same.

Jessie called back with the roster. Unit 29: Lieutenant Dmitri Vlotsky and ten enlisted men, all on leave.

"Let's go," I said.

"Are we going to talk with the Vlotsky family?"

"Later. Chief of Detectives Banks will call them if he hasn't already. The Vlotsky story's going to break in less than an hour. We have to talk to his unit while we have the chance."

I didn't have my car, so we decided to take the river. We started hoofing it for the pier. The five hours of daylight were almost over, the sun just dipping below rooftops. Cool shadows had begun to draw people out of their homes. They sat on their stoops waving paper fans. The Koba winter was currently serving up seventeen hours of night and taking the worst of the stifling heat out of the jungle. The thankfully shortened days were symptomatic of Koba's polar location. Go much farther south and you'd hit uninhabitable deserts.

I adjusted my pace to keep a half step ahead of my partner. I didn't want her thinking she was my equal. This was my case.

We made our way through the Phra Kaew market area. I spotted an offworlder at a fruit stand; his too-tall body and two-tone designer skin were dead giveaways. The suck-up fruit stand owner hustled out from the back with a crate of fresh fruit and picked out the choicest pieces for his newfound offworld friend. The prospect of landing some offworld currency was enough to set just about any Lagartan to performing tricks.

The sidewalks were crowded with merchants. Shopkeepers were busy moving racks of wares onto the walk. Vendors on the street side were propping open boarded-up windows, cutting the sidewalk down to a narrow path for pedestrians to navigate. It was like walking through a tunnel with walls made of butchered chickens, cheap sunglasses, stacked cigarettes, and skin vids. I bought some 'mander tacos—extra hot.

We turned into a narrowing alley. On the left, we passed a window filled with fried fish wrapped in newspaper; on the right, skinned iguanas hanging on hooks. We took a left, to the river. At this point, the walkways were made of sandbags, three layers deep. Rank water lapped the sides of the sandbag bridge. Fish innards bobbed on the surface among iridescent swirls of oil. Planks ran from the sandbag bridge to a row of shops on stilts.

We emerged from the market. The river rolled in front of us. We hopped a skiff downriver. Maggie ate quietly. I ate with my left and made a damn mess.

Private Jimmy Bushong from Tenttown wasn't first on the list of ten enlistees in Vlotsky's unit, but he lived the closest to KOP station. I checked my watch. Jessie would be running the story on the news any minute. The military was about to be cover-their-ass alerted to Lieutenant Vlotsky's death. They'd be snapped to attention and engaged in Operation Roundup That Unit. They didn't like civvy cops and civvy reporters nosing around in their business. I hoped we'd be able to get to Bushong first.

We rode the skiff down one of the canals that ran into the Tenttown neighborhood. The water took on the familiar sewage smell that I remembered so vividly from my childhood. Women stood knee-deep washing clothes. Young children swam naked as youths hauled buckets of water for boiling.

My great-grandparents settled here in Tenttown along with countless other families that made the fourteen-year journey from Earth. They came lured by the promise of work. The brandy market was surging. The plantation owners needed labor, so they advertised all over Earth's third world, and my great-grandparents answered the call, selling everything they had to buy their way here on a cargo freighter. They came for the high wages, the free housing, and the bright future.

But by the time they arrived, the brandy market had collapsed. Somebody had smuggled a pair of brandy tree saplings offplanet, and soon after, all the settled planets began raising their own fruit. Why pay extra to import Lagartan brandy when the local variety was just as good? Especially when it took anywhere from five to thirty years to ship it in from Lagarto?

In fact, the brandy market had already been dead for twenty years by the time my great-grandparents landed. The plantation owners had sent message to Earth that they didn't need any more labor, but even at light speed, it still took ten years for the message to reach Earth, and by the time it was received, my great-grandparents were already four years into their journey. When they finally made landfall, they found that all but a few of the sprawling plantations had already reverted to jungle, and all the great riverboats had been sealed up and left to rust.

My great-grandparents were taken to Tenttown, nothing more than a succession of slashed and burned fields upon which do-gooders raised tents for the twenty-four-year stream of immigrants that landed after the economic crash. No jobs, no homes, no medicine, no food—welcome to Lagarto.

Jimmy Bushong's address was listed simply as "Tenttown." A half hour's worth of asking around my old stomping grounds and we located him at a canal party. It didn't matter that it was still early afternoon. As soon as the sun went down in Tenttown, the youth came out for good times. I checked out the four-piece band cranking out the tunes. I scoped the sweated-up dancers, barefoot in the mud, their whites rolled up to the knee. I took it all in: buckets of shine with enough tin cups to go around, eye-straining strobe lights, mud-coated topless chicks speaking in tongues. My heart swelled with teenaged memories.

We led Jimmy away from the party, to the canal's edge, which was coated with slippery-wet moss. Reptilian eyes reflected from the water below. Maggie was silent. I took the lead. "You serve under Lieutenant Dmitri Vlotsky?"

"That's right." Jimmy was dressed in his whites. His pants were rolled up, exposing mud-caked bare feet. His sleeves were rolled to the shoulder, showing off his Army tats. He had a boy's face with Army-cut hair. His eyes had been replaced with metallic night-vision implants. He was sipping from a tin cup, drinking shine. My mouth watered.

"Where were you last night?" I asked.

Jimmy said, "Right here. Why?"

"Lieutenant Vlotsky was murdered last night."

"Murdered? Shit, you serious? Can't say I'm surprised, but shit, that's fucked up."

"Why do you say that?"

"You gonna tell anybody I talked to you?"

"No."

"Know what? I don't care if you *do* tell anybody. My two years is up next month, that's right, next month. It ain't worth it to 'em to send me back out on patrol, so I'll be workin' a

desk while the rest of the Two-Nine is goin' back to the jungle.
Not me, man. I tell you, I'm through with that jungle shit. I
can't wait 'til they pop out these night vision eyes and give me
back my biologicals. As long as they didn't lose 'em like they
lost my cousin's. He had to wait almost a year for them to get
a new set grown 'n' flown from the Orbital. Say, man, you
guys're cops, you think I got a chance of landin' a job like that?
I'm not talkin' no detective shit. I know you gotta be smart for
that. I'm talkin' phones, filin', you know, 'ministrative shit. I
did some of that in basic before they sent me out on patrol
with the Two-Nine. I was the best they seen in a long time.
Sorry to see me go. That's what they told me."

I threw the kid a bone. "I can put in a good word. You look
me up when they let you out. KOP can use a smart and honest
guy like you."

"You serious? Yeah, you're serious. Ha, ha, what's your name
again?"

"Just ask for Juno."

"Juno. Okay. Thanks, man."

"Why weren't you surprised about Vlotsky?"

"Yeah right, the lieutenant. We all wanted to kill that asshole. I didn't sign up for the shit he put us through."

"What did he do?"

"You see, we was workin' out of a base upriver, you know,
jungle duty. We'd spend two weeks doin' maneuvers, then one
week on the base. Now these maneuvers was fucked up.
They'd give us a truck. Four walk in front, four in back. Two
guys take turns drivin'."

We didn't have time for this. The mils would be here soon.
"What about Lieutenant Vlotsky? We just need to know about
Vlotsky."

Jimmy sounded insulted. "Shit. I know, man. You want to
know about the lieutenant, but you got to have some back-

ground in order to understand; you see what I'm sayin'? I ain't goin' to waste your time. You're goin' to want to hear this."

"Sorry. You're right, Jimmy. Go ahead."

"Now, when the rest of us are doin' maneuvers, Vlotsky takes a bedroll, ties it to the top of the truck, and sleeps. You believe that shit? I'm talkin' all day. I don't know how he does it—these roads are rough. I couldn't sleep like that. The truck'd get stuck in the mud all the time. We'd be shovelin' out, and Lieutenant Vlotsky'd be up their snoozin' away. Only time you see him's when it rains, then he sits in the cab."

Maggie Orzo asked, "What's the purpose of these maneuvers?"

His metal eyes swiveled inhumanly. "That's the kicker, man; there *is* no purpose. We ride around all day lookin' for this hill, that creek—shit like that. Shit, this ain't no real war. If it was, we'd be invadin' and shit, but they never give us those kinds of orders. We could wipe them out inside a year, I guarantee it. Shit, they ain't nothin' but a bunch of farmers."

"They're drug lords, Jimmy," Maggie emphasized the words *drug lords* like it proved something.

"Shit, I know that, but they ain't so dangerous. There ain't no money in brandy no more, so they growin' poppies. So what? Who's it hurtin'? They sell most of that O to offworlders anyway. It's the politicians that make them out to be some kinda threat. You know they do that 'cause they just want to keep those offworlders sendin' in that aid. Shit, man, they gettin' rich off that money."

"That aid keeps us from getting overrun by the warlords. Without it, we'd lose our independence." Maggie was wasting time, getting into it with the kid.

"You believe that shit? They just talk all that freedom and democracy bullshit to keep that aid money comin' in. I know for a fact that they don't want to win no war. If they did, we'd a won it thirty years ago. The politicians hold us back from goin' all out on the warlords. They know that if we took the warlords out, there'd be no more reason for them offworlders to keep sendin' in that aid, you hear what I'm sayin'. I'd be surprised if half that money makes it to the Army. Shit yeah! They keep us runnin' around the jungle doin' a couple raids here and there to make it look good, but they ain't serious about winnin' no war."

Maggie started to speak, but I cut her off before she could parrot more bullshit propaganda. "Tell us about Vlotsky."

"Nobody likes the lieutenant. For my first few months, things was pretty smooth, but then things got real bad when they swapped in six new soldiers. Two of them enlisted like me, but the other four got sentenced."

Maggie interrupted. "What do you mean sentenced?"

"Yeah, you believe that shit? These assholes are criminals—I'm talkin' hard-core. Some dumb-fuck judge gives them shorter jail terms in exchange for service. I guess they're havin' trouble recruitin', so now they got to start sendin' convicts."

Jimmy leaned in close like he was telling us a secret. "Now, Kapasi is the baddest of these convicts. The others, they do what he says. They started by shakin' the rest of us down. You know, they'd take our shit, eat our food. We went to Lieutenant Vlotsky and told him what was happenin'. He didn't do a goddamn thing. It took me a while to figure out what was goin' on. One day, I went into Vlotsky's tent to pick up some reports. I didn't know he was there, so I just unzipped my way in. He had this big-ass pile of brown sugar right there on the floor."

Maggie sounded shocked. "Lieutenant Vlotsky was an opium addict?"

"Damn straight he was. That's how come he sleeps all day. It didn't take no genius to see that Kapasi was his supplier. That's why the lieutenant let him get away with all that shit."

I told Maggie to take notes; I could barely write legibly any-more. I told Jimmy to give us names. Make Jhuko Kapasi the ex-con ringleader. Make Pardo, Magee, and Deng the other three ex-cons. We'd have to look up their records. Make Cardoso, Jiang, Jiabao, Sarney, Serra, and Jimmy Bushong the non-ex-cons. Maggie entered it all into her digital paper pad, one of her rich-girl toys. The molecule-thick paper was seriously expensive. They only made it offworld. Somebody had explained it to me once. The molecules were white on one side, black on the other. When you talked to it, the molecules would flip from white to black, forming words on the page. The thing could hold an unlimited amount of information. It'd just keep flipping molecules and changing the display.

I said, "Tell us more, Jimmy."

"Kapasi started runnin' games when we was on the base, you know, bettin' games—dice, cards, shit like that. His guys'd be up half the night, and then the next day, they'd take these long naps, make the rest of us do all the work. They started runnin' maneuvers the same way. They'd stay up all night then sleep in the truck all day."

"What would Vlotsky do?"

"Shit, man, I already told you, he'd be sleepin' on the roof. Things stayed real smooth between Kapasi and the lieutenant for a long while. Kapasi wanted to run his games, and the lieutenant wanted a cheap supply of O. But that all changed when they gave us a real mission."

"What was that?"

"The One-Seven, they're one of the elite units; they raided a farmhouse where they was storin' opium. They killed a bunch of enemy, torched the place, and captured six. We was ordered to meet up with them and escort the prisoners back to the base. All the sudden, Lieutenant Vlotsky is awake all day, givin' orders—Mr. Big Shot on the job. He doesn't do shit for two years, but now he's in charge, orderin' us around. We picked up the prisoners, six of them. I was expectin' soldier types, but these guys was just farmers." His metal eyes focused on my partner. "Before you say different, I'm tellin' you, they was farmers. Anyway, we marched them for two days and tied them to trees at night. We took shifts guardin' 'em.

"On the second night, me and Pardo was on guard. Kapasi came out of his tent, started the truck, then told us to go to bed. I went to my tent and watched Kapasi load the prisoners into the truck and take off. I waited to see if Lieutenant Vlotsky would get up. He never came out of his tent. He *had* to hear the truck; that thing is loud. I figure he must've been too doped up to notice. When Kapasi came back, he came back without the prisoners."

"What happened to them?"

"Shit. I don't know, man. You think Kapasi talks to me? I wasn't about to ask, either. The next morning, Lieutenant Vlotsky wanted to know what happened to the prisoners, and Kapasi just said, 'They escaped.'"

This Kapasi was getting more interesting by the minute. "What did Lieutenant Vlotsky do?"

"He told Central Command that twenty men came out of the jungle, armed to the teeth, and took the prisoners back— you believe that shit? He didn't tell them the truth, 'cause then he'd have to explain why he didn't get up when he heard the truck. He don't want his superiors knowin' he's a hophead."

"Was Lieutenant Vlotsky angry at Kapasi?"

"Shit yeah! The lieutenant fuckin' came to life. He got on the radio every day volunteerin' us for missions. He wanted to prove somethin' to Central Command. You know, he was tryin' to get their confidence back after he lost the prisoners. I'm tellin' you, he was on that radio all day. It took a couple weeks, but he landed us another mission. That's when things got real fucked up."

"What was the mission?"

"They told us to attack a distribution center on the river. We scoped the place for an hour—counted four guards, all armed. Lieutenant Vlotsky split us into two teams of five. He told us to avoid the road and charge the place from two different angles. He sent some guys back to the truck to retrieve the weapons. They was just cheap Army-issue lase-rifles, just like the ones we learned on in basic.

"He had us sync our watches, and he told us to get into position and attack in exactly ten minutes. 'Kill the guards and burn the place,' is what he said. He would wait with the truck. We creeped right up to the jungle's edge. Then when the time came, we flew out of the jungle. We was tearin' across this open space, gettin' real close, and the guards hadn't spotted us."

Jimmy was fully into the story, his ball-bearing eyes sliding back and forth between us with robotic precision. "Both our groups stopped, and we raised our weapons. We had them in a wicked crossfire. I pulled the trigger and nothin' happened. I'm tellin' you, nothin' happened. I figured my gun was frozen and looked around and everybody was fiddlin' with their guns. None of 'em worked. The guards on the dock saw us and ran for cover while we're all tryin' to figure out what the fuck's wrong with our guns. Deng turned and *zoom*, he's off for the jungle. I was thinkin', shit yeah! So the rest of us dropped our guns and ran after him. I'm tellin' you, you've never seen a bunch of guys run that fast in your life. The four on the dock finally figured out that we was runnin' away, so they quit hidin' and started firin'. You ever been shot at? Their laser fire was burnin' the humidity out of the fuckin' air. Shit, the steam can kill you without you even gettin' hit. They taught us that in basic. They came close, but we hit the jungle fast. The worst that happened to us was we got our eyebrows singed. We went back to rendezvous with Lieutenant Vlotsky, but he was gone, and he took the truck with him. You believe that shit? Lieutenant Vlotsky rigged the guns. The fucker set us up."

"He rigged the guns?" I was dumbfounded.

"He sure as shit did. Now I can understand him doin' somethin' like that to Kapasi for takin' the POWs and makin' him look bad. But sendin' all ten of us in to die? That shit ain't right."

We had our killer's motive. I asked, "When did this happen?"

"Couple weeks ago. We was left out in the middle of the fucking jungle. We marched south for half a day and got lucky meeting up with the Two-Six. We hitched a ride back to the base. The day after we got there, in came Lieutenant Vlotsky ridin' that truck. You should've seen the look on his face when he saw us standin' there. He was shocked; there was no doubt about that. Then he acted all happy to see us. He made up some story about bein' attacked by the enemy, and he had to run for it. He even showed us the scorch marks on the truck. You believe that shit? He left us for dead and shot up the truck hisself. He told us how he came back for us when it was safe, but we was already gone. He thought we was dead.

"We was due to go back out to the jungle a week later, but Lieutenant Vlotsky got us this leave time instead. He knew he couldn't go back out to the jungle without payin' for what he did to us. He told Central Command how we was involved in all this heavy combat, and we needed some time off. I heard he even asked for a transfer. Central Command came through with the time off, and here I am."

"Do you think Kapasi killed Vlotsky?"

"Kapasi might have killed him. Shit, we *all* wanted to kill him after what he did to us."

"You say you were here last night. Can anybody back that up?"

"Yeah. Do you want to talk to them now?"

We headed back to the party. The music pulsed. Mud-spattered dancers glistened with sweat. I lost a shoe suctioned into the mud. Maggie and I proceeded barefoot.

Jimmy took his cup and refilled, scooping up a cupful of white mash from a bucket. "You want some?"

We declined.

He took careful sips, letting only the alcohol through by using his upper lip to filter out the mash. We asked around to make sure Jimmy was telling us the truth about being here last night. Everybody we talked to backed him up—another all-nighter party last night. We cleared Jimmy Bushong off the suspect list.

I spotted two Army uniforms looking lost on the far side. They stopped to ask for directions. I pulled Jimmy aside. "You want that filing job with KOP?"

Jimmy's metal eyes reflected the lamplight. "Shit yeah! I'm gonna need a job."

I pointed to the two mils coming this way. "You don't tell them anything."

"You got it, Juno."

We walked down to the canal's edge, startling a pair of monitors into a scramble for the water. We rinsed our feet in canal water that was slick with algae. We slipped our shoes on and found another skiff.

six

THERE was no point in trying to get to the other members of Vlotsky's unit. The mils would have them all under wraps by now. They could be efficient when they wanted to be.

The skiff took us out of Tenttown and we grabbed a cab to Vlotsky's neighborhood—one of the nicer parts of town. No drug dealing or prostitution permitted here; this was one of the city's safe zones—people around here voted. We rode with the windows down. The night air ran through my hair, drying the sweat on the back of my neck as well-to-do houses with manicured gardens ticked by.

The driver pulled into a driveway. I told him to wait for us. We ambled up the stone path, which had been freshly torched and was still dusty with blackened moss. Vlotsky's house had carved wood columns on either side of the door and a glassed-in porch with a rooftop cooling unit to the left. A plaque by the door read "Neimenans." I remembered how Rose had told us he'd just bought a new house. He must not have gotten around to changing out the plaque.

The door was opened by a heavy man in a freshly starched suit with bulk-minimizing vertical stripes. His face was a blank mask.

Maggie held up her badge. "Hello, I'm Detective Maggie Orzo, and this is Detective Juno Mozambe."

"Yes, we've been expecting you. Please come this way."

We trailed sooty footprints into the sitting room. Offworld

artwork hung on the walls—pasty-skinned nude women lying on settees and prim horsemen surrounded by hunting dogs. One of the paintings shifted from a group of Victorian women on a garden stroll to a foo-foo picnic scene with dainty ladies and jaunty chaps. The Vlotskys had expensive tastes—digital art wasn't cheap. It worked off the same premise as Maggie's digital paper, but added color and texture. Very expensive indeed.

Peter Vlotsky dropped his mass into an armchair and took up a sweaty drink in his meaty hand. Jelka Vlotsky sat with her legs crossed and didn't get up to greet us. Her hair was pulled back, so taut that when you looked at her dead on, you couldn't see her hair at all.

"We are so sorry for your loss," I opened.

Mrs. Vlotsky met my eyes with an icy glare. "Where have you been? Our son was *murdered* this morning, and you waited until now to come?"

"Didn't you get a call from the chief of detectives, Diego Banks?"

"Yes. He *called* to tell us our son was dead."

"I know it's hard to hear that kind of news over the phone. We're sorry we couldn't be here earlier, but we needed to wrap up the crime scene first. We have to gather the physical evidence while we can."

"Are you telling me that the two of you are the only police officers in the entire Office of Police? Surely that must be the case, or you would have assigned other officers to that task while you came to tell me my son was dead."

"I understand how you must feel at a time like this, but I want you to know that the Office of Police is giving your son's case the highest priority. Chief Chang has taken a personal interest in this case, and he won't rest until it's solved."

Mrs. Vlotsky turned away from me; she made no attempt to hide her contempt.

Mr. Vlotsky spun the ice around the inside of his glass and took a quick sip. "Please, Jelka. I'm sure they are doing the best they can." Focusing his attention on us, he said, "What can we do for you?"

"If it's not too much trouble, we'd like to ask you some questions."

"Ask us anything if it will help you catch this savage."

"When was the last time you saw your son?"

Mrs. Vlotsky answered with a tone clipped as tightly as her hair. "Yesterday afternoon."

"Did he say where he was going?"

"No."

"Does your son have a girlfriend?"

"No, not currently."

"Has he received any threats?"

"No."

"Can you think of anybody who might want to hurt your son?"

"No, of course not."

"Did he tell you about the other members of his unit?"

"No."

"Did he tell you about the operations he's been involved in?"

"No, that's classified. He couldn't talk about it."

"Did he seem nervous or agitated yesterday?"

"No."

"How about you, Mr. Vlotsky? Do you have anything to add?"

Peter Vlotsky looked lost in thought until my question brought him back to the conversation. "No, I'm afraid not. I wish I could be of more help."

"I understand you work for the city?"

"Yes, I do."

"What do you do?"

"I chair the board that issues business licenses."

"And you, Mrs. Vlotsky?"

"I don't work."

"Does your son have a room here?"

"Yes. It's upstairs."

"Can we take a look around?"

"Yes, but I don't think you'll find anything."

"Why's that?"

"We just moved in two weeks ago. Most of his things are still boxed up. This was the first time Dmitri had been here. He didn't bring much more than a bag."

"Still, we'd like to check it out."

I hit the lights. Geckos dashed under the floorboards.

Vlotsky's room was sparse, nothing but an unmade bed and an Army-issue bag on the floor. Maggie looked at the bag tentatively. I nodded, as if to say, "Go for it." She pulled the drawstring and dumped the contents on the bed. Mostly clothes. I searched the pockets—nothing but condoms and a matchbook.

I looked out the window and checked out the new car in the drive. New house, new car, offworld artwork . . . Mr. Vlotsky had another source of income. Nobody who worked for the city made that kind of scratch. I should know.

We hopped back into the cab and rode shoulder to shoulder.

The mils were going to make it red-tape tough to proceed on the investigation. They weren't going to let us interview any soldiers until they figured out what was going on. They'd protect themselves first, and for once, they'd have good reason—Army officers high on O, POWs set free, an entire unit sicced on the enemy with sabotaged weapons and left for dead . . .

Lieutenant Vlotsky learned a lesson in that alley last night. If you were going to set somebody up to die, you'd better make sure it worked. We had ten members of Unit 29 with a murder motive. Number one on my list was ringleader and ex-con Jhuko Kapasi.

"What now?" Maggie asked.

"We call it a day and start fresh in the morning." I didn't tell her about my banquet plans.

"Where do we start?" Maggie's voice was flat. Her face was shadowed, but I could see the way her shoulders were slumped in fatigue.

"You've got a good nose for this; why don't you tell me?"

She looked at me, searching my face, looking for a trace of sarcasm. I meant what I said. I hoped she could see that. It must've been too dark to read me since she answered cautiously. "I think we need to talk to Kapasi. He has to be our top suspect."

I played the devil's advocate. "But Jimmy Bushong told us that the whole unit wanted to kill Lieutenant Vlotsky."

"Yes, but Jimmy also told us that most of them answered to Kapasi. If one of them did it, my guess is Kapasi put him up to it. It sounds like they don't do anything without his say-so."

"What do you think of the Vlotsky family?"

"Mrs. Vlotsky is a cold woman. How do you lose a son and not shed a single tear? Mr. Vlotsky is hard to read. He was very subdued."

"I agree on both counts. Why do you think Mr. Vlotsky was so quiet?"

"I'm not sure. It could be he was in shock . . . or drunk. Maybe he's just docile around his wife. She seems like the domineering type."

"What do you think of their house?"

"I guess it's okay."

"The new car?"

"What are you getting at?"

"Do you think he can buy those things on a city salary?"

"I don't know, maybe not. I guess I didn't think about it." Maggie Orzo's rich-girl upbringing was coming through strong.

The cab dropped her at a hotel that had lizard statues guarding the entrance. She said she was staying there until she could find a place of her own, something about needing to get away from her mother. I didn't ask her for details.

Since Private Jhuko Kapasi was from Loja, we made plans to meet at the north dock—early.

On the way home, I made a quick stop at the Lotus Club. I wanted to see if our peed-his-pants peeper was back in his erogenous zone. No luck. The perv was probably scared he'd be next to get his lips stripped.

seven

When I finally got home, I keyed through the front gate into the courtyard. The fountain in its center was completely over-grown with greenery. I could hear just the slightest trickle of water muffled by the layers of foliage. Niki was the one who had wanted the fountain. I'd told her it was crazy to have a fountain on Lagarto. You might as well put a giant fucking petri dish in the courtyard.

I went through the front door. A voice came from the bed-room, "That you, Juno?"

"Yeah." I went into the kitchen and cut some bread and cheese, trimming off the mold.

I heard her feet coming up behind me. I turned around to see her showing off her dress, red and heavy on the sequins. "What do you think?"

"I love it." And I did. Her obsidian hair was pulled into an updo, leaving her brown shoulders bare except for the spaghetti straps holding up the dress. Just for the chance to see her like this, I should've agreed to go to the banquet long ago.

"I have your tux ready," she said.

"Thanks."

"So what's this case about?"

"It's just a case."

"Is it the Army lieutenant?"

"Yeah. How do you know about that?"

"Jessie ran the story on the news. She and I were going to go shopping this afternoon, but she canceled. Why is Paul so interested in this one?"

"I don't know. I'll talk to him tonight."

"You have to tell him no."

"You know I can't."

"Yes you can, Juno. Paul doesn't own you. A few years ago, you told him you weren't going to enforce for him anymore. Remember how crazy you were about that?"

"He needs my help."

"Why?"

I took a bite of cheese. I didn't want to talk about it.

She kept staring me down. "You promised me you wouldn't do his dirty work anymore."

I was instantly aggravated. "Give it a rest."

She cranked up the intensity of her stare. "I will not give it a rest. We had an agreement."

"This is different, Niki. He's in trouble."

"What kind of trouble?"

"I don't know."

"Paul is very capable of taking care of himself you know."

"He wouldn't ask for my help if he didn't need it."

"What's so important about this case that he needs your help?"

"Jesus, how many times do I have to tell you? I don't know."

"Okay, so you don't know. Can't you just say that without getting so nasty?"

I could feel myself turning red. "Dammit, Nik, I *did* say it. Now can we just drop it?"

"Sure." She turned away, sending a chill in my direction. She walked out, certain to make her footsteps louder than necessary.

I rolled my eyes. I knew I shouldn't have been short with her, but we'd been having this same stupid argument since

I gave up enforcing. Whether it was a case or a bagman job for Paul, I'd tell her I had to do this. It was important. She'd come back with "you need to be home more," "you're getting too old," "it's too dangerous." Eventually she'd hit me with "you promised you'd quit." She was right of course, which is why I always got so sore.

I'd made the promise a few years ago. Back then, my drinking was out of control. I'd become an ugly drunk. It got so bad that Niki threatened to leave. That was when I promised her I'd quit KOP. And I'd truly meant it when I said it. I *was* going to quit.

But actually following through was another matter.

I just couldn't do it. I kept putting it off. Day after day, I'd tell myself tomorrow would be a better day to do it. Pretty soon, the tomorrows added up to a week, then a month. I couldn't quit being a cop. It was who I was.

I'd apologized a thousand times for letting her down. I'd explained it as best I could, yet she insisted on continuing to beat me over the head with it. *"You said you'd quit. You promised."* *Yeah, yeah, yeah. I fucking get it already. What do you want me to say?*

It wasn't like I'd totally blown her off. I eventually did work up the courage to cold-turkey my enforcing. I demoted myself to a collections man—no investigatory responsibilities. If a cop or pimp got out of line, I'd make the referral to Paul, who would take care of it with one of his young-buck thugs. Giving up the enforcing was the key. Without the need to constantly anesthetize my soul, I'd been able to drop myself down to a two-glass-a-day habit. Wasn't that the important part? How about a little credit?

I started hurrying into my tux. I got hung up on the shirt, damn hand. These buttons were a bitch, especially the ones on the cuffs, but I'd be damned if I was going to call her for help.

I'd get it done without her. It wasn't like she was so perfect. Shit, she popped more painkillers than a damn cancer ward.

There. I'd finally gotten the last button. Now for the bowtie. *How the hell am I going do that?* Fucking hell. I swallowed my pride and apologized.

We took the car. I'd bought it straight off the manufacturing line in '84. I had it classed up with black paint, silver trim, and a monitor-hide interior. Niki talked the whole way, about shopping and then I didn't know what. My head was back on the case. Why was it that the mayor's man, Karl Gilkyson, got to hang out in Paul's office? Paul had never answered to the mayor's office. He operated KOP independently.

It was true that Mayor Samir was the most powerful politician on Lagarto. Lagarto's planetary government was a joke. More than half the planet's people lived inside the Koba city limits, and Lagarto's entire economy was controlled out of Koba. Whoever ran the city ran the planet. Despite the mayor's political dominance, he had no standing with KOP and no right to station one of his lawyers in Paul's office. Beyond the technicality that the mayor appointed the chief, there was no relationship between the two entities, and everybody knew that it was really the previous chief who appointed the next chief; the mayor would just sign off on it. It was the way the system worked.

Yet, Karl Gilkyson had been planted in Paul's office. How much trouble was Paul in? *What's been happening since I stopped enforcing?*

The Iguana King loomed ahead, ten stories of Lagartan luxury. A sign ran from the ground to the roof, the words "Iguana King" riding the back of the largest lizard you've ever seen, outlined in bright green neon, with a curled red-neon tongue that whipped out at a neon fly buzzing ten meters above the rooftop, in a four-stage repeating capture sequence.

I stopped at the back of a line of cars waiting for valet service. I left my keys in the ignition and walked around to the passenger side to open Niki's door. We walked past the cars, every one of them freshly washed and waxed. There were a few offworld cars in the mix—miners and orbital-station entrepreneurs networking with Lagarto's rich and politically powerful, looking for ways to save money on Lagartan food or lobbying for development projects like the half dozen resorts in the works. They liked to run their own resorts. That way, vacationers wouldn't have to come in contact with us natives. Not at all what Paul intended when he set out to increase offworld tourism so many years ago.

We made our way toward the main entrance. Tuxedos and evening gowns crowded into a who's-who mass of winks, handshakes, and pecks on the cheek.

When we finally made it in, I said, "I have to talk to Paul. Then I'm yours. Okay?"

Niki went off without answering. She moved effortlessly from one social circle to another, an elbow grab here and a formal hug there. I immediately felt naked without her. She would class me up enough to hang in high-society circles like these. She was the one who could talk the talk and fill the conversation lulls. She elevated me beyond my Tenttown upbringing. I was out of my league without her in a place like this.

I went off to find Paul. Tall windows ran down both sides of the ballroom. Plush red drapes were tied back with gold ropes. A twenty-piece band kept the dance floor busy. Waiters carried silver trays loaded with drinks. Hoity-toity dilettantes and pseudo-intellectuals gathered in small cliques speaking snob to one another. I betted my new partner's parents were around here somewhere. I passed a group of brown-nosed Lagartans hanging on some offworlder's every word. The offworlder was probably twice my age, but looked like a thirty-year-old vid-star.

I navigated the perimeter of the room, looking for the police table.

"Juno!"

I turned to the voice.

Matsuo Sasaki said, "Come have a drink with me."

Shit, I didn't need this right now. I sat down. You didn't snub Sasaki. "Hey, Matsuo. Long time no see."

"You can say that again." He snapped, and a waiter appeared. "A glass of brandy for my companion."

Matsuo Sasaki was the number two man of the Bandur cartel. He'd served under Ram Bandur from the beginning. Since Ram's death, he worked for Bandur's son, Ben. He was wearing a white tux that went well with his silver hair. He clapped me on the back with his four-fingered hand. "It's been too long, Juno. What have you been up to?"

"I'm still working the streets, making collections and keeping my head down."

"You are a wise man, Juno Mozambe."

"Where's Ben?"

"He couldn't make it." He spoke crisply, like he was unhappy about Ben's absence. It sounded like there was a little trouble in the Bandur camp. Sasaki normally kept his emotions corralled.

I didn't ask why Bandur didn't come. You didn't question Sasaki. His toughness was legendary. The story went that Sasaki was one of many lieutenants working for Ram Bandur in the early days of his organization. They were all vying for Bandur's favor. At one of their meetings, Bandur joked that his lieutenants should be willing to cut off their own fingers to serve him. Sasaki saw his opportunity and abruptly left the meeting, returning ten minutes later with a pair of pruning shears and his severed pinky. The sick fuck didn't even use a lase-blade. That way, at least the wound would have been partly cauterized and a hell of a lot less painful. Ram Bandur instantly made him his pinkyless right-hand man.

Somebody was on stage, making a toast. Holy hell, it was Bandur's chief rival, Carlos Simba. Sasaki gritted his teeth. I was stunned. What was he doing up there?

Simba was wearing an ill-fitting tux. High-water pants showed sock, and a purple cummerbund clashed over a blue shirt. He loved his uncouth image. It endeared him to the impoverished Lojan people. He stuck it to the rich. Nobody cared that he was a drug-dealing mass murderer.

He held his glass high. "I won't speak long. I know you are all having a good time, so I'll make my comments brief. I want to speak on all of your behalf by thanking Mayor Samir for inviting us to this fantastic banquet."

The room sounded gentle applause. Sasaki looked ready to blow. The audaciousness of the *Loja* crime lord toasting the mayor of *Koba* was too much for him. He stamped out. A collective intake of breath ran through the neighboring tables.

Ben Bandur should've been here. Simba wouldn't have been so daring as to affront him in person. I realized for the first time that the outcome of the war between Simba and Bandur's cartels might not be as predetermined as I thought. I had deemed Simba's attempt to take over Bandur's organization nothing but megalomaniacal folly. Loja was a mere fraction the size of Koba and had no tourist business to speak of. I thought Bandur's monetary dominance was impenetrable. Tonight, I wasn't so sure.

Simba finished his toast and chinked glasses with the bandleader. A spotlight illuminated Mayor Samir. He held up his glass like he was returning the toast. Then he slowly poured it out on the carpet without taking a sip. He turned his back on the stage in a show of contempt. The crowd went pin-drop silent. The mayor was letting everybody know he was anticorruption pure. He didn't consort with criminal elements.

I slugged down a hit of brandy to quell my nerves. Simba left the stage with a broad smile, not missing a beat. His goal wasn't to score points with Mayor Samir. He wanted people to notice his presence and Bandur's absence at a major Koba social function. The signal was clear: I'm the new man in town. The Bandur kid had better grow up fast and quit staying home before Simba took away his Koba empire in a self-fulfilling prophecy of greatness.

I knocked back the last sip of brandy and moved on. I found C of D Diego Banks at the police table. His mousy wife gave me an abbreviated smile.

I dispensed with the niceties. *This asshole wants Paul's job.* "Where's Paul?"

Banks stared at me. The hostility between us pushed his wife back in her chair. Banks pointed to the dancers.

I waited on the edge of the dance floor. The band was playing an upbeat number slowed down to a geriatric tempo. Haughty old men moved in slow motion. Their dates danced with hankies to dab the sweat off. I mentally relocated to the Tenttown canal party—dancers spraying starlit mud and sweat with every gyration. Poor people knew how to party.

The tune ended. People spilled off the floor to the surrounding tables. Paul had his arm around his wife's waist. Her dress was conservative, covering shoulders and knees. She saw me and gave me a strong hug for such a small woman. Paul and I shook hands and found an uncrowded spot near the can.

Paul looked sharp in his tux. He looked good in everything. He said, "Did you see the shit Simba pulled?"

"Yeah, the guy's got cojones."

"I don't even know how he got in here. The mayor never invited him. He must've bribed his way in through the kitchen."

I changed the subject to the reason I came. "What's this case about, Paul?"

Paul's permanently pasted-on smile disappeared. "I don't know."

"What do you mean you don't know?"

"I mean I don't know. Listen to me, I got the mayor's office investigating me, and their man Gilkyson's been like my fucking shadow. Then the Vlotsky killing came up, and I found out his father worked for the city, so I thought I could get some good PR with the mayor's office if I made a show of the investigation, maybe get them to lay off a little. Then Gilkyson started telling me the mayor didn't want special treatment. Give me a break. Since when does a politician not want special treatment? So I got to thinking they might have something to hide. I started talking big, saying things like we have to nail the SOB that killed Vlotsky, or people will think it's open season on city employees. It was a total stab in the dark, but Gilkyson got all nervous. He kept trying to downplay the whole thing. I'm telling you, Juno, I've had that weasel in my office for two weeks. I can read him. The more I talked about ramping up the investigation, the more he resisted."

"You think the mayor had Lieutenant Vlotsky popped?"

"That, or he has a good reason for covering it up. Either way, I need you to connect him to it. I have to kill this corruption investigation. I'm getting desperate. You get me the goods on this one, and I'll extort the mayor into laying off of KOP."

"Why don't you just kick that asshole Gilkyson out of your office?"

"Don't you get it, Juno? I work for the *mayor*. He wants Gilkyson to follow me around. There's nothing I can do."

"Just give them what they want. Hand over a couple crooked cops, and they'll leave you alone. You have a whole police force to choose from. Use it as a goddamned opportunity to clean house."

Paul became visibly angry, very un-Paul. "You don't think I

tried that? Do you think I'm a fucking idiot? The mayor won't take the deal; he wants *me*, Juno."

I snagged a brandy from a passing waiter and tossed it down my throat. The alcohol quashed my rapid-fire nerves. "Why?"

"He wants control of KOP, and he knows he won't get it as long as I'm here. He wants a fucking yes-man."

"How bad is it?"

"Bad. My informants in the mayor's office say he's getting ready to make a move on me."

I rejected the notion. "He can't touch you."

"The mayor is flexing some serious muscle. He's got cops on his payroll, and he's got Chief of Detectives Diego fucking Banks working against me. He's the mayor's little lapdog, and he's drooling all over himself, thinking about my job. He's been sucking up to Mayor Samir so he'll get appointed chief when I fall. I never should have let Samir get elected. I thought I could buy him off like the other mayors. I should have sabotaged his campaign the minute he started in on KOP. Now it may be too late. It's only a matter of time before Gilkyson ties me to the Bandurs. Shit, we've been allied with the Bandur cartel for twenty-five years. We worked hard at covering our tracks, Juno, but we've been sanctioning criminal activity for over *twenty-five years*. You can't tell me they won't find something."

"I can't believe what you're saying. Why haven't you told me about this?"

"I couldn't do that to you. You've been working so hard on getting your life under control. I wanted to keep you out of it."

"But now you want me back in?"

"I don't want to drag you into this, but listen to me, Juno. You're the only one I can trust. Since Mayor Samir started in heavy on this corruption bullshit, I've been trying to take him down, but nothing's worked. Even my extortion scheme fell through."

I waved for another brandy. "What kind of extortion scheme?"

"I put some of my most loyal cops on it. They started checking into Mayor Samir's personal life. Turns out the mayor's daughter is a real slut. 'Sounds promising,' I thought. We catch some vids of her poking every guy she meets and threaten to go public with them, and the mayor will lay off. We've been tailing her for a month, and we've got squat. All the sudden, her legs lock together at the knees. It's like she's a fucking nun. Somebody in the inner circle's a rat."

I squeezed my glass. I was growing double angry—angry at a cop who was a rat and angry at myself for letting Paul down. Ferreting out rats used to be one of my specialties.

Paul said, "So then I figured that if I can't trust my own men, I'll give Sasaki a crack at it, but somebody keeps ratting his plans, too. You know Sasaki; he does his best to run a tight ship, but that fucking Bandur kid is fucking worthless. Ram was always too soft on him. He's too worried about his looks to do anything productive. When I told him that he's got a rat in his organization, he listened, then asked me how he'd look with a more pronounced chin. I wish his father was still alive. Shit, they're so worried about the Simba cartel moving in that they don't care about the mayor anyway."

I tried to soak it all in. Mayor Samir was trying to take KOP away from Paul, and Paul thought the Vlotsky case was related. My stomach started to flop. I downed the brandy in my glass. The mayor was up on the bandstand now, dancing with his wife. They were hamming it up, twirling and dipping, taking full advantage of the photo op.

Paul asked, "What have you got so far on the case?"

Paul's question took a minute to register. "We were going to look at an Army guy who has a record and a good motive. But

I don't see how that could be related to the mayor. Do you want me to drop it and focus on the mayor?"

"No. Work it like any other case. I need you to find out what happened in that alley. You work the case from the bottom up. I'll work it from the mayor down. Hopefully we'll meet in the middle."

"Can you get me in to see this Army guy? His name's Jhuko Kapasi. The military has him under wraps."

"I'll do what I can."

The place went quiet. The band had stopped playing, and the mayor had moved to the podium, throwing grins and waves at the audience. A hundred holographic replicas of the mayor floated over the tables of the people too far away to see his charming mug. Paul and I waited quietly as he spoke a few brief words of thanks then ticked through his political agenda. Straight through the mayor's anticorruption stumping, Paul kept his true feelings hidden behind his public face.

The crowd was still applauding when Paul said, "Are we square on this?"

"Yeah," I said. "But you have to get rid of Maggie. I work alone."

"No. I handpicked Maggie for this. Everybody knows how far back the two of us go. If we manage to nail Mayor Samir, we'll need somebody with a good rep, somebody they can't slander as a dirty cop. Somebody that they can't dig up any dirt on. Maggie is crystal. She hasn't been corrupted like the rest of us. She was first in her class, and she comes from a prominent family that can't be pushed around. Plus she's got that honest face—the public will believe anything she says. I'm hoping that we can force the mayor into a deal, but if we have to go to the public with it, she'll make the perfect face for it. You don't have that kind of credibility. If I put you in front of the cameras, they'll spin it as a ploy to save ourselves. I made up all that stuff about her mother calling me so Gilkyson wouldn't suspect anything. He thinks I'm doing her mother a favor."

"Does she know about this?"

"No. She just thinks she's my favorite. Keep her out of the loop. You do the dirty work, let Maggie take the credit."

Niki appeared at my elbow. "Who's Maggie?"

Paul smiled at Niki, happy to see her. His smile faded when he caught her evil eye. Before he moved off, he said, "It's nice to see you, Niki."

Niki evil-eyed Paul until he disappeared into the crowd. Niki used to like Paul. It was hard not to like him, the way he could charm you. With that broad smile and that easy attitude, you'd think he was the nicest guy you ever met. Niki blamed Paul for my drinking problem and my nightmares, and everything else that was wrong with me. To her, it was all Paul's fault for making me do all the things I'd done as his enforcer. While it was true that I was following his orders, I had free will. I knew there was nobody to blame but myself.

Even when I'd gotten to the point where I'd have to down half a bottle to work up the nerve to go into a beatdown session, and then drink the other half to try and forget what I'd done, I'd still kept going. It made me sick to think about all the times I'd slammed my fists into some defenseless sap's face.

"Who's Maggie?" Niki repeated.

"My new partner."

"Seriously?"

"Yeah."

"Why do you need a partner?"

"Paul has his reasons."

Niki and I got home late after having a surprisingly good time. It had started off rocky, but once I'd explained away my new partner to a jealousy-prone Niki, things got loose. I pounded down enough brandy to grease the friction between us, and I slipped into my old hard-partying habits. We danced ourselves sweaty and ran the waiters ragged on brandy refills.

On the way home, I drove with one hand on the wheel and one on Niki's thigh. A full day of looking at Maggie Orzo had me feeling frisky. At home, Niki went into the bathroom and came out in the sheerest of negligees, her dark nipples visible through the red fabric. Already buzzed on brandy, my buzz notched higher as I took in her long legs. She smiled coyly.

I took off my clothes then took her in my grasp. I started on her neck then moved in to taste her mouth. My hands slid down and around and back again. She pressed into me, her need as great as my own. I stripped her negligee off, tasted her breasts, her nipples, her shoulders. We moved to the bed, touching and fondling, trying to stretch out the moment. We couldn't resist any longer. She crawled on top of me, sinking me into her. We moved together, slow at first, then faster when it became apparent we wouldn't last long. I watched Niki's face. Her eyes were closed, her mouth was open, the corners curled upward in pleasure. I closed my eyes and couldn't resist picturing Maggie Orzo's face with that same expression, closed eyes, open mouth, maybe biting her lip to keep from screaming . . . I lost control and released into her, feeling ashamed even before the last spasm. I kept my hips moving when I was through, only stopping after Niki reached her destination.

I held Niki from behind. My liquor and lovemaking high starting to fade. Niki asked, "Is she pretty?"

"Who?"

"Your new partner."

"Yeah, I suppose she is." I tried to sound casual despite the guilt I was feeling.

"I thought so."

"What makes you say that?"

Her voice turned cold, accusatory. "I haven't seen you this horny in a long time."

Her words doused the last embers of my high, and my eyes stung from the smoke. I tried to blink them normal, but they stayed stung. I rolled away from her, looking up at the ceiling, but not really looking at it, mostly just looking up. Was this all we had? She'd needle me, and I'd say ouch, then I'd needle back, the two of us constantly yanking each other's strings, neither one of us able to stop.

eight

'Sixty-two was the year everything changed. For better or for worse, I still wasn't sure. I never set out to change the world. Shit, it had never crossed my mind that it was even possible.

I was a vice cop and I thought that was the greatest gig there was. A cop's take-home afforded what seemed to me to be a good life. When the bus was inconvenient, I could take a cab and not worry about the cost. I didn't have to barefoot it anymore. I could afford to buy two pairs of shoes a year, and not the crappy ones with the laces that snap off in a month. Best of all, I was renting my own place, a place with actual walls and a floor that was raised off the ground. After spending my whole life in a tent, I felt like I was living large.

I'd even been able to afford a proper death for my mother. Once the rot had set in, there was no way to save her, but with my KOP paychecks, I was at least able to pay for her antibiotic injections. Without those shots, the rot would have spread to her face, and she wouldn't have been able to have a wake when she died. Most rot sufferers would be so disfigured by the time they died that they had to be cremated, but my mother was buried whole. She meant something.

I was just your average clock-punching cop with aspirations of being nothing more. Things were good. Other vice dicks were making names for themselves and rising through KOP ranks while I was content to work the shit details. I wasn't

scoring any flashy busts, but I was doing my job, arresting one
pimp or pusher at a time.

Paul Chang was different. He was a dreamer, a big-picture
guy. He never cared much about the daily grind of police work
or about the individual victims we saw. To him, such things
were just pieces of a pattern, cogs in a system that he needed
to understand. Paul was all visions and designs. I was all nuts
and bolts. But for some reason, when the two of us were partnered together, we were electric, instant best friends.

Our big break came when we caught a hot tip from Chow
Lin—an opium dealer who we'd flipped a few months earlier.
We pinched him for pushing, which carried a minimum seven.
We held the evidence and told him he could serve the seven in
prison or serve seven working for us. He made the easy choice
and kept pushing while he passed us information on the side.

He put us onto an offworlder named Mai Nguyen who had
just come down to the surface from the Orbital. He told us she
was a big offworld buyer who smuggled O up to the Orbital
and sold it to the freighter crews that passed through the Lagartan System. He heard she was on the surface, shopping for
new suppliers.

It took Paul and me a full day to pick up her scent. We
bribed hotel clerks all over the city, finally scoring a hit at the
Nirvana Palace. We staked out the place for an hour before
spotting her leaving from the back entrance. Like all offworlders, Mai Nguyen was easy to pick out. She was physically
perfect. She had a doll's face, an athlete's legs, and cleavage up
to her chin. She strutted down the grassy steps accompanied
by two heavies who came out into the steamy heat wearing
thick jackets, gloves, and long pants. Nobody dressed like that
on Lagarto. It could mean only one thing—the suits were covering some serious technological voodoo. Retractable finger
blades? Recessed lasers? Mechanical limbs stronger than a

crane? Who the fuck knew? You never could tell with off-worlders.

They turned and walked onto the street. Crowds gave them a wide berth, making them easy to tail. They strolled into the Old Town Square, a busy thoroughfare crammed with souvenir shops and sidewalk stands. Hawkers flocked around them, peddling chess sets with lizard-shaped pieces and old bricks with jungle scenes painted on.

Mai Nguyen stopped at a small stand and bought a cloth that she used to mop her brow and cleavage. Her goons stayed on her heels with their perspiration-soaked jackets buttoned all the way up. She weaved from booth to booth trying on sandals. She finally found a pair to her liking and talked the old woman into a trade: Nguyen's shoes for the sandals. The old woman gladly stuffed paper into the toes of Nguyen's shoes then slipped them on.

They stopped for dinner at an Asian place on the square. Paul and I sat on a park bench and watched them through the restaurant window. "Some drug dealers," I said.

Paul looked at his discount store watch and chuckled uncomfortably. "Tell me about it. So far, it looks like a nice family on vacation."

Paul was knotted with frustrated ambition. He came onto vice after only two years as a beat cop compared to my three. He became fast friends with our lieutenant, passed all the tests with high marks, and got reports done on time but was still passed over when promotions were handed out. I told him it was because he was young, but we both knew the real reason. You had to earn your stripes with a big bust, simple as that. He wanted to nail Nguyen. An arrest of an offworld trafficker would put our pictures all over the news and land him a lieutenancy, maybe even get him his own squad.

Nguyen and her keepers finished their dinner and ambled

back to the hotel, stopping once so that one of the thugs could buy a shellacked monitor head mounted on a slab of wood with its jaws spread wide enough to bite off a limb.

I wasn't worried about promotions for myself. Since I'd never graduated from school, I would never rise above sergeant anyway. I just liked the idea of bringing down an offworlder. Lagartans have always held a grudge against offworlders, and I was no exception. I hated the way they'd act like they were superior coming down here showing off their far-out tech and their bottomless bank accounts.

Nguyen was from the Orbital, or Lagarto Orbital-1 as it was officially known. The Lagartan government came up with that name. They numbered it like someday there'd be an LO-2 and an LO-3. They'd originally built it as a trading post for brandy exports, but it had ceased being a trade route hot spot long ago and therefore its successors had never been constructed. However, in recent years, the Orbital had been returning to prominence thanks to the flourishing mining operations in the asteroid belts. Freighters were coming through regularly now, which meant big opportunities for drug traffickers like Nguyen.

Two days of tailing her finally paid dividends when she and her goons came down the hotel's back stairs in the middle of the night with three large cases. They flagged a cab and counted off enough offworld bucks to convince the driver to rent out the car. The driver danced to the sidewalk counting his good fortune.

Paul and I waited for them to pull out then ran for the street. We flashed badges and weapons at the first cab we saw. We took the car, leaving the driver and a pair of bar floozies on the curb.

I drove with the lights off while Paul hung out the window trying to pick up their trail. We caught up to them just as they turned east, heading for the river. I stayed back as far as I could, while they drove into an old industrial area. We passed broken-windowed bottling plants and caved-in lumber mills. As we got closer to the river, more and more of the road was enveloped by dense green weeds that slapped and scraped at the car's underside.

Nguyen and her thugs drove up a concrete ramp into the cargo bay of a dilapidated brick building. I pulled around to the backside of the building and parked out of sight.

Paul and I high-stepped through the deep weeds to an old fire escape that barely clung to the side of the building. We climbed slowly. The rusted metal squeaked and swayed as we made our way up to the third story and through a window. Paul flicked on a flashlight. Dozens of lizards dashed for cover. One held her ground, guarding a nest of eggs and hissing. We worked our way to the front side of the building, ducking our heads to avoid the face-tickling moss that drooped from the ceiling. We stopped at a door that opened onto a catwalk over the cargo bay.

The door was half open. We could hear mumbled voices right below us. We would have to get what we could from here. There was no way we could go out onto that catwalk without being detected.

Paul took the flycam out of its case. We'd stolen it. There was no other way for us to get our hands on good tech. Lagartans couldn't buy any of it with our worthless currency. We couldn't even purchase the cheapest offworld products because of the steep shipping charges. The closest planet is five long years away. The only tech Lagartans could enjoy was vids, net access, and communications equipment—all provided by the Orbital. The communications equipment was useful. The whole planet had phone coverage—as long as you could pay the charges. The vids and net access were a curse. All they'd do was advertise a bunch of shit we couldn't afford.

This flycam was an unbelievable catch. Nobody manufactured cameras on Lagarto—too sophisticated for us. Paul and I had scammed our way into the top-notch equipment a couple months earlier. An offworld dignitary had come planetside for some conference, and we arrested one of her bodyguards on trumped-up charges. We impounded everything in the body-guard's hotel room. Upon his release, we informed him that somehow all his surveillance equipment had gotten "lost" on the way to the evidence room.

Paul set the flycam, which was no bigger than a coin, down in a bare patch on the floor. He used the control mechanism to lift and guide it silently into the cargo bay. We huddled on the floor, studying the display.

Vines hung down from the catwalks. Green grasses sprouted from old loading equipment. The cargo bay held two cars, posi-tioned to illuminate the area with their headlights. One of Nguyen's heavies kept lookout at the door, while Nguyen and the other heavy showed the cases to a balding man, definitely a local. Surgery and genetic manipulation protected offworlders from suffering from such a hideous deformity.

Nguyen popped open the cases, revealing stacks upon stacks of pesos. Paul and I exchanged big-eyed glances. The camera gave us a bird's-eye view as the local emptied the cases into a mail sack then hung the sack from the hook of a butcher's scale. When there was too much money to count, just weigh it and call it good.

From above, Nguyen was all cleavage; couldn't even see her feet. "All there?"

The local did some math with a stick in the dirt. "Yeah. It looks good."

"And the opium?"

"Start loading," the local said to a holographic accomplice. The real accomplice was surely located at the spaceport. To Nguyen he said, "You should be able to confirm that loading has begun."

One of the heavies' faces went lobotomy-blank as he

mouthed words to the offworld communications implants in his head. After a moment, his face returned to human, and he nodded affirmative to Nguyen.

Nguyen made a show of mopping her perspiration, starting with her brow and moving to her neck and arms, a little show for the native. Her sexed-up looks were downright cartoonish. It was hard to believe that she was a real woman. She said, "Excellent, now we wait until loading is completed."

She sauntered over to the thug guarding the door, leaned in, and whispered something—couldn't hear what she said. She walked back and sat on the hood of one of the cars.

Her thug started acting strange. He had this ultradumb expression on his face. His mouth was open; his eyes were closed, and his fingers were twitching. Then he looked right into our camera. My breath caught in my throat. OH SHIT! He saw the camera. Then he turned to look back out the door. Paul exhaled, thinking the same thing I was—calm down, you're just paranoid. He couldn't have spotted that camera—too small, too dark. He just happened to look that way.

We watched and waited. It felt like forever.

The local's holographic accomplice spoke up. "They're done. The cargo's onboard."

One of the thugs confirmed with a gloved thumbs-up.

Mai Nguyen said, "Pleasure doing business with you, sir. The money is all yours."

They all made quick business of packing up and leaving. Paul recalled the camera. It came slowly out of the shadows and landed in his palm—offworld magic.

I whispered, "We got it?"

"Yeah. We got it." He grinned large.

"Let's go."

Paul hightailed to the fire escape. I was just a step behind. We did it!

The rest of the plan was easy—rush back to HQ, show the vid to the lieutenant, and hit the hotel with a whole squad to make the arrest. We knew better than try to arrest them ourselves. Two cops with antique lase-pistols didn't stand a chance against three offworlders.

We jumped down from the fire escape and bolted for the car, tearing through the weeds at full bore. We came upon our car . . . HOW? SHIT! SHIT! Nguyen was sitting on the hood. The goons came up behind us and pinned our arms behind our backs. *FUCK, that hurts!*

Nguyen took out her already dripping cloth and drew it across her face and chest. She wrung the sweat out into a small puddle. She vamped over and frisked us, tossed our weapons out into the weeds.

"It's nice to finally meet you boys. I feel like we already know each other, we've been spending so much time together for the past couple days." She turned to me. "You'll forgive my being blunt, but who the fuck are you?"

I didn't answer.

The thug yanked my left arm backward.

PAIN, unbelievable PAIN! I heard a crack. PANIC! "Juno! Juno!"

"What's that? Did you say Juno?"

The thug loosened up—just a touch.

I had tears in my eyes. I couldn't catch my breath. "J-Juno, Juno Mozambe."

"And who do you work for, Juno Mozambe?"

"We don't work for anybody." My arm was yanked farther. I felt bones scraping. "COPS! We're cops."

Nguyen started to laugh. "Cops? And I thought this might be something serious. Let them go."

The thug let me go. I fell to my knees and vomited, feeling ashamed that I broke.

"Which one of you has the camera?" Paul pulled it from his pocket and handed it to her.

"And who are you?"

"Paul Chang."

"Well, Paul Chang, at least you have the good sense to answer me without forcing me to resort to this . . . unpleasantness. You are unusually civilized for a Lagartan. You people really are just dirty little animals. Take your little monkey of a partner for instance . . ."

BITCH! I charged, my right hand going for her throat, thugs too slow to react. My hand closed in on her throat. SQUEEZE HARD! Crush it before they grab me. My palm made contact. I could feel her damp skin. WHITE FLASH—PAIN, oh god pain!

I fell to the ground convulsing, my nerves on fire.

Nguyen's voice mocked. "As I was saying, take your little monkey of a partner for instance. He sure tries hard. You might be able to teach him a few tricks, but he's just too dumb to think for himself." She patted my head.

I couldn't move. The air reeked of burned flesh and my own shit.

She straightened up. "We must be going, Paul Chang. I trust we won't be hearing from the two of you again."

". . . s'okay Juno, you're gonna be okay. I'll get you to a doc. . . ."

". . . might hurt. I just have to pull you up into the car. On three, okay? One . . . two . . . three . . ."

". . . almost there, Juno. Stay with me, okay? You have to . . ."

". . . palm is burned pretty badly. We'll have to graft some skin. . . ."

✠

"Hey, Juno. You awake?"

Everything was blurred, white walls, white sheets. Paul's smile came into focus. "Paul?"

"Yeah, Juno. It's me. Doctors say you're going to be fine. How do you feel?"

"How long?"

"Three days."

"Nguyen?"

"Gone, she's gone . . . best I can tell, the shipment of O is gone, too. We have nothing on her except maybe assaulting an officer. No evidence, though. It's just our word. A cop's word is normally good enough, but not with her money. There's no way we could make it stick. She's offplanet now anyway."

"What happened?"

"You don't remember?"

"I remember going for that bitch's throat."

"Shit, that temper of yours is going to get you killed one of these days. She was rigged, micro wires under her skin. She electrocuted you when you touched her."

"Wires under her skin?"

"Yes."

"You've got to be fucking kidding me."

"You have the scars to prove it."

"What can we do against these people?"

"I think we've been going about this the wrong way." His trademark smile was gone.

nine

"THE doctors clear you yet?"

I flexed my right hand. "They say I can start in two days."

Paul beamed. His smile was infectious. "That's great, Juno! It's been tough working alone."

"It's only been two weeks."

We sat at the counter of a fish bar near the pier. I was careful to sit on the edge of the stool. They'd grafted a piece of skin from my thigh to my hand. I'd already opened the thigh wound once when I'd sat too hard, and I didn't want to bloody another pair of pants. I forked through the bowl of fish and noodles. Chopsticks were too hard to control—left arm in a cast, right hand too stiff from the skin grafts.

Paul finished his bowl. "Are you ready for me to fill you in yet?"

"Sure."

"I IDed the local that sold the O to Nguyen. His name's Pavel Yashin."

"How'd you find him?"

"I thought the guy looked at least forty. I figured that if he's dealing at age forty, he must have a record. Nobody goes that long without getting picked up for something, right? I pulled the records on all offenders aged over thirty-five."

"You looked at mugs?"

"Yeah, but most of the mugs were too old. I didn't think I could pick him out of a lineup when he was twenty years younger, so I called up to the Orbital and had them pull all their current phone records and beam down their holos. I didn't have to go through more than a few dozen before I recognized him."

"What do you have on him so far?"

"Nothing. I've been waiting for you to get better."

I hurried the last few bites. "Let's go."

"I thought you had to wait two more days."

"I won't do anything strenuous. Let's go."

Pavel Yashin lived in an upscale neighborhood, in a house that was large by Lagartan standards, two stories with an attached garage. We hid in a nearby alley and waited for him to show himself. Mosquitoes sucked our blood for a full hour before the garage door opened and a car pulled out. We leaned back into the foliage as the car passed, our balding local at the wheel.

Paul went over the outer wall. With me unable to give him a boost, he had to climb my body like a ladder to get to the top. I kept lookout while Paul put six of our stolen cameras in place. These weren't as sophisticated as the flycam we'd lost to Mai Nguyen. These were stationary but next to impossible to detect. All you had to do was stick one to a window, like a piece of rubber cement. It dried clear so you could only see it if you knew to look for it. As long as Pavel Yashin didn't have the same tech as Nguyen and her heavies, we'd be able to spy in as long as we wanted. More offworld magic, thanks to our offworld bodyguard friend.

Six cameras: living room, kitchen, dining room, office, and two upstairs bedrooms. The cameras had a limited broadcast range, so we found somebody in Yashin's neighborhood to rent us a room with a private entrance. The cameras' audio feed was excellent, even the kitchen's drippy faucet came through, but the 2-D image was seriously low quality. No depth to the picture and no ability to rotate your viewing perspective around the room. Wouldn't matter, the important thing was stealth, not quality. The monitor had buttons labeled A through F, that you could use to cycle through the six cameras.

We flipped through all the cameras: nobody home. We left it on the kitchen: button D. Paul turned off the recorder.

I tilted my chair back. "I guess this could take a while."

Paul looked apprehensive.

"What is it, Paul?"

"Do you like being a cop?"

I held up my cast. "Some days better than others."

"You ever wonder what we accomplish?"

"What do you mean?"

"We bust all these pimps, hookers, and pushers and what does it ever accomplish? As soon as we lock one up, there's another one ready to take their place. What's the point?"

"Where are you going with this?"

"Lagarto is always going to be poor, Juno. The pols are always telling us times will get better, but you know they won't. Our currency is worthless. You saw it yourself. It takes so much of our money to be worth anything that you can't count it all. Yashin had to *weigh* it; you understand that? We don't even deal in single pesos anymore. Our smallest denomination is a hundred. Offworld money isn't like that. Pols say it's just a trade 'imbalance.' No fucking kidding. We have nothing to trade. We export a few illegal drugs to the Orbital and the mines, maybe a little food. That's it. We get a few tourists coming down here looking for a good time, but half of them are too afraid to leave their hotels. We can't make anything that offworlders can't make for themselves faster and cheaper. Their tech is centuries ahead of ours, I mean *centuries*. We're using fossil fuels for god's sake. What does that tell you?"

I knew he was right, but I spewed the same shit the pols did just to piss him off. "That's where you're wrong. We keep whining that offworlders have all this tech we can't afford. We don't have to buy it; we can build it ourselves. All the information we need is on the nets."

Paul was heating up. "What the hell have we done with the information we have? Nobody even understands it."

I tried to keep a straight face as I egged him on. "That's why they're starting to teach tech in schools. Those kids are whizzes. We'll catch up in a few years."

"Jesus, Juno, you know most kids can't afford to go to school. You know that better than anyone. School is worthless anyway. When I got my degree, they taught us all kinds of useless tech shit like how an antimatter drive works. You see an antimatter store around here? What the hell good does it do to know how antimatter works when we don't have any?"

I toed the optimist's line a little longer. "So what if we don't have the resources of other planets. We just need to make a few products that we can export. Then we can import all that other stuff in."

"That's just it," he said excitedly. "We can't even do that. Any information on the nets is years old by the time we get it. They can't transmit any faster than the speed of light, so whatever information we get is already out of date by ten years or more. So say we take a year to learn to build whatever it is that you think we can export. That's eleven years already, then we have to ship it fourteen years back to Earth. You think they want a twenty-five-year-old product? It'd be worthless."

"So you're saying we have no hope?"

"That's right. No hope at all. And what do people with no hope do? They abuse drugs, gamble . . . sell their bodies, that's what. Now tell me how a couple vice cops can accomplish anything?"

We broke out the booze, put our feet up, and watched the screen—still no action.

"Okay, Paul. If you're so sure we're wasting our time, why are you sitting here on your day off?"

"So I can learn."

"Learn what?"

"Learn how to run a drug operation."

"You want to be a pusher?"

"No. I just need to understand how it works."

"Why?"

"So I can harness it." Paul's fist was clenched; his smile was dangerously high-wattage.

I wanted to know what he was talking about but was afraid of where it might lead me. I'd noticed a tendency in myself to follow Paul, no matter how crazy his ideas were. I told him, "You are seriously fucked up." We laughed as I poured another round. "Whoa, somebody's home."

A woman came through the back door into the kitchen. She had long legs, long hair, and was dressed to the nines. She kicked off her shoes, losing a few centimeters in height. She just left the shoes in the middle of the floor. She stopped at the fridge, popped some ice into a glass, and headed for the living room. I flipped channels to B. She pulled open the liquor cabinet and poured enough to cover the cubes. She took a sip and headed upstairs. I flipped back and forth between E and F until she showed up on F.

She stripped off her gown, showing black underwear on coffee skin. She slumped into a chair and nursed her drink. I fixated on her eyes. I felt like they were speaking to me, like they were calling me. My insides hummed. Her eyes also said something else. It was there, under the surface. I just couldn't seem to peg what it was.

She slinked into the adjoining bathroom and closed the door.

"Who was that?" I wanted to know.

"Must be Yashin's daughter. Her name is Natasha. She's twenty-four. Strange she still lives at home."

"It's not that strange. Not everybody marries young."

"I know, but a looker like that in her prime years? She should be living it up at her own place. She doesn't need Mommy and Daddy cramping her style."

I nodded without looking at Paul. My eyes were riveted to the bathroom door, waiting for her to come back out.

ten

PAUL stared at the papers tacked up on the walls of our stake-out pad—the results of a month's spying. The mold-speckled notes detailed Pavel Yashin's drug trade. "What do you think, Juno?"

"I say we arrest the SOB."

"We don't have any evidence."

"We have all kinds of evidence, Paul."

"We've gathered all this evidence illegally. We can't use any of it in court."

"All we need is a surveillance warrant. I told you about Judge Saydak. She's got huge gambling debts, and she's selling warrants. It won't even cost that much. All we have to do is get her to backdate the warrant, and we're set."

"But Yashin's strictly small-time. Don't you want something more?"

He was right about Pavel Yashin being small-time. He ran a good business, though. He was making weekly trips upriver to meet representatives of the warlords, and placing opium orders. They'd ship the brown sugar by barge to a drop point a few klicks upriver from Koba. Yashin would take a skiff out on the water and send flashlight signals. They'd dump his O overboard, and he'd fish out the floating packages by flashlight. He'd motor the goods to shore and load it into his car. Then he'd drive home, his weighted-down car scraping the pavement at every bump in the road.

Yashin worked solo. He trusted no one. He made an easy target driving around with all that dope by himself. You'd think he'd have some bodyguards riding shotgun, but he was too paranoid to let anybody near his contraband. He'd pull the car into the garage and haul the dope down to the basement, working himself into a heart-attack-intensity sweat.

He had a network of dealers who came to the house to buy his shit, but he wouldn't let any of them into the basement. He'd go down alone and bring up the right quantities. The dealers would turn around and sell it at high-class hotels and restaurants. Most of them had jobs as waiters, bartenders, or bellhops. That must've been how the electric bitch, Mai Nguyen, found Yashin. She'd probably been approached by one of his dealers who had set her up with Yashin. Up 'til recently, his business was small potatoes, but he was hoping that the Nguyen deal would change that.

Nguyen had been looking for a new supplier, one that could deliver high-grade O at a good price. Yashin thought he was just the guy so he made his sales pitch, and she bought it. He wanted to impress her with his ability to deliver in quantity so he went upriver and he bought up tons of product—literally. He sank all his funds into the down payment. He sold Nguyen a fourth of his stock the night we were watching, and he made pricing agreements on six more shipments.

At first, Paul and I were optimistic that if we could keep close to Yashin, we could get another shot at Nguyen when she made her next O buy. Yashin was calling up to the Orbital every day to see if Nguyen was ready for the next order, but she wouldn't answer his calls or return his messages. After a month of failed attempts to contact her, it had become abundantly clear that she was screwing him over.

We figured Nguyen was too spooked by us to deal with Yashin anymore. She knew we were likely to be onto Yashin, so she had probably moved on to another supplier. She had handled Paul and me just fine that night, but for all she knew, the whole of KOP would be waiting to pounce the instant she made another buy from Yashin. There were plenty of dealers for her to choose from. She could afford to play it safe by ditching Yashin even though she had little to worry about since Paul and I had kept Yashin's identity from our superiors. We'd been conducting this entire investigation on our own. Paul and I had learned the hard way that when you kept the bosses informed, you'd get your collars stolen out from under you.

When Yashin bought all that dope, he had thought he and Nguyen were going to have an ongoing business relationship, but now he'd finally caught on that she'd hung him out to dry. He was stuck with this huge stockpile of opium in his basement and had nowhere to unload it.

Yashin was unraveling. He'd gone from three to seven drinks a night. He'd overextended himself, and he was having major cash flow problems. He still owed money on his mammoth purchase, and he wasn't selling it fast enough to keep up on his payments. He kept trying to return it, but the warlord he bought it from wouldn't hear of it—all purchases were final.

He tried to increase his sales by getting two dealers to start pushing on the street. One had already gotten knifed, compliments of Ram Bandur. Bandur had his initials, R.B., burned with cigarette butts into the dealer's forehead, chest, and scrotum—antemortem. He wasn't taking kindly to anybody encroaching on his territory.

I wanted to arrest Yashin while we still had the chance. He'd become vulnerable, and I was afraid the sharks might get him first. Paul wanted to use Yashin to chum the water, see if we could snag us a shark.

I asked, "Just who do you think we can get?"

"We should go for Bandur. We already have him on murder."

"He's way too big, Paul. He's got Phra Kaew under his control. That's a big neighborhood, and he's not just peddling drugs, he's taking a piece of all the gambling and prostitution profits, too. He's got the money and the muscle to keep us from laying a finger on him. He knows we can't touch him. Why else would he burn his own initials into a vic?"

"You don't think we can take him down?"

"There's no way. Listen, busting Yashin would be perfect. We could get the warrant and nab him ourselves. We wouldn't have to share the collar with anybody. Going for Bandur will just get us killed."

"Okay, forget Bandur. Maybe we can get somebody else. Don't you want to run this up the ladder, see who Yashin can lead us to?"

"No, I don't. The lieutenant is already all over our asses. We can't just keep putting him off. We're way behind on our quota."

"So what? We can catch up anytime we want."

"You've been saying that for a month now, but we just keep falling further behind. You said we could run this whole operation on our personal time, but we've been watching this screen so much I doubt we've put in twenty hours of regular work this whole week."

"Don't worry about it, Juno. I can handle the lieutenant. He likes me."

"He's not going to like you for much longer if we miss our quota for the second month in a row. Listen, Paul, we don't need to be greedy. This arrest will give us everything we want. You know how much O he's got in his basement. A haul like that is the kind of thing they always put on the news. Shit, they'll take vids of the two of us posing next to that stash. They'll put you on the fast track for a lieutenancy. What more do you want?"

Paul didn't answer. He turned his gaze back to the papers on the wall. I couldn't figure out what had gotten into him lately. I didn't know what he was thinking half the time. I decided to drop it. We'd just wait and see like Paul wanted. We had what we needed on Yashin. There was no rush.

Paul got up. "I'm gonna run out for kebabs. You want anything?"

"Yeah. Set me up with one fish and one liz."

Paul closed the door behind him. I poured myself a drink and went back to watching the Yashins. Pavel was sulking on his couch. His wife, Gloria, was packing a suitcase, and daughter Natasha was reading in her bedroom. You'd never see any two of them in the same room.

I stayed on F. Pavel Yashin wasn't doing anything anyway. Natasha sat on the bed, flowery pillows propping her up. The book's cover was of a tuxedoed man dipping a woman on the dance floor. Natasha twisted her raven hair around her finger, untangling it every couple minutes to turn the page.

She kept checking the clock and returning to the book. Finally, she got up, reading all the while, like a kid reluctant to give up a favorite toy. She finished the page, bookmarked, and stripped off her clothes—petite breasts on svelte physique. She walked into the bathroom.

She came out a few minutes later, naked except for the towel wrapped around her head. She pulled a pair of red sheer panties up over her coffee skin and blow-dried her hair. She was sitting on the bed, using the window as a mirror, unknowingly looking right into the camera, looking right at me. My heart drummed in voyeuristic bliss.

Then she took two dresses out of the closet—one red, one black. *Go for the black.* Like she heard me, she hung the red dress back up, took the black one off its hanger, and slipped it over her head. The dress hung loose, but clung at all the right curves.

The smell of greasy meat preceded Paul's entrance. He glanced at the screen. "You watching her again?"

"Yeah. Can't take my eyes off her."

Natasha dabbed on just a touch of makeup and pulled a pair of heels out of the closet—black with thin straps.

"She is hot. I'll give you that, but she sulks too much for me. She looks like a real downer." He tossed me a kebob.

I unwrapped it from the soggy paper.

Paul took a bite. Sauce dripped down his chin. "Yashin up to anything?"

In response, I licked my fingers and kicked it over to B. He was up out of his seat, pouring himself another drink.

"Where's the missus?" Paul wanted to know.

"She's packing. She must be going to stay with her mother again."

"Again? Shit. Natasha's going out; Gloria's going to her mother's. He's gonna have another one of his party nights. We won't learn a damn thing tonight."

This would be the third time this week. Yashin had a thing for young poon. Once he was home alone, he'd call down to one of the prosty joints and get them sent over two at a time, the younger the better.

I finished off the first kebab. "You want to call it a night?"

"Yeah, we can record it. Scan through it tomorrow."

"Sounds good to me."

"You wanna hit the bars?"

"Not tonight, Paul. I'm beat. I just want to have a quiet night."

"Are you shittin' me? Since when do you want to stay home?"

"Since tonight."

We hopped separate cabs. I told my driver to let Paul get out ahead of us then made him turn the cab back. I had him wait three doors down from the Yashin house. No more than a

minute later, another cab pulled up. Two women with tall hair
sat in the back. After a couple honks, Natasha came out the
door and down the walk. She took the front seat.

I made the driver follow them. They stopped in the Old
Town Square at a restaurant called Afrie's—chic and ritzy. The
women got out of the cab deliberately, showing plenty of leg.
I waited a few, tossed some bills to the driver, and went in.

The place was done up in style. The floors were covered
with thick rugs that you sank into as you walked. The chairs
were upholstered with monitor hide. Nice. The lighting was
dimmed down with candles on the tables, setting the right
mood. People dressed in fancy clothes. I looked like a square in
my white linens. The maître d' pretended not to notice. "Will
you be dining tonight, or would you like to go to the bar?"

I scanned the restaurant and didn't see her. "The bar."

"Excellent, sir. Let me show you the way."

I parked on a stool at the bar, ordered house brandy on ice,
and checked out the room. I saw the three of them sitting in
a round booth. The two tall-haired women were laughing
over their drinks. Natasha sat opposite them, watching and
smiling when they looked her way. I could see she was too
smart for them. They bored her, but she was too polite to let
it show.

Natasha sipped at her drink, which was already almost gone.
It was some kind of special rainbow-colored drink with pieces of
fruit on the rim. I was mesmerized by her. She had the goods—
gorgeous, sophisticated, mysterious. I was flying high.

For the first time I noticed the man next to me. *What the
hell?* His forehead was glassed in with three goldfish swimming
about. Offworlders would come up with the strangest shit. This
place was a big offworlder hangout. At the end of the bar was a
super buxom broad with vampire fangs. A table of quintuplet-
clones in low-cut sundresses with cat faces—whiskers, fur, and

all—giggled at the pumped-up muscle-head miners flexing in front of a mirror. Offworlders looked like models most of the time, but when they went out partying, they'd pull out all the stops, morphing into the freakiest characters. *I can't believe they get off on that shit.*

I felt self-conscious in my linens. I was tempted to run home for a change of clothes, but a mental survey of my closet yielded nothing but more of the same. I asked the bartender to bring Natasha a second drink. I watched as he poured, scooped, shook, then blended the drink into a tall glass. He put some fruit on the rim, stabbed it with a straw, gave me a nod, and headed for her table. I picked up my drink and took a swig.

The bartender stopped at her table. The two chatterbugs stopped talking as he gestured in my direction. All three of them looked at me, but I made eye contact with Natasha only. She took the drink and held it up in a silent toast. I toasted back and took a long sip of brandy, hoping it would drown the butterflies in my stomach.

She excused herself and brought her drink with her to the bar. Straight black hair brushed her shoulders as she walked. I picked up the scent of her perfume as she took the barstool next to me.

"I'm Juno."

She gave my threads the once over. "What brings you here, Juno?"

"You."

She gave me an odd look.

I said, "I was walking by, and I saw you and your friends come in. I followed you."

"Why would you do that?"

"I want to get to know you."

"Are you sure?" She smiled the same coy smile I'd seen her get when she read her romance novels.

"Yes."

"I'm Natasha." She put her hand out for a formal shake. "What do you do, Juno?"

"I'm a cop."

"What kind of cop?"

"I work vice."

She raised her eyebrows at that. Thoughts of her father's business must've been running through her head. "So you chase down drug dealers?"

"Yeah. Drugs, prostitution, gambling."

"And you think I would be interested in a guy like that?"

"I don't know. Are you?"

The early morning sunlight beamed through the window, toasting the blanket beyond comfortable. I got up, cranked the aircon, and crawled back into bed. Natasha rolled over and laid her head on my shoulder. I held her and stared at my bedroom ceiling. Geckos came out of the walls to sip water from a ceiling leak. Most days I'd chase the pests away, but today I felt generous. I started to think up pet names for them.

The rage that lived in my gut was blissfully silent. I felt drunk on a night of fantasies come true. I held Natasha tight, my mind rocking to the rhythms of last night's lovemaking. I ran my fingers into her hair. I thrilled on the smell of her, the way her body curled against me.

Natasha said, "Juno."

"Yeah."

"Do you know who my father is?"

"Yeah."

"You're after him, aren't you?"

"Yes."

"Are you trying to use me to get to him?"

"No."

"Then why are you with me?"

"Because I want to be."

Paul and I watched the monitor. All the Yashins were home. Another couple weeks had gone by, and we still hadn't decided what to do about Pavel Yashin. I was more than ready to run him in, but Paul kept insisting on waiting to see if he could lead us to a bigger bust. Even after this morning, when the lieutenant gave us both a hellish reaming for our lackluster performance these past six weeks, Paul still remained unfazed.

Pavel Yashin was pacing the house, from one room to another. Paul kept flipping channels trying to keep up with his restless movements.

"The guy is getting desperate," I said.

"Yeah. It's like he's sitting on a time bomb with all that dope in his basement."

Yashin had stopped trying to sell it on the streets since his two dealers got clipped by Bandur's outfit. Now, he was spending most of his time on the phone trying to find a buyer—nothing but hang-ups so far. Paul changed to channel E. Yashin's wife, Gloria, was in their bedroom, kneeling in front of an altar made of candles and pinned-up pics of the Virgin Mary. She kept her long-sleeved nightgown buttoned to the top. She crossed herself, and then the room and slipped into bed.

Paul said, "No wonder Yashin goes for hookers. She's such a prude." It was true. We'd been spying for a month and a half, and we hadn't even seen them kiss.

Over to F: Natasha was reading again, another romance novel. My heart thumped in exhilaration. I watched her read, unable to stop despite my mounting guilt over deceiving her by intruding on her privacy. It looked like she'd be staying in for a change. She'd been out every night for the past two weeks, half those nights with her friends, the other half at my place. Paul didn't know about us. I told him I was seeing somebody but didn't tell him who. It was getting harder to cover my tracks. Yesterday, she sat in bed and wrote me a letter. If you zoomed the cam in, you could read my name. I had to erase that section of the recording to keep Paul from seeing it. I'd eventually have to come clean with him.

Back to B: Pavel Yashin wasn't there. Paul ran through the channels hunting for him, stopping on F. There he was, standing in Natasha's doorway. Somehow, he'd managed to open her door without her noticing. She was on her bed, engrossed in her book, unaware of his presence. He just stood there, staring long enough that I started to feel uneasy. Eventually, he pulled the door shut as silently as he'd opened it. She kept twirling her hair all the while—lost in her fictional world.

Paul jumped back to B in time to see Yashin settle on the couch. "What was that about?"

I said, "I don't know."

"That is one strange family, Juno. You ever notice how they don't talk to each other."

"Yeah." My stomach clenched. *What am I getting into with Natasha?* Why was it that I had such a thing for women with problems? Tall, dark, and fucked up. That was my type. I needed to be careful around her. We were having a good time together, but I didn't want to fall for her. I really didn't.

Yashin poured a drink for himself, downed it in a hurry, and poured another. He placed a call. A holo of Ram Bandur flickered into his living room. Both Paul and I perked up. Why would he be calling the man who killed two of his dealers?

Yashin said, "I have a proposition for you."

"What is it?"

"I have surplus product that I thought you might want to take off my hands."

"Is that why you're poachin' my territory? Just 'cause you

have some extra shit you want to dump, you think you have the right to sell in my territory. You steal from me and then you want to do business? FUCK YOU!"

Yashin winced at the fury coming from Bandur's cheery-faced hologram. "I'll give you a good price," he said.

"What you got?"

"Eight hundred kilos of O."

"What you askin'?"

"Kilo for kilo."

"Are you fuckin' kidding me! What kind of fucked-up deal is that? I did you a favor by not killing *you* for poaching my terri-tory. Is this how you show your 'preciation, you cocksucker?" Bandur hung up.

Paul smiled wide. "This is our chance, Juno."

"What chance?"

"When Yashin sells the opium to Bandur, we'll nail both of them."

"Bandur didn't sound too interested in buying."

"Kilo for kilo—that's hardly a bargain." One kilo of opium for a kilo of pesos. "They're just negotiating. We have to be patient."

I took one last bite and put my fork down.

"Do you want some more?"

"No, I'm full."

Natasha had cooked up a chicken with apricots over rice. She was nervous about it. Her mother taught her how to pre-pare it, but her mother used 'guana instead of chicken. When I'd asked her why she didn't use 'guana, she said it was a special occasion. I thought the chicken was a little dry. I told her it was delicious.

Natasha took her brandy to my couch and pulled her feet up. "What was your family like?"

I joined her on the couch. She listened with rapt attention as I open-booked my life for her. I could tell her anything— judgment free. I told her about Tenttown. I told her how my father would tie me up while he beat my mother. I showed her the rope-burn scars. I told her how I was always getting kicked out of school for fighting. When she asked if I had any regrets, I told her that I wished I had killed my father before his liver beat me to it.

"Really? You wouldn't feel guilty killing your own father?"

"The bastard deserved it. I deserved the chance to kill him myself. His liver robbed me of my vengeance. It was my only chance to see the world as a fair place."

She wouldn't let it drop. She kept asking questions about my father and how I could possibly kill him, my own flesh and blood. He beat my mother. I didn't know how much plainer I could make it.

She asked me if I'd had any happy times when I was growing up. I told her about how my mother and I used to make shab- bakia together. Natasha had never heard of it. No surprise there. Nobody had ever heard of it. I'd never seen the honey- soaked pastries anywhere on Lagarto, not once. It was an Earth thing. Moroccan was what my mother would say. I didn't even know how my mother learned to make it, but whenever she managed to scrape a few coins together, that was what we'd do. It would take the entire day, buying the ingredients, mixing the dough, forming it into rosettes. Then we'd stack up the trays and carry them to the public deep fryers. Next we'd bring the hot golden pastries all the way back to our tent and soak them a pot of honey that sat over the fire. I was amazed Natasha was still listening when I told her that we'd finish it off by sprinkling the shabbakia with toasted sesame seeds.

She had more questions, but I refused to answer until she answered some of mine.

Her favorite flower was a lily. Her favorite food: lamb.

She told me she'd had a big brother who died of pneumonia before she was born. She wished he were still here. She would've loved having a brother. She was proud of the fact that her mother saw to it that his first name would be her middle name. That way her brother would always be with her.

She liked school. She didn't like sports. She loved to read. She hated to play games—cards, dominoes, mahjong . . . She didn't like any of them.

I asked about her father. She told me he was a bellhop who dealt O on the side until he made enough money to start his own drug business. When I asked about her mother, she said her mother didn't know what her father did for a living, and if she did, she'd have to Hail Mary for eternity. She thought her mother had to know on some level, but it was too scary for her to confront, so she just stayed away from the basement.

I wanted to ask more about her father. I'd seen the strange ways she'd interact with him. I knew she was holding something back, but fair's fair. I held back the fact that I spied on her every day.

I woke with the sunrise, Natasha's arm across my chest. I traced the scar on her wrist with my finger.

"That tickles," she said as she pulled her arm away and rolled over.

I curled up next to her, "Where did you get that scar?"

She tensed under my hold. "I ran into a glass door when I was little. I thought the door was open. It was stupid."

I tried to sound natural but came off guarded. "Oh . . . that must've been awful."

"It was."

The room began to warm with the sun beaming in. I didn't want to let go of her but I forced myself to get up and turn the aircon to full. By the time I went back to the bed, Natasha was already up and getting dressed.

I didn't want her to leave yet. "Do you want some coffee?"

"Sure."

The sink was full of dishes from the previous night. I worked around them, rinsing the coffeepot and starting some water on the stove. "You like it black, right?"

Natasha came out buttoning her shirt. "Yeah."

I was pulling two mugs out of the cupboard when Natasha came up behind me and put her arms around me. "Are you my knight in shining armor?"

I wanted to be. "I don't know. . . . Am I?"

"When are you going to arrest my father?"

"I don't know. Soon."

"What are you waiting for?"

"We need more evidence," I lied.

"How soon will you have it?"

"Why do you want me to arrest your father?"

"Because I hate him."

"Why?"

After a pause she repeated, "How soon?"

"I don't know."

She held on to me while I poured the coffee. Then we sat across the table from each other. I watched her blow on her coffee before each sip. She barely moved her lips as she blew, like she knew a pucker would be unbecoming. She was all cool grace on the surface, but if you looked close, you could see what I now thought of as the slow burn smoldering behind her eyes.

I asked her, "What about your mother?" She puzzled at my question. "Do you hate her, too?"

She put the mug down. It clunked on the table. "I don't want to get into it."

❖

Another week had passed. Natasha and I had seen each other every single day. We would meet for lunch. We would meet for dinner. We would talk for hours.

For me, the highlight of the week came two days ago. I'd left Natasha at my place while Paul and I spent the day beefing up our arrest numbers. We busted a pair of pimps that we'd busted six months earlier, and then we nabbed four dealers, all of them repeats of earlier arrests. As long as nobody paid much attention to the fact that we'd begun arresting the same people over and over, we'd be able to keep up our numbers indefinitely.

After Paul and I had finished a long work day, we went back to the stakeout pad to fast-forward through a day's worth of video. Nothing new. I'd finally arrived back home at a little before midnight. Natasha was still there, but she'd fallen asleep on the sofa. I didn't want to wake her, so I went quietly into the kitchen to grab a snack. I flicked on the light. The counters were covered with platters stacked high with shabbakia.

Tonight, I pulled a piece free from a cluster of rosettes that had stuck together. I took a bite and savored every bit of it. I said, "I still can't believe you made this for me."

She smiled. "Why don't you tell me another one of your stories?"

She loved cop stories, the ones where the good guy catches the bad guy. Her fiery eyes would glow as I spun the police tales. Some nights, we'd stay up the entire night, her curled up on my shoulder, me churning out yarn after yarn. It didn't take long for me to run out of stories, so I began making them up. The one time I'd admitted that most of the stories weren't true, she'd just hushed me and made me tell her another.

I was eighty-sixed on stories. I had to think on it for a few.

I ate another piece of shabbakia while she waited for me to start. I couldn't come up with anything else so I started with this: "A little while back, Paul and I caught a tip on an offworld buyer who was on the surface looking to score some O."

"Really, an offworlder?"

I licked my fingers. "Yeah. Her name's Mai Nguyen, and she has two badass bodyguards. . . ."

I told her how we found Nguyen and her heavies at a hotel and tailed her out to an abandoned factory where a big drug deal was going down. When the seller turned out to be her father, she was tip-to-toe captivated. To Natasha, he was the baddest of all bad guys. I told her the whole story—the abandoned factory, the flycam, how I wound up shitting myself when I got zapped, how everybody got away.

She kissed the scars on my hand and said, "That was the best one yet."

"But it didn't have a happy ending. The bad guys got away."

She smiled that delicious smile of hers. "They didn't get away. The story's just not over yet."

eleven

I WAS early—couldn't sleep. Thoughts of my past had kept me awake all night.

I sat on the north dock, waiting for Maggie Orzo. A half hour ago, the dock had been bustling with fishermen loading bait into their boats. Now it was mostly quiet, just the peaceful slosh of waves and the creak of ropes pulled taut by the boats they tethered. Slowly, the stars dimmed and disappeared as the first of the sun's rays kicked off the five hours of daylight.

I called down to HQ and had them pull Kapasi's record: sentenced to five years for running a gambling ring. Released to the Army after three. The prosecutor's name was Wilhelm Glazer.

I rang up Prosecutor Glazer. I could tell by his voice that I woke him, even though his holo looked wide awake with a holographic diploma floating over its shoulder—pretentious jerk.

I asked, "You remember a guy you busted for running games named Jhuko Kapasi?"

"Yeah, I remember him. He was running 'guana fights. I sent him to the Zoo for a nickel. Why are you interested in him?"

"We're looking at him for a murder."

"Is he out? Has it been five years already?"

"No, he got two years cut off his sentence to serve in the Army."

"That figures. I want to know who came up with that

idea—an Army of ex-cons. Dumbest thing I ever heard in my life. Someday they'll join in with the warlords and attack *us*."

"Do you think he's capable of murder?"

"Not the guy I sent up. He was strictly a hustler, but you never can tell what a few years in prison will do to a man."

"I need to know what he's been up to lately. Can you tell me who he ran with back then that we could talk to?"

"I don't know anybody that could help you there. He made more enemies than friends with his hustles. He lived with his brother who raised the 'guanas in the basement. You could try to talk to him, but I don't think you'll get much out of him. He's slow—some kind of retard. My guess is he'll still be living at the house. He was living with a younger sister named Isabel who used to take care of him. She was maybe sixteen, and a real looker, but she disappeared the same day Kapasi got sentenced. It must've been tough for the poor retard to lose a brother and a sister the same day. He didn't have any other family to speak of."

"What do you mean she disappeared?"

"I mean she disappeared. She went missing. The police got on it, but they never found her. If you ask me, she was lookin' at a life of taking care of her half-baked brother all on her own, and she took off. Can't say I blame her."

"Can you think of anybody else Kapasi may have associated with?"

"No, that's it."

I hung up after getting the brother's name, Sanje Kapasi. I already had the address.

Maggie arrived with coffee. She was dressed smartly, loose-fitting blouse over color-coordinated ironed pants. Her clothes were too good for a cop, but not fancy enough to betray how rich she was. "Good morning, Juno," she said with a casual smile, her hair still damp from a morning shower. She *was* pretty, there was no denying it. I had to remind myself of how easy it was to look that good with her kind of money. To her, getting nipped, tucked, lifted, and lipoed was as easy as getting a haircut.

"Morning, Maggie. Thanks for the coffee." I took the coffee with my left and took a sip—too hot. I wanted to take off the lid and get it to cool faster, but there was no way to do it without spilling. I'd just have to wait a while.

We chartered a boat to take us to Loja, two hours upriver. The river was the fastest way. There were no good roads to Loja; the damn things would get overrun by jungle so fast that the government couldn't keep them clear.

Loja was founded at the junction of the Koba and Vistuba Rivers. It was only a fraction of the size of Koba; still, it was the second largest city on Lagarto. In its glory days, it was a bustling port, but now it was just a hollowed-out husk of a city. The smart people migrated downriver by the boatload and left that second-rate town to rot.

The Army would be interrogating Jhuko Kapasi by now. No way we'd get to see him, but with any luck we'd be able to get something out of the brother, find out what kind of rackets he was into. Jimmy Bushong's story repeated in my mind. Jhuko Kapasi: hustler ex-con, running games in the Army and selling O to his lieutenant. One night he took six POWs out in the jungle and came back without them. His lieutenant was so incensed that he sent the whole unit into combat with sabotaged weapons. And now that lieutenant was dead, lipless.

And somehow the mayor was involved. Paul's instincts were rarely wrong. My hands clutched. I felt juiced, back in the game. Paul needed me to connect this to the mayor. One way or another, I'd do it. *Who the fuck does the mayor think he is, making a play for KOP? That's Paul's turf.*

Maggie and I sat on mildewed cushions and rode slowly away

from the dock. Buoys bobbed on either side, guiding the way. Once in deeper water, the driver opened up the throttle and turned into the current. The sun rose but was quickly overtaken by thick clouds from the east. The city gradually faded behind us, and we were alone on the river, leaving a wake of black-green water rolling into the reeds and mangroves of the riverbank.

I sprayed on a thick coat of bug spray and relaxed into the cushions, settled in for the ride.

"Juno, can I ask you something?" I could barely hear Maggie's voice over the motor's roar.

"Yeah."

"Are you dirty?"

I hesitated—damn it. Then I looked at her expectant eyes: second mistake. "Yeah, I'm dirty."

She looked disappointed.

"We all are, Maggie. You will be, too."

Deafening rain pounded onto the rusted tin roof of the boat as we pulled up to the Loja wharf. We hurried through the sting-ing downpour, past the rusted-out robotics and ducked into a café. A good time to have breakfast and wait out the showers. We ordered a flatbread with honey drizzled on. It'd be easy to eat with my left.

Maggie said, "You're wrong."

"About what, Maggie?"

"Me becoming dirty."

"How can you be so sure?"

"I didn't get into police work for the money."

"Then why did you?"

"I want to help people."

"Help people? You should be a teacher."

"I don't like kids."

I smiled at that. "I don't like them either." I looked out the window. "Looks like the rain is slowing down."

Maggie wouldn't drop the subject. "Just because KOP is corrupt doesn't mean it has to stay corrupt."

"Give me a break, Maggie. KOP will *always* be corrupt."

"How can you say that?"

"Until the city starts paying us more than the pimps and pushers, it will always be corrupt. It's the natural order."

"That's not true. The city can stop hiring people like you and start hiring cops who care more about serving the people than lining their pockets with a little cash."

"Now you sound like Mayor Samir."

"At least he's trying to do something . . . clean things up."

"You think the mayor's clean?"

"Of course."

"Trust me, there's no such thing as a clean politician."

"How can you say that?"

I just shook my head. *She'll learn.*

She wouldn't let it drop. "Hey, I know the government isn't perfect, but they try to do the best for the people."

"If they wanted to do the best for the people, they wouldn't have sold off the Orbital and the spaceport to a bunch of off-world corporations. They sold out Lagarto for their own profit. This planet would be sitting pretty by now if we were running the mining operations."

"That happened a long time ago, and they had no choice. They needed to get the government out of debt."

"They had a choice, and they chose their own interests over ours."

We sat silently for a few moments, then she said, "All I know is I've met the mayor a few times. He seemed genuine to me."

"Friend of your parents?"

"Acquaintances. My mother supported his campaign."

Figures. She couldn't find out we were hunting the mayor. She was liable to run to her mother. "What about your father? Doesn't he support the mayor, too?"

"My father's dead. Murdered during a mugging. They executed the son of a bitch that did it."

I creaked out an apology as I began to understand why the rich girl had gone into police work.

"It was a few years ago," she said. "I was just a teenager."

"Do you miss him?"

Maggie's raised eyebrows voiced a silent, "What do you think?"

"Sorry. Stupid question," I said with the sad realization that to me the answer to that question wasn't at all obvious.

Maggie said, "I especially missed him last night. My mother can't stand it that I'm a cop. I made the mistake of calling her last night to tell her that I got my first case. You should've heard the way she laid into me. It's that kind of crap that made me move out before I could find a proper place. I figured living in a hotel was better than listening to her every night. If my father was still around, he'd be able to settle her down some. He was good at keeping her off my back. He wouldn't be happy with me being a cop either, but he'd respect my decision."

"Why does being a cop make your mother so upset?"

The bread arrived, steaming and golden brown. Maggie broke it down the middle, careful not to burn herself. "She wants me to work for my brother in the family business."

"That doesn't sound so bad."

"Yeah, but she wants my brother to be in charge of everything. I'm just supposed to do all the grunt work while he gets to make all the decisions."

"Because he's a man?"

"That, and he's older. Listen, I love my brother, but I'm not willing to take the backseat."

"Do you think you would do a better job than he would?"

"I doubt it." Maggie pushed a piece of bread through a puddle of honey at the plate's edge. "You used to be partners with Chief Chang?"

"Twenty-five years ago."

"Is he dirty, too?"

"Whoa, you're getting into dangerous territory now."

"So he is dirty."

"I didn't say that."

"No, but you didn't deny it. Are the rumors true about Chief Chang and the Bandurs?" Maggie looked at me with her blue, blue eyes.

"You've got no sense asking me a question like that. If he was dirty, how do you think he'd react if he found out you're checking up on him? Trust me, Maggie; you don't want to go down that road."

"If I'm going to work with you, I think I should know who you are, where your loyalties lie. How else can I depend on you?"

"As far as this case goes, my only priority is to catch Lieutenant Vlotsky's killer. Nothing else matters."

"I'm not sure that's good enough for me."

"It'll have to be."

We asked the waitress for directions to Jhuko Kapasi's neighborhood—close enough to walk, which was good since cabs were hard to come by in Loja.

It was still misting when we left. It felt cool on my face. Water flooded the intersections. An occasional car splashed through with a salamander's tooth of clearance over the high water. Shopkeepers swept brown water off the walks with wide brooms. When the sun broke through, steam rose off the asphalt, and sweat ran down from under my arms.

We found Kapasi's house. A falling-apart pigsty set behind a
trashed-up yard. We climbed the caved-in steps to the door and
tried knocking—no answer. I went in with Maggie right behind
me. A blast of cage-rattling hisses and snaps scared the shit out
of me. Maggie jumped and let out the smallest scream. I could
feel my heart pounding in my ears. Caged lizards were stacked
to the ceiling on every side. Some sat on their haunches clicking
and spitting; others puffed out throat pouches and bobbed from
side to side; still others watched indifferently as we tried to recapture our composure. Since Jhuko had been gone, and his
sister disappeared, Sanje Kapasi must've decided to move his
lizards up from the basement.

"Who the f-fuck are y-you?" Sanje Kapasi, Jhuko's brother
and 'guana keeper, appeared from behind a pen. He wore an
unevenly buttoned shirt and falling-down pants. His oil-slick
hair poked out on the sides, and his mouth hung perpetually
open, revealing half a mouthful of brown-to-black teeth.

I said, "We're the police, Sanje. We want to talk to you.
We're sorry we scared your lizards."

"Th-that's okay. I'm Sanje."

"I'm Juno, and this is Maggie."

"Hi, J-Juno and Maggie. I'm Sanje."

I scanned the surroundings—no chairs. "Is there a place we
can talk?"

"Yes, this is a good place to talk."

"I was wondering if you had a place that is quieter. I'm not
sure I'll be able to hear what you have to say."

"Okay, quieter, quieter." He tottered down the hall, head
bowed, arms held stiff at his sides. We followed him. The
stench was incredible. Lizards crawled loose on the walls and
ceiling. Dried excrement crunched under our feet. We entered the kitchen. A monitor, the heavyweight of fighting
lizards, was chained to the stove. It was straining for a piece

of maggot-covered meat on the floor. Its teeth were metal implants that snapped like a spring-loaded trap. In some places, its skin clung taut over rippled musculature. In others, it bunched into loose folds like a sheet on a used bed. A clumsy Sanje Kapasi almost tipped himself over kicking the meat into the dragon's reach, where it was snatched up and swallowed whole.

I stayed a safe distance from the monitor. Maggie stayed safer by standing behind me.

"Thank you, Sanje. It is much quieter in here. Now we can talk." Again no chairs. We'd have to interview him standing.

"Y-you're welcome, Juno and Maggie."

The kitchen was a lizard free-for-all. Scope the iguana bathing in the sink. Check out the tuatara sunning in the light fixture. I kicked a gecko off my shoe, sent it tumbling into the wall.

I refocused on the metal-mouthed monitor. There were burn marks on its sides, some healed over, some fresh. The floor was lined with hundreds of scorches. I asked Sanje what they were from.

"Oh, they're funny. Here, watch, watch." He grabbed a broomstick and poked at the monster, tapping its sensitive nose. The monitor's claws extended in anger, two centimeter lasers burning black lines into the wood as it scrabbled to defend itself. "W-when he sleeps, sometimes he dreams and his claws come out, a-and he burns himself. It's funny."

I said, "We want to ask you some questions about your brother, Jhuko. Will that be okay?"

"Jhuko's not mad at me anymore."

"Was he here?"

"Yes, b-but the Army man came, and he took him away."

"When did the Army man come?"

"Last night."

"What about the night before last night? Was your brother here then?"

"No."

"Where was he?"

"I don't know. He w-went out."

"All night?"

"All night. Yes."

I added opportunity to our already established motive. "You said your brother wasn't mad at you anymore. Why was he mad?"

"Because he told me he wasn't."

"I know, but why was he mad at you before?"

"That's a secret."

"It's okay, Sanje. We're police officers. It's okay to tell secrets to the police."

He balled his hands into fists. "N-NO! Y-you're wrong. B-brothers d-d-don't tell secrets."

Maggie took over, talking like a mother to a baby. "It's okay, Sanje. You're right, brothers don't tell secrets. Can you tell me about your lizards?"

"Th-they're my pets."

She soothed with her voice. "What do you do with your pets?"

Sanje was already fully calmed. *This guy has a quick switch— happy to furious and back in thirty seconds.*

"I breed them and train them," he said, beaming a rotten-toothed smile.

Maggie kept up the questions. "What do you train them for?"

"I sell some of them, but I keep the best ones."

"What do people do with the ones you sell?"

"I keep the best ones."

Maggie took a deep breath. "Tell me about your sister."

"Isabel."

"Yes, Isabel. What happened to her?"

"She went away."

"Did she say where she was going?"

"No. Sh-she just went away."

"What about your brother. Can you tell us about him?"

"He's not mad at me anymore."

"Why was he mad?"

"That's a secret."

Maggie gave me a frustrated look.

This was going nowhere. It was time to get things moving. "Listen to me, Sanje. We know you raise lizards for fighting. You know 'guana fighting is illegal, so we're going to take your lizards away."

"N-No. Y-you can't d-do that!"

"We can, and we will."

He pulled at his greasy hair. "NO!"

"We'll take all of them away from you. We'll make sure you can't get any more."

"No, no, no." Sanje started rocking from foot to foot and beating his head.

I talked as I pulled my piece. "We'll have to kill them, of course." I aimed at the monitor's head, trying to keep my wobbling hand steady.

Sanje rushed me.

I sidestepped and shoved him in the back as he passed, using his own momentum to send him crashing into the wall head first.

He fell to the floor with a rough thud. Sound erupted from under the floorboards, the growls and snaps of an unknown number of monsters like the one in my weapon's sights. Sanje Kapasi pulled his hands away from his head. They came away bloody. Scalp wounds were always the best bleeders.

"Ow! . . . Ow!" he sniveled.

"That's right, Sanje. We're going to kill your pets, and there is nothing you can do to stop us."

"N-no, y-you can't do that."

"I'm starting with this one." I made another show of aiming at the surgically enhanced monster, ready to fry it with one sustained burn. It had to be at least twice the size of any monitor I'd ever seen.

"No, don't kill him! DON'T!" He started to cry. Tears ran from his eyes and snot poured from his nose.

"I'm gonna start with this one, but I'm going to kill them all, Sanje." The monitor stared at me coldly unaware, testing the air with its tongue.

"Stop, Juno!" About fucking time Maggie stepped in, good cop to my bad.

"No. I'm going to kill this one right now!"

"No. Why can't we tell Sanje to stop fighting 'guanas? He'll stop if we tell him to. We don't have to kill them."

"Y-yes, I'll stob," he sobbed through clogged nasal passages.

I lowered my piece. "How can we trust him? He won't even answer our questions."

Maggie leaned in close, put her hand on his shoulder. "He's right, Sanje. How can we trust you?"

"I b-bromise I won't fight them."

"Will you answer our questions?"

"Y-yes."

I looked at Maggie, at the expression on her face. She was enjoying this. I put the lase-pistol back in my belt and tossed Sanje a musty towel, telling him to blow his nose and wipe the blood off. He wound up just smearing it all over.

Maggie baby-talked. "We want to know about your brother."

"H-he's not mad at me anymore."

"Why was he mad at you?"

"I-I was s-stubid. He t-told me I was stubid."

"What did you do that was stupid?"

"I didn't give Vishnu the bill."

"Who's Vishnu?"

He pointed to the reprieved reptile.

"What kind of pill?"

"A w-white bill."

"What does the pill do?"

"Makes him bleed and bleed."

"I don't understand. What do you mean it makes him keep bleeding?"

"When he gets cut, it makes him bleed and bleed and bleed."

"An anticoagulant?"

Sanje just looked at her, his mouth hanging open.

Maggie asked, "Why did Jhuko want you to give the pill to Vishnu?"

"I told him Vishnu was the best. I c-couldn't give him the bill. He w-was the best."

"Did Vishnu win the fight?"

"Vishnu was the b-best."

"So your brother told you to give Vishnu a pill, and you didn't do it? Is that right?"

"Yes."

Maggie took a long breath. "What happened next?"

"H-he couldn't bay. B-because I didn't g-give the bill to Vishnu."

"Who did he have to pay?"

"A-a lawyer was after him."

My mind went instantly to the pretentious prosecutor. "Was it Wilhelm Glazer?" I asked.

"N-no. A lawyer." Then thinking I wasn't understanding him, he clarified, "A LAW-YER."

Fuck, this is driving me crazy. "Why was a lawyer after him?"

"B-because Jhuko couldn't bay. Then Jhuko s-stobbed c-coming to see me."

✲

Maggie and I tracked along the river, in the direction of the wharf, Sanje Kapasi's less-than-shack of a house falling out of sight.

I said to Maggie, "How come you helped me manipulate him? That wasn't exactly police procedure in there. I thought you were the honest cop."

"I didn't do anything wrong."

"Don't even try it, Maggie. You know we manipulated him. And don't tell me you didn't enjoy it. I saw you."

"I just questioned him. You're the one who assaulted him." She played it innocent, but her foxy grin betrayed her. Was that a wink? My stomach flipped at the thought, in a good way.

We walked back onto the wharf. Arboreal robotic loading arms lined the water's edge. The last one had died decades ago. Ivy had greened over the rusted metal, and lizards had nested on hydraulic pistons.

We found the same boat captain at the wharf playing cards on an upturned barrel. He must've waited around, hoping he'd catch us for the return trip. We climbed down into the boat and sat next to each other on the shady side, our knees bumping with the river flow. The electricity of each knee bump set my heart sparking.

A flyer launched from behind the wharf. It buzzed the wharf then headed upriver. It was probably filled with offworld tourists who had stopped in Loja for lunch. The sun hung low in the sky as we plowed our way out into the thick water. The temperature was just starting to drop. I tried to fan my shirt, but it was plastered to my body.

I tried to piece things together. My theory went like this: Jhuko Kapasi was running 'guana fights. He got greedy and rigged a fight. He gave good odds on Vishnu and took big bets. He gave his 'guana keeper brother some anticoagulants and told him to give them to Vishnu before the fight. Real simple— Vishnu gets cut, doesn't clot, bleeds to death; Kapasi makes a killing. But his brother Sanje was attached to Vishnu and didn't give him the pills. Vishnu won the fight, and Kapasi didn't have the money to pay out.

Assuming I was right, I was surprised Kapasi was still alive. A guy who pulled a scam like that paid one way or another . . . and since he didn't have the money . . .

He must've had enough dough to pay off Carlos Simba. The Loja crime lord totally controlled that city. No 'guana fights would have gone on without a fee going his way. If it was illegal, he'd get his piece. Simba would've whacked Kapasi by now if he hadn't paid. Not even prison could have protected him.

The way I saw it, Kapasi must've used the purse to pay off Simba and any bookmakers he was afraid of—fuck everybody else. According to his brother, one of the fuckees was a lawyer, almost certainly Prosecutor Glazer. He wouldn't have taken kindly to getting stiffed on his winnings. He had Kapasi arrested and sentenced to five years. I still found it hard to believe Kapasi made it through alive. He would've had to cough up some serious bucks.

Fast forward three years and Kapasi opted for a stint in the Army rather than serving the full nickel. According to Jimmy Bushong, Kapasi got back to his old tricks running games and supplying brown sugar to his lieutenant. Then he took six prisoners out in a truck for reasons unknown. Lieutenant Vlotsky was forced to cover for Kapasi and came up with a BS story about getting attacked rather than being made for a guy who was dosing on duty. Vlotsky resented being made the fool and armed the unit with bum guns and sent them into combat. The logical conclusion was that Kapasi killed Vlotsky out of revenge.

Where Mayor Samir fit in, I had no idea.

twelve

By the time we made it back to Koba, early afternoon darkness had already fallen. Seventeen hours of darkness before the sun would rise again.

We hit the station. The basement was naturally cool. Condensation seeped from the walls, and the ceiling had sprouted dense green growths. The stone floor was ridged for better footing. Even so, muckish puddles had to be avoided. We entered the morgue. "Seen Abdul?"

"He's in room four."

We pushed our way through the swinging doors into room four. My eyes burned from the smell of morgue-sterilizing acid. Frigid air gusted from the overhead cooling unit. Bright lights shone on a steel table that was topped by an open body. Abdul Salaam was ripping the rib cage apart.

He looked up and spotted us through his thick glasses. His magnified eyes lit. "Juno."

"Hey, Abdul. This is Maggie Orzo. You remember her from yesterday."

"Yes, yes—of course I remember." He tore his gloves off, revealing bony hands creviced with age. Maggie and I followed Abdul to his office, grabbed up a couple mugs of coffee, and took seats on wooden chairs.

Abdul pulled a folder from a squeaky drawer. "Your vic bled to death." He held the folder out for me to take, but I had coffee in my left! *Put the coffee down first; take the folder with your left—that'll look strange . . . quick snatch with my right? Take the folder.*

Maggie took the folder. *I'm off the hook.*

I set my coffee down.

Maggie said, "What am I thinking? You should probably look at this first, Juno. I can look at it when you're done." She passed the file to me.

What just happened? She knew about my hand, and she was covering for me. That was what happened. She thought I was trying to hide my hand from Abdul, when it was her I was hiding it from; Abdul already knew. I wrenched my mind off the horror of Maggie knowing about my hand and forced my attention onto the horror of the crime.

Abdul said, "The throat wounds did the trick. He hardly lost any blood through the stab wounds. He was well on his way to dead by then. The recovered maggots were eighth generation since the wounds were opened. That puts the time of attack at twenty-two minutes after midnight. Time of death about two minutes after that."

"How about the murder weapon?" I wanted to know.

"I won't be able to help you much there. The perp used a regular butcher knife. We only have one company on Lagarto that makes them. The problem is they sell thousands of them every year. This one was definitely not new or recently sharpened. Even if you find the exact one the killer used, I won't be able to give you a positive match with the wounds; the maggots did too much damage to the flesh around the openings. You better find prints on the handle and your lieutenant's blood on the blade."

"How about the perp?"

"Based on the incision angles on the throat, I can determine that your killer is right-handed. The killer was strong, almost certainly a male. He put the vic in a headlock and cut his throat. That means he's tall. Now, Lieutenant Vlotsky was slightly shorter than average, so put the killer at above average height."

"Do you think it could be the work of a first-time killer?"

"It's possible, but I don't think so. I can see a first-time killer sticking the body fourteen times . . . make sure he's dead, maybe a fit of rage. What I can't see is a first-time killer mutilating the face that way. He took his time cutting off the lips. He did some delicate cutting. That's hard to do with a butcher knife. Even with a lase-blade, it would've taken a steady hand. I really don't think a first-time killer is going to have that kind of patience. He'd be too worked up. I think this guy had practice."

An image flashed in my head of six dead POWs, lying in the jungle with lipless smiles.

Maggie decided to push the point. "What if he used a butcher knife for the stabbings then used a scalpel for the face?"

"Nope. He used the butcher knife on the face. I found small pieces of the vic's liver in the face wounds. He used the same knife for everything. Any ideas on why he took the lips?"

Maggie answered, "I've been thinking a lot about that, but everything I come up with sounds harebrained."

"Like what?" asked Abdul.

"The killer is clearly fixated on the lips, and lips are for kissing, right? Maybe his mother never kissed him, and this is some twisted reaction to that. Or it could be that he was seriously verbally abused as a child, and he takes the lips as a way to *own* his victim's mouth. It's a control thing. The lips are in his possession where they can't hurt him anymore."

Abdul nodded agreement. "Doesn't sound harebrained at all, Maggie."

I stayed out of this one. Since my conversation with Paul, I'd been operating on the theory that the lip cutting was just a ruse. Whoever killed Vlotsky just wanted it to *look* like a serial. "Can you give us anything else to go on, Abdul?"

"I'm afraid not. Your killer was careful . . . he must have been dressed head to toe. Lieutenant Vlotsky had to have been kicking and scratching, but there's no skin under his nails. You might ask yourselves how the killer got home. He would have been covered in blood. Oh, and the Orbital returned the results on the porn mag fingerprints. They also returned DNA results from some . . . ah . . . stains on the page. No matches in the system. Looks like he doesn't have a record."

"Actually, Abdul, the magazine isn't the killer's. It belongs to a potential witness."

"You have a witness?"

"*Potential* witness, and since there's no matches in the system, we don't even have that."

Abdul sighed. "That's all I have for you, Juno. How's your arm?"

Maggie turned to look at me. She definitely knew.

I said, "It's okay, Abdul. Just a little stiff."

Abdul confided to Maggie. "He took a nasty spill a while back and broke his arm. I fixed it up for him."

Maggie said, "Oh. How did that happen, Juno?" Her expression was pure devil.

I'd never broken my arm. All cops would go through tests every five years to prove you were fit for duty. When mine came up, I passed all the written tests but knew I would never make it through the marksmanship test since this hand started shaking a few years ago. I talked Abdul into putting a cast on it and fooled KOP into waiving the shooting portion. I wore that damn cast for weeks.

I could have gone to Paul. He would have fudged the shooting test for me, but I didn't want him to know about my hand. I didn't want him thinking his old enforcer was a weak old

man. Now here was Maggie asking how I broke my arm. She'd
seen my hand, and she was onto the charade. She was messing
with me, wanting to see me squirm my way through this one.

I deadpanned, "I broke it backhanding a surly partner."

Maggie restrained a smile.

I pulled up a chair for Maggie, and we sat at my desk. We decided to finish canvassing our list of johns from the Lotus. I
was still hopeful one of them might have seen something in
the alley. After an hour, we succeeded in cutting the original
list of thirty-three down to just eight that we still hadn't talked
to. So far, nobody had seen a damn thing.

Maggie looked worn. "You hungry?"

It had been hours since the café in Loja. "Yeah . . . I buy, you
fly?"

"Deal."

I handed her some bills. She took them without pause, like
my hand was a normal hand. I tuned into the way her fingers
brushed mine. "I'll get the drinks downstairs," I said. Then I
watched her go, jazzing to the wag of her hips. Now that she'd
gone, the vice squad room felt graveyard quiet. Vice was always dead calm during the day—all the action was at night. I
stood up. My neck ached from sitting too long. I left the office
empty and headed downstairs to the newsstand to buy a couple bottles of soda.

I came back through the lobby. The water-stained ceiling
flaked plaster to the floor. Musty flags hung like rags from
poles by the door. I passed by Yuan Kim who was hanging with
a young officer in uniform. "Hey, Juno. How's that murder
case going?"

I didn't want to talk to this hump. "Slow," I said.

He shoved his glasses up to the bridge of his nose. "Got any
good leads?"

"Naw, you know how it is."

"Yeah, tell me about it. Me and Josephs are hitting dead ends at every turn, too. It's probably just as good that you took that Army case. We've got fucking MPs coming out our asses. Two new ones since the last time I saw you and that's only been what—since yesterday." MPs: missing persons.

I gave him the kind of uh-huh that said, "Stop talking to me because I don't care."

He rolled on, oblivious. "We just got back from Tenttown. There's a fourteen-year-old girl that's been missing for two weeks. It doesn't take a genius to figure this one out. A fourteen-year-old girl from Tenttown, you know she's a runaway. Only her mother is so grief stricken that she calls the police. When we ask her if her daughter was upset about anything before she disappeared, she said, 'No, she's a very happy child.' I'm thinking, 'Gimme a break. Nobody's happy in Tenttown, especially a teenager;' am I right? You know what kind of hole that place is."

I almost picked a fight right there. *Did you know I'm from Tenttown, motherfucker?*

Yuan Kim pushed his glasses up and rambled on. "Even her father thinks she ran away. Let me tell you, she's no child, either. According to the neighbors, she'll bang anything with a dick. For two weeks now, we've tried to talk the mother out of filing a report, but she won't hear it. Now Josephs and I are stuck with the paperwork."

He didn't even realize how close he was to getting those glasses permanently tacked to his nose. I let out another uh-huh.

"Hey, how's Maggie doing on her first case?"

"Good."

The uniform standing with Kim snickered. "Maggie? Is that Magda Orzo?"

Kim said, "Yeah, her real name is Magda. What of it?"

The uniform pointed over his shoulder to the rookie wall. Photos of all the recent graduates grinned in their frames. *What—where?* Now I saw it . . . Maggie's face with the caption "Officer Magda Orzo" underneath. There was a dripping penis doodled next to her smile and nippled breasts drawn over her uniform.

"Who did that?" I wanted to know.

"Josephs. Who else would find that funny?" Kim answered.

"You knew about this?"

"You know how he is, Juno. He doesn't know when to stop. He screwed around with her picture, then came and got me and told me my girlfriend was in the lobby, waiting for me. I came down here wondering who he was talking about. I mean, I see a few girls, but none of them regular. He followed me down, bringing half the squad with him. I was wandering around looking for whoever she is, and he pointed the picture out and yelled, I mean yelled, 'She's right here, Kim!' Then the dumbass started laughing like crazy."

"Why didn't you take the picture down?"

"Trust me, the best way to deal with Josephs is to ignore him. If he knows he's getting under your skin, he won't let up."

"Hold these." I handed Kim the soda bottles and reached up for the picture—too high. I told the uniform to get it down. He had to stand tiptoe to get it.

I went straight for the stairs, carrying the picture in my right. My hand was quivering—didn't care. Kim trailed behind, asking me what I was doing. I didn't answer. My vision narrowed down to a burning red tunnel.

I charged into homicide. *Where the fuck is he . . . ?* There, sitting at a desk, his back turned to me. The people around him looked up at me and stopped mid-sentence. Josephs sensed something. He started to turn . . . .

I slammed the picture glass side down over his head. Glass

shattered, and the frame broke apart. Only the photo itself held it together.

Josephs wheeled in his chair. *Shit he's fast.* He swung. *Move!* My body couldn't move fast enough. His fist connected with my jaw . . . .

". . . Juno! Juno! You in there?"

I opened my eyes.

Yuan Kim knelt over me. "He's awake, guys."

I tried to sit up—too dizzy.

A hazy Mark Josephs sat at his desk holding a bloodstained towel to the top of his head. *Don't tell me . . . Shit! He knocked me out. Shit!*

Two Kims pushed their blurred glasses up their blurred noses. "You okay, Juno? You been out for about a minute. He clocked you good. Do you need a doctor?"

"No." Shit, my head hurt.

"Is your jaw broken?"

"I don't think so. Help me up."

"Maybe you should wait a few minutes . . . take it easy."

I sat up. This time I was less dizzy. Kim pulled me wobbly-legged standing.

"Where's my soda?"

"Here, right here."

I grabbed the bottles and took short steps to keep upright. I walked down the hall, found the toilet, and rained vomit on floating cigarette butts. I made my way back to vice, got to my desk, and dug around for aspirin. I cracked open a soda and washed down the pills. I felt my teeth with my tongue—all there, one a little loose. *How the fuck did Josephs get so fast?*

Maggie came in wielding a fresh loaf, a chunk of cheese, and a hell-bent attitude. "Who the hell do you think you are?"

"You heard?"

"I just ran into Kim. He told me what happened." She launched into a string of rants. "I can take care of myself . . . I don't need you to protect me . . . I can fight my own battles . . . You're not my father." That last one hurt.

I hung my knotting head and took it all. Why did I go after Josephs like that? It was the way that asshole treated Maggie. It just set me off. You don't treat women like that.

thirteen

I WALKED through the alley entrance to the Lotus. Perfume and incense-scented aircon tickled my nose. I turned down the houseboy's offer of a clean shirt and sent him off to get Rose. I needed to ask permission to see if our peeper witness was back. I'd be surprised if he was back so soon, but it was worth a check.

Rose sauntered out with gaudy makeup and a dress slit on one side, exposing some thigh. "My word, Juno. What happened to you?"

The bruise on the side of my face had already developed—purple on my brown skin. I'd gone home after the fight. The aspirin wasn't strong enough. Niki went through her stash, picking out the best painkillers for me. She gave me an ice pack and left me napping on the sofa after some appreciated babying. I slept the afternoon and early evening away in a drugged euphoria.

I told Rose I got into a little scuffle.

She said, "You have to take it easy, Juno. Would you like to lie down?"

"No thanks, Rose. I'm fine." My face didn't hurt. I was still looped. "It okay if I head on up?"

"Sure." She checked her watch. "They should be done in room two any minute now. Do you mind waiting a bit for them to come out?"

"No problem. Is it okay if I wait upstairs?"

"You go right ahead."

I climbed up the back stairs and waited at the end of the hall. I sat on a frilly bench and watched the door to room two. The sounds of somebody's good time came through the walls at high decibels. I probed my jaw, finding the tender spots. What the hell was I thinking attacking Josephs like that? I knew he might kick my ass. And now that he had, the whole police force knew he could kick my ass. What the hell good was an enforcer nobody was afraid of?

The door opened. Out came an offworlder—genetically engineered perfection. Every one of them an Adonis. He buttoned his last button, and his hair self-straightened—never seen that before. Lagartans were starving to death while these narcissistic bastards thought up ways to obsolete combs. Attached to his elbow was one of Rose's hookers, wearing yellow satin with lacy edges. They giggled their way to the opposite stairs.

I went into fuck-chamber two and surprised a couple on the floor, he on his knees, she on all fours getting her throat checked by his Doctor Johnson. The scene reflected off the mirrored walls with hundredfold intensity. She startled at my entrance, then grinned and went back to work with renewed relish. My face burned red. She pulled her mouth free and said, "It's okay, honey. You can watch." Both of them had offworld-white skin, not Lagartan brown. Holograms—used to get the johns in the mood. Rose forgot to shut down the system.

My embarrassment turned to anger at being fooled. The holograms adjusted to my frame of mind. Leather, spikes, and chains faded in. He had a hold of her hair now, yanking her head back and forth with rough jerks. These weren't the cheap holos we got with the phone system. These auto-adjusted to your emotions. The Orbital must have been charging Rose a hefty fee to have these images beamed down.

They sensed my lack of arousal and shifted into two women. The system was searching for that perfect image, the one that sent my blood gushing south. I walked through the scene, my legs momentarily disappearing under their sweaty flesh. I approached the window, pulled my piece, and climbed out onto the roof.

I beelined across the roof, heading straight for the peeper's hideout—couldn't see shit. Somebody dashed out of the shadows and vaulted over the wall, landing on the fire escape with a loud clang. The peeper's feet clomped down the metal stairs.

I jogged to the fire escape and looked over the wall. He clunked his way to the bottom and sputtered down the alley. He chanced a look back to see if I was in pursuit. He was going to run right into Maggie who had stationed herself at the end of the alley. She held her weapon firm and called "Freeze!" He tried to stop, skidded, and fell on his ass with his hands up. "I got him, Juno! Come on down."

I put one hand on the rusted fire escape rail, thought better of it, crossed the roof, and crawled back through the window. Houseboys were giving the room a makeover—fresh sheets, replacement candles. By the time I made it into the alley, Maggie had him on his knees, hands cuffed behind his back. He was just a kid.

I stood over him. "How old are you?"

He had to crane his neck back to look at me. He had a smirk on his pudgy face. Clean clothes stretched over his chunky body—kid had a home. "Fifteen," he mumbled.

"What did you say?"

"Fifteen." He said it louder this time.

"What's your name?"

"Pedro Vargas."

"Did you say Pervo Vargas? Who do you live with, Pervo?"

"My mother."

"Where's your father?"

"I don't have a father."

"Why's that?"

"I just don't. Okay?"

"What does your mother do?"

"She's a waitress."

"Is she working tonight?"

"Yes."

"Does she know you're a pervert?"

No answer.

"What's she gonna think when she finds out her little piggy boy has grown up into a sexual deviant?"

"Fuck you."

I slapped him across the face.

"You can't do that! I'll—" I slapped him again. He was 100 percent smirkless now. My heart kicked into high gear.

"Do you have a girlfriend?"

"No."

"That's right, girls don't go for pervs." Another slap for good measure. "You have a boyfriend?"

"NO!" That struck a nerve. *Remember that.*

"Pedro the Homo."

"NO! I like girls."

"How about Officer Orzo here? You want to spy on her?"

"No."

"Do you think she's pretty?"

"I don't know."

"Is your mother pretty?"

"I don't know."

"Does she have boyfriends? Do you like to spy on her when she's with them?"

"NO!"

"How long have you been coming here?"

"This was my first time."

"You're lying, Pervo. You make a habit of peeping."

No answer.

"Were you here two nights ago?"

No answer.

"Did you see something go down in the alley?"

No answer.

"What did you see? Tell me now."

"I didn't see anything. I wasn't here."

"You were here. We found your stash of skin mags. We know the kind of sick shit you're into. We got your DNA from the mags. You jizzed all over them, Pervo. Don't tell me you weren't here. You saw something that scared you, and you pissed your pants."

"No, I didn't see anything." He was shaking now.

"If you want us to let you go, fatboy, you'll tell us what you saw."

"I-I didn't see anything."

We rode back to the station in my car. The triple palm print I'd put on Pedro's cheek had faded. His lips were zipped up tight. He was too scared to talk. The things he saw were enough to haunt him for life. I couldn't blame him for being afraid, but it didn't change the fact that I had to break him.

We hauled him up to the second-floor lockup. Eddie was working the desk. "Hey, Juno. How's it going?"

"You know how it is, Eddie. You look like you could use a cup of coffee. Why don't you guys take a break? I can watch the desk for you."

Eddie beamed. We hadn't played this game in years. He called out the interior guards, and they made like they were leaving. They weren't really going anywhere. In a couple minutes they'd be gathered around the monitors to watch the show.

"Did you turn off the cameras?" I asked.

"You bet." Eddie flipped a couple switches to make it look good. You couldn't really turn them off. What Eddie really did was flick the holding tank lights on and off. We had no more control over our cameras than we did our phone system. Like most of the tech on Lagarto, it was provided by the Orbital. Paul told me that the fat cats on the Orbital got a bigger cut of the KOP budget than police payroll did. Damn offworlders would never just sell us the tech. Instead, they'd rent it and then have the gall to tack on maintenance fees. They'd say we didn't have the expertise to maintain it ourselves.

I seized Pedro by his shirt and led him in as the door opened upon detecting my DNA.

The holding tank consisted of three cages on the left. The night's catch looked bored until they saw us. A chorus of teeth sucking started Pedro to shivering. I paraded him up and down the hall, close enough to the bars that the prisoners could just about touch him. I surveyed the detainees: drunks bloodied from bar fights, tweaked-out dealers, freaked-out johns caught wagging their wangs. Not the toughest group I'd ever seen, but there might've been one or two actual rapists or murderers in there. More than enough testosterone-laden malice to get the kid blabbing his life story.

They barraged the kid with catcalls. "Sooo weee! Piggy boy." "Look at that big juicy butt." "The bigger the cushion, the better the pushin'."

I egged them on, telling them his name was Pedro the Homo.

His lip quivered. "Why did you turn off the cameras?"

I got up in his face. "I'm not a fucking perv like you. I don't want to watch." The kid looked pale. "Time to pick a door, Pervo. One, two or three . . ."

Prisoners whooped.

Pedro avoided my eyes. He was on the edge. . . . *Push him.*

I whispered in his ear. "You hear them? They can't wait to pop your cherry. You talk now, or I leave you here."

"I'll talk."

I popped a couple more pain pills while Maggie filled out a witness report with the kid.

Vice was now in full swing. The veterans were gathered around the coffee machine, passing a flask and putting on an early buzz. They were swapping stories and laughing up a storm like always. They quieted down when I passed. News of my ass-kicking by Josephs must have been the hot topic.

The younger cops sat at desks, talking to the air, their words caught by the dozen voice pickups around the office, sending their dictation up to the Orbital to be digitized and fed into the system as arrest reports, nightly activity logs, citation journals, and evidence entry forms. The vets made the younger cops do all the paperwork. It was called paying your dues. I had had to do the same tedious bullshit work until I latched onto Paul's coattails.

I rang up the kid's mother. I could barely hear her over the bar's din. "What's the little fucker done now?" Her hologram smiled sweetly.

"Nothing, ma'am. He's a witness to a crime. We just need to question him."

"You keep him for the night. Teach the brat a lesson."

"He hasn't done anything, ma'am. Would you like us to call you when we're done questioning him so you can take him home?"

"No. I need my sleep. He knows the way."

"I'm sure he does, ma'am, but he's seen some things no boy his age should see."

"Don't think I won't punish him for it, officer. He may be bigger than me, but I can still beat his ass."

I got off the phone and entered interrogation room two. Maggie and I sat on one side of the mildewed table, the kid on the other.

Maggie said, "Tell us what you saw . . . from the beginning."

Pedro wiped away a tear. "I was on the roof, you know . . ."

"Peeping."

"Yeah . . . peeping. And I heard something in the alley. So I looked over the wall. I saw two guys, one holding the other from behind. The guy was struggling—kicking and grabbing at the other guy to get loose, but the first guy held him tight, and he couldn't get away."

"How did he hold him?"

"He had him in a headlock, from behind. Like this . . ." Pedro held his fleshy arm across his throat.

"Then what happened?"

"The guy stopped struggling, and the man dragged him farther into the alley."

"Dragged how, by his feet? Hands?"

"No, he kept him in the headlock and just walked backward."

"Then what?"

"The man let him go, and he fell down. It was sick the way he fell."

"Why do you say that?"

"He landed wrong. He hit his head on the ground, and his arm was all bent up under his body. I thought he had to be dead, but I guess he wasn't, 'cause then the man got on top of him. You know, he got on his knees over top of him."

"He straddled him."

"Yeah, he straddled him. Then I saw the knife in his hands, and he started stabbing him."

"How?"

"Like this . . ." He held his hands together over his head, brought them down to the table with a quick stroke. "He stabbed him a whole bunch of times . . . I didn't count. Then he took the knife and started cutting on the guy's face." Maggie shuddered.

"Then what?"

"He undressed. He wrapped the knife in his clothes and stuffed them in a plastic bag. You know, the kind you get from a store."

That bag was guaranteed bottom of the river. "Then what did he do?"

"Then he pulled clean clothes out of another bag and got dressed."

"Did he leave then?"

"Yeah, but first he stopped to take the piece with him."

"Piece?"

"Yeah. The part of the guy's face. The part he cut off. He wrapped it up in a cloth."

Maggie asked, "Why did you go back there tonight? Weren't you scared?"

Pedro looked down, guilt written all over his face. I'd seen his type before. The kid was a born voyeur. I'd seen the twinkle in his eye as he described the murder scene. He was into it. Two nights ago, he had been so terrified that he wet himself. He had never felt anything so intense before. Now he wanted that feeling back. His little bondage books looked like kid's play now. He returned to the alley hoping to catch a double feature, sex through the windows and violence in the alley.

Maggie looked puzzled. She didn't get it. "Could you see the killer's face?"

"It was kinda dark, but I saw him."

Maggie and I walked back to my desk. I connected to the Orbital and surfed the KOP system for mugs. Our own computer system had fried in '41. A lot of cops still had the old terminals on their desks as if they still worked. That way we didn't appear to the public as helpless as we were. I voice-navigated to an old mug of Jhuko Kapasi and then had the system bring up five shots of males with matching skin, hair, and eye colors. I put them in an array and had them holo-beamed to the interrogation room.

Maggie and I went back in. Pedro looked spent. He was slumped in his chair.

"If you recognize anybody, point him out."

He studied each of the images, one by one. "Nope. He's not here."

"What do you mean he's not there?" Maggie asked.

Pedro looked at the holograms again—Jhuko Kapasi in spot four. "What do you think I mean? He's not there."

"You're sure you got a good look at him?"

"Yes. I'm sure. The guy in the alley had a messed-up face. None of these guys has a messed-up face."

"Messed up how?"

"I don't know . . . like he was in an accident or something."

"We'll be right back, Pedro. Just sit tight, okay?"

"Okay. Can I have something to drink?"

"Sure, no problem. You like soda?"

"Yeah."

Maggie and I stepped out. We downloaded mug shots of the other cons in Vlotsky's unit—no messed-up faces. We downloaded phone holos of the remaining members of Unit 29. Normal faces all around.

"Dammit to hell!" Maggie said. "We've wasted two days on Kapasi, all for nothing."

My stomach sank. Lieutenant Vlotsky's entire unit was cleared by witness testimony. Two days and no closer to the mayor.

Maggie wasn't ready to give up. "You think the kid is lying?"

"No. I scared him pretty good. He's telling the truth."

"It was dark. Maybe Pedro didn't get a good enough look. Hey! Maybe Kapasi wore a mask."

I shook my head no.

We remained in silence for a moment. I looked out over the vice room, which was hopping with action. Pimps crowded around the violations window waiting for their numbers to be called so they could pay off their tickets and free their hookers. If they got through quickly, they could still notch a sale or two before the night was over. Jose, the night janitor, sat on his up-turned mop bucket, selling the low numbers while the toilets stayed dirty.

Maggie asked, "Would you have gone through with it?"

"Gone through with what?"

"Put the kid in one of those cells. Let him get raped."

"No, but I would have put him in a cell and let him sweat it out a while."

Maggie nodded approval. "What do we do now?"

"Get the kid a soda and start him going through mugs. We have to hope he recognizes somebody. It's going to be a long night. We can take turns."

Maggie volunteered for the first shift with Pedro.

I crashed on the padded floor of the psych room, falling straight into a pain pill–induced sleep.

fourteen

"JUNO . . . Juno, you awake?" I did my best to ignore the words that were invading my dreams until a hand began shaking my shoulder. "You awake?" I knew that voice, Niki's voice.

"Yeah, I'm awake," I croaked with my eyes closed.

"What are you doing?"

"Sleeping."

"Why didn't you come home?"

"What time is it?"

"About six."

"Really?" I couldn't believe it was morning already. I was still so tired, and I still felt doped on painkillers. I didn't know how Niki could function taking these pills all the time.

"I tried calling you, but you wouldn't answer," she said.

"I was sleeping. I guess I didn't hear it."

"I was worried sick all night."

My eyes were open now, and as I was looking at the expression on Niki's face, I was beginning to realize how badly I'd screwed up. "How'd you find me?"

"I called Paul, and he put me in touch with Maggie who told me you were here."

"You talked to Maggie?" My heart skipped, like I was caught with my hand in the candy jar. I told myself I was being stupid reacting like this. I hadn't done anything with Maggie.

Niki gave me a long look before answering. "She was surprised you hadn't called to tell me you were working all night."

"Sorry. I should have called." I struggled upright then had to limp for the first few steps as we exited the psych room. The vice room was empty as was usual in the early mornings. The door to the interrogation room was shut, a sure sign that Maggie was still inside, going through mugs with Pedro the Peeper. She hadn't come to wake me up for my turn. I rubbed the sleep out of my eyes, careful to avoid touching my jaw. I stopped for a cup of water and rinsed my mouth out as I drank. Then, Niki and I settled at my desk with a couple cups of coffee.

Niki said, "You going to tell me what's going on?"

"I told you. Paul's in trouble. He needs my help."

"Paul's always in trouble."

"I know, but this time it's serious." The words sounded hollow, but it was the truth.

Niki shook her head in disappointment. Then she took hold of my hand. "You're scaring me, Juno."

I didn't have an answer for that.

Niki let go of my hand and took a sip of coffee. She looked at the floor as she talked. "I'm afraid that if you keep this up, you'll end up going back to your old ways."

I didn't tell her how far down that path I'd already gone. *Did I really slap that kid last night?* "It'll be okay," I said, "I've got it all under control."

She looked doubtful. "But—"

I interrupted her, "I have to do this, Niki. I have to see this one through."

Niki looked into my eyes. "Why?"

"Paul needs me."

"Forget what Paul needs for a minute and think about what *you* need."

"What I need is your support."

The door to the interrogation room opened, and Maggie

poked her head out. "We got him. Pedro picked him out." Her head disappeared back behind the door.

Niki was still looking at the floor. Her expression was unreadable.

"I have to go," I said.

"I know."

We both stood. I leaned over to kiss my wife, and when I did, she moved in for a hug that I felt I didn't deserve. I returned the hug halfheartedly. I was eager to get back into the interrogation room. When Niki didn't let go, I felt myself succumbing to the full force of the hug. I held Niki's head to my chest. We stayed like that for while, long enough that I stopped thinking about the case and started thinking about Niki and me, and how comfortable it felt to hold her, and how that had to mean that we still had something. Then Niki suddenly let go and walked out without another word.

I entered the interrogation room. Pedro and Maggie were seated at the table. Four soda bottles were lined up, mold already forming on their insides.

"I found him!" Pedro said excitedly.

"That's great, Pedro. You did a great job." Poor kid must have been attention-deprived if he wanted approval from *me*. It wasn't that long ago that I'd threatened him with gang rape.

I strode up to the killer's hologram and walked around it. "He has a harelip," I said.

"See, I told you his face was messed up."

"You were right, Pedro."

Maggie had already pulled his record. "Ali Zorno, age twenty-nine. He was arrested once for burglary. He served three years and was released three weeks ago."

"Who was the arresting officer?"

"B. Redfoot. You know him?"

"Yeah. Brenda Redfoot; she retired last year. Let's call her."

"It's still early, Juno."

I called anyway. Brenda answered. "Hello?" Her hologram looked good; she was made up nice, far nicer than I ever saw her in person.

"Sorry it's so early, Brenda, but I need to talk to you about a guy you sent up."

"No problem, Juno. I've been up for a while. I don't sleep as good as I used to. Who do you want to know about?"

"Ali Zorno. He has a harelip. You put him away on a burglary."

"What happened; did he kill somebody?"

"We think so. What can you tell us about him?"

"I arrested him when I was off duty. He broke into an apartment in our building. You ever heard this story?"

"I think you told it to me once, but I don't remember too well."

"My husband heard something in the middle of the night. He woke up and saw this asshole outside our window. He was on the fire escape, fiddling with the window, trying to get it open. We keep the windows locked, so he couldn't get in—not without breaking the window, anyway. You do police work for twenty years and you learn not to trust anybody, am I right? By the time my husband woke me up and I found my piece, he was gone. So I went to the window and opened it as quiet as I could. I looked down to see if he was still out there, then I heard him up above me. I looked up just in time to see him go in the window of the apartment above ours—the Benzels' place. They were the family that was living there at the time.

"I trailed him up the fire escape, real slow so he wouldn't hear me. I didn't know if he was armed or not, and I didn't want him to find me before I found him. I reached the window, and I saw him come out of the kitchen with a butcher knife."

"Butcher knife," I said.

"Yeah. One of those big long ones." Brenda asked, "Is that how he killed your victim?"

"Yeah, mutilated him pretty bad."

"Mutilated him how?"

"Cut the guy's lips off."

"Shit, Juno. I knew he was a sick bastard. I interviewed his family. They said that when he was a kid, he got picked on something awful with that face of his. I wanted him put away on attempted murder, but the damn judge wouldn't believe me."

"What judge?"

"Judge Heifetz, he was the one that sentenced him. Here, let me back up a minute. I was looking through the window, and he went down the hall to one of the bedrooms, carrying the knife. I climbed in the window and snuck up behind him. He was in the doorway of the kids' bedroom. He had turned the light on, and he was just standing there with that creepy smile of his. He had the knife in his hand."

"Do you remember which hand he held the knife in?"

"Yes. It was his right."

Right-handed, butcher knife, witness testimony—the evidence list was piling up on Ali Zorno. "Then what happened, Brenda?"

"So then I came up on him and yelled, 'FREEZE!' He dropped the knife and didn't resist. I guess I should be thankful that he didn't. I was worried he was going to try to grab one of the kids, you know, as a hostage. If he took one step into that room, I would have fried him right then. But he just gave up and stood there with that freaky grin."

"You did well, Brenda. It must have been tough to keep your head like that when you'd just woken up."

"Not really, Juno. When you wake up with somebody trying to break in to your place, you wake up fast."

"What about this judge?"

"Oh yeah. Zorno's case got assigned to Heifetz's court. You know how thick-headed that guy is. Zorno's lawyer pleaded him guilty to a charge of burglary. You believe that? This guy had murder in his eyes. He wasn't there to steal anything. The judge bought it, sent him up for three years."

"What about the knife? The judge had to see he was up to no good."

"Get this; Zorno claimed he took it to defend himself. He said he heard me coming up after him, and he saw me come in the window with my weapon. He said he was afraid for his life—thought I would shoot him, so he snatched a knife from the kitchen in self-defense. I was floored. I couldn't believe he was trying to get away with a story like that. Meanwhile Judge Heifetz was eating this bullshit up. Since when does a judge trust a criminal's word over a cop's? I'm glad I'm not police anymore. Who needs it? You're getting up there in years, Juno. When are you going to call it quits?"

I chose not to answer. "Is there anything else you can tell us about Zorno?"

"Not much, just dead ends. When it started looking like the judge was going to let him slide on the attempted murder charges, we starting thinking maybe this wasn't the first time he killed somebody, so we started checking around. He comes from a stand-up family. They own a souvenir shop a block off the Old Town Square, and they live upstairs. He'd hang around the shop all the time when he was little. The neighbors said he was a real mama's boy. He'd run to mommy all the time when kids would pick on him. Have you seen his picture?"

"Yeah. I'm looking at his mug right now." His dark and mis-shapen maw resembled an ink blot. Vacant eyes stared out from under a loose mop of hair. I anchored onto the humanity of his nose, which rose from his face like the only island in an abnormal ocean.

"They used to call him Fishhook. They'd put their fingers in their mouths and pull like they were hooked. When he got older, the other kids stopped picking on him, because they were afraid of him. As a matter of fact, they still are afraid of him—scared to death. I interviewed at least a dozen of them. They were all real reserved at first, but once they started feeling comfortable talking to me, they told me all I needed to hear. All the shops on that block have these connected basements, so you can go from one building to another without ever going outside.

"Anyway, all the kids that grew up on that block swore that he'd come through the basement and come into their rooms at night to watch them sleeping. They'd wake up screaming, but he'd be gone by the time their parents would come. One of the kids, well he's an adult now, he told me that he would sneak his father's lase-pistol into his room and hide it under his pillow and try to stay awake so he could fry the Zorno kid when he came in, but he always fell asleep. They'd find missing pets down in the cellar, staked open, blood and guts all over. You know, the usual serial-killer-in-the-making kind of shit. Even if he only did half the things they think he did, we're still dealing with a major psycho."

"Did he do anything to the pets' faces?"

"He sure as hell did. He'd cut the lips off just like your vic. That's how they all knew it was him that was doing it. He had a real obsession with lips. I had two theories on that: either he cut the lips off to make the pets ugly like himself, or he keeps the lips as some kind of substitute for his own. Either way, the guy's nutsville."

"Did you tell all this to the judge?"

"Of course I did—didn't make a difference with that idiot. Get this; when Zorno turned eighteen, he got a job on a barge as a loader. He traveled up and down the river all the time. I subpoenaed the barge's records, matched up the ports of call with reports of missing persons. I found seventeen matches— *seventeen*. And the judge gave him three years for burglary. That asshole judge said, 'No body, no crime.'"

Maggie and I looked at each other, the same shock in her face as mine—*seventeen*. Then Maggie's face struck with a revelation, "Kapasi's sister."

She was right. The time frames matched up. "Brenda, do you remember if one of your missing persons was named Isabel Kapasi from Loja?"

"It sounds familiar, but I'll have to check. Give me a minute to look it up."

Her hologram froze on hold while my brain did anything but. I tried to change gears . . . from Jhuko Kapasi to Ali Zorno with his twisted fishhook grin. I stretched for a connection to Mayor Samir and came up empty.

Brenda came back on the line. "I do have Isabel Kapasi on my list. How did you know?"

"I'll have to explain it later, Brenda. We've got to go." I clicked off the line, forgetting to say thanks. I'd make it up to her later.

Maggie looked like she was having the time of her life. Her eyes were thrill-of-the-hunt glowing. "Let's go get the son of a bitch."

I was still trying to come to terms with the new facts. Private Kapasi: hustler, but not a murderer. His sister disappeared the day he got sentenced for running 'guana fights, possibly a victim of Ali Zorno's. "Yeah. Let's go get him."

"Do we need backup?"

"Never share a collar unless you have to, Maggie. You heard Brenda; he gives up easy."

I called the prison and found out which boardinghouse Zorno had been placed in. Ex-cons got thirty days of free housing, supposedly enough time to land work before they were tossed onto the street.

On the way out, I stopped to tell the kid he could go. I had to wake him up. "You're free to go, Pedro. Here's some money so you can get a cab home."

"Are you going to get the guy?" he asked looking up at me, squinting from the bright lights. The kid was tired.

"Yeah. We're going to get him now."

"Are you going to kill him?"

"Only if we have to, Pedro."

"Can I come?"

"No, but we'll have to bring you back in to ID him after we pick him up so get some rest."

Pedro looked let down. He wanted to come and watch.

We hopped into my car. We'd be better off in it than a police prowler. We didn't want him alerted to our presence.

We crossed the Koba to get to Zorno's boardinghouse. It was slow going on the bridge—caught behind a flock of skeletal old women on bikes, their handlebars stacked high with roped bundles of rugs. They pedaled at walk-speed in sweated-up dresses, heading for the Old Town Square. Even an off-world car got stuck behind them, no room for it to pass. They should've taken a flyer.

We parked a block from the boardinghouse. It was a drab three stories, built after the boom—no arches or tile work. The building was boxy concrete, not even painted. We three-sixtied the place, no fire escape—good. If he was in his room, there wouldn't be an escape route. The first-floor office door was hidden behind a locked steel gate. The building manager demanded our badges before opening the gate and letting us in.

There was a worn-out rug on the floor, and the walls were decorated with faded nature-scene posters spouting bullshit inspirational messages. The manager took a seat behind the counter. A selection of keycards sat in cubbies behind her. She was past her prime, with a cracked-leather smoker's face and a voice to match. "What do you want?"

I said, "We need to talk to one of your tenants, Ali Zorno. Which room is he in?"

She talked like she had gravel in her throat. "You're going to have to help me out, doll. I see a lot of guys come through this place. It's hard to remember 'em all. It's not like any of 'em are worth remembering. They're all rotten, if you ask me. Most of 'em get back to doping and stealing the day they get out."

"Ali Zorno. He would have come in about three weeks ago."

She ignored me and continued. "I'm not joking. Just yesterday, I got a new guy. Jacob is his name. He told me he served ten years. He was very happy to be out, and I was happy for him. He told me how he's going to get a job waiting tables and settle down and start a family. I told him that sounds like a good idea. You know, I was encouraging him, building up his spirits."

How hard is it to answer a simple fucking question? "Ali Zorno. He has a harelip. What unit is he in?"

"Hold on, I'm trying to tell a story. So last night another boarder starts banging on my door and tells me Jacob is in the hall, all strung out, sleeping on the staircase. He tells me he puked up all over the hall and it stinks. I told him I ain't coming out there. I know better than to go out there at night. I open that gate and one of 'em will break in here and have his way with me. I tell you, these guys ain't had any front-door lovin' in a long time. I hear they do it with each other when they're in jail, but that can't be the same as having a woman."

"Ali Zorno. First name A-L-I, last name Z-O-R-N-O."

"I know how to spell, doll. Anyway, I opened the door but not the gate, and I peeked out to see Jacob lying on the staircase just like the boarder told me he was. He was right about the puke, too; it did stink. I told him it will just have to set there until morning. I called the cops; they came and took him. You see what I'm trying to tell you, there ain't one of 'em that's worth a damn. Now who was it you said you were looking for?"

"Ali Zorno."

"Sure, I know who you're talking about. He's the quiet type. If you ask me, they're the kind you really have to worry about. You never know what they're thinking."

"Which room?"

"He's in room thirty-four."

"Is he in now?"

"How should I know? I don't keep track of 'em. That ain't my job."

"Give me a key to his room."

"That ain't my job either."

I reached over the counter, snatched the key in cubby number thirty-four with my shaky hand. She started to protest but thought better of it and backed the hell out of my way. Maggie and I climbed the three flights of stairs, drawing our weapons as we approached the door. I tried to slow my breathing. I was winded from the stairs and more than a little scared. *This fuck butchers people, cuts their lips off.* I knocked, and we waited silently. If he asked who was there, I was going with, "I'm a new tenant, just got sprung from the Zoo this morning. I got a bottle of brandy that I don't want to drink by myself."

No answer. I knocked again . . . still nothing. I took the keycard out of my pocket and waved it at the reader. I held up three fingers for Maggie then mouthed, "One . . . two . . . three . . ."

We stormed in, weapons raised in two-handed grips. . . . Empty. *Damn.*

Maggie holstered her weapon.

My piece was wobbling in my hands. I self-consciously put the gun away. "Let's search the place."

"Don't we need a warrant for that?"

"How do we know what we need a warrant for until we know what he's got in here?"

She gave me a sly grin. She was catching on. Maggie rifled the dresser drawers while I checked out the bed. The sheets were stained brown in several places. The blanket looked chewed upon. I lifted the mattress. Bugs ran for cover, disappearing into mattress holes.

Maggie closed the last of the drawers. "There's nothing in the dresser. Find anything?"

"Not yet." I upended the mattress and braved the insects by reaching into any hole big enough to fit my hand. I felt them skittering over my skin as I probed around the moist insides of the mattress. Every time I pulled my hand out, I flicked my wrist and sent the hangers-on skipping across the floor. *There! Something . . . plastic.* I managed a grip and extracted a shopping bag.

Maggie said, "What are you waiting for?"

I opened the bag. Lying on top was a magazine. The cover showed some actress with her mouth cut out. A quick thumb-through showed mouthless celebrities on every page.

I went back into the bag and grabbed hold of two bundles of money. Talking to myself as much as Maggie, I said, "Where the hell did he get that?"

I passed a stack to Maggie who ran through the bills. "They're all ten-thousands. There has to be at least a million pesos here, maybe two." Enough money to buy a house . . . a nice house.

Maggie turned the bundle over. There was something on the bottom. She stripped off the rubber band and unfolded a photograph of Lieutenant Dmitri Vlotsky saluting in uniform—Vlotsky's address scribbled on the back. "What the hell?"

I reached into the bag and removed a roll of cloth. I began unwrapping the plain white fabric with red stains at the center. We both knew what we'd find, but I continued with morbid obligation. I pulled over the last fold of cloth, exposing a piece of red flesh—Vlotsky's lips.

Maggie asked, "What's that string for?"

There was a string running from the backside of one cheek to the other.

"I don't know. It's like a . . ." I couldn't finish.

"Like a mask," she said.

"Yeah. A mask." An image of Ali Zorno standing in front of the mirror with Vlotsky's lips strung over his ears, his patchwork face reflecting back a set of normal lips, seared itself into my brain.

Maggie shivered the horror away and said, "We've got the bastard, Juno. When Abdul matches this up to Vlotsky's body, we'll be able to give the case to the DA. Between that and Pedro's testimony, Zorno won't stand a chance. He'll be executed."

"Zorno's just the hitter, Maggie. This wasn't a serial killing. He was hired to whack Vlotsky. That's where the money came from. He got half the money up front along with Vlotsky's picture and address, the other half after he did the job."

Ali Zorno: psycho for hire. Paul's mayoral suspicions came to me front and center.

Maggie asked, "How are we going to get him to talk, tell us who paid him?"

"He won't squeal," I said. "I say we tail him—see who he talks to."

Maggie looked skeptical. How could we let a serial killer roam around untouched?

She was right, but I was tasting mayor. I was already envisioning Mayor Samir's head on a platter with me as the waiter. I'd be damned if I let him take KOP away from me and Paul. We took it a quarter-century ago. It was ours.

fifteen

WE put everything back the way it had been, locked the door, and went back down to the building manager. I slapped the keycard on the counter, told the old hag, "We were never here."

I moved the car across the street for a better view of the front and got a spot in the shade. I kept the car running with the pedal floored to keep the aircon pumping.

I settled into my seat. Maggie had her head leaning on the window—probably fell asleep. She'd been up all night.

I scoped the parade of ex-cons passing in and out of the boardinghouse—zeroed on harelips.

"Juno?"

I guess she wasn't asleep. "Yeah."

"How's your jaw?"

"It hurts a little, not too bad anymore. It looks worse than it is."

"You know I can take care of myself, don't you?"

"Yeah. I know."

"Then why did you attack Mark Josephs like that?"

"I was angry."

"You're always angry."

"Yeah."

"Yuan Kim talked to me about you."

"The guy's an idiot, Maggie."

"I know he is, but don't you want to know what he said?"

"What?"

Maggie tucked her hair behind her ear. "He said he's sorry that I have to work with you."

"Why's that?"

"He had a lot of reasons."

"Tell me."

"He said you're just a hothead, and you're still working vice because you have no smarts for being in homicide. He said the only way you got anywhere at all was by using muscle to intimidate people, and you're too dumb to see that nobody is afraid of you anymore. He called you a shaky old man that should have been bounced out of the force years ago."

"Gee, thanks for sugarcoating it, Maggie."

With an amused look, she said, "There was more."

"I can't wait to hear it."

"He said you're the chief's bitch."

"He said 'bitch'?"

Now she was laughing as she nodded her head. "He said Chief Chang tells you what to think. He'd be surprised if you ever had a thought of your own."

"Was that it?" I asked as I wished that I'd pounded that asshole when I had the chance.

"He said you would have lost your job a long time ago if you weren't the chief's yes-man. He thinks the only reason that the chief threw this case to you is as a favor, so you could prove you can still perform."

"What do you think?"

"He's right about you being a hothead, but he's wrong about everything else, especially the part about you being stupid. He shouldn't underestimate you like that. I think Chief Chang put you on this case because he wants it solved, and he knows you'll do whatever it takes to get results. Now, I've been honest; you tell me why you got so angry at Josephs that you attacked him."

"Hell, I don't know what to tell you, Maggie. I know you can take care of yourself, and I know you don't need me to protect you, but when I saw what he did to your picture, it made me angry that he would disrespect you like that. You're my partner." I braced for another lecture.

Maggie didn't say anything for a while. "Thanks." She patted my hand—the shaking one—then let her hand rest over mine. I froze. *Pull away!* My hand stayed where it was. My heartbeat picked up, and my body went prickly.

She took her hand back and focused on the door.

I scrambled for words. The silence was stifling. "You surprise me. I thought you'd still be furious with me."

She thought before responding. "I guess I'm realizing it's just who you are. I just can't believe you're still alive with that temper."

"Sometimes I can't believe it either."

"I looked up your record. It surprises me even more that you've never killed anybody."

"Don't believe everything you read." I let my statement hang. I wished I hadn't said it.

"You scare me, Juno."

"I wouldn't hurt you."

"No, not like that. You scare me because you bring out parts of me that I didn't know I had."

"Bad parts?"

"Yeah."

I was sick of sitting in the car so I sat on a mossy stoop, sipping an icy soda. The boardinghouse was directly across the street. I kept one eye on the front door and the other on the occasional gecko attracted to the smell of dew gathering on the soda bottle. Maggie would be back in a couple minutes. She'd run out for some food.

Luckily, the sun had gone under dark heavy clouds. I felt a raindrop on the back of my quivering hand. Yuan Kim told Maggie I was a shaky old man. *Does everybody know?* It didn't take long for Maggie to figure out I had a problem. *Look at the damn thing shake.* It would take a blind man not to notice. *What the hell were you thinking?* I was like one of those guys who combs his hair over his balding head and thinks nobody will notice the difference.

The rain was coming down hard now. It stung like hot needles. My hand swayed back and forth as I let the downpour massage my neck and back. I'd told only Niki and Abdul about my hand. Niki because I couldn't hide it from her and Abdul because he knew more about medicine than any other doctor I ever met.

I remembered lying on the cold steel autopsy table. Thinking about it, I could still smell the formaldehyde. I remembered how the gutters that ran down the table dug into my back, making me squirm as he examined me. "Please stay still, Juno. I'm not used to patients that move."

"Sorry, Abdul. It's these damn gutters. It's a wonder you don't get more complaints."

"I don't hear the janitors complaining when all they have to do is empty a bucket. You'd be surprised how many fluids come out of a body."

Abdul spent more time on the nets than he did looking at my hand. He scanned through terabytes of data on the nervous system. His eyes strained through his thick glasses at floating bubbles of holographic text. He grabbed out the relevant snippets and diagrams and tossed them around the autopsy room until the place looked like a fragmented 3-D comic book. Finally, he pulled up a stool. "Looks like you have some nerve damage, old friend. It's taken twenty years to manifest itself this way, but it's just going to get worse."

My hand tingled as I thought of wrapping it around that bitch Nguyen's throat. "Can you do anything for it?"

"No. We don't have the right equipment."

"Does anybody?"

"Not on Lagarto. Nobody has anything that sophisticated down here."

"Offworlders could fix the damage?"

"Of course they could. They could even grow you a new hand."

By now, the rain had completely soaked through my clothes. I squeezed my hand into a trembling fist—offworlders. Sons of bitches would float across our nighttime sky, a mocking bright light that crossed from horizon to horizon every hour and twenty-three minutes. They could have grown me a new hand. They could have cured my mother's rot. They even could have repaired Ali Zorno's harelip. He could have had a childhood without being tormented over his looks. Instead the offworlders *sold* medicine to us—*sold it.* It didn't matter if we could afford it.

I realized how conspicuous I looked sitting in the sheeting downpour, so I moved into the doorway of the potato woman. She sat on a three-legged stool in her tiny alcove with potatoes piled on the dirt floor. She lightly flogged the potatoes with a long bundle of grass to keep the lizards away. I dripped rainwater into a muddy puddle around my soaking shoes. I picked out a half dozen potatoes, looking for ones that hadn't sprouted roots.

An offworld woman hopped into the alcove. She had her normal-person look going. There was no telling what she could morph into, but she currently looked like one of us except for her drop-dead-gorgeous looks. Nobody looked that good naturally. She crowded next to me. I felt warmth kick off her tech-heated skin. Rainwater steamed off her clothes.

She beamed plumb teeth and luxurious lips. "Some weather you get down here."

"Uh-huh," I responded.

"And the days are so short here. I thought it was supposed to be summer."

"Go figure," I said.

The calendar was just one more thing that was fucked up about this planet. The Mexican scientists that first colonized this place were a bunch of sentimental shits. They liked their *Cinco de Mayo* on May fifth, and they liked their *Navidad* on December twenty-fifth, so they kept the Earth calendar. They accommodated the fact that our days are only twenty-two hours long by making every month three days longer and leaving February at twenty-eight, giving us a three-hundred-ninety-eight-day year instead of the Earth three-hundred sixty-five. They ignored the fact that Lagarto cycled around the sun every six hundred eighty of our days, yet we would cycle through their three-hundred-ninety-eight-day calendar two-hundred eighty-two days faster. One year June might land in our early winter, like this year. And the next it might be in the dead of summer.

The offworlder kept up the small talk. "Do you know how to get to a restaurant called the Starry Night? I'm meeting a friend there."

I knew the place. "No. Never heard of it."

The potato woman volunteered directions, drawing a map in the dirt.

Somebody was running down the street. I couldn't see his face, but I knew it was Zorno. There was something about the way he ran, upright with his arms barely moving at his sides. His gait was clumsy and uneven. His legs were running, but the top half of his body wasn't. He tried leaping over puddles only to land in their centers, kicking up big splashes that he didn't seem to mind. His sopping shirt clung to the broad shoulders of a man that looked like he'd loaded barges for a living. Lieutenant Vlotsky never stood a chance against this guy. Once those gorilla arms clamped around his neck, it would have been impossible to break his grip. Only an offworlder would've had the strength to do it. If they didn't just electrocute you.

Zorno made it to the door of the boardinghouse and stopped to shake off some of the water. He wrung out his shirttails and pant legs, his mouth frozen in a lopsided snarl. He looked over, seeing me and my bag of potatoes. He grimaced and turned into the building like somebody who has had people staring at him all his life and didn't like it.

I interrupted the potato woman's direction-giving to pay. I noticed Maggie was back in the car and hurried through the rain and sat down uncomfortably in my wet clothes. "He's inside. He saw me buying potatoes. When he comes out, you'll have to follow him; he might recognize me. I'll call you, and we'll keep the line open the whole time. I'll follow in the car at a safe distance. You keep me updated. You got it?"

"Got it."

"This is for real, Maggie."

"I know."

Maggie kept the wipers going. My eyes strained through the water-blurred windshield. Maggie used her napkin to wipe off the fog that formed on the inside. We waited, and we waited.

After two hours, I started feeling antsy, so I rang up the Zoo. Zorno had only been out of jail for a few weeks, yet he'd landed a contract for a hit. I was figuring that he must have made some contacts in prison.

I got prison guard Fatima DuBois on the line. Her image sat in the backseat. I conferenced it so Maggie could participate.

I said, "We need to talk to you about Ali Zorno."

DuBois wore her hair up, streaks of gray ran throughout. "You mean Fishhook? Yeah, I know the guy. They never should have let him go. He has no business being on the street. He just isn't stable."

I got chummy, making her feel like she was one of us cops rather than a cop wannabe. "You're sure right about that. People like us can just spot 'em, can't we?"

"You bet we can. They ought to get rid of juries and put us in there. Regular citizens can't tell if somebody's guilty. They have to guess. They don't know guilty like we do."

"You're onto something there, Fatima. Can you tell us who he associated with?"

"Why?"

"We're looking at him for a murder. We're hoping we might find somebody that he was friends with, somebody he'd confide in."

"That's kinda tough. He was mostly a loner. The only guy he ever seemed to talk to was his old cellmate."

"Can we talk to him?"

"Nope. He was released a year ago."

"What's the cellmate's name? We'll try to look him up."

"Kapasi. Jhuko Kapasi. Check with the Army, he went in—"

I stopped listening to her, the name sinking in. Kapasi. *What the fuck?*

The sun eventually burned through the clouds and doused the street with rays that made wet cars twinkle as they drove by.

Maggie said, "I can't believe they were cellmates."

"I can't believe it either." My brain short-circuited every time I thought about it. Our hitman was cellmates with our original suspect. I slouched into the seat cushions.

Maggie was pumped. "What about Kapasi's sister? Brenda Redfoot was looking at Zorno for her disappearance. Can you believe it; Kapasi gets sent up to the Zoo and ends up rooming with his sister's killer. Can you imagine his grief, losing a sister like that and not knowing that the murderer was sleeping in the next bunk? He was the last person he saw every night;

the first person he saw in the morning. Do you think Zorno knew?"

"I'm sure he did. Serials have long memories. I wouldn't be surprised if Kapasi told him about how he had a sister that disappeared. Zorno would have figured it out—probably played it real cool asking questions like, 'How old was she?' and 'What did she look like?' Meanwhile he's sitting there the whole time, knowing what he did to her. He probably still has her lips stashed away somewhere."

"Do you think Kapasi hired Zorno to kill his lieutenant?"

My mind said, "No. It was the mayor. Paul couldn't be wrong about this." My mouth said, "Could be. We know Kapasi had motive. If somebody gave me a bum gun and sent me into combat, I'd be angry enough to kill." I left it at that. I was stringing her along, letting her think whatever she wanted. It was the mayor who was behind this. Kapasi and Zorno being cellmates was just a coincidence. It had to be.

Maggie started questioning herself, reasoning it through. "But why hire Zorno when you could kill Lieutenant Vlotsky yourself? Maybe Kapasi was just a tough talker. He didn't have a violent background. He was just a scam artist. He didn't have the guts to do the job himself, so he hired Zorno. Little did he know that the guy he hired, the guy he roomed with in prison, killed his own sister."

"Where'd he get the money? That was a large pile of cash we found in that mattress."

"Kapasi was dealing opium and running games in the Army. He used the profits to buy Zorno. That has to be it. Maybe he sold the mystery POWs back to the warlords. That might net him enough money."

Pieces were falling into place. I tried to mentally poke holes in her reasoning, but the more I poked, the more her theory made sense. But it had to be the mayor that bought Zorno. Paul needed it to be the mayor.

Maggie asked, "Can we get in to see Kapasi?"

"Not yet. Paul's trying to get the mils to let us in to see him. He'll tell us when he gets through."

Maggie nodded.

Zorno came out and tromped in our direction. I sank down as far as I could with this creaky old body. I felt his shadow crawl over me as he passed by.

Maggie waited impatiently for ten seconds and stalked out after him. I immediately rang her up. I set it up as a hologram-free phone connection.

"Yeah, I'm here," she said.

"Okay, Maggie. I'll be just a step behind you."

I U-turned onto the street and crept up behind her. *Where is he? Don't worry about him . . . just keep your eyes on Maggie.* Maggie had to double-time to keep up with him. Her shirt was instantly perspiration-stained under the arms and down the center of the back.

A flyer roared overhead. Zorno paused to watch, and Maggie ducked into a shop in case he looked back. I pulled to the side, letting traffic roll by. The flyer buzzed the rooftops. Offworld passengers were sure to have their heads pressed against the glass, looking down at us savages. It was painted camouflage style, as if that thing could ever blend into the surroundings. There were at least a dozen offworld resorts on Lagarto, and one of their main attractions was a flyer ride out to the remote jungle for a monitor shoot. Offworld tourists would rough it in airconned tents while trappers let caged monitors loose right outside the tent flaps for them to pop with scatter-shot lase-rifles that couldn't miss.

The resorts were offworld owned and operated. This was

our planet, yet Lagartans were relegated to cleaning the rooms and washing the dishes at cut-rate salaries. Paul never saw that one coming. He always thought Lagartans would be the main benefactors of increased tourism. It had never occurred to him that offworlders would develop their own resorts and keep millions of tourist dollars from entering the Lagartan economy. Zorno watched until the flyer dropped out of sight then renewed his fast-paced walk.

Maggie turned into a vacant lot that kids used as a playground. I pulled over to the side and saw Zorno already on the far side of the lot. *Damn, he's heading for Floodbank.* That neighborhood floated on pontoons—no cars. When the rainy season came, the Koba River flooded that area. It stayed underwater for three-fourths of the year. It was a large expanse of useless mud for the rest of the year.

"Maggie, I'm going to have to ditch the car. I'll follow on foot."

"Yeah, I was just thinking the same thing."

I left the car curbside and hurried into the lot. Maggie was out of sight. I said, "I'm on foot. Where are you?"

"I'm about to cross the canal bridge—the one by the church."

I jogged until she came back into view then slowed to a quick march as I tried to bring my breathing back under control. I closed the distance between us so I could keep her in sight once we started into Floodbank's intricate system of makeshift walkways.

Following the Lagartan economic collapse, the unemployment rate ran sixty percent, yet for years immigrants like my ancestors continued to arrive, victims of the incredibly slow speed of interstellar travel and communications. They arrived at the spaceport, received their papers, paid their citizenship fees, and were bussed to Tenttown. *Here's a tent with a little free space. You and your family will like it here.* Disease and starvation took out a third of them.

The Tenttowners desperately wanted land of their own to settle, but the Lagartan government claimed ownership over the whole damn planet. They'd sell off parcels of land to anybody who had the cash. Tenttowners had no money. Most arrived destitute, having spent everything they had on passage to Lagarto. Some fled upriver to the remote jungle and squatted, eventually coming under the control of the warlords. Many others moved to the Floodbank area of Koba. It was free. It flooded every year, so it wasn't considered land—no point developing it.

To build a Floodbank home, you'd start by lashing together some old brandy barrels or empty oil drums. Then steal some scrap wood from an abandoned factory and attach plank floors and walls. Then just top it off with a corrugated metal roof, making sure you stacked rocks on top to keep the wind from ripping it off. For indoor plumbing, just cut a hole in the floor and use the river as your toilet.

They built these junkyard homes in the ankle-deep mud of the Floodbank using salvaged concrete blocks as anchors. When the rains came, their homes floated on the river water only to sink back into the mud in the dry season. Floodbank had grown over the years from a small collection of homes to a floating city in its own right. They had their own schools, brothels, churches, and bars—all tied together with a never-ending series of knotted ropes and cords.

Zorno led us through the labyrinth of haphazardly connected structures. We were surrounded by the moan of ropes tug-of-warring against each other and the sharp cracks of buildings bumping into each other at the whim of the river currents. Maggie stopped and turned to look back my way.

I hurried to catch up to her. "What is it?" I asked, afraid she might have lost him.

"He went into that bar." The place looked pretty dead, too early for all but the hard-core drinkers.

"Did he see you?"

"No way, he never looked back."

"Is he still in there? Can you see him?"

"Yeah. That's him sitting at the bar."

Now I saw him. Thankfully, his back was turned to us, so he couldn't see us gawking through the window. We snagged a pair of stools at the end of an open-air fish counter that had a view of the bar. Hopefully, Zorno would stay put long enough for us to scarf down a bite—I was starving. I ordered mine fried on noodles. Maggie asked for hers steamed, but it came fried anyway.

We kept an obsessive eye on Zorno as we ate. He downed brandies, one after another. People stayed clear of him; nobody sat within three stools of the guy. Even the bartender kept himself busy at the far end of the bar.

The fish was greasy-wet, the noodles soggy-wet, but I was hungry enough that it didn't matter. I leaned over until my chin almost touched the bowl. I spooned it up and in as fast as I could with my left; didn't spill much that way. I left nothing but a pool of oil on the bottom. Maggie just picked at hers.

The sun had dropped. Cool evening air lured throngs of people out onto the Floodbank walkways. The fish counter creaked and rocked to the footfalls of customers and passersby. The cook scrambled to keep up with the orders. His grease-stained T-shirt dripped with sweat as he toiled over the deep fryers, stopping only to give Maggie and me nasty looks for hanging around and nursing our drinks, taking up two valuable seats.

Inside the bar, the bartender passed Zorno his check. After

paying up, he was back on the move. I downed the rest of my soda and dropped a few bills on the counter.

Maggie said, "Same plan?"

"Yeah. You follow him, and I'll follow you."

sixteen

MAGGIE and I trailed behind like a piece of loose fishing line hooked in the fish's mouth. We snaked our way back toward the riverbank. At times, I could see Zorno's sturdy build in the distance ahead, but mostly, I just eyed Maggie's sweat-soaked back.

We were near the edge now. The walks were wider and more solid. If not for the slight sway, you wouldn't know you were actually on the water. Maggie talked in my ear, "I'm on the street now . . . . He's taking a cab. Hurry up, Juno. He's taking a cab."

I caught up quickly—I hadn't been far behind. We were on land now. The two of us made for the line of cabs that waited at the entrance to Floodbank. There was no way to get back to my car so Maggie crawled into the back of an empty taxi while I hopped in the passenger seat. Zorno was haggling with the driver of the cab in front of this one, no more than a couple meters away. *Where the hell is the driver?* There was a crowd of people playing dice on the street. I made eye contact with a woman who didn't seem too interested in the game. She nudged a player who was on all fours, waiting for the next throw. He looked over and saw us sitting in his car. He held up a finger to say, "Wait a minute." *Holy shit, hurry up!*

Zorno was getting in his cab. *What the fuck is keeping our driver!* He was arguing with a man holding a wad of cash, trying to settle his account. He kept pointing at us. The man counted out some bucks and passed it to our driver, who finally got in the car just as Zorno's cab pulled off.

I flashed my badge and pointed to Zorno's cab.

He whipped the cab out onto the street and set out in pursuit of Zorno.

I told him, "Leave some space between us. We don't want him to know we're tailing."

"You gonna pay me for this or what? You ain't gonna give me some bullshit about this being an emergency, are you?"

"We'll pay. Now shut up and drive or I'll toss your ass out and drive it myself."

"That's cool, man. If you're paying, I'll do whatever you say. You're the boss." I wanted to tell him to shut up again but held my tongue. Sometimes the best way to keep somebody from yapping was just to stay quiet.

There was only one model of car built on Lagarto. Distinguishing between individual vehicles at night could be next to impossible. Luckily, Zorno's cab had a driver who liked to stand out. His rear windshield was bordered by tacky running lights that cycled in a marching-ant pattern. We headed out from the city center into a residential area. I said as much to Maggie, who was slow to respond. I stole a look back at her. She looked wiped. She hadn't gotten any sleep last night— spent the whole night with Pedro Vargas, going through mugs. "You can take a nap, Maggie. I'll wake you up when we get somewhere."

"No, I'm okay. Just a little tired." She opened her eyes wide and sat up in her seat.

The traffic thinned, so the driver hung farther back, letting Zorno's cab get way out in front of us. I sneaked another peek at Maggie, whose eyes were now closed. I decided to leave her alone and let her get some rest. We drove for a long time on the Cross Canal Road then turned into a dingy development of single-story apartments. The drive was overrun with branching weeds, candy wrappers caught in the cracks. We rode along slowly, people checking us out the whole way.

The apartments were run down. The paint was peeling; pieces of cardboard were taped over window holes. Many apartment fronts had been converted into small stores or food counters. People were out enjoying the evening. Men were grouped into card games and drinking circles. Women worked the stores and food counters. Their kids were running loose with the chickens while lizards hung out on the rooftops, observing without moving.

Zorno's cab drove around to the back one of the apartment rows. He didn't want anybody to know he was here. He got out of the cab and walked to the building. I couldn't see which unit he went in; our view was blocked.

He was here to meet somebody, and I had to find out who it was—could be the person who hired Zorno to snuff Lieutenant Vlotsky. I was afraid he might spot me if I got out too soon, so I waited a minute before I rushed up to a row of crooked mailboxes, leaving a sleeping Maggie in the backseat.

Not all of the boxes had names written on, but I read off the ones that did. Scheid . . . Nunes . . . Rhyne . . . Vargas . . . OH SHIT! Vargas in unit 7! I sprinted to the back of the building, the weeds grabbing at my ankles. I struggled to pull my piece as I ran, finally managing to get it out of the holster as I sped up to the door of unit 7. How could I be so stupid? FUCK! The door was cracked open. I threw it wide and burst in.

Zorno was on his knees, lopsided smile and bloody knife in his hand. Pedro Vargas fish-flopped around the floor with his hands to his throat, blood running through his fingers—too goddamned late.

I was trying to keep my weapon leveled at Zorno, but it was wavering wildly—keep it cool, just relax.

Zorno held onto the knife. He was studying my wobbling gun, measuring his chances.

I held my piece with two hands but couldn't control the tremors—RELAX! He got up, slip-sliding in Pedro's blood. I started squeezing the trigger. My shots burned high and wide, my hand quaking so much that I wasn't even close.

He was charging now. I kept firing and missing. I stopped pumping out short bursts and held the trigger down creating one long burn that I swept side to side like a fire spraying garden hose. He was still coming.

The frying sound of laser fire came from over my shoulder. Zorno buckled. Two more shots and the knife fell harmlessly from his hand as he collapsed.

"You okay, Juno?"

"Yeah, Maggie. Thanks."

"You have to do something about that hand."

The air smelled charred. The walls and furniture smoked with black singe marks. Zorno's burnt flesh smelled well-done. Maggie kept a bead on him as she approached. She kicked away Zorno's knife while I stood there, useless and fucking impotent. Pedro had stopped struggling, and Zorno wasn't moving. Their blood mingled on the floor.

Maggie looked at Pedro's body trying to figure out who it was. "Oh god. Is that Pedro?"

"Yeah."

"How did he know about Pedro?"

I checked them both for a pulse—dead and dead. Then I searched Zorno's pockets, pulling his bar bill out of his back pocket. There was a handwritten note on the backside.

PEDRO VARGAS

BUILDING II, UNIT 7

BAINE'S CANALSIDE DRIVE

KOBA

MALE

AGE 15

SAW YOUR HANDIWORK!

Maggie paled. "Oh my god, Juno. It's my fault. I filled out the witness report. I knew where Pedro lived."

"It's not your fault, Maggie. Zorno did this."

"But I should have known! I knew his address. I should have known that was where Zorno was leading us. I could have stopped it."

"You were tired. You didn't sleep last night."

"I don't believe this. I fell asleep and let him die. He was counting on us. . . ."

"Zorno did this, Maggie. You can't blame yourself. Zorno and the fucking barkeep that passed him this note. I was the one that pushed you into following him. If we had arrested him right away, this wouldn't have happened."

Maggie didn't look convinced.

She found a dry spot and sank down to the floor, the lase-pistol still in her hand. I studied her shock-seized face, unable to help . . . another example of how fucking useless I was. *Somebody is going to pay for this.*

Some punk kid poked his head in the door.

"GET OUT!" I scared him so bad that he smacked into the door frame as he bolted away. I looked out and saw there was a whole crowd out there. Just like the flies and lizards, people were attracted to dead bodies. I closed the door and sealed us off from the scavengers.

I called down to HQ—told them to send out a body wagon and to get some cops here quick for crowd control. I went through the apartment and found Pedro's mother in the bedroom, lying on the bed with an opium-glazed look on her face, ashtray on the pillow. She'd been here the whole time, too hopped to notice her son being murdered in the room next door.

I dried the cup with a moldy towel, dropped in a bag of green tea that I found in the cupboard, and poured boiling water. I left the tea bag sunk in the water and brought it to Maggie. It looked like some of the color had returned to her face, but I wasn't sure.

I took a seat. Abdul worked from a kneeling position, plastic bags meticulously rubber banded over his clothes. His fingers spread Pedro's throat wound open. "He did this one the same way—from behind pull right, push left, pull right. The incision isn't as deep this time. He used a smaller knife, but the cutting motion is the same. It's not as exact as fingerprints, but it looks like Pedro Vargas and Dmitri Vlotsky were killed by the same man."

Greased by Pedro and Zorno's combined blood, he slid more than crawled over to Zorno's body, which lay facedown. "There's your killshot," he said, pointing to the charred region on the top of Zorno's head. "Help me turn him over, Juno."

I got down low, careful to stay out of the blood, and tried using my legs to help power him over. I pulled hard on one of his bulky arms as Abdul turned the torso. I almost fell when the body slid on the slick floor—damn, he was heavy. When we finally succeeded in getting him over, Abdul surveyed the corpse like it was a fine meal. "Ah, we have a stomach wound. I can see it now. The first shot burned into his stomach; he doubled over, and the second shot bored into the top of his head. How am I doing, Juno?"

"You've got it."

Abdul took his eyes off Zorno's body to look at Maggie sitting silently on the sofa. "That was nice shooting, Maggie."

She met his eyes after a pause, reluctant to speak. "Only two hits; I fired three times."

"Two out of three is excellent. I know thirty-year veterans that can't match that ratio." He smirked in my direction.

Two white coats entered. "You have somebody for us?"

About time! "Yeah, she's in the bedroom, right down the hall."

"Is she injured?"

"No, just drugged out of her mind. She missed the whole thing."

They headed into the bedroom and came out a few minutes later with Pedro's mother on a stretcher. They had mercifully pulled a sheet over her head, so she wouldn't have to see her dead son. As soon as they left, in came Paul with that asshole Karl Gilkyson.

Gilkyson looked ill the instant he laid eyes on the gory scene.

Paul noticed his queasy stance. "Why don't you wait outside? We'll come right out."

Gilkyson gave Paul a thankful nod and stepped out.

Paul told Maggie to take a break. She was deeply offended; after all, she'd just killed a man, working this case. She'd earned the right to be in the inner circle.

Paul said, "I'm sorry, Maggie, but I need to talk to Juno and Abdul privately."

She left in a rush. *Are those tears in her eyes?*

The three of us were alone with the two bodies. Paul took charge like always. "We won't be able to talk for long. Gilkyson will be back in here as soon as he gets his stomach back. I need to know what happened."

I said, "The kid's name is Pedro Vargas. He was a witness to the Vlotsky killing—saw the whole thing go down. He picked Ali Zorno out of the mugs last night."

"Zorno? I thought you were looking at the military guy—Kapasi. I've been busting my hump trying to get you in to see him."

"Keep on it. He and Zorno were cellmates at the Zoo. I still want to talk to him. Zorno got arrested by Brenda Redfoot when he broke into an apartment in her building. She had him pegged as a serial killer but couldn't sell it to the judge, so he got sent up for burglary. He just got released from the Zoo a few weeks ago. Get this: Brenda put together a list of missing persons that she thought Zorno could have taken, and Kapasi's missing sister is on the list.

"At this point, Maggie was thinking Zorno was a serial killer and Lieutenant Vlotsky was just a random victim. But when we busted into Zorno's place this morning, we found a pile of cash in his mattress along with Vlotsky's lips. We're talking a big pile of cash with Vlotsky's picture and address. That locks it, Paul. Vlotsky was a hired hit. Maggie wanted to arrest Zorno right away, but I wasn't sure we'd be able to get him to squeal, so I talked her out of it. I thought we should follow him to see who he contacted. We wound up following him here. By the time I realized this was the kid's place, it was too late."

"How did he find out about the kid?"

"I had Maggie fill out a witness report."

"A cop tipped him off? Is that what you're telling me?"

"Yeah, unless it was Gilkyson. Is that guy glued to you or what?"

Paul looked ready to explode—must be what I looked like most of the time. "No. Gilkyson's too busy crawling up my ass to read witness reports. It has to be one of ours. Odds are it's the same asshole that ratted the frame job I tried to put on the mayor last month."

Abdul stopped working the stomach wound to talk to Paul. "Why'd you put Juno on a homicide? You could have gotten him killed."

That made me angry. "Since when do you talk about me like I'm not here?"

Abdul raised his spectacle-magnified eyebrows at me. "Since you don't know how to take care of yourself."

"I don't need you to take care of me, Abdul. I need you to butt the hell out."

"The hell you don't. You practically fried the whole apartment and didn't hit him."

Paul looked at the burn-scarred room. "Did you do all that? Is your hand that bad?"

"How do you know about my hand?"

"Abdul told me."

I was getting angrier. "What the fuck did you do that for, Abdul?"

"Because I'm your doctor. You are my responsibility."

"You're not my doctor. You're a fucking coroner."

"I am your doctor. And you're not fit for a homicide investigation. You shouldn't be on the street at all. I called Paul as soon as I found out you were on this case and told him about your hand. I knew there was no point in trying to talk you out of it, so I appealed to Paul."

"Fuck that! I won't leave the street."

Paul tried to settle the argument. "You're right to be worried, Abdul, but I need Juno on this case."

Abdul resumed work on the stomach wound, wiping the blood away as he talked. "What's so important about this case?"

Paul sat down on the sofa. He fingered his tie tack. "I need somebody I can trust."

Abdul asked, "Why?"

Paul took a minute to explain his mayoral involvement theory to Abdul. It was cut short when the door opened, and Karl Gilkyson came back in—bastard couldn't leave us alone.

Gilkyson was making a concentrated effort to keep his gaze off the carnage. "Fill me in."

Paul jumped in before I could respond. "The kid's name is Vargas. That's him with the cut throat." Paul pointed to Pedro's body, trying to get Gilkyson to look, but he wouldn't bite. He stayed focused on Paul. "He witnessed the Vlotsky killing and picked out the murderer's mug shot. The murderer's name is . . . what was it again, Juno?"

"Zorno. Ali Zorno."

"Yeah, Zorno. That's him with the head wound." Again he pointed.

Gilkyson fell for it and took a swift glance at the burned-out hole in Zorno's head then jerked away.

Paul mocked him with a devilish grin. "He killed the kid to protect himself from prosecution. That's when Juno and Maggie arrived and tried to arrest him, but he resisted and they had to use deadly force."

Paul led Gilkyson out for some fresh air before the lawyer blew his dinner all over our crime scene. The door closed behind them before Paul returned with a take-charge attitude. "I only have a minute before Gilkyson comes back in. Here's the plan: I'm going to tell him the Vlotsky case is closed. Let him think we don't suspect anything. I'll put Maggie's picture out with the story. We'll get her introduced to the public as the hero cop that brought down a serial. Getting her image built up now will only help if we end up going against the mayor publicly with her as the front man. Sound good?"

"What if he asks how Zorno knew about our witness?"

"How 'bout this? I'll tell him it's irrelevant. We already have our killer, so case closed. When I tell him that, he'll just assume we don't want to dig into it because we're trying to cover for a bad cop who leaked the info on the kid to Zorno. No harm done."

I agreed. Gilkyson already knew we were corrupt. What was one more violation on his list of unproved accusations? I nodded to Paul who slipped out.

I stewed while Abdul worked, silent tension between us. He moved up to the head wound but stopped at Zorno's harelip. "I guess we know what his lip fixation was about."

"I guess we do."

Maggie appeared at the door. "Is the boys' club over yet, or do I need to wait outside?"

"Maggie, we need to talk."

We were standing in an open area next to Pedro's apartment building—nobody near enough to eavesdrop. Most of the curiosity seekers had moved on. Only a few die-hards still milled around, waiting for the bodies to be brought out.

A light breeze ruffled the scratchy weeds that stretched up to our thighs. Thousands of nocturnal insects chirped all around us, their song blending together into an arrhythmic drone. A mosquito cloud stayed bug-spray distance from our heads. I looked up at the sky; I spotted the Orbital, the brightest star in the heavens.

Maggie spoke abruptly. "What did you talk about in there?" The dark night sky hid her face from me. I couldn't see the anger I knew was written there.

"Here's the way it is, Maggie. You have to decide how committed you are to solving this case."

"I just killed a man and caused the death of a boy. I think I'm a little committed now, don't you?"

"Zorno killed that kid, Maggie. You can't let yourself get all torn up over it. We both made mistakes, but we're not respon-

sible for the kid's death. Our hearts were in the right place—
you understand me? You never intended any harm toward Pedro. Your conscience is clear."

"But—"

"Stop blaming yourself and put the blame where it
belongs—on Zorno and whoever hired him to kill Lieutenant
Vlotsky. They put us on this path. It's their burden, not ours."

"I should have been paying attention. If I had stayed awake,
Pedro would be alive. You can't deny that."

I was getting nowhere. It was hard to talk somebody out of
guilt. "Do you want to catch the bastards that hired Zorno?"

"Yes, I want to catch them. What the hell do you think?"

"I know you want to catch them, but how bad do you want
to?"

"I want to catch them, okay? Quit beating around the bush
and say whatever it is you want to say."

"I know why Paul's so interested in this case."

"Why?"

"Because Karl Gilkyson encouraged him to downplay it."

"Why would the mayor's office want to downplay it? Vlotsky's father works for the city."

"Because the mayor's behind this whole thing, Maggie. He
hired Zorno."

"No he didn't. It was the Army guy, Kapasi."

I shook my head no.

"Do you have any proof?"

"Not yet, but the mayor wants control of KOP, and this case
is related. I have to find out how."

Maggie looked tired. "I don't see how there can be a connection between Mayor Samir and this case."

"Hey, if you're afraid to stand up to the mayor, I understand."

I was being unfair, and she called me on it. "Quit the bullshit. I
want to catch these guys, Juno. I don't give a shit who they are."

"Even if it's the mayor?"

"How can you be so sure it's the mayor?"

"I'm sure. Why else would his office try to downplay it?"

"That's all you're basing this on?"

I wanted to say no, there were other reasons, but the truth was I had nothing else. "I'll make you a deal, Maggie. The two of us, we take this case to the end, no matter what, whether it leads to the mayor or not."

"Fair enough," she said. "I think you're crazy with this mayor stuff, but if he is involved, I'll cuff him myself."

The bodies were being carried out under Abdul's supervision, two black bags dragged across the weed tops to the truck. The truck pulled off, and the onlookers went back to their boozing and betting.

I looked at Maggie's silhouette. "You understand that I won't be playing by the rules? The mayor is trying to take KOP away from Paul. I can't allow that."

"I've seen the way you are. I can handle it."

"We have a deal then? We take this case to the end."

"On one condition. You can't keep any more secrets from me." When I didn't answer, she said, "You proved tonight that you can't do this alone. You need me, Juno."

I flexed my hand. "What do you want to know?"

"I want to know if Chief Chang is dirty. I want to know about his relationship with the Bandurs. I want to know everything."

I though about making up a bunch of bullshit to tell Maggie, but she'd just saved my life. She deserved the truth about Paul and me. To make her understand I had to go back to '62. . . .

seventeen

NATASHA and I sat at a window table. The restaurant bobbed with the flow of the Koba. Boats lights skimmed by, dimmed by a haze of falling rain. I'd been seeing her for months now. Things were going well, real well, but not tonight. Tonight she had something on her mind.

I offered the last mussel to Natasha. She refused, so I sucked it down and returned the shell to its plate.

Natasha had her hair pulled up. An open-backed black dress made me wish I was sitting behind her, getting lost in neck shadows and nape hair. She dabbed her mouth with a napkin for the third time. "Juno, can I ask you something?"

Here it comes, what she's been stewing about all night. "Yeah."

"Are you really going to arrest my father?"

"Yes. Why? Don't you want me to?"

"Yes, I want you to. I just don't understand why you haven't done it yet."

"I told you. We're still collecting evidence. We'll do it as soon as we can."

"It's just that you've been saying that for a long time."

"And you're starting to wonder if I've been honest with you?"

She looked down at her empty plate and nodded.

"I swear to you, Natasha; I'm going to arrest him myself. He'll spend the rest of his life in the Zoo."

"You're not just saying that?"

I reached across the table and took her hand. "I'm not."

She nodded again, but I could tell she wasn't convinced.

"Listen, maybe it would help if I knew why you hate him so much."

She pulled her hand away and looked out the window. There was a gecko hanging on the other side of the glass, his pale underbelly exposed to me. I put my napkin on the table and unintentionally scared him away.

Natasha said, "It's the way he treats my mother. He doesn't love her . . . and she deserves better than that."

"How do you know he doesn't love her?"

"He sleeps around."

"Does your mother know?"

"He doesn't do it in front of her, but she knows. She has to know."

"Maybe your mother should leave him."

"She can't do that."

"Why not?"

She was starting to raise her voice. "Because he controls her, Juno. She's afraid of him."

"Why is she afraid?"

"She just is."

"Does he threaten her?"

She looked out the window.

"Is she worried about money? Doesn't she think she can make it on her own?"

Nothing.

"Why is she so afraid?"

"You want to know why? I'll tell you why. He rapes her! I hear him at night yelling at her, telling her it's time to give him a son. She begs him to stop, but he forces her. I can hear her crying while he grunts away."

I looked away—wrong thing to do.

"You just had to make me say it, didn't you!? You treat me like one of your snitches. You push and push, wear me down until you break me. Well, you broke me. Now you know why I hate my father. Does that make you feel big? What are you going to do about it, cop? Have enough evidence now?"

She hurried to her feet, bumping the table and making the plates jump. She took the napkin with her, using it to wipe at her eyes as she stomped out of the restaurant.

I wanted to chase after her, but I couldn't move. I felt like there was a giant ball of lead in my stomach, holding me down like a paperweight. What the fuck was I doing? I was spying on her. Spying on her family. Leading her on while Paul cooked up his bullshit schemes. It needed to stop. If we were going to have a future, it needed to stop.

I found Paul watching channel F. Natasha was lying on her bed, bawling. She hadn't bothered to take off her dress or let her hair down. My eyes stung with salt.

Paul said, "What do you think happened to her?"

"I don't know," I managed to rasp out. I felt sick.

She began to moan when it took too much energy to wail. I couldn't take it anymore. I turned down the volume.

Paul asked, "How was your date?" He still didn't know about Natasha and me.

"Not so good. We had a fight."

"Really. What about?"

I didn't answer. Pavel Yashin was at Natasha's door. *What is he doing?* Natasha didn't see him; her back was to the door. He came into the room and crossed over to her bed. Her face was buried deep in her pillow. Yashin slowly, tentatively set his hand on her shoulder, where my hand should be. Natasha's body went rigid. He started to rub her shoulder, moving toward her neck. She jerked away.

I could see it now. She had lied about her mother.

Yashin stood still for a moment with his hand outstretched. She stopped crying; she stopped breathing. She had the pillow gripped like a life preserver. He withdrew his hand and walked out.

I finally understood. He'd never raped her mother. I'd seen how he never even touched her; he had a thing for young girls, substitutes for his grown-up daughter. Natasha was the one he'd raped.

I went red. In my mind, my father's face superimposed itself over Pavel Yashin's. The rage boiled over.

"Hey. Are you okay, Juno?"

I knocked the display over.

"It's okay, Juno! Whatever it is, it's okay."

I ran outside into the stinging rain. Lizard eyes mocked me. I stomped a gecko, kicked at a too-fast-for-me iguana. I pulled my piece, took two shots at the iguana. The second one blew it apart. People came out of their houses. Paul badge-flashed them back in.

I counted breaths, bringing myself down from memories of frenzied struggles against my father's wrist restraints. I tucked my piece away. I ran my fingers into my hair and squeezed, the pain nudging me back toward center.

Paul tried to lead me inside. "Are you okay?"

I stayed where I was, letting the rainwater cool my over-heated body. "We have to talk, Paul."

"Let's go have a drink." Paul didn't ask what my blowup was about. He knew I'd tell him when I was ready.

Paul and I walked into the first bar we could find, the Jungle Juice. Fake trees lined the back wall, and fake vines hung down from the ceiling, nothing more than ropes with paper leaves stapled on. The bartenders were in Tarzan garb, the waitresses sporting zebra-stripe dresses.

We nabbed a couple seats at the bar. Bar noise invaded my thoughts. I teetered on the edge. I slugged down a shot of brandy, warming the skin under my wet clothes. My nerves dulled. A security blanket of logical thought wrapped itself around me. "It's time to move on Yashin."

"Not yet, let's give it a little more time."

What the hell was his problem? We'd been having this argument for months. The lieutenant had reached the end of his rope with us. He was threatening to split us up as partners, but Paul still wouldn't let it go. The guy was obsessed.

I wasn't going to let Paul talk me out of it, not this time. "We have all we need. All we have to do is call Judge Saydak, and get our warrant. I want this to be over, Paul. We've had those cameras up for *months.* I'm sick of us sitting on our asses when we could have dropped the bastard a long time ago."

Our case against Natasha's father was airtight. We had more vids than a jury could watch—Yashin making flashlit pickups on the river; Yashin cutting piles of brown sugar on his kitchen table; bowtied waiters coming to the door and exchanging cash for butcher-paper wrapped packages.

The only thing we needed was witness statements. My plan was to run a sweep—Paul and I would pick up Yashin. We'd get vice officers to pick up all his dealers. The whole thing would be coordinated, so it all happened at the same time. We'd make their heads spin. We had vids of all his dealers making midnight buys from Yashin. We'd use the vids to turn two dealers on Yashin—first come, first served on two reduced sentences; fuck the rest of them. The first two to take our deal would authenticate our surveillance.

But Paul was still hooked on the bigger fish—Ram Bandur.

Pavel Yashin and Bandur were *still* negotiating the sale of Yashin's overstock from the busted Nguyen deal. Paul swore that the deal would eventually go through, and when it did, we could get Bandur.

Paul tried to disarm me with one of his smiles. "I'm telling you, we can get Bandur. Just give it a little longer."

"We don't *have* anything to pin on Bandur. You've been waiting for months for this deal to go down, and you don't have shit. Even if he and Yashin come to terms, and we get the whole deal on vid, it still won't matter. Bandur is out of our reach. He's not a small-time drug peddler like Yashin. The guy's a fucking kingpin. I wish we could bag the guy, but we can't. He can buy his way out of anything we get on him. The vids we take will go missing, and we'll go missing with them."

Paul took a hit of his drink. He talked without looking at me. "We don't have to arrest Bandur."

"What are you talking about, Paul?"

"We can use the vid as an in. I'll take it to him and offer to hand it over to him."

"I don't get it."

He looked at me. "We've got Yashin whether we move now or later, right?"

"Yeah."

"So we wait and maybe score some evidence on Bandur. Nothing he can't beat on his own, but if we turned it over to him, he'd be appreciative; wouldn't he?"

"Maybe so," I admitted. "Where the fuck are you going with this?"

"We should make a deal with him. Bandur can rat out his competition to us, and we'll arrest them. Think about it, we'll make so many busts that we'll be stars in KOP."

Was he serious with this? "You're talking about teaming up with a *murderer*, Paul. He had his initials burned into those dealers' balls. How can you think of making a deal with a guy like that?"

"Don't give me the goody-good bullshit, Juno. Crime isn't the real enemy. It's poverty. Why pretend that we can beat crime when we'd be better off partnering with it, controlling it? I'm sick of these college-educated pinhead politicians riding their fucking white horses, telling us cops to clean up the city. Who are they to deny people the right to gamble or take a few hits of O? It's the only thing that's keeping them all sane. It takes their minds off how hopeless their lives are. The only thing we achieve by arresting them is filling up the Zoo with prisoners— just more people living off the government peso. In the meantime, the people keep gambling, whoring, and drugging as much as ever."

I couldn't believe he was seriously thinking about this. "And you think that you can change things by giving our evidence away?"

"Why not? I'll go to Bandur and tell him that I can make him the most successful crime boss Lagarto's ever seen. We'll arrest all his competition. The whole city will be his. Who would turn down a deal like that?"

"And what do you get in exchange?"

"Some rules, that's all. Just some rules. We'll carve the city up into zones—areas where illegal activity is accepted and areas where it's not. Maybe we can get some more tourists to come down here if they know there are areas where it's safe to go. We'll be able to regulate the illegal areas. Whores won't have to hide out in alleys anymore. We'll have whorehouses as classy as anywhere. We can even run honest games. That way offworlders won't be afraid to play, because they'd know they wouldn't be cheated. You know the mines are doing well. There's going to be more and more people up there. They all need to take a vacation somewhere. What do you think?"

I was shaking my head. Was he insane?

Paul grinned at me. "It comes down to this. We need off-world money; that's the best thing we can do for Lagarto."

"This is too far out for me, Paul."

"Hey, man, I wouldn't ask you to do this with me. I'm okay doing it alone. Just let me do it if you don't want to be part of it."

I was tempted. Despite it all, I was tempted. Crime-free zones could actually work. Paul's ideas, no matter how fucked up, could be infectious. Then Natasha's picture came front and center. "I can't let you do it, Paul. If you don't want to arrest Yashin, I'll do it myself."

Paul clenched his drink. "You would do that to me? We're supposed to be partners. You can't just go and take a collar for yourself. We've been working Yashin together."

"I'm going to do it tomorrow. I'm going to walk in there and arrest the fucker. Are you coming with me or not?"

"Why are you so hot to do this? We've got Yashin sewn up. Why the rush?"

"I'm sick of waiting. I don't want to watch that family anymore."

"What are you talking about? You love to watch them. What are you going to do if we arrest Yashin, and you can't watch Natasha anymore? I've seen the way you look at her."

"It's weird to watch them like that—in their own home."

"You didn't think it was weird when we started. You told me yourself that you liked it. You said that watching them made you feel invisible. You could move from room to room, and they couldn't see you."

"That was at the beginning. I don't feel that way now." *Let it go, Paul.*

Paul downed his drink and held up two fingers for the bartender. An overweight Tarzan filled our glasses halfway and hurried back down the bar to keep up with the late-night rush. Paul looked like he was going to say something. He took a couple long pulls on his brandy before he spoke up. "There's something you're not telling me. What made you have a change of heart?"

He was going to find out anyway. "I've been seeing Natasha."

Paul just about busted a vein. "What? How long?"

"Since April."

"Is that who you've been seeing all this time? Shit, what are you thinking? Does she know you're a cop?"

"Yes."

"Does she know we're after her father?"

"Yeah. She knows, but she won't tell him."

"Why the fuck not?"

"She hates him."

"Does she know about the cameras?"

"No."

Paul rubbed his face with his hands. "How could you do this? We put too much effort into this case for you to risk it all for some tail."

"It's not like that."

"What is it like?"

"We're serious about each other."

Paul finished off his drink with a gulp and put two fingers back up. The bartender came and filled Paul's glass then gave me an irritated look when he had to wait for me to empty mine.

Paul frowned. "How serious?"

"Serious."

Paul took a deep breath and let it out slow. "Is that why you're so gung ho on getting Yashin? You feel guilty about those cameras, about watching her without her knowing."

I didn't have to answer. I just took another drink. The brandy burned all the way down to my stomach.

"Why did you go off on those lizards?"

I told him about the fight I had with Natasha and how I thought her father abused her. I told him about the suicide scars on her wrists that she wouldn't admit to. Her father put them there—like my father put scars on my wrists. I was going to arrest that asshole. He had to pay for what he did to her. I hoped he'd resist arrest. Any excuse to get a few licks in would suit me fine.

We sat for a long time without talking. Finally, I said, "So are you coming with me when I arrest the bastard or not?"

"You're really serious about her?"

I nodded.

"You love her?"

I nodded again.

Paul put his true-friend hand over mine. "Okay, Juno. I guess Bandur can wait. We'll pinch Yashin tomorrow."

eighteen

I POUNDED on the door. "Get up, Josephs!"

After two minutes of continued pounding, Mark Josephs finally opened the door, heavy lidded with cowlicked hair. His voice was a half-awake croak. "What the fuck are you guys doin' here?"

"You going to let us in or what?" Paul challenged.

Josephs let us through. We didn't bother wiping our shoes. The stone floor was already covered in muddy footprints. We settled in his living room. Dried up tea bags were stuck to the walls—he'd do the same shit at the office, make his tea and whip the tea bag at a wall to see if it stuck. I had to move an empty liquor bottle to make room on the sofa. A gecko scuttled out from underneath. A poof of moldy air came up out of the cushions as I sat down, making me sneeze.

Josephs sat on a chair that looked ready to collapse. "It's too early for this. What do you two want?"

Paul said, "We're going to make a sweep this morning. We need your help."

"Can't it wait?"

"No, it can't. You know that morning is the best time to catch drug dealers, when they're still sleeping."

"Shit. I wish I was still sleepin'. Who are you bringin' down?"

"Pavel Yashin. He sells O to a high-class crowd. You know him?"

"I don't know him, but I know who he is. What do you need me for?"

"You're just our first stop. We're going to wake up Reyna, Cheng, and Banks next. We have names and addresses of the top guys that work under Yashin. Juno and I are going to arrest Yashin in two hours, and we want all of you to pick up the scraps."

"You have evidence?"

"We have a bundle. Convictions will be a cinch."

"Damn. Who would have thought you two could put together a bust like this?"

A female voice came from the back. "Are you talking to somebody?"

Josephs yelled back, "Yeah, it's just some guys from work. Go back to sleep."

"Are my clothes out there?"

Josephs ignored her, spoke to us. "How do you want to do it?"

I could see a bra on the floor. I handed Josephs a name and address. "When you get set in position, you call me or Paul. When everybody's set, we'll call and tell you to move in. It'll be synchronized."

"Did you find my clothes?" The woman came out from the bedroom with a dingy-gray sheet as a wraparound. She snatched up her clothes from the floor. When Josephs turned her way, she said, "Thanks a lot, asshole. Some gentleman you are."

Josephs turned back to us and spoke in a voice that didn't care if she heard. "Don't mind her, guys. She's just a round-heels I picked up last night."

She was gone to the back—I couldn't tell if she heard him or not.

"I never should've brought her home," Josephs said. "If I didn't work vice, I would just pay for a pro. Sure it costs some money, but by the time I bought that skank enough drinks to get in her pants, I just about could have paid for a hooker, and then I wouldn't have to deal with this broad's attitude."

A door slammed. Josephs grinned. "Good, she's gone. Hey, speakin' of hookers, are you gonna to nab Yashin's daughter while you're at it?"

Did I hear that right? "What the fuck are you talking about?"

"Yashin's daughter, I can't remember her name."

"Natasha."

"Yeah, that's it. Natasha. She's a high-class hooker and a hot one at that. When I leave vice, I think I'll look her up. I'll probably have to save up two months' pay, but it'd be worth—"

My world turned red. I was on top of him in a flash. I socked him in the face once, twice. Paul grabbed me from behind. "LET ME GO!" I shouted. I fought against the arms holding me back. "LET ME GO!"

I was wrestled to the floor from behind. Paul buried my face into the mildewed rug. My nose tickled uncontrollably. I went into a sneezing fit. Can't BREATHE. I turned my face to the side and heaved as much air into my lungs as I could with Paul on top of me.

Josephs was yelling at Paul, "Let him go! I'm gonna fuck him up!" Josephs started trying to pull Paul off me. "Let him go!"

Paul managed to stay on top, his hands clasped under my stomach in a bear hug. As Josephs's rants petered out, Paul's pythonlike hold began to loosen. Once Paul was sure we'd both calmed, he whispered in my ear, "Are you all right? Can I let you up?"

I nodded, my cheek scraping carpet.

Paul let up superslow. I stayed still. When he let go, I rolled over, sat against the wall, and blew my nose into a dirty napkin.

Josephs was on the couch, nursing a bloody lip.

I said, "Natasha's *not* a hooker."

"She sure as hell *is* a hooker," he said. "I arrested her myself. Check the fuckin' books if you don't believe me."

My insides went to jelly. "Tell me about it."

"Apologize first."

I gritted my teeth. "You're right, Josephs. I shouldn't have come at you like that."

Josephs thought it over, deciding whether or not I was sincere. I wasn't. He said, "Okay, Juno. I'll tell you, but only because we go back a few years."

"Thanks."

"Why are you so interested in her? You seein' her?"

"Yeah."

"Shit. I didn't know. I wouldn't have said those things about her if I knew you were pokin' her. You know I'm not the kind of guy that talks about another guy's woman."

"I know. I just lost it, okay? I wasn't thinking straight."

"You can say that again. You were like some kind of fuckin' animal, man. You were flashin' your teeth. I was afraid you were gonna bite me."

"Sorry, Josephs."

"Hey, man, that's okay." He wiped his lip with a towel.

"Tell me about Natasha."

"It must have been a year ago. Back then I was all jazzed to arrest an offworlder. I'd only arrested Lagartans up to that point, and I thought it would look good on my record to have a few offworld collars. I got all dressed up, got my clothes ironed and everything. Then I hit some of the nice restaurants near the Town Square, you know, the touristy places. I'd hang out in the bar and wait for an offworlder to proposition a hooker. Didn't have to wait long."

Josephs wiped his lip again. This time it came away clean, and he tossed it on the floor. "You ever been in a restaurant called Afrie's?"

"Yeah." That's where I'd met her.

"Your Natasha was there with two other hookers. They didn't look like hookers though. I thought they were just out partyin' together. There was also this group of five miners there. The two groups were makin' eyes at each other, then the miners started sendin' drinks over. One of the miners went over and sat with Natasha and her friends. You should've seen this dude. He had this fish skin—you know, scales and shit. They was all into touchin' it, seein' how it felt. He was turnin' it on and off. One second he's a fuckin' fish, and the next, he's a normal person. Natasha and her friends were oohin' and ahin' like schoolgirls. At this point, I wasn't suspicious at all. I'm thinkin' it's just some innocent flirtin', but then he goes back to his table, and the five of them pool together a bundle of cash. Then the guy goes back over to Natasha's table and leaves the money with a hotel key. I followed them to the hotel and busted the whole lot. All eight of them."

"You're sure we're talking about the same Natasha?"

"Yeah, I'm sure. When I booked her, she said her name was Yashin. I asked her if she was related to Pavel Yashin, and she said he was her father. I just about shit when I heard that. I asked her why she was hookin'. She's got all the money she needs. She wouldn't answer."

I went for the door—had to get out of there.

Josephs stayed seated. "Sorry to break it to you. You were gonna dump her anyway, weren't you?"

I stopped, my hand on the doorknob. "Why do you say that?"

"You're about to arrest her father. Aren't you gonna sting him? Give him a line like, 'You're under arrest, and I've been fuckin' your daughter.' Shit, that's cold! That would sting him good, Juno. You could even dress it up a little—"

Paul put his hand on my shoulder and guided me out.

I couldn't think straight. All this time she'd been with me, she'd been . . .

Paul yelled over the rattle of rain on the aluminum overhang. "What do you want to do?"

"I don't know. I have to talk to her."

"Are you sure that's a good idea?"

"No."

"Can you keep that temper under wraps?"

"I don't know."

"Do you want me to come with you?"

"What good would that do?"

"I can watch while you talk. The second I see your switch go off, I'll stop you before you hurt her."

"You think you can stop me?"

"I just did."

I called Natasha, told her to come down to my place right away. Paul and I sat together wordlessly waiting. My emotions cycled with alarming speed—anger, hatred, disgust, grief, resentment, hostility . . . They all burned through me—their combined combustion nearing a flash point. A knock on the door launched me from my seat. Paul went in the bedroom, leaving the door cracked.

I opened the front.

Natasha's gray dress matched the sheeting downpour. The smile on her face didn't last long. "What's wrong?"

I let her in and led her into the living room, into Paul's view. "I talked to Officer Josephs today."

Her defenses snapped into place. "So?"

"He told me he arrested you a year ago."

"So what if he did?"

"You're a prostitute. That's what you do when you say you're going out with your friends."

She looked away.

"How could you do that to me?"

When she turned back, her eyes had ignited. "How could I do what? Open my legs for money?"

My vision started to blur. "Yes. How could you do that?"

"Because they fucking paid me."

"I don't pay you."

"Yes you do. You'll pay me when you arrest my father—a onetime fee!"

"Is that all I am to you? A means of getting rid of your father?" I was pacing now.

"Yes. That's all you are, just a cop that can get me what I want. And I'm getting sick of you stringing me along!"

I could feel my pulse in my temples.

Natasha unleashed. "I came here expecting you to tell me you were going to arrest him today. For months, you've been leading me on. A real man wouldn't be so chickenshit scared of my father!"

My head pounded; my stomach churned. My whole body ached for release.

She kept at me. "I'll tell you another thing. I didn't have to fake it with my johns!"

I wanted to lose control. The only thing holding me back was the fact that I knew she was deliberately provoking me. She wanted me to strike her . . . punish her.

I wouldn't give her the satisfaction. I just hit her with the truth. "You hurt me, Natasha."

She was positively fuming. My emotions suddenly shut down, like they'd overloaded. I watched her with a strange detachment. It finally occurred to me why I was so attracted to her in the first place. She was the only person I knew who was filled with more rage than me.

Nothing left to say, we stared at each other for long minutes.

I saw her expression move from bitter to smoldering, then from smoldering to little-kid scared.

Questions ran through my head. . . . How long has your father been raping you? . . . Is your shame so great that you punish yourself by selling your body? . . . Would you stop if I took your father away?

Instead I said, "Get out."

"What?"

"Get out. I don't want to see you." I wanted her to pay for how I felt.

"Please, Juno. I didn't mean those things I said." She was misting up now.

"Get out."

"But I quit. I quit! I quit after I met you." Tears rolled down her brown cheeks. "Don't do this, Juno. You can't do this to me. Don't leave me!"

I went to the door and opened it.

"I'm sorry. I should have told you, but I quit. I didn't think it mattered. Don't do this!"

She stepped out the door where elongated raindrops were stabbing the ground like glass pencils driven into the mud. She slipped and just managed to catch herself by dropping her hands to the ground. She pushed herself back up and pulled her hands free from the wet earth, her fingers coated with mud. She flicked her hands in an effort to get the clumps off but just wound up spraying the front of her dress with muddy water. She looked at me. Her eyes imploring.

You can't do this to her, Juno, Don't be an asshole.

I closed the door in her face.

Paul and I were still at my place. I called off the Yashin arrest. "Wait and see if we can get Bandur," I said.

Paul tried to talk me out of it. "Are you sure? It's going to kill your chances with Natasha. If we nab her father, you'll still have a chance to patch things up."

"After what she did to me? She can go to hell."

"You know what her father did to her. She's been carrying all that guilt. She hooked to punish herself, Juno. We work vice. How many hookers do we know that have the same story? Besides, the way Josephs told it, she didn't sound like a serious hooker. Maybe she was just experimenting. Maybe it was peer pressure. You don't know. She did quit. Doesn't that count for something?"

"She's been lying to me, Paul."

"And you've been honest with her? How do you think she'd feel if she found about you spying on her?"

"That isn't the same."

"It isn't?"

"Dammit, Paul, you're supposed to be on my side. Quit making me feel like a shit."

He grinned. "But it's so easy."

"Fuck you."

"Listen, Juno, I've never see you like this. You must love her, right?"

I begrudgingly nodded.

"Do you think she loves you?"

I nodded again.

"Then at least give it a couple days. You need to cool down first, so you can think straight. Will you at least do that?"

I gave him a reluctant yes.

"Good. Now let's go get drunk."

nineteen

PM became AM and Paul slowed the drinks down. My buzz started to fade. Paul and I had been living large since we'd left my place—a two-person bar-hopping blowout. I'd been knocking back drinks with forget-Natasha abandon the whole night.

The crowd was thinning out. Where there'd only been standing room, there were now open tables. I hadn't had a drink in at least an hour, and I was beginning to see straight. I wasn't liking the idea of being sober one bit. The same strippers that I thought were hot an hour ago were now playing ordinary in my eyes—bad dancing, bad thighs, and bad sags were suddenly coming through strong. I wasn't ready to shift from drunk-and-happy to depressed hangover. "You know where we should go, Paul?"

"C'mon, Juno, it's late. The sun will be up in a few hours."

"You haven't even heard my suggestion yet."

"All right, what is it?"

My phone rang. "Yeah."

I couldn't hear a damn thing over the late-night hubbub, but Natasha's smiling hologram was blocking the stage. I read her holo-lips. "Juno," she said.

Her sweet face soured in my mind, yet I couldn't keep myself from cranking up the call's volume. "Yeah?"

"I need you to come over. Something happened." Her voice rang an alarming note over the go-go music.

"Be right there." I clicked off. "We have to go to Natasha's."

Paul asked, "What do you think she wants?"

"I don't know, but there's something wrong."

We went to the back door and knocked. Natasha opened up and let us into the kitchen. It was my first time inside the house that I had spent so much time spying on. I turned on the lights—knew right where they were. "Oh god, Natasha. Are you okay?"

Her shirt was covered in blood. There were spatters on her face, in her hair.

"Somebody broke in . . . my parents . . ."

"Are you hurt?"

"No, I'm okay."

Paul and I sprinted through the house. We bounded upstairs like we lived there. We found her parents in the bedroom. There was blood on the walls, the carpet, the lamp. Pavel Yashin was lying in bed, stab wounds all over his body. His blood had run through the mattress and puddled to the floor underneath. Blood spatters doused geckos drinking their fill. Flies were already bouncing around the room. We waved our hands in a futile attempt to keep them away. Pavel's wife, Gloria, was huddled in a defenseless ball under her Virgin Mary shrine; white candles were spotted red. A lase-blade handle protruded from her back and smoke rose from her charring flesh as the blade burned an ever-widening hole. Half the hilt was already sunken into her back. I flicked it off before it burned through to the floor and set the house ablaze.

Paul said, "Go take care of Natasha. I'll scope the place out."

I returned to the kitchen. Natasha was sitting at the table, blood-smeared Formica under her hands.

"Tell me what happened."

Her face was unreadable. "I'm sorry I called you. I know you don't want to hear from me, but I didn't know who else . . ."

"It's okay, Natasha. I'm here now. Tell me."

"I went out with my friends . . . and no, I wasn't hooking. When I came back, I saw that my parents' door was open. I peeked in to see if they were home, and I found . . ." She couldn't finish. Tears began to stream.

"Then what?"

"I checked to see if they were still alive, but they weren't breathing. That's when I called you."

"Do you know who did this?"

"No. Somebody must have broken in and sneaked back out. There was nobody here when I came home."

Paul came around the corner. He checked the kitchen window then asked for a key to the basement. Natasha told him to look in the silverware drawer. He ran down to the basement for a minute, came back up, and waved for me to follow him to the living room.

"Excuse me, Natasha; I have to talk to Paul for a minute."

Paul and I went into the living room. Paul spoke in whispers. "They're both dead."

"Do you think Bandur could have done this?"

"Is that what she said?"

"No. She said that somebody must have broken in."

"I checked all the windows and doors, Juno. There are no signs of forced entry. The basement is fucking packed with O. He's also got a couple cases of money down there. Nobody touched any of it."

I couldn't purge brandy-buzzed go-go tunes out of my mind. "What are you saying?"

Paul scratched his head. "You know what I'm saying."

I dropped onto the couch. What had I done? She needed my help; she begged me for it. She asked me to deliver her from her home, and I shut the door in her face. "It's my fault. I knew how desperate she was to get rid of her father. I made her do this. I left her no other choice."

"It's not your fault."

"Yes, it is."

He put his hand on my shoulder. "What do you want to do? Nobody knows about the cameras but us. We can play it however you want."

"You want to take the opium and the money, don't you?"

"It's your call on this one, Juno. I'll do whatever you say."

I dropped my face into my hands and tried to concentrate. The upstairs massacre scene dominated my internal vision. A film of Natasha murdering her parents set to go-go music looped continuously before my eyes. I pushed the heels of my hands into my eye sockets, creating kaleidoscopic color patterns that drowned out the butchery.

Two paths emerged in my head. One path promised a life free of Paul and his cooked-up schemes. I could live free of Natasha and her wounded psyche. All I had to do was walk out that door. I could leave it all behind—*adios*.

The second path was risky. I'd have to break all the rules. I'd have to sacrifice my conscience. . . .

I didn't have to think long. "What time is it?"

Paul checked his bargain-basement watch. "We have two hours until sunrise."

"Let's do it."

I put Natasha in the shower and bagged her clothes. I made her scour her body. I even got in with her to scrape under her nails. "Here's what we're going to do, Natasha. When the sun comes up, you are going to call the police. You'll tell them that when you woke up, you saw your parents' door was open, and you peeked in—just like you told me except you'll say you found them when you woke up in the morning. Do you understand?"

"Yes."

"You didn't hear anything last night. You're a sound sleeper, and you like to fall asleep watching vids. You were watching vids last night. Think up a couple titles that you could've downloaded last night, in case they ask."

"Why do you want me to lie? Don't you believe me?" Natasha's coffee skin was flushed from the steamy water. Her smoldering eyes burned less fiercely; vulnerability was seeping through.

"I believe you, Natasha. But the people that did this might try to blame you. They might say that you're the one that did it. I'm going to protect you. I'm going to take you away from this. Okay?"

"Okay."

"You have to be strong for this, Natasha. Paul and I will come right after the police get here. We'll say we were investigating your father, which is true. But we won't be the ones interviewing you. They'll have homicide cops talk to you. Paul and I know most of those guys, so we'll soften them up a little. We'll let them know you and I are dating. They'll take it easy on you. Do you understand?"

"Yes."

"Did you finish your hair?"

"Yes."

"Scrub it again." I continued giving instructions. "You don't have any idea who would do this to your parents. You don't know anything about your father's business."

"Okay."

"Stay in here and keep washing. I'll come get you when it's time to stop."

"Okay." Her eyes were dull.

I went downstairs and went to work on the kitchen, cleaning the table and chairs. I remembered to wipe down the undersides, where you put your fingers when you slide your chair in. I worked my way down the hall and then moved upstairs, erasing her bloody tracks.

Paul came up the steps dripping wet. "I got the last of the cameras. They're a bitch to take down. I'm gonna start in the basement."

"Yeah, I'll come down as soon as I'm done here."

I moved into the Yashins' bedroom. Natasha had left bloody footprints on the carpet. I didn't have time to clean them out. I found a pair of Yashin's shoes in the closet. I shooed geckos away and dipped the soles into his blood. I tied them on my feet and walked in Natasha's footsteps, superimposing my tracks.

I finished my clean-up job. I got Natasha out of the shower and had her get in bed. "Try to take a nap if you can. That way the bed will look natural." I bleached the shower walls and poured the rest of the bottle down the drain. I bagged the towels, Yashin's shoes, and the cleaning supplies.

By the time I made it to the basement, Paul had already worked up a lathery sweat running opium out to Yashin's car. It took four carloads to get it all over to our stakeout pad. Paul gave the car a thorough wipe-down. I went to check on Natasha. She was sound asleep—at peace.

I took the murder weapon, put it in a separate bag, and threw it in with everything else. I scraped under the corpses' fingernails just in case one of them had gotten a scratch in on Natasha. I went out the back door, locked myself out, and broke back in, putting my elbow through a windowpane and popping the lock.

Once inside, I made one last run through the place, wiping fingerprints everywhere I went. The sky was starting to lighten. I dashed back into Natasha's room and stopped by her bed. "Natasha."

"Mmm."

"The sun will be up in about fifteen minutes. Do you remember everything I told you?"

"Yes."

"I'm going to leave now. Everything's set. Just remember what I told you." I kissed her forehead and then left to go meet Paul at the stakeout pad.

We had opium stacked to the ceiling. Paul was counting the money into neat piles on the table.

Paul looked up. "Hey. How're you holding up?"

"This is quite a stash."

"You can say that again. What do you want to do with the vids?" He motioned toward the monitor.

"Did you watch it?"

"No. Should I destroy it?"

"No . . . I have to watch it."

"You don't have to do that to yourself."

I voice-activated the monitor.

Paul sighed and said, "I'll leave you alone. I'm going to listen to the police bands. I'll let you know when Natasha calls it in."

I sat in front of the screen, skipping backward through time until I found the right spot. The camera brought the dark room into perfect focus. The Yashins were sleeping on far sides of the bed, careful not to touch each other. The door opened. Natasha stood in the doorway with a blade in hand. She crept over to the bed, slow high steps, like she was walking on eggs. She hovered over her father, lase-blade raised in a two-handed grip. She held that position for a full minute before she flicked it on.

She wanted him to know who it was—let him die with the knowledge that his own daughter did this.

She waited for him to open his eyes. "Natasha?" he said. Then he jerked back—too late. She plunged the blade down; Gloria Yashin leapt out of bed; Natasha struck her father again; blood fountained from an artery. Gloria made a frantic dash to her Virgin Mary altar. Pavel Yashin held his hands up in defense. Natasha stabbed through them. He stopped struggling, then he stopped breathing. Natasha continued to stick him, motoring back and forth from chest to groin. She moved off him, staring at his corpse, his flesh bleeding and burning, her smoking eyes in full brilliance.

She wheeled on her mother, who was rubbing her rosaries, whispering to herself with closed eyes. Natasha stalked across the room, crying, "You make me sick! You knew!" Gloria rosary-rubbed right up until the moment Natasha plunged the blade into her back—up to the hilt. Two more violent stabs and the rosaries fell from her mother's fingers.

Natasha left the blade in its flesh-scorching place. She paced the floor, surveying her handiwork. Pavel was dead still. Gloria kept breathing for a few moments then slouched into her final resting position.

Natasha strode out of the room. I flipped channels until I found her in the kitchen. I watched her call me and talk to my holo. She reached out for my cheek, touching nothing but air. After she hung up, she grabbed a soda from the fridge. She stayed at the table and nursed the soda, wearing a disturbingly flat affect.

I moved the vid forward. She heard the knock—put the partly finished soda back in the fridge and let Paul and me in. When the kitchen lights came on, the camera momentarily went into light overload then compensated swiftly for the brightness, bringing back a clear image.

It hit me like a fucking bolt of lightning. OH SHIT!

Paul and I raced up to Natasha's house. The call went out twenty minutes ago. There were already cops fucking all over. Paul and I badge-flashed our way in.

Natasha was sitting on the couch with homicide dick Yuan Chen. She ran into my arms, laying on the waterworks. "Juno!"

Paul made quick business telling them how she and I had been dating and how he and I were investigating her father's drug business.

Yuan Chen caught us up to speed on his investigation so far. "Intruder or intruders, we don't know which, busted the kitchen window and unlocked the door, then proceeded upstairs and committed the crime, then exited through the kitchen."

My heart beat at unprecedented speed. "You didn't hear anything, Natasha?"

"No, nothing. I was sleeping."

Chen said, "It's a good thing she didn't wake up. Who knows what would have happened if she walked in on them."

Natasha sobbed. "But I could have saved them."

Chen calmed her. "You can't let yourself think that. If you had tried anything, they would have killed you, too." Chen looked at me. "I know you two probably want some alone time, but is it okay if I ask her a few more questions?"

"Natasha," I said, "can you do that?"

She nodded a watery-eyed yes.

Paul leaned in. "I'm sorry to interrupt, Chen, but did you check the basement yet?"

Chen blinked through his glasses. "No. The door was locked."

"They say Yashin keeps a stash in the cellar."

Natasha chimed in. "My father is *not* a drug dealer." Playing the clueless daughter bona fide.

Even though he already knew the way, Paul thought to ask Natasha, "Where is the door to the basement?"

She gave directions to the door and the key. Chen and Paul headed through the kitchen to the basement door.

Natasha and I were alone—coast clear. "Let me get you something to drink, Natasha."

I went into the kitchen, my nerves on edge. My eyes sought out the refrigerator. Damn—two uniforms were in the kitchen. Neither of them paid much attention to me, so I opened the fridge with my shirtsleeve over my hand. I ran it up and down the handle then I pulled open the door, trying to look natural. I saw Natasha's half-empty soda bottle on the top shelf—bloody fingerprints all over the glass.

I reached for it. SHIT! I heard one of the unis slide his chair. *Is he watching me?* I panicked and took out a different bottle. I rummaged through the drawers, found a bottle opener, and flipped off the cap.

Paul and Chen entered the kitchen through the basement door, Chen saying, "We have our motive. The basement's been picked clean. Looks like a robbery/homicide."

Paul gave me a questioning look. I frowned a negative; the bottle was still in there. They moved back into the living room. I followed with a sparkling clean soda bottle in hand.

Chen went back to questioning Natasha. She did great—had him feeling sorry for her. My heart reached for her. I knew she was putting on that act for me as much as for Chen. She started off wanting me to save her from her father, and now that she had saved herself, she wanted me to save her from the police and the make-pretend monsters that did this to her parents. She needed me to be her rescuer one way or the other.

Chen said to Natasha, "The coroners are here. It would be best if you waited outside while they work. I'll come out and check on you." He brought her out through the rain to sit in one of the cars.

I stayed on the sofa. One of my knees bounced up and down with telltale jitters. I crossed my legs to keep it still. Cops were

all over the damn place. I tallied up our violations: illegal surveillance, evidence tampering, accessory to murder, and add a
robbery to top it off. That soda bottle would land all three of us
in the Zoo.

Hommy dick Yuan Chen was directing traffic from the living room. "Dust every fucking inch of that basement . . .
search the alley for our murder weapon . . . nobody talks to
a reporter—anybody talks, they answer to me."

I made three trips to the kitchen—always somebody there.
I needed that bottle. I sat still, mortified through and through.
The lab techs were already moving away from the bedroom,
working their way downstairs. They'd be all over the kitchen
soon.

Paul caught my attention with a subtle wave. He winked
and went upstairs.

Paul had a plan! I leaned forward in my seat, primed to leap
into action. I eyeballed the kitchen door, anticipating Paul's up-
coming distraction.

He jogged back down and shouted, "You guys gotta see this!
Yashin's got vids up there of himself doing two girls at a time."
Cops started up the stairs, men and women alike. Paul yelled
into the kitchen. "You guys gotta come check this out, come
upstairs."

The unis filed out of the kitchen and followed the crowd up
to the bedroom. *Paul, you're a fucking genius!*

I went for the kitchen—just nab the soda bottle and take it to
the sink for a quick rinse. I speed-walked through the door and
stopped in my tracks. The refrigerator door was open and
Deputy Coroner Abdul Salaam was putting *the* soda bottle into a
bag. "I found something," he said, blinking through his glasses.

twenty

I LEANED over the rust-eaten rail of Koba's tallest bridge. My eyes strained to see through the dead of night to the black water below. I pulled one very expensive soda bottle from its evidence bag and held it tight as I looked down into the blackness, my gut heavy with the realization that I was a criminal.

I wondered how far I was willing to go for Paul and his plans. He wanted to change Lagarto, and he was willing to do anything to achieve it, including getting in bed with Ram Bandur. Paul had made his intentions clear to me after we'd bought off the deputy coroner. He was going to take over KOP, and he wanted my help. He was going to need somebody to help with the dirty work.

Were we really that bad off that saving this planet required such desperate measures? I scanned the riverbanks, taking in the city lights. I could see the capitol building with its well-lit marble façade and golden dome. It was there, inside that building that they sold us out, making the decision to sell off the Orbital and the mining rights, dooming this planet to economic isolation. *Fuck the rich politicians and their picture-perfect lives.*

I could smell the mold that was growing thick on the bridge rails. Try as you might, you couldn't ever get away from that smell. *Fuck this lizard-infested jungle planet.*

I looked over at Tenttown. Its tents looked like lanterns

when they were lit up at night. I couldn't believe I used to live in one of those things. My skin reflexively itched as I remembered how the mosquitoes would swarm through holes you could never seem to find. *Fuck that fucking place.*

I watched the tangle of Floodbank lights shimmering on the river, each one bobbing independently of the others. There was a carnival going in the Old Town Square. A Ferris wheel was spinning slowly in front of the cathedral's steeples. The city would've looked beautiful if I didn't know better. *Fuck the drunks that piss and vomit all over the street. Screw the O-heads hiding in their cardboard boxes. To hell with the unemployed, the lazy fucks. Fuck the wife beaters and the wives who keep going back for more. Fuck the pimps and whores, and the kiddie rapers. Fuck those tech-hoarding offworlders. Double-fuck Nguyen and her bug-zapper skin. Fuck everyone!*

If any of them got in our way, they'd deserve what they got.

I held the soda bottle up to the beam of a street lamp, the glass reflecting back sharp points of light. I heaved the fucking thing into the darkness.

When I made it back to the stakeout pad, Paul had holo-mugs of Yashin's dealers lined up against the wall. We went through them together, methodically evaluating their records. We discarded the holo-heads one by one, tossing them into a pile like stones until there was only one left: drug dealer and stick-up artist Elvin Abramson. His history of armed robbery would go well with the fact that as one of Yashin's dealers, Abramson would know about the basement stash. The perfect fall guy for our first frame job.

We concocted a plausible line for lead-dick Yuan Chen. We told him about an imaginary snitch who worked for Yashin. We said that we leaned on him hard, made him spill everything he knew. According to our fake snitch, Elvin Abramson dropped by and started acting like he was the new O supplier. When our pseudo-snitch asked him where he came up with an O supply, Elvin responded with a sham story about some cousin who put him in touch with a high-grade but low-cost supplier. Elvin even tossed our snitch a quarter-kilo free sample.

The implication was clear. Elvin Abramson killed the Yashins, took the dope, and was now trying to take over the business. Yuan Chen fell for our ruse and elevated Elvin Abramson to suspect number one.

Chen set up a raid on Elvin's place. He wanted to run it by the book, but I talked him out of it when I laid on the let-me-take-this-one routine. "He may be the guy who killed my girlfriend's parents," I said. Chen was thinking, sure, why not? Let hothead Mozambe go in and knock him around a little, see if he can get anything out of him.

Paul and I smashed through the front. We charged the bed, our weapons drawn. Elvin Abramson and his lover rolled out from under the sheets and fell to the floor. It was early morning—always the best time to make arrests. The two of them froze, lase-pistols in their faces. We cuffed Elvin naked.

The lover was on his knees, begging. "Please, I didn't do anything. I don't even know him. We just met last night. I have a wife and kids at home. . . ."

I said, "Get dressed and get out."

Paul shoved the warrant in Elvin's face. "Can you read this? It says you're fucked."

The apartment was a one-room. I scanned for possible stash locations. Kitchenette cabinets held dishes only. Dust bunnies under the bed. I went into the closet. Glitzy shirts hung on hangers, and hats hung on the back of the door—all fedoras and panamas. I shoved the clothes aside, pulled out a trunk. "Where's the key?"

Elvin said, "In my pants."

I snatched up a pair of white pants draped over a chair and retrieved the key. I opened the trunk—brown sugar, spoons, scale, plastic bags, and rubber bands. I cinched up my trouser leg, plastic bag tied to my calf.

Elvin saw me. "HEY! What the fuck are you doing?"

Paul stomped on his foot and shushed.

I untied the bag from my calf and emptied it into the trunk, adding one bloodied lase-blade to the contents.

I closed the trunk, closing the case along with it. Natasha was safe. It wasn't her fault that she did what she did. The fault was all mine. To set things right for her, I had to frame a man innocent of the crime. The price was cheap. What was the conscience of a flatfoot like me worth?

"It's over," I said. "Detective Chen probably called to tell you we got the guy."

Natasha's eyes were staring off into nothingness. I leaned back in my seat, the back of the iron bench chilling my skin. I looked at the lilies. There were all kinds, orange, pink, purple. It had taken me a while to find her. She'd told me to meet her here at the Koba Gardens. I'd wandered around for a good ten minutes before I thought to ask somebody where the lilies were.

Natasha's voice was barely a whisper. "How did he end up with the blade?"

I knew what she meant. It was in her mother's back that last time she saw it. "Paul and I had to plant it on him," I admitted. "But we *know* he did it. This wasn't the first time he's killed somebody." That was a total lie. I didn't want Natasha to feel guilty about somebody else getting punished for her crime. She'd have enough guilt to deal with. This way she could tell herself that Abramson deserved his fate.

"He's killed other people?"

"Yes. Two that we know of, but his lawyer got him off both times."

She stayed silent for a few minutes. I sat quietly, wondering what she was thinking.

"So what do we do now?" she asked.

"We don't have to do anything. It's over."

"No. So what do *we* do now?"

"You mean us?"

She nodded.

I knew what a regular guy would think. He'd think she's a fucking psycho. Did you see what she did to her parents? But I wasn't a regular guy. I rubbed at the scars on my wrists. I understood what she did. I *understood*.

I said, "I'm sorry I closed the door on you."

She shrugged. "I should've told you."

"It's none of my business what you did before we met."

She looked into my eyes. "You mean that?"

"I do," I said.

"So you think it's possible to have a fresh start in life?"

I could see the hope in her eyes. I said, "I do."

"Do you think we could have a fresh start? You and me?"

I wanted to ask her for forgiveness. I wanted her to forgive me for spying on her. I wanted her to forgive me for failing her when she needed me most. But I couldn't ask. Not without her learning that I knew the truth about her father, about how her parents died. Maybe a fresh start was the best I could do. It wouldn't be easy to put all this behind. But I didn't want easy. I wanted *her*. I wasn't ready to say good-bye.

I said, "I do."

She squeezed me in her arms. I squeezed her back. I kissed the top of her head. "I love you, Natasha."

I felt her tense in my arms.

"What's wrong?" I asked.

"It's nothing."

"No, tell me. What's wrong?"

She kept her face buried in my chest. "You said my name. I don't like my name. I never liked it."

"What's wrong with Natasha?"

"I don't know. I just don't like it. I don't like it when you call me that."

"Why?"

She didn't answer.

Her father used to call her Natasha. I pictured him on top of her, saying her name, whispering it in her ear . . .

I shivered. I could feel my face flushing with anger. Now I hated the name, too.

I thought about how she'd been Natasha for her whole life. A life she hated. A life she desperately wanted to leave behind. I thought about her father's final word, a second before the lase-blade stabbed down into his chest. I wondered if the memory of that moment would come back to her every time somebody said her name.

"Change it," I said.

"Change what?"

"Change your name."

I could feel her head shaking left and right against my chest. "I can't do that. People would think I'm strange."

I didn't think there was anything strange about it. "Who cares what they think? You can pick whatever name you want. That's what fresh starts are all about."

She squeezed me tighter. "Maybe you're right."

Minutes passed, and we stayed in that position, holding each other.

She asked, "Remember how I had a brother who died before I was born?"

"Of course I do."

"Remember how my parents gave me his name as my middle name?"

"You want to be called Nikita? That was you're brother's name, right?"

"How about just Niki?"

twenty-one

MIDNIGHT had passed. The men had gambled their last pesos and drunk their last cups of shine. The women's cliques were long since gabbed out and had moved inside. Lights were flicking out from behind taped-over windows.

Maggie and I sat on Pedro's stoop. She knew the whole story. How Paul approached Ram Bandur using Yashin's opium as a good-faith offering. How Bandur took Paul's deal and how they helped each other take over the city. She knew how Paul used Yashin's money as a bribe fund and that the first person he put on the payroll was Deputy Coroner Abdul Salaam, who became his *numero uno* evidence tamperer and star witness.

She had listened to how Paul and I tore through the city. How criminals had two choices: work for Bandur, or go to jail. Paul ran the evidence room and the Office of the Coroner. He could trump up anything he wanted. He arrested his way to the top.

I'd told her how Paul seized control of KOP with his *plata o plomo* policy. The choice was yours: silver or lead. Paul dished Bandur money to anybody who would take it, and for those who didn't, I dished out the lead. I was the enforcer in a skull-cracking, reputation-smearing rampage through KOP. I learned how to turn my temper on in an instant. I wreaked vengeance on all who opposed Paul. Everybody feared me.

She'd learned how Paul picked tourist neighborhoods that Bandur had to keep crime free. In exchange, Bandur was permitted to war with his enemies, immune to prosecution. Paul molded the city to his vision of what was best for Lagarto. So what if he got rich along the way? You couldn't expect him to do a job without getting paid. What did it matter that crime never dropped? Who cared that Paul's attempt to bring more tourists to Lagarto only resulted in a boom of offworld-operated resorts that kept all the big money in off-world hands? At least he did *something*.

I'd unloaded twenty-five years of sin on Maggie, only holding one thing back: that Niki murdered her parents. Niki still hadn't even admitted it to me. Some secrets are best left buried. I let Maggie think our patsy really did it. The poor bastard didn't even survive the first week of his incarceration before he was tortured to death by some inmates who were trying to make him spill where he'd hidden Yashin's stash.

We sat quiet for a while. Maggie looked at me, her features hard to read in the dark. She put her hand on my shoulder and leaned in close. My skin tingled; my heart raced. She kissed my cheek. I turned to her lips, but they were already gone. I wanted to put my arms around her, but I held back as my brain struggled to interpret her gesture. I wanted to believe she was attracted to me, but . . .

Could be she was just delirious—she hadn't slept for two days. Could be she just felt sorry for me. Could be she was thanking me for making her feel less guilty about Pedro's death by dwarfing her error with the quarter-century of broken dreams, broken lives, and broken skulls I'd left behind. Then again, it could be she wanted me to kiss her. I was on the verge . . .

She stood before I got the chance. "Let's get going. We have work to do," she said.

Maggie followed me into the Floodbank bar. The place was empty except for the bartender, who was sweeping up after closing. "We're closed," he said.

Maggie held up the bar bill with Pedro's address written on the back. "You passed this note to one of your customers. Who told you to do it?"

He stopped sweeping and leaned on the broomstick handle in a belligerent fashion. "I don't know what you're talking about. I didn't pass no note."

I ran at him. He reflexively swung the broom. The handle bounced off my arm. I drove my shoulder into his chest, and brought him down hard to the floor. I was on top of him. Years of pent-up enforcer rage drove my piston fists, my right doing as much damage as my left. My blood pumped through my veins, while his pumped from nose and mouth. He gave up the struggle and covered his face, submitting to the beating.

I started taking my time, a cat playing with its prey. I picked and chose shots through his guarding hands. I felt better than I had in years. The enforcer was back. So what if I couldn't shoot anymore?

Maggie strode forward. She stood over us, her legs spread wide, hands on hips, her face pure cool. She held out the bar bill. He moved his hands off his face and looked at it through teary eyes. She spoke slow and deliberate, enunciating every syllable. "Who told you to give this note to Ali Zorno?"

I was primed for the words *Mayor Samir.*

He sobbed through a wrecked mouth. He said, "Mdoba, Sanders Mdoba."

Maggie gave me a look that said, "I told you so."

Son of a bitch! Sanders Mdoba: I knew him. He ran the East Side O dealers for the Bandur cartel. They were supposed to be on our side.

twenty-two

My eyes stung when I forced them open. Fuck me—it was early. The sky hadn't even begun to brighten with the coming dawn. Ali Zorno had come to me in my dreams, wearing a lip mask and charging with a butcher knife while my father held me down. Two sweaty wake-ups later, I'd used a triple-shot of brandy to put myself under.

I sat up; Niki stirred. I imagined a lip mask strung over her face. A shake of my head couldn't dispel the image. I labored my aching body out of bed. The brandy fog made me wonder if two hours of uninterrupted sleep was worth going to bed at all. I bumped my way into the shower and let the warm water massage me awake.

In a perverse attempt to shake the image of Niki wearing a lip mask, I recalled Pedro's death, his hands to his throat in a futile attempt to keep his blood from spilling. If only I'd gotten there a minute earlier . . . What good would that have done? I would've burnt the whole place down before I hit Zorno. I looked at my hand shaking under the trickling water—fucking useless.

I rubbed soap into my scraped fists, relishing the sting. I found a deep cut on one of my knuckles. I hadn't realized I'd cut myself so badly. With so much of the bartender's blood on my hands last night, I hadn't noticed. The cut was only a couple centimeters long, but an open wound was an open wound. Taking a close look, I could see the tiny wriggling shapes of maggots. Shit, I'd have to get it cleaned out.

Last night's events ran through my mind. When had I turned into such a joke? Zorno killed our witness *while* we were following him. How could I have let that happen? It had been my idea to follow him. I should've arrested him the first time I'd seen him. I could've crossed the street with my gun under the bag of potatoes. I could've made up some shit to say to him like, "Helluva downpour." I could've walked right up to him, real close, then dropped the bag, my piece right in his face, close enough that I couldn't miss if he tried anything, shaking hand or not.

If I had just arrested the fishhook-faced asshole, I could've beat the truth out of him. I used to strong-arm all the time. I was a first-rate expert with over two decades of experience. I probably didn't even need to torture him. I bet I even could've gotten him talking with some sick game like showing him holos of his mommy with the lips cut out, or maybe pasting a holo of Zorno's own fubar lips on top of hers. Instead, I had pushed Maggie into following him.

Maggie was blaming herself for the kid's death, but the fault was pure Juno. She was going to carry that guilt for the rest of her life. It would eat her up. I knew what it was like, a hundred times over.

Dammit, all of that was in the past. Nothing to be done about it now. I hit the brakes on my thoughts and changed gears from reverse to drive. *Where do we go from here?* I was supposed to find a link to the mayor, and instead I'd found Sanders Mdoba. He was the one who passed Zorno the skinny on our witness, and he was a high-ranking member of the Bandur organization, the same outfit that Paul and I had been conspiring with for all these years. Hell, Paul made the Bandur organization what it was. Without Paul, they'd still be just a neighborhood outfit.

Reluctantly, I turned off the faucet and watched the ankle-deep water swirl down the rusted drain before I got out and dried off with a towel that smelled like mildew. I needed to tend to the cut on my knuckle. I rummaged under the sink, trying to find the fly gel.

"Juno, what are you doing?"

I looked up from my kneeling position to see Niki in the bathroom doorway. My first instinct told me to hide my hands, but I could see it was already too late. Niki was looking at my hands with a resigned look on her face. She gestured at the toilet, and I took a seat while she took my hands in hers. "You have to be more careful." She didn't say it as a nag. She said it like she meant it.

"I know," I said.

She opened a drawer and pulled out a tube of fly gel that hadn't been opened in a long time. She parted the skin around the cut. Blood oozed out as she squeezed a bead of the yellow gel into the cut. She walked out, coming back a minute later with a magnifying glass. She moved my hand under the faucet, rinsing the gel free along with the now dead maggots and eggs.

Niki asked, "Who did you . . . ?"

"A bartender." I remembered what he looked like, lying on his back, one of his popped-out teeth stuck to his forehead. *Did I really do that?* "He wouldn't talk. He passed on some information that got our witness killed."

"Hold still." I held my hand steady. Luckily it was my left hand that had been cut. Niki was looking through the magnifying glass, using a pair of tweezers to pull the maggot corpses out. "Sounds like he deserved it," she said.

How many times had we had this same conversation, with me sitting here on this same toilet while Niki nursed my damaged fists? The conversation always ended with that same line about how whoever it was deserved it. For over two decades, I'd beaten down anybody that opposed Paul. I'd destroyed countless lives with these fists, and no matter how lame the reasoning, Niki always told me I was doing the right thing. We were increasing tourism. We were bringing offworld money into the economy. We were serving the greater good. And it was true . . . at first.

The great upsurge in tourist money eventually plateaued as offworld businessmen began to take over the industry, effectively erasing any progress Paul had made. Over the years, Paul became less worried about Lagarto and more worried about holding on to his power. I no longer knew what purpose I served, yet I kept up my enforcer's ways, demolishing Paul's opposition and collaborating with a murderous crime lord, the flames of hell licking at my feet. It was Niki who saved me, pulling me out of the fire, telling me I had to quit enforcing. Niki always took the right side, my side.

I rested my head on her hip as she stood over the sink, squeezing a fresh bead of gel into the cleaned wound. She placed a bandage on it and declared me good as new. I knew I could never leave her.

Maggie wasn't interested in me anyway. I was deluding myself if I thought any different. Maggie was young, smart, honest, good-looking. I wasn't any of those things. There was absolutely no way a woman like that would ever be interested in a guy like me. I remembered how she'd kissed my cheek. I wasn't sure what that was all about, but it wasn't romantic. That was just wishful thinking on my part. Some kind of midlife crisis–induced hallucination. Hell, even if she were interested in me, what were we going to do? Go out on a date? Go dancing? Go meet her high-society mother? Give me a fucking break.

I stood up and embraced my wife. I kissed the top of her head. I dropped my nose into her pillow-head hair and kept it there, breathing *her* in. I held her tight as I said, "Thank you."

⁜

Benazir Bandur's home sat on a rise, no neighbors within a hundred meters. The surrounding jungle was immaculately controlled. The house was ivy free, and the walk was mossless. Shrubs were formed into topiary animals, a bird on the left with a goat behind. Check out the two rabbits and a chicken just over the little brook. The former Kingpin of Koba, Ram Bandur, used to love his garden. He'd rave about it all the time. The way plants grew around here, he must've had to get the shrubs trimmed every day to keep their shape. Today they looked a bit shaggy, like they all needed haircuts.

Detecting my DNA, the door opened on its own. A bodiless voice welcomed Maggie and me, then instructed us to go out to the pool. We walked through the foyer—polished stone floors with a car-sized chandelier glimmering above. We cut through the kitchen, which was bigger than my entire flat, and my flat wasn't small. We stepped down a set of Spanish tile stairs to the poolside door, which slid open to let us pass.

The pool area was done up in desert landscaping. Offworld desiccators buried two meters underground would suck the moisture from the soil, leaving a caked and cracked surface, perfect for cactus imported from the nonpolar regions of Lagarto.

Was that Ben Bandur floating in the pool? I couldn't tell with his face all bandaged up.

"Juno! What brings you here?"

I turned to see longtime Bandur right-hand man Matsuo Sasaki poolside. Who was that sitting next to him? Tip Tipaldi—Bandur strong-arm. He'd once beaten a chef to death with a slab of frozen meat, for overcooking his fish. The crime scene was still fresh in my head—blood trail from the kitchen to the freezer. Freezer contents included the following meats: two sides of beef, twenty three 'guanas, and one blue-skinned chefsicle with grill marks on his face, hands, and ass. Paul had the incident buried.

I said, "Hey, Matsuo. Is that Ben out there in the pool?"

"The one and only. Please, come join me."

"Thanks. Matsuo Sasaki, this is Detective Maggie Orzo."

"Pleased to meet you, Detective. I see Paul is making them better looking these days. I've always thought the Office of Police lacked a certain . . . elegance."

"Thank you," she said uncertainly.

We took seats at the table. Aircon blew from vents in the decking. The air rushed by us in a cool gush then dispersed into the jungle heat in a colossal waste of energy.

Sasaki waved at Tipaldi. "Tip, would you please leave us alone for a bit?" Chef-killer Tipaldi ambled off. "Would you like something to drink?" he asked Maggie.

"A glass of ice water would be nice."

"Ice water? Wouldn't you prefer something with a little kick?"

"I'm on duty."

"You're not going to let some silly rules stand in your way, are you?"

Maggie was emphatic. "Yes I am."

"How about you, Juno? You wouldn't mind sharing some brandy with me; would you?"

The early morning hour didn't bother me. "You know I can't turn down the good stuff."

"Very well." Sasaki made no move to get up for the drinks— no need to; our orders had been picked up by some unseen microphone and forwarded to the help.

I relaxed back into my chair. It responded with a light massage for my back. Damn, that felt good. I looked out over the pool, a blue-gem oasis surrounded by stark desert. Ben Bandur floated on a half-submerged lounge chair, only his toes and his bandaged head above the surface. "What happened to Ben?"

"You're referring to the bandages?"

"Yeah."

"He went up to the Orbital to have some work done. That's why he didn't make it to the mayor's banquet the other night. He's obsessed with his looks. I don't know where he gets it, certainly not from his father. They built up his cheekbones and enlarged that less than masculine nose of his. He won't stop talking about it. He pulled off the bandages to show it to me. You would've loved it. His nose was swollen up like a tomato, except it was purple. Funniest thing I ever saw. I can't remember the last time I laughed so hard." Sasaki let out a rare smile. His teeth reflected sunlight.

"What did Ben think of you laughing?"

"He threw a fit, just like when he was a kid. He's still spoiled rotten to the core."

I'd never heard Sasaki be so disrespectful. When he worked for Ram, he was the consummate loyalist. "How's he doing with the business?"

"I suppose he's learning, but he's still more focused on which whore to invite to his room every night. I wish his father were still alive, so he could knock some sense into him."

"Did you tell Ben that?"

"Sure, I told him. He makes me so angry sometimes I can't help myself. One of these days, he's either going to shape up, or he's going to burn a hole in my head. Half the time, I don't care which."

The houseboy approached, carrying a tray with our drinks. I could almost taste the brandy already. I sipped and took the time to enjoy the flavor before swallowing. "How's the Simba situation?" Koba had been exclusive Bandur territory for over twenty years. I thought Koba would be Bandur domain forever. But now I wasn't so sure anymore. Not since the Loja crime lord offered that gutsy mayoral toast.

Sasaki looked me in the eyes and nodded in Maggie's direction as if to say, "Is it okay to talk in front of her?"

"Yeah. I'll vouch for her."

"Your word was good enough for Ram, so it's good enough for me. I'm going to level with you, Juno. Simba's becoming difficult. There's no chance that he'd try to pull this on Ram. Ram would have killed him by now. Ever since Ram died, Simba's been pecking away at us. He's like a damn child always testing the limits. I keep telling Ben that we have to slam the door on Simba, but he just doesn't have the balls to do it. Please excuse my language, Officer Orzo. Once I start hitting the hard stuff, I find my tongue has a mind of its own."

Maggie said, "That's okay. My father had a foul mouth as well. I didn't think any less of him for it."

"A very reasonable attitude."

I asked, "How bad is it?"

Sasaki swirled brandy in his four-fingered hand. "Oh, it's sufficiently contained for now, but the potential for disaster is right around the corner. We've got people in Floodbank paying double protection. They're paying us and paying Simba's people. How long do you think it will be before they quit paying us altogether? We're supposed to be protecting them from other crime bosses. What else is protection money for? I explain this to Ben, and he just doesn't get how serious the situation is. I told him about the stunt Simba pulled at the mayor's banquet, but he was too excited about his new nose to care. You tell me, how do you get somebody motivated when he has everything he ever wanted handed to him before he even knows he wanted it?"

I shook my head and grimaced with a what-is-this-world-coming-to look.

Sasaki was struck by a thought. "Maybe you could talk to him, Juno."

"What the hell good would that do?"

"He has no sense of what his father had to do to build this

business. You were there at the beginning, you and Paul. You could tell him some stories about his father. Tell him what a ruthless man his father was. How he had to fight for everything he got. The kid's almost twenty-five, and he still hasn't learned how to be tough. It would do him some good."

I shook my head.

Sasaki persisted in trying to convince me. "Come on, Juno. It would be fun. You and Paul could come over. I'll have a big dinner fixed up. We'll split a couple bottles of brandy and swap some stories about the old days. What do you say?"

"I'll tell you what, if you can talk Paul into it, I'm in. I hardly know Ben. I wouldn't feel right talking to him about his father without Paul."

"No problem. I understand what you're saying. I'll talk to Paul and let you know. All right? I really think it would help. He doesn't listen to me anymore. So what brings you over?"

"We wanted to talk to you about one of your people."

"Who?"

"Sanders Mdoba."

"Why are you looking at him?"

Here we go. My heart started pumping nervous beats. *Gotta play this one just right.* "His name came up in a murder investigation."

"Murder? I thought you were working vice."

"I was. Paul asked me to work this case."

"Why did he do that?"

"The victim's father works for the city, and Paul's trying to score points with the mayor by putting Maggie and me on the case. He gave the mayor a line about me being the best detective he's ever seen, and he ought to know since he used to be my partner. Then he told him that Maggie was the best recruit he's seen since he's been chief. He's hoping that by playing nice he can get the mayor to cool his corruption investigation."

Sasaki said, "I see. How did Mdoba's name come up? Is he a suspect?"

"No." I hoped I sounded truthful. "We know he didn't do it. We already got our killer—a real schizo. Maggie fried the son of a bitch dead last night. As far as we're concerned, the case is closed, but the mayor's investigator—Karl Gilkyson—you know him?"

"No, but I know of him."

"Well, then maybe you heard how big a shithead he is. It turns out that our killer made contact with Mdoba yesterday. I told him that the killer was probably just scoring some brown sugar off Mdoba. Who cares? But Gilkyson can't let it go. Best I can tell, Gilkyson got wind that Mdoba's one of your dealers, and now he wants us to 'chase the lead.' Can you believe that? This suit from the mayor's office saying shit like 'chase the lead.' What an asshole. I told him there was nothing to find, but he won't take no for an answer. He wants to get dirt on Mdoba so he can run it up the ladder to you and Ben."

"What exactly do you want from us?"

"Your permission to talk to Mdoba." I was holding my breath.

Sasaki savored a slow sip of his brandy. "You're right to come talk to us first." He paused to consider. I needed to breathe. I eased the air out of my lungs, and took long slow breaths so he wouldn't notice.

A splash of water called my attention to the pool. Done with his morning swim, Ben Bandur stood on the pool's edge, dripping water into puddles at his feet. The houseboy rushed over with a towel and dried him off while Bandur stayed in place, raising his arms and legs at the right times.

He strutted over to greet us. It was hard to believe this loser was Ram's son. Ram was the most successful crime lord in the history of the planet, a powerhouse of a man. His control over Koba had been absolute. Nobody dared to challenge him. He would've ruled Koba forever if it weren't for the stealthy, un-derhandedness of a killer like cancer. Ram had the money to go up to the orbital station for treatment, but he absolutely re-fused to see an offworld doctor. Sasaki was right that he was the meanest SOB you ever saw, but he was a true Lagartan.

"Juno." Ben used my name as a greeting. The center of his face was wrapped with pool water–drenched bandages. His bathing suit emphasized an unnaturally large bulge—his nose wasn't the only thing he got extended.

"Hey, Ben. How's it going?"

Ben ran his eyes up and down Maggie, checking her out. The bandages failed to hide the lascivious look in his eyes.

I said, "This is my new partner, Detective Maggie Orzo."

Ben's eyes focused on her crossed legs. "Nice legs," he said in a nasal timbre.

Maggie was unsure how to respond, so she didn't.

He said, "When do they open?"

Again, she didn't answer, but I could see the flush in her cheeks. I wanted to throttle the little prick, rip those bandages off, and squeeze the hell out of his new nose—maybe fuck it up good. Even Sasaki shook his head in disapproval.

Sasaki spoke in an appeasing tone. "Juno and Officer Orzo want to talk to Sanders Mdoba."

"Why do you want to talk to that fatass?" Ben's nasal whine would have been funny if I hadn't been so busy wanting to rip his nose off.

"They are investigating a murder case and—"

"What murder case?"

"An Army lieutenant," I said. "Dmitri Vlotsky."

"Never heard of him. Why do you want to talk to Sanders?"

Sasaki interjected. "He was seen talking to the murderer yesterday. They want to know why."

"How the fuck should I know?"

Sasaki breathed deep. "They don't expect you to know. They just want permission to talk to him."

"Talk to him all you want. I don't give a shit." He turned his back on us and swaggered into the house.

Sasaki closed his eyes until his frustration passed. "You see what I have to put up with?"

I said, "He got some work done downstairs, didn't he?"

"Yes. He had 'erective surgery,' as I like to call it. Ben doesn't get the joke. Every time I say that around him, he tells me to stop talking like a chink."

I laughed loud and long, fueled by nervous energy.

Sasaki got back to business. "You can talk to Mr. Mdoba. But you can only talk to him about your murder case. His relationship to Ben is strictly off-limits. Do you understand?"

"I understand just fine, Matsuo. If it were up to me, we wouldn't talk to him at all. We'll go, and he'll make up some excuse why he met with our killer—end of story. Then, once Gilkyson sees there's nothing there, he'll drop it."

I swallowed the rest of the brandy and got up to leave. I felt a slight alcohol fog in my head. We walked back through the house, taking the same path to the front door, which opened by itself when we approached.

I hopped into the car, and I aimed it for the Phra Kaew docks.

Maggie spoke while looking dead ahead. "Are you sure that was the best thing for us to do?"

"No."

I wasn't sure of anything. I had thought it best that we come to Bandur and Sasaki for permission to speak with Mdoba. If we had talked to Mdoba on our own, he surely would've told Sasaki we'd contacted him. That would've sent up red flags all over the damn place. Credit for my twenty-five years of loyal service to them would've evaporated instantaneously, and Sasaki and Bandur might've decided to just kill Maggie and me rather than bother to find out what I'd been up to.

I'd made up the story about Gilkyson as a cover. The way I saw it, it should've worked either way. Either Bandur and Sasaki hired Zorno to whack Vlotsky or they didn't. If they did hire Zorno, they would be alarmed that we connected Zorno to Mdoba. I figured all that bullshit about Gilkyson, and how we considered the case closed, would set their fears to rest. They would be thinking, what harm would it do to let Juno talk to Mdoba? Act like there's nothing to hide. Even if Juno figured out we put out the contract on Vlotsky, Paul would shut him up before it went too far.

And if they hadn't hired Zorno, they wouldn't be worried at all about us talking to Mdoba. If anything, they would want to know if Mdoba was into something they weren't aware of. Maybe he was moonlighting on them.

Maggie said, "Do you think Sasaki bought our cover story?"

"I couldn't tell."

"Neither could I."

twenty-three

SANDERS Mdoba lived on a boat that was usually tied up to one of the docks in Phra Kaew. Maggie and I walked the labyrinth of walkways and rickety docks looking for the *Tropic of Capricorn*—an old tug turned houseboat.

We focused on the docks that held the larger vessels—worn-down trawlers leaking and listing, beat-up passenger boats with empty frames where seats used to be. It was still a big fishing time. Many of the moorings were vacated, making our job marginally easier.

The resort-owned *Lagartan Queen* was in dry dock. It was painted white with red trim, and it had a paddle wheel on front that gave it that old-timey feel. The ordinarily underwater nuke-powered props ruined the steamer illusion. The banner pinned to the rail read, "Sunset Cruises—One for $30, Two for $50." Convert that to pesos, and you could buy a car. Lagartan workers were at work, scraping barnacles off the hull under the supervision of an offworld foreman who probably paid them by the hour.

We finally found the *Tropic of Capricorn* loosely roped to a crumbling pier. The rusted hull had left orange stains on the stone landing. We had to step across the water to board—no gangway. Colored lights hung on strands that ran bow to stern. Taped-down power cords snaked across the deck. The cabin door was cracked open. I pushed through. Maggie followed me in.

We passed through the galley. Half-eaten cans of food were strewn about, lizard tails poking out of the tops. Maggie closed the door behind us. Startled geckos upended themselves and sprang from the cans in a panic.

I took a quick look into the common room. Nobody there. We clanked our way down metal steps to the cabin, which welcomed us with a dirty-laundry odor. The messed-up bed was empty. Nobody home. Odd that the door was unlocked.

I hit the dresser: nothing but elephant-sized clothes, hypodermics, and sex toys. Maggie pulled down a cardboard box from the closet and dumped the contents across the bed—vids and pics. We sorted through the pics: Mdoba fishing topless, his bulk hiding his belt all around; a younger and thinner Mdoba boogying on the dance floor; Mdoba posing with both Bandurs, father and son, all wearing hunting clothes and holding dead reptiles up by their tails.

Maggie stopped and held up a pic for me to see. I'll be damned—Vlotsky. Not Dmitri but his father, Peter. There was a whole stack of them. Vlotsky walking up to his house, Vlotsky in his car, Vlotsky eating dinner.

I grabbed up one of the vids and held it up for the entertainment system.

Holograms appeared on Mdoba's bed. Mdoba was lying on his back with a heavy-breasted woman riding on top, her legs spread uncomfortably wide to straddle his body. I held up the next vid. Same woman on all fours, Mdoba behind.

I flashed through three more vids of Mdoba's greatest hits before finding something interesting. A new room superimposed over the reality of the cabin. A different woman was on the bed, naked with a drink in her hand. She looked bored. From a bathroom came a man with wavy hair and dark skin. She traced a teasing finger up and around her breasts. His member traveled from six o'clock to high noon. He crawled on top, and once he did, she went back to looking bored—definite hooker.

They writhed around on the bed. I rotated our vantage, taking in the details of the room. I zoomed to the door, which had a deadbolt and peephole—hotel. I zeroed in on the bedstand. There was no money—she was giving him a freebie. By the time I moved back to the bed, the writhing was already over, done in sixty seconds—record time.

Snap conclusion: classic extortion scheme.

I could picture Sanders Mdoba rigging the room with cameras then squeezing himself into a closet, peeking through a cracked door. I could imagine his hooker in a smoky bar, making eyes at Mr. Sixty Seconds. Letting him buy the drinks; letting him think she's not a hooker; letting him touch her back, then her ass, cooing as he grabbed and tickled until he brought up the idea of getting a room. She knew just the place.

I'd run the same scam a hundred times.

Next vid: another man getting busy, this time with a teenage boy who cried when they were done.

Next vid: woman locking her toddler in the closet while she fired up some O. Her kid crying and knocking on the door the whole time.

Next vid: Peter Vlotsky at the Lotus with one of Rose's 'tutes.

New possibilities blossomed in my brain.

The boat moved, just barely, then it moved again. Somebody was coming onboard. Bare feet crossed in front of the porthole. I pocketed the handful of vids and helped Maggie shovel the rest of the vids and pics back into the box. The top deck door opened. Maggie tossed the box back onto the closet shelf. We moved to the steps, climbing quietly. Sounds issued from the galley.

We could see her now: the heavy-breasted woman catalogued in Mdoba's vids. Wearing a bikini with a puddle of river water gathering at her feet, she was digging through the fridge. We moved up on her without her seeing us.

Maggie said, "Boo," and just about startled the woman into jumping out of that bikini.

It took the woman a moment to figure out that there were two strangers staring at her. "What the fuck is wrong with you?" She was trapped-animal scared.

"Mdoba," I said as I held up my badge with my left.

"Sanders isn't here."

"No fucking kidding. Where is he?"

"I don't know."

"Who are you?"

She was starting to get her confidence back, a hint of defiance in her words. "I'm Malis."

"Are you his girlfriend?"

"I don't know. I guess so."

She was probably some rich-girl groupie who thought she was living large screwing a high-roller like Mdoba. "Where's Mdoba?" I repeated.

"I don't know. He doesn't tell me his business." She sized Maggie up then ran her hands into her hair for me, churning out the foxy wiles, trying to take control of the situation. I reevaluated my opinion of her. She wasn't the well-to-do daddy's girl. She was more likely street trash with the looks and moves to land a big fish like Mdoba from across a packed dance floor.

I said, "Tell him Juno wants to see him."

"Yes, officer," she pouted as she played with her bikini's shoulder strap.

We left. On the way out, Maggie gave Malis that supernasty kind of look that women save up for each other.

I stopped at the next boat down. A former barge, now an apartment building. There was a girl on a tire swing that was suspended from the rigging.

I asked her, "Do you know the man that lives on the *Tropic of Capricorn?*"

"Yes." She put a finger over her lips and blew her cheeks out in imitation of Mdoba.

I smiled and handed her a thousand pesos on the upswing. "You call me the next time he comes home, and I'll give you another thousand."

She jumped off the tire when it reached its highest point and landed running. She disappeared into the boat and returned seconds later with the family phone so our phones could exchange numbers.

Maggie and I hustled back to the car and started toward the Cap Square. I peeked at Maggie as I drove. She wore a stern look, no longer the wide-eyed rookie. I was starting to wonder if she would come through all this with her sanity intact. She pushed her hair back and closed her eyes, trying to reason her way through the latest piece of information. There was a connection between Sanders Mdoba and Peter Vlotsky, our murder victim's father. The further we went on this case, the more complicated it got. Lip-obsessed Ali Zorno killed Lieutenant Vlotsky; Zorno and Private Kapasi were cellmates; Mdoba tipped off Zorno about our witness; Mdoba worked for Bandur, who was tied to Paul and me. And now the latest mindbender, Mdoba had some kind of extortion scheme running that involved Vlotsky's father.

I wanted to call Paul, but I couldn't talk to him without Gilkyson listening in. I called Abdul instead, and we apologized to each other about last night. I told Abdul we needed details on Vlotsky senior's finances. New house, new car. We needed to trace that money. Abdul had the numbers streamed into Maggie's digital paper pad.

✳

Peter Vlotsky's office building looked like most government offices, a plain rectangular structure, constructed from drab concrete blocks that were cracking apart from the years of mosses and ivies digging into the porous surface. Inside, the halls were antiseptic clean and the elevators were slow and jerky. The Koba Office of Business Affairs was on the seventh floor.

We entered Vlotsky's office. A receptionist put on a polite face until we breezed past him and into Vlotsky's inner office without stopping. Peter Vlotsky sat at his desk. A dark-skinned man with wavy hair sat across from him. *Well I'll be, Mr. Sixty-Seconds Flat.*

Peter Vlotsky stood to greet us. "Hello, officers. It is so good to see you." The receptionist left the doorway with a wave of Vlotsky's hand. "Officer Mozambe and Officer Orzo, this is Judah Singh."

Sixty-Second Singh rose from his chair. "Pleased to meet you both. I'll leave you alone."

Vlotsky offered us seats across his desk. "I'm glad you're here. I was hoping I'd get a chance to thank you for catching my son's murderer. I can tell you that Jelka and I will be sleeping better knowing that he can't do this to anybody else's child."

Maggie took the lead on this one. She had a better bead on his finances. "We would like to know if you know this man." She showed him a picture of Mdoba that she had five-fingered from the *Tropic of Capricorn.*

He hesitated . . . too long. "No. I don't. Who is he?"

"Could you please explain the deposits made to your account on the third and seventh of last month?" She read the dates from her high-tech pad.

"What deposits?" His voice cracked.

Again she looked at the pad. "The deposit on the third was eight million, and the deposit on the seventh was another five. Both transfers were made from an account owned by the DHC Corporation. Can you tell us who they are?"

Peter Vlotsky was positively pale. I saw a picture hanging behind his desk showing the entire seven-person board seated at a table with name plaques and microphones. I stood to go study it. Vlotsky was in the middle, chairman of the board. Mr. Sixty-Seconds to his right. Opium-smoking child abuser on the far right. Homo with a thing for teenage boys to the left. Mdoba's extortion scheme was taking shape.

Vlotsky said, "I don't think I should talk to you without my lawyer present."

I rushed up into his face, making him just about tip over in his chair. "You will tell us what we want to know. You hear me, you piece of shit? No lawyers, no games, you understand me?" I popped him one in the face. My body sizzled electric.

"I can't help you," he whined. "They'll kill me."

I pulled a vid from my pocket. I backhanded him with it.

His nose started running blood.

I got nose-touching close. "We've got some great footage of you down at Rose's. We've got half your coworkers caught in compromising positions. You don't think we'll learn what we want to know from one of them?"

"No. I can't talk." Nose blood ran in his mouth, staining his teeth red.

"We'll find out anyway, shithead. When we do, we're going to arrest Mdoba, and I'll let it slip that you're the one who snitched."

"You can't do that! He'll have me killed." He was teetering on the edge.

"I'm sure he will. Tell me what I want to know, and I won't tell a soul." I whispered the last part.

He was visibly sweating; his lips quivered. Blood ran down his chin and soaked into his white collar.

Maggie pushed him over with "Your son is dead, and we know it's your fault. It's time to clear your conscience."

Vlotsky rained bloody snot and tears. His wails brought his receptionist back to the door. Again, Vlotsky waved him away.

We waited him out. Finally, he brought his cries under control. "They killed my son."

"Who did?"

He pointed to the picture of Mdoba held in Maggie's hand.

"Why?" she asked.

"We were going to vote on a business license for a shipping company called Lagarto Lines. He told me he wanted it to pass. He came to me one night and threatened to release the vid of me at the Lotus to the public if I didn't."

"What did you tell him?"

"I told him it wasn't my decision. The whole board had to vote. He told me that he'd worry about the rest of the votes."

"What did you do then?"

"I told him I'd do what I could. At the time, I didn't think the license had a chance of passing anyway."

"Why not?"

"Everybody knew the company was a front for the Simba organization."

Carlos Simba. The Loja crime boss was reaching in every direction. Trying to eat into Bandur's Koba monopoly and now trying to start a shipping company.

I asked, "What does Simba want with a shipping company?"

Vlotsky raised his hands and sniffled. "I don't know, but only two members of the board were advocating for the company. Everybody else was going to reject it."

"Why would they advocate for a business that they knew was a front for Simba?"

"They thought it would be good for Lagarto if we had our own shipping company. They insisted it would mean lower rates because Simba's line would be able to compete with the offworld lines."

"*Offworld* lines?" I had assumed he was talking about a regular shipping company—running boats on the river.

"Yes, offworld lines. Simba wants to start a shipping line that runs from the surface to the Orbital."

I was stunned silent.

Maggie said, "How could he do that? He'd have to buy a ship."

"He already has. He bought a freighter that's getting refitted at the spaceport as we speak."

I got my voice back. "Did the mayor chime in on this?"

"No. He stayed out of it. With all his anticorruption talk, you'd think that he would be all over me, making sure this license got rejected. Instead he was strictly hands off. If it ever comes back to bite him, I'm sure he'll use me as the fall guy. He'll say I didn't keep him properly informed."

Maggie brought us back to the money. "Is the DHC Corporation another one of Simba's fronts?"

"No. They're an offworld company."

"What did they pay you for?"

He wiped his nose with his sleeve then was immediately disgusted by the red stain running from elbow to cuff. "They wanted me to reject the license. DHC is the parent company that owns TransPort, the biggest offplanet shipper. They didn't want any local competition."

"So you decided to take the offworld money and vote against Simba?"

"Yes. My wife and I are getting a divorce anyway. We've been cheating on each other for years. I didn't really care if she saw the vid or not, so I went with the money."

"Then what happened?"

"He"—pointing to Mdoba's picture—"visited me the morning after Dmitri was murdered. He showed up at my door and
told me Dmitri was dead, and I was next. I didn't believe him at
first. I thought he was just trying to intimidate me, but then we
got the call from Chief of Detectives Banks. I didn't even care
that much about the money. Why didn't he warn me he would
do something to my son? If he had threatened to kill Dmitri, I
would have done what he said. He didn't have to kill him!"
More pathetic sobbing.

"When's the vote?"

"We already had it." He managed between sobs. "We issued
the license yesterday."

twenty-four

WE found a free bench in the Old Town Square and sat to eat kebabs we'd picked up from a street vendor. I ate leaning far forward so any greasy spillover would fall safely to the ground instead of in my lap.

There were still a fair number of people on the square. A little unusual for this early in the afternoon, but the dark clouds were taking some edge off the heat. Even so, it was intensely hot, but bearable when you sat still.

The walks were blanket covered. Vendors offered jewelry, wood carvings, lizard jaws, rugs, paintings, spices, and anything else that was cheap to produce, displayed in neat rows, small items in the front, larger ones in the back. Tourists crowded the narrow trails between blankets, looking for that special bargain that they could brag to their friends about; "guess how little I paid for this." Every so often, children approached us, trying to get us to come back to their space: "Good quality, good prices." A quick dose of ignoring them and they moved on. Never make eye contact.

Maggie finished off the last of her kebab. "What does a crime lord want with a shipping business?"

"I don't know." I said.

"It can't be legit. I mean he *bought* a freighter. It would take years, maybe decades for him to turn a profit if he was on the up and up. He can't have that much patience or he wouldn't be a criminal in the first place."

"Yeah."

Maggie was incredulous. "Are guys like Simba and Bandur really that rich? They can just buy spaceships and bully the government? How can you work for somebody like that?"

"I don't work for Bandur. I just don't work against him."

"Right," she said sarcastically.

"Hey! You wanted to know my history, and I told you."

She let out a sigh. "You're right, Juno. Sorry."

She sounded genuine, so I let it drop.

Maggie wondered aloud, "How much does a freighter cost?"

"A bundle." My brain raced. Where could he have gotten that kind of money? Loja was tiny compared to Koba and hardly made any tourist money. Even if he took 100 percent of the gambling, prostitution, and drug profits, I couldn't believe he would have enough to buy a freighter. Not even the government could afford to buy one.

Maggie called Abdul. His hologram stood straight, without his real-life stoop. Maggie set the coroner to tracking down the sale of that ship.

I returned to the last few bites of my lunch.

Maggie kept her eyes on her pad. When the data came in, she told the pad to sort through the docs and highlight the relevant portions. The regular-looking paper shifted from one document to another. I couldn't keep up with her. I just watched the people on the square and waited for her synopsis.

"The freighter cost over thirty billion pesos."

"Thirty billion?"

"Yeah. Can you believe that? That translates to almost fifty million Earth dollars."

"How did he pay for it?"

"He put up fifty-one percent of the money. It took loans from four separate offworld banks to front his share. The other forty-nine percent came from two minority investors, both offworlders. Fernando Mendietta, who is the vice president of Universal Mining, and Mai Nguyen, who you already know."

My stomach seized. I looked at my hand.

Maggie continued. "She had to take out two loans to come up with her twenty percent. Mendietta paid cash for the rest."

Mai Nguyen. It had been twenty-five years since I'd tried to strangle her . . . I still wanted to.

Maggie put her notes away. "It's opium, isn't it? Simba'll use the shipping company to smuggle opium up to Nguyen, and she'll distribute it to the orbital station and the mines."

I couldn't answer; my thoughts were swimming. I got up without saying a word and tried to walk it off. *Nguyen.* Anger welled up from my gut, spilling into my head. My face felt flushed. I wanted to smash something.

I held on until the tide of blood slowly receded from my head and my locomotive breathing chugged out of steam. Some deep breaths soothed me back toward level. I rubbed my face with my hands. My forehead was running sweat.

Maggie looked concerned. "You okay?"

I nodded.

She hurried over to a street vendor, returning with a cold soda.

I chugged down half the bottle.

"Are you okay?"

"Yeah. Just give me a minute."

Simba, Nguyen, and Universal Mining. Simba: known O dealer. Nguyen: known smuggler and dealer. Vice president of Universal Mining: ???

It made no sense that the VP of a mining company would invest in an opium-smuggling scheme. The last thing he'd want to do is turn his employees into junkies—bad for productivity. He had to be going solo on this one, putting up his own money—screw the company.

How big was the mines' opium market that they needed a freighter to keep up with demand? It couldn't be that big . . . but what else could it be but opium? Everything else on Lagarto was worthless. . . .

A thought popped. Clarity overwhelmed. My nerves fired in a surge of understanding. We had missing people at every turn: six POWs, Kapasi's sister, Brenda Redfoot's list of suspected Zorno victims, Josephs and Kim busy investigating MPs . . .

Pieces snapped together—not all of them, but enough.

I called Abdul immediately. "I want the name of a missing persons case in Tenttown that Josephs and Kim have been working."

"Sure, Juno. Hang on."

Maggie looked at me strangely.

Abdul's holo unfroze. "Got it."

"Give it to me."

We tracked down the Wolski family in an hour's time. Their Tenttown home had a flap for a door. Maggie called inside.

A woman came—short with ratty hair. "Yes?"

"We are police officers, ma'am. I'm Detective Mozambe and this is Detective Orzo. We'd like to talk to you about your daughter. We understand she's been missing."

"The police were already here. Don't you talk to each other?"

"I know, ma'am, but we are carrying out our own investigation which may be connected to your daughter's disappearance. We'll only take a few minutes of your time."

She waved us in. Two open sores stood out on her arm—looked like they needed treatment. We made ourselves comfortable on pillows. She hiked her dress up to her knees as she sat down, exposing more sores on her ankles.

"Would you like some tea?"

"No thank you, ma'am." Too hot without aircon.

Bright blankets covered the tent walls, and the tent's ceiling was concealed behind more blankets that were tied to the center post and slung out to the corners. A cookstove in one corner had a stack of dishes sitting next to it. Bedrolls were lined up along the wall. I counted six. No other furniture. The surroundings felt childhood-familiar.

Mrs. Wolski scratched at her ankles. I caught a whiff of rot. There was no mistaking that smell.

Mrs. Wolski said, "What you want to know?"

Maggie said, "Please tell us what happened to your daughter."

"Shamal's gone." She fanned her face—the heat suddenly too strong for her. "My husband took her with him to the work tree and she—"

Maggie interrupted. "Work tree?"

"Sure. You want work, you go to the work tree. My husband, Dominick, he goes there every day. If he gets lucky, some rich people come needing a hand for the day. When they do, we eat good that day. How come you never heard of the work tree? You ain't some rich girl now, are you?"

"I don't live on this side of town." *Nice cover.*

"Anyway, he took her down there with him. She needs to get out of the house, you know. He was waiting by the tree, and she got bored, so he let her wander around a bit. She always been good at taking care of herself. After a while, he starts to wondering where that girl is. He tried to find her, but he can't find her nowhere. We ain't seen her since."

"How many children do you have?"

"Four."

"Did any of the others go to the work tree with your husband?"

"No, he only took Shamal. She's the oldest."

"Can you think of anybody who might have taken her?"

"I think it was that man that came here. I didn't trust him."

I asked, "What man?"

"I told the other officers about him."

"I know. I'm sorry to make you go through it again. Could you please tell me about this man?"

"He was going door to door, trying to find people to work the mines."

"Was he with Universal Mining?"

"I don't know. He didn't say. I suppose he could have been, but he didn't look all fancy like an offworlder."

"What did he say to you?"

"I tried to shoo him away, but Dominick invited him in. He told us how they had good jobs out in the mines. I asked him, 'Why do you want a fourteen-year-old girl?' He told me they needed all kinds of people; not everybody was going to be a miner. They needed cooks, maids, waitresses. . . . He said they could find a good job for her. Something that she liked to do— all depended on what she was interested in."

"What did you tell him?"

"I told him no. We ain't interested. Sure, it all sounded good, but I had a funny feeling about him. I didn't trust him straight off."

"Did he leave when you said no?"

"He left. He went on next door, but not before he got my husband all fired up. Dominick kept telling me how good it would be for Shamal. He told me how happy she'd be, because she'd have all this food and money. I told him food and money don't make up for losing a mother. That ain't a fair trade for a child. When she's older, she wants to go, I'll kiss her good-bye, but she's too young to be away from home."

"And you think this man could have taken her?"

"Yes, I do. I think he made that whole story up about working

in the mines. Like I said, he didn't look like no offworlder. I saw
it on the news . . . how men that like raping little girls and boys
make up some excuse to get into your house and see your kids.
It's like they're shopping. They remember the ones they like
and come back for them. I think he came back for Shamal."

"Did you tell all this to the officers who talked to you a few
days ago?"

"Why do I have to say everything twice with you people?
Yes, I told them, but they kept trying to tell me that she ran
away. I know my daughter . . . she did *not* run away."

"Did you get the man's name?"

"No." Her eyes misted over.

"Can we talk to your husband?"

"He went to the work tree first thing this morning. He'll
still be there if nobody hired him today. He's broken up about
Shamal. I've never seen him so upset. He even started drinking
again. I have to chase him out of the house in the mornings.
We got three other kids to feed, so he's got to keep working."

I had Maggie jot down Abdul's name for her. I told her he'd
treat those sores. Maybe the rot hadn't fully set in yet.

There had to be fifty people under that tree—some leaning up
against the trunk, others sitting on wide boughs, legs dangling,
watching traffic roll by. My deadbeat father used to spend most
of his days under this same tree, supposedly looking for work,
but mostly just pissing time away. A few were already moving
off, the setting sun a sign that there was no more work to be
had today. We walked under the umbrella of green foliage just
as raindrops began to patter on the leaves above. We stepped
over sleeping bodies and approached a trio of chatting men.

I put on a friendly smile. "Do any of you guys know Dominick Wolski?"

The shortest of the three stepped forward, his sleeveless

T showing off a scar tattoo of a naked woman in sunglasses. He was too poor to afford the real thing, so he'd had it burned into the skin with a makeshift branding iron. "You mean Nicky? Yeah, we know him."

"Is he here?"

"What you want with him?"

"Mrs. Orzo here needs him to lay some tile in one of her bathrooms." I tried to make it look like I worked for her.

"You don't need Nicky. I can do tile. I'm the best tile man out here. Isn't that right?" His buddies agreed. The rain was finding a way through the leaf canopy. Large drops fell on our heads and shoulders.

"No. She wants Mr. Wolski. He did her mother's bathroom, and she wants hers done the same way." I threw in an eye roll to show how crazy rich people were.

"He isn't here." He looked at Maggie. "You take me to your mother's bathroom. I'll look it over and do yours the same way. You won't be able to tell the difference. I'll give you a good price."

"No," she said, turning on an I'm-better-than-you voice. "I want Mr. Wolski. Tell us where he is."

"He doesn't work anymore. I'm your man."

"Tell me where to find him."

"You think I'm lying? I told you he doesn't work anymore. He's been hanging out at PT's." He pointed down the street to PT's Lounge. "You wait and see, he'll tell you he doesn't work anymore."

She walked away without thanking him, playing up the rich-bitch persona. I slipped him a few pesos and followed her out into the now pounding rain.

He yelled at our backs, "I'll wait right here for you. When he tells you he doesn't work anymore, you come back."

PT's Lounge had the aircon running low, just enough to take

the heat down a notch from smothering to uncomfortable. There were about a dozen tables scattered around, half occupied by men drinking and playing cards. We headed for the bar, a window covered in chicken wire with a slot at the bottom for passing out the hooch.

We waited our turn, three men ahead of us. Shine looked like the house specialty. Each customer passed a tin cup and a couple coins through the slot. The woman behind the bar took the coins and scooped out a cupful of mash. Her face was scarred-up from a botched plastic surgery. There were hacks all over Koba that lasered up faces. Make you look like an offworlder—guaranteed. Maggie gave her a pitying look, probably feeling guilty that she'd been able to afford getting her own fake face properly done. The burden of being rich.

When we got to the front, Maggie said, "We need to talk to Nicky Wolski."

The bartender pointed him out. I looked across the room and sized him up—my enforcer juices were flowing strong. He was a scrawny guy. Based on the dopey look on his face, he was drunk off his ass. He'd be easy for me to take, even at my advanced age. We just had to get him outside so his friends wouldn't jump in. My muscles tingled with anticipation. My nonviolence kick was strictly a thing of the past.

He was playing cards, showing off a big pile of money. The fuckhead was *gambling* with the money. Enforcer juices reached tidal wave proportion.

I walked over and stuck my badge in his face. "We need to talk to you."

He clumsily gathered his money from the table and tried to stuff it in his pocket. Some coins fell to the floor, and he teetered down to get them. We walked him out the back door to an alley littered with garbage, but otherwise empty. All three of us hugged the wall to stay out of the worst of the rain.

Maggie had her arms crossed. "What happened to your daughter Shamal?"

His dopey face went serious. "I don't know. She disappeared."

I socked him in the gut, using my legs to put all my weight into it. He went down to the ground, his face landing in a dirty puddle. He sucked in a breath, choking on puddle water. I felt a power surge in my shaking right. It could still do some damage.

When he stopped gurgling and sputtering, Maggie repeated, "What happened to your daughter?"

"I don't kn—"

I kicked him in the side. A good futbol kick, where foot met leg, no toe. He rolled on the ground, out into the rain.

Maggie was all cold steel. "What happened to your daughter?"

This time, there was no denial. Broken ribs were telling him to cooperate.

"Where did you get that money?"

Wolski vomited shine and puddle water. The rib pain threatened to make him pass out. I lunged in, grabbed his hair, and turned his face up into the driving rain until his eyes looked alert.

Maggie started the questioning again. "What did you do to your daughter?"

"I got her a job."

I had to lean in to hear him.

She bent over him. "You mean you sold her."

He didn't respond.

"Answer me! Did you sell her?"

"Yes. What of it?"

I put my foot on his rib cage and pushed, sending him squirming.

"Who bought her?"

"Carlos Simba."

"What's he going to do with her?"

He didn't answer.

I rifled his pockets and took every last peso before we left him moaning on the ground.

Quick stop at the Wolski house. I gave Mrs. Wolski her husband's money and padded it out of my own pocket. When we told her that her husband sold Shamal, she broke down.

One of her children entered, looking terrified to see his mother crying. He drew close and rubbed her back the same way she had probably calmed him so many times.

It didn't help.

Lagarto had finally found something new to export. Slaves.

twenty-five

MAGGIE and I rolled through the dark afternoon streets. Conversation was impossible as sheets of rain slapped onto the car's metallic roof, leaving me alone with my thoughts.

Knowing what to look for, it had only taken us a couple hours of surfing financials to figure out the basics of the operation. Carlos Simba had been running a slave trade. The buyer was Universal Mining. Free labor equals big profits. The middleman was the electric bitch, Mai Nguyen. We'd checked the shipping manifests. There were four shipping containers a week sent to Nguyen Imports from Vanguard Supplies, a warehouse located on the Loja waterfront that was probably a front for the Simba organization.

The slave business must have been going gangbusters. Four shipping containers a week simply hadn't been cutting it anymore so Simba, Nguyen, and Universal Mining had gone in together on a freighter, an outright slave ship.

Since there was only one spaceport, Simba had to run the operation from Koba. To get approval from the city, he tried to pass the thing off as a legitimate shipping company. He submitted a business plan to the board of the Koba Office of Business Affairs. He played up the patriotic angle—a shipping company owned and operated by Lagartans.

Simba didn't stand a chance with the board. They didn't like dealing with kingpins, plus the fix was in—Chairman of the Board Peter Vlotsky had been scoring big money from an offworld shipping company trying to maintain its monopoly.

Enter Sanders Mdoba—a Bandur crony who must've liked the looks of Simba's slave money. He ran a blackmail scheme on the board, using compromising vids of board members to buy votes.

Chairman Peter Vlotsky didn't play. His wife already knew he was screwing around, and the offworld money was too good for him to pass up. Mdoba turned up the heat—killed Vlotsky's kid—and Simba got his shipping company signed and sealed.

The still missing pieces were Private Jhuko Kapasi and the grand prize, Mayor Omar Samir.

We rode through the outskirts of the city. Kicked-up mud from dirt roads stuck to the windshield. The towers of the Koba Spaceport were now visible, poking up through the jungle.

The cab dropped us at the spaceport gates. We used our badges to get past the guards minus our weapons.

The cargo docks housed five massive freighters that towered like high-rises while cranes dangled metal boxes going into and out of gaping cargo holds. Simba's new purchase, the *Sunda*, stood in the second position. Trucks on the ground cannoned the ship with water, hiding all but the tip behind falling clouds of mist.

We entered the command tower and marched down the cinder-block halls. The walls were alive with molds and mosses. We looked for the office of Clay Reinholt, nightshift supervisor. His signatures were on almost half of the delivery receipts from Vanguard Supplies to Nguyen Imports.

We found his office, ignored his receptionist's protests, and strode for the door. She jumped up and blocked our path. Maggie's dirty look convinced her to move out of our way.

We headed through the door with the adrenaline-pumped

confidence of three successful bully sessions in a row. I was revved—hadn't felt like this in years.

I stopped face to face with Mai Nguyen. *NGUYEN!* Maggie bumped into me from behind. The corner of my eye picked up something coming from the side. Before I could turn, I was tackled. My face bounced off the floor. Maggie screamed. My vision went red, and my gasket blew sky high. I thrashed against hands that held me stock still. I jerked violently to no avail, my body overheating with the effort. When my flame finally burned out, the hands lifted me off the floor and sat me in a chair. Maggie was already seated. The hands pinned my arms behind the chair. I couldn't move.

Mai Nguyen stood before me like a déjà vu doomsday. She studied my face with her not-a-day-older eyes. She extended her index finger toward my nose. I slipped into a fried-nose panic. I strained against the hands that held my head. She gave my nose a poke.

She retreated to a desk and sat on its front edge, leaning forward so her impressive cleavage offered a view with the utmost titillation. "How nice to see you, Officer Mozambe. I thought you looked familiar, but I wasn't sure. I'm not used to people who age. I stole a few skin cells off your nose for a DNA test which verified your identity. I'm sure you don't mind." She spoke to the hands. "You can let them go."

Hands released me. I looked over my shoulder at the offworld bodyguards. The one behind me didn't look familiar, but I recognized the one behind Maggie from a quarter-century ago. I took in the rest of the room. Off to the side stood a nervous-looking local man. It had to be the nightshift supervisor we'd come to see. Nguyen shot him a look, and he made a quick exit.

Nguyen aimed her cleavage at Maggie. "Who are you?"

Maggie spoke with straight-ahead cool. "Detective Magda Orzo."

"Are you partners?"

"Yes."

"I'm so sorry for the rough treatment you just received, but you can hardly blame my bodyguards for reacting that way. You didn't give them much choice, entering unannounced the way you did. What brings you here, officers?"

My hand was outright gyrating. I tucked it under my leg. I didn't want her knowing how badly she'd hurt me. "We'd like to know about your dealings with Carlos Simba."

Nguyen wore an amused expression. "Mr. Simba is an entrepreneur. He approached me to see if I would invest in his new shipping company. Lagarto Lines looked like a sound investment, so here I am."

"Carlos Simba is a known figure in organized crime."

"He's nothing of the sort. He's a very successful businessman. He's going to be the first Lagartan to compete with non-Lagartan shippers. That means jobs and affordable shipping prices for Lagartans. I would think he'd be a hero to your people."

"What goods does he plan to ship?"

"Does it matter?"

"It matters if he's going to sell our people as slaves."

"Don't be so shortsighted, Officer Mozambe. Mr. Simba will be able to cut into Lagarto's trade deficit. That means the peso will be stronger. Think of all the things Lagartans could buy with a peso that's worth something—medicine, robots, computers. This is the first step for Lagarto to enter the galactic economy."

"Don't bullshit me. You don't care about Lagarto. You're selling slaves for your own profit."

"Look who is suddenly the moralist. That's quite the attitude from a hatchet man for the Bandur organization. Bandur enslaves his people with their own vices for his profit. I fail to see the difference."

"But . . . but . . ." I stammered like a fool. I couldn't find the words to defend myself. Maybe because there weren't any. Maybe there was no difference between Nguyen and me.

"You tire me." She looked to her bodyguards, "Escort them out, will you. See to it that the guards don't let them back in without a warrant."

I stood up and dropped my right into my pocket. My gut stirred anger, vengeance, and guilt into a vile stew that I couldn't vomit.

Nguyen's voice stopped us at the door. "You know I have camera implants in my eyes. Whenever I'm feeling down, I recall the recording of our last meeting. It never fails to cheer me up."

My hand went spastic within the confines of my pocket. Maggie led me out to the sound of Nguyen's tech-amplified laughter.

I felt shell-shocked from my run-in with Nguyen. She'd gone from moving O to moving slaves, and she wasn't shy about letting people know it. I dropped Maggie at her hotel. Seeing all the offworlders coming in and out, I once again marveled at how rich she had to be to afford that place.

I headed home for dinner with Niki. I was looking forward to seeing her. I felt bad about being gone so much. Since I'd stopped my enforcing, we'd spent a lot more time together, and I wasn't used to going this long without seeing her.

My phone rang. The young girl from the dock dropped into the passenger seat. She looked at least a year younger than her real self—overdue for a holo-update.

"Is Mdoba back?"

"He was," she said. "But he's gone again. He took his boat out on the river."

Thanks for nothing. "Call me when he gets back, okay?"

"Yep." She disappeared in a flash.

I pulled into the drive and entered the house. I found Niki sleeping on the sofa. "Hey, Niki. It's me."

Silence.

"Niki?"

More silence. An empty pill bottle sat on the table.

My mind slid six years to another episode. In an instant, I remembered a blue-skinned Niki breathing shallow, and then the sirens and the stomach pumps. *Not again!* I flew to her side, checked her pulse. *Both* my hands shook. Her pulse ran strong and regular; her color was good; her skin felt warm to the touch. I let out the breath I'd been holding and sucked at the air. Ever since that night six years ago, I'd always think the worst. No OD tonight; she'd just double or triple dosed to get to sleep. I'd been neglecting her.

Niki's mini-relapse complemented my total one with foreboding clarity. My life was running full speed in reverse. I was running around fists first, doing Paul's bidding, and chasing the hot skirt in some kind of pathetic attempt to recapture my youth. Looking at Niki, my Niki, I could see the ridiculousness of it all.

My galloping heart was slowing to its normal beat. I brushed Niki's hair off her face and listened to her breathing. I sat on the floor and rubbed my too-sore knuckles. I'd see this case out, because Paul needed me, but then I would be done. I'd quit the force altogether. It was time to put all my energy into Niki. We still cared about each other. We could make it work again.

Niki barely woke when I picked her up. I carried her to bed, whispering soothings in her ear.

I was munching a sandwich when Paul called. Holo-Paul sat across the table from me. "How are things going?"

"Are you alone?"

"Yeah, we can talk. Catch me up."

It was hard to know where to start. "Sanders Mdoba is the son of a bitch that tipped off Ali Zorno about our witness."

Holo-Paul looked delighted. Real-Paul sounded pissed. "Mdoba? SHIT!"

"The kid's blood is on his hands, Paul. We still don't know who told Mdoba about our witness, other than it must be a cop. We tossed his boat, a rusted-up number in Phra Kaew. We found vids of Vlotsky's father and four other board members caught with their dicks out. He blackmailed them into approving a business license for Carlos Simba's shipping company, Lagarto Lines. He had Vlotsky's kid killed to keep him in line. He's moonlighting for Simba."

"Bandur is losing control. I can't believe Simba flipped somebody that high up. Does Sasaki know?"

"No, I didn't tell him. I was afraid Mdoba was working under Sasaki's orders."

"What's this shipping company about?"

"They're shipping slaves to the mines, Paul. Simba sells them to Universal Mining. We found a man today who *sold* his daughter to Simba. It's only one instance so far, but when we start combing through all the missing persons cases, we'll find lots more. Guess who the middle man is?"

Paul replied, "Mai Nguyen."

Surprised, I said, "How'd you know?"

"I've been digging into Mayor Samir's funds. There are connections between him, Nguyen, and Simba all over the damn place."

The alliance between Mai Nguyen, Carlos Simba, and Mayor Samir solidified in my mind. "We're getting close, Paul." I was up out of my seat, pacing. "The Vlotsky hit looks like Simba's doing, but the mayor must have a stake in the slave trade. Simba must've asked him to try and keep us from digging too deep."

"Do you think that your Army guy has anything to do with it?"

"Yeah. I keep trying to discount him, but it's too big a coincidence that he and Zorno were cellmates. Why?"

"Private Kapasi's back on leave as of this morning. Once the Army heard the news reports that we caught Vlotsky's killer, they decided the murder wasn't Army related. He should have made it back to Loja this afternoon."

"Hold on." I froze Paul's image and had the system dial up the little girl from the dock.

"Hello?" she said.

"Which way did he take the boat?"

"Upriver."

I hung up and unfroze Paul. "I gotta go, Paul. Mdoba's heading upriver. How much you want to bet he's going to meet with Kapasi?"

I was already out the door. Holo-Paul followed me through the courtyard. "Get me proof, Juno. We're running out of time."

I sped to Maggie's hotel, honking through the intersections. I tried calling, but she didn't answer, so I left a message. What the hell was she doing?

I recklessly rounded the last corner, the hotel dead ahead. Hell with it. If she wasn't there, I was going to Loja without her. I rolled the car up near the entrance and caught sight of Maggie getting out of somebody's car. My heart involuntarily jumped in excitement. I kiboshed the feeling—I was a one-woman guy. I almost called out to her, but my instincts kept me silent. *Whose car is that?*

She walked through the double doors into the hotel. The car she'd exited was turning around. I swerved onto the street;

I had to get close. The car drove right by me. The driver—Karl Gilkyson.

I braked, my mind in a stupor. I couldn't think straight. Maggie and Gilkyson? I decided I had to ditch Maggie. I needed to swing the car around. I cruised into the hotel turnaround, getting stopped behind another vehicle with an open trunk. Two offworld tourists were supervising a group of bellhops on the proper way to carry their luggage. Like they'd never seen luggage that hovered.

Before I could pull all the way through, the passenger door opened, and Maggie dropped into the seat. "I just got your message. Why are we going to Loja?"

My brain went haywire on a conflicting mixture of being excited to see her and a double-crossed rage.

"They released Private Kapasi," I said.

My skin slithered as I drove. I could be sitting next to the mayor's plant. I tried to ice my firing thoughts with careful deliberation. A cop informed Mdoba about Pedro. Could it have been Maggie? *Can't be.* She'd saved my life last night. She could've waited for psycho Zorno to slice me up before she came in. She didn't have to come in at all. Better yet, she could have lost Zorno's trail; she'd had plenty of opportunity to claim she'd lost him in the labyrinthine Floodbank corridors. She wasn't the mayor's plant—simply couldn't be. My nerves cooled from a boil to a simmer.

What then? The mayor was worried about me. The mayor was making a play for her. He wanted her to start informing for him. He wanted her on his side. She probably told him to fuck off, but I couldn't be sure.

The boat tore through the water. I paid extra for a high-powered fishing boat instead of a skiff—should cut the trip to Loja down

by a half hour. We'd arrive well before midnight. I sat on a fish
chest, my brain dazed by plots and subplots. My eyelids began to
feel weighted. My barely open eyes blurred fishnets into what
look like whip-wielding slavers.

Maggie's voice sounded next to me. "I had a visitor today."

I tried rubbing my face awake. "Who?"

"Karl Gilkyson. He brought me to see the mayor."

I tried to keep a level expression. "What did you talk about?"

"He wanted me to tell him about our investigation."

"What did you say?"

"That I was under orders from Chief Chang not to talk."

"What did he say to that?"

"He just asked more questions."

I was already feeling less suspicious of her. If she wanted to
hide things from me, she'd be hiding them instead of talking
about them. "Tell me more," I said tentatively.

"Mayor Samir tried buttering me up, asking me about my
family like he was all concerned about how they were doing.
He talked about how good my mother looked when he saw
her at the banquet.

"Then he asked about you—how I felt about partnering with
you. I wanted to sound believable, so I decided to tell him I
couldn't stand you. When he asked why, I told him that you
were dirty, a disgrace to KOP. He went on to ask me why I didn't
refuse to be your partner. I said that I had no choice; Chief
Chang gives the orders. I have to play the game to move ahead."

"Go on," I said.

"Then he started asking how I felt about taking the chief's
orders. I said I didn't like it, and that I'd heard the rumors
about him and the Bandur cartel. Then when he asked if I believed those rumors, I told him that I was inclined to believe
them, especially after I'd seen how dirty Chang's old partner
was."

"Then what?"

"Next, he wanted to know how I'd feel about taking his orders instead of the chief's. He offered me a deal. He wants me to snitch for him, be part of his anticorruption investigation."

I was studying her closely, her voice, her body language. I could tell she was being honest with me. "What did he offer?"

"A fast track to a lieutenancy after Chief Chang's forced out."

"Do you still think the mayor's innocent in all this?"

"Not anymore. He was pushing me hard to take the deal. When I finally told him I'd take it, he wanted to know all about the Vlotsky case. He has to have a personal stake in it."

"What did you tell him about the case?"

"Just that we solved it."

"Did he believe you?"

"I think so."

Maggie had played him flawlessly, telling him things he already knew about Paul and me, getting him to think of her as an anticorruption zealot, and an ambitious one at that. She was a natural—maybe better than Paul.

"Why'd you decide to tell me about this?"

"Because you're my partner."

I grinned at that. She trusted me, and I trusted her. We were true partners. "Tell me something, Maggie. Why did you kiss my cheek last night?"

"I don't know. I think it's because you remind me of my father."

If I had any romantic notions left, that put an end to them, once and for all. "Are we a lot alike?"

"Actually, you're nothing like him. It's the way you and I interact that reminds me of him. He and I never agreed on anything, but that never got in the way of us caring for each other. Even when we were dead set against each other, we always had this respect for each other. That's the way I feel when I'm around you."

I nodded my head, *very* glad I hadn't made a move for her last night. I thought of Maggie and me having a father-daughter relationship and decided I was just fine with that.

Maggie said, "I want you to help me construct lies to tell the mayor."

"So now you want to be my double agent?"

"No." Maggie was wearing a sly grin. "I want *you* to work for *me*."

I laughed. "For what purpose?"

"To take over KOP. I'm going to be chief one day, Juno. Things have to change. Lagarto can't go on this way. A clean police force can change everything."

"What do you want with me?"

"Who better to help me take over KOP than somebody who's already done it once?"

"Are you asking me to overthrow Paul?"

"Of course not, but he won't want to be chief forever."

"I don't enforce anymore."

"I won't ask you to enforce for me. I want to do this clean."

"That's impossible. It can't be done."

"Is that a no?"

"Yes, that's a no. I'm quitting after this case."

twenty-six

THE lights of the Loja pier appeared off the bow. I hung up
with Niki. She'd called when she woke up, giving me the usual
postbinge earful. "It's late. . . . Where have you been? . . . Paul
doesn't own you. . . . I thought you told him you wouldn't run
his errands anymore."

The understanding attitude she'd had this morning was
long gone. I knew it wasn't entirely about me. She was feeling
bad about herself since her pill-popping relapse, and she was
redirecting all that self-loathing at me. I came back with the
standard excuses. . . . "This time is different. . . . Paul really
needs me on this one. . . . It's almost over." More bitterness
than normal slipped into my voice—I was angry at her for
scaring me by pain-pill binging and angrier at myself for neglecting her and then angry at her again for calling my neglect
to my attention when I already knew. It wasn't going to be easy
getting things right between us.

We rode past Mdoba's docked boat. His bikini-clad girlfriend
Malis was on the deck grooving to a tune. She didn't see us. She
was too involved in self-involvement. We landed on an empty
pier. Maggie and I hopped off without waiting for the skipper
to tie up.

I broke into a heavy sweat as the two of us kept up a brisk
pace on the walk to the Kapasi brothers' falling-apart home.
Sneaking up from the outside, we checked the front and back
windows—nobody home. I went for a basement window,

closed my eyes, and stuck my head through the jungle shrub-
bery that had overrun this side of the house. Thorns scraped
my skin; twigs slapped my cheeks and forehead. I pressed my
face against the glass, straining to see through the basement
window . . . holy fuck.

I reached a hand back through the brush and gave Maggie a
come-here finger curl. Mosquitoes bit on my face as she rus-
tled her way through the shrubs. Her cheek slid against mine
into position at the window.

I tried to keep a cool head as we took in the scene. A dozen
laser-clawed and razor-jawed monitors thrashed in their pen.
Their metal teeth sparked as they gnashed on the bars that ran
floor to ceiling. Their laser-claws scratched at the cement floor
in a frenzied scramble to push through the gaps. A piece of
meat flew through the bars and landed on the floor where it
was torn into a half dozen pieces.

Outside the pen, Sanders Mdoba's oversized frame was on
all fours, lase-blade in hand, sawing through human bone.
Body parts lay all over, blood streaming into a floor drain. He
successfully severed an arm and slid it through the bars, then
moved to the head, his lase-blade slicing clean through neck
flesh, getting hung up on the vertebrae. He sawed the blade
back and forth, finally cutting through in a cloud of bloody
steam. He stood up, his tent-sized clothes stained red and
black, and tried to shove Sanje Kapasi's larger-than-normal
head through the bars. It stuck momentarily, monitors snapping at the backside, until Mdoba used a shoulder to shove it
the rest of the way through.

I counted the remaining limbs—three legs, one arm. Jhuko
and Sanje Kapasi.

Maggie and I pulled free of the jungle scrub. We jogged
around to the front door and into the house. We strode pur-
posefully through the house as lizards screeched all around us.

I slinked through the basement door and crept down the stairs, Maggie following sure-footedly. Mdoba was hacking through ribs, the lase-blade blinking on and off from overload. I moved up on him from the rear, the racket from the monitor pen covering my approach. Smoke-filled air made my eyes water. Mdoba pulled a side of ribs free—BBQed at the edges. I pushed my piece into the middle of his back, sinking it into his ample flesh. He froze. Maggie moved around front, her piece held level.

He let the blade drop from his hand; the beam flickered out. He put his hands over his head and submitted to the frisking like a pro. I relieved him of his lase-pistol. When he saw who I was, he tried to act all buddy-buddy saying, "It's good to see you, Juno. How's Niki?"

I led him upstairs without speaking. He tried to bullshit me the whole way, telling me he was here doing Bandur's business, and that Sasaki was gonna be pissed when he found out I'd interfered.

I made him sit on the kitchen floor. Sanje Kapasi's prized monitor strained at its chain, the smell of carnage driving it near insane. I thought about frying it just to shut it up.

Mdoba rested his back on the wall, looking defiant instead of defeated. It would be tough to break him. My stomach sickened at the thought of torturing him. Maggie was waiting for me to take control, but I procrastinated as I tried to summon my temper. I was drawing blanks. I wanted a drink.

I told myself, fuck this. Just do it already. I tucked my piece away and moved in on him, my fists ready to do some damage.

Living room lizards suddenly went berserk. Somebody was here. Maggie wheeled on the kitchen door, her body in a crouch, her weapon extended. I stuck my piece under Mdoba's double chin, pushing through the fat and pressing on his Adam's apple.

Matsuo Sasaki came into the kitchen with his muscle, chef-killer Tipaldi. Both their hands up.

"What are you doing here?" I wanted to know.

"Paul called and gave me the news that Mr. Mdoba betrayed us to Mr. Simba. We called his girlfriend, who was gullible enough to tell us where he was."

"That dumb cunt." Mdoba wheezed.

I shoved my weapon deeper into his throat.

Maggie butted in. "You can't have him. We're going to arrest him."

I shot her a warning look.

Sasaki didn't take offense. "I'm afraid I can't allow that, Maggie. You see, the criminal justice system doesn't offer a punishment severe enough to fit the nature of Mr. Mdoba's betrayal."

Maggie's eyes drilled into Sasaki. "You're going to kill him."

"Why of course we are, but not until we've had a spot of fun. You don't know the kind of anguish we've felt since your chief told us how disloyal Mr. Mdoba has been. But fear not, I will give you the opportunity to speak with him first. However, you will limit your questions to Mr. Mdoba's involvement in any schemes masterminded by our Lojan friend, Mr. Simba. It is only along these lines that our interests overlap with police interests. You will not question him on any illegal activities outside of that realm. Is that satisfactory?"

Maggie stayed silent.

"Deal," I said, glad to be relieved of torture duty.

"Excellent, Juno. You've always been most . . . practical."

"Where's Ben? Shouldn't he be here?"

"That he should, but he had to stay home. He's suffering from an infection in his reconstructed nose. The doctors told him not to swim, but he didn't follow their instructions, and now he is suffering magnificently." He turned to Tipaldi. "If you'll do the honors, Tip."

Tipaldi darted in, dropping knucks on Mdoba's nose, barely giving me time to step back. A few quick shots and he had Mdoba seeing double, his nose swollen beyond the confines of his already fat-swollen face. Tipaldi pinned Mdoba's arm under his own and dragged Mdoba's heavy form across the floor. Mdoba was squealing now, his heels kicking at the floor, failing to find purchase.

Tipaldi yanked and pulled the resisting Mdoba into the monster's reach, holding Mdoba's hand out as a snack. It came back less three fingers.

Maggie turned her back. I eyeballed the whole scene. I'd done worse. Four fingers later he was ready to talk—the reward: a quick death instead of a part-by-part dismemberment.

Sasaki told Tipaldi to get him cleaned up. "You can't expect a lady like Officer Orzo to look at such a mess."

Tipaldi found a couple towels and wrapped what was left of Mdoba's hands. Maggie stayed planted where she was, her back turned on the ugliness.

I wiped the sweat off my face, and spoke slow and clear. "You work for Simba."

"Yes," Mdoba answered.

"When did you start working for Simba?"

He couldn't answer, the pain too great. Tipaldi slapped him lucid. "Two years ago," he croaked.

"Why?"

Again he couldn't answer. Tipaldi slipped him a needleful of morphine. I waited a few, until he started getting happy. "Why did you start working for Simba?" I repeated.

"He paid well."

"What did he want from you?"

"He wanted somebody high up in Bandur's outfit to pass him information on what we were doing. Don't get me wrong;

I'm not a traitor or nothing, but the money was good. Besides, I was hired by Papa Bandur, not that pussy kid of his."

"What other kinds of work did you do for Simba?"

Mdoba went into a coughing fit. His belly rolled with every hack. After a glass of water, he was talking again. "I was help-ing him get his shipping company going. Shit, it was a sweet deal, Juno. He has some bitch on the Orbital that buys up peo-ple, ships 'em to the mines."

"What kind of people?"

Mdoba had entered a morphine euphoria. His words were coming out fluidly now. "All kinds. It don't matter. Kids are good, because they're easy to kidnap. Some people even sell their kids cheap."

"What happens to them?"

"They send 'em to the mines. From what I hear, the ship captains keep the pretty ones for themselves. You ever heard of a harem? They used to have 'em on Earth. They knew what they was doing back then. A harem's when you got all these women and they do whatever you say; they have to please you. You know what I'm saying? Beat 'em, rape 'em—whatever you want."

"YOU DON'T TREAT WOMEN LIKE THAT!" My piece was in his mouth.

Mdoba ranted garbled pleadings, begging mercy.

Tipaldi and Sasaki didn't move to stop me. Maggie said, "Juno."

My hand tremor spread over my entire body. Sweaty shivers ran up and down. My face burned red. I pulled my piece free, revealing a newly chipped tooth in Mdoba's blubbering mouth. I stepped outside and sucked early evening air. My muscles adrenaline-twitched. I struggled to calm my out-of-control thoughts.

Maggie stayed next to me with a look of pity on her face. I'd spent a lifetime proving I wasn't weak by exacting brutality in abundance, and in the end, I came off pitiful. I gave her my weapon and headed back in.

Mdoba was as calm as could be expected. Sasaki had moved to the stove to prepare tea. Tipaldi was nursing his bruised knuckles with ice from the freezer.

I took a place on the far side of the kitchen—safely out of throttling distance from Mdoba. I concentrated on self-control. "What do they do with the rest of the slaves?"

Mdoba answered, "They make 'em work."

"Don't they have robots to do the mining?"

"They need people to run the robots. The more people, the more machines they can run. They don't need just miners, though. They need people to grow food and shit, same as here."

"Why can't they hire labor? Twenty percent of Lagarto is looking for work."

"This way's cheaper. Why pay for something when you can get it for free?"

"Aren't they afraid of getting caught?"

Mdoba's speech was getting labored. "Who's going to catch them? Even if somebody found out, it would take years for the message to get to Earth or anybody else that can do anything about it. By the time they send somebody out here to investigate, twenty or thirty years go by."

"How were you helping Simba get started?"

Mdoba turned to Tipaldi. "More. I need more."

Tipaldi administered a morphine booster. Mdoba instantly became more relaxed.

I started back in. "How were you helping Simba?"

"He told me how he wanted his own ship. I thought he was crazy. I don't know how he did it, but he bought a fucking ship. I'd like to see Bandur pull that off. Maybe Papa coulda done it.

I seen that man do some amazing shit, but the kid ain't got it in him."

"Simba needed approval from the city."

"That's right. He wanted me to handle it. He needed somebody that knew Koba. It was a test. You know, to see how I did. If it went well, he was going to see about putting me in charge of Bandur's operations when he took them over."

"So you took vids of board members."

"You know about those? Yeah, it was easy. Everybody's got something they don't want people knowing about. I took vids and used them to get the board to vote the way Simba wanted."

The questions were ticking off my tongue in a strictly professional manner. "What about Peter Vlotsky?"

"I caught that prick screwing hookers, but he didn't care. It took me a while to figure out that he was getting paid by an offworld shipping company to kill Simba's business proposal dead. I needed him. He was the fucking chairman. Without his okay there was nothing we could do. He's got some kind of veto power."

"What did you do then?"

"Simba gave me the go-ahead to play it rough with Vlotsky. Simba said he couldn't compete with offworld money, so he said we'd have to use intimidation to get what we wanted."

"You went after his family."

"Right. I'd already done my homework on the family. I told him about how Vlotsky had a wife and a son, but the problem with his son was that he was in the Army. How do you whack a guy in the Army? He's surrounded by guys with guns. So Simba told me to go for the wife, but I told him that if Vlotsky doesn't care about his wife seeing him fucking another woman then he probably won't care if we kill her either. We'd be doing the guy a fucking favor."

"So what did you decide to do?"

"When I mentioned that Vlotsky's kid was stationed at the base upriver, he told me he knew somebody stationed there."

"Jhuko Kapasi."

"You know about him, too? What the fuck are you asking me all these questions for?"

Pieces were coming into focus. "Go on."

He looked at Tipaldi, not needing to ask. Tipaldi gave him another mini-injection. Mdoba looked at his wrecked hands then closed his eyes. "I checked out this Kapasi. He was a hustler—got sent up to the Zoo for a gambling deal that went bad. He got early release from prison and was sent into the Army. It turned out he was in Vlotsky's unit."

"How did Simba know Kapasi?"

"He told me that Kapasi sold him some POWs—farmers that brought a good price when he sold them to the mines."

"What about Kapasi's sister? Did he sell her to Simba?"

"Yeah, he sold her, too. He ran that crazy gambling scheme that blew up in his face, and he had to pay off some big debts before he went to jail, so he sold her to Simba. That was when Simba was just getting started on the slavery thing."

My brain locked the pieces into place. "So you approached Kapasi."

"Yeah. I told him I'd pay him to snuff Lieutenant Vlotsky. He got all excited about it. He told me how big a prick Lieutenant Vlotsky was and how the lieutenant screwed his whole unit over on some operation. I thought he was onboard. He'd kill Chairman Vlotsky's kid, and I'd go tell him he's next if he doesn't vote our way, but Kapasi fucked the whole thing up."

"How?"

"I gave Kapasi half the dough up front. I was going to give him the other half after he did the job. He was running around in the jungle with Vlotsky for days. How hard could it be to pop the guy?"

"He didn't do it?"

"He didn't do shit. I don't know if he ain't got the cojones or what. I figured that a guy who sells his sister as a slave won't mind killing somebody, but this guy must not like to get his hands dirty. I called him on it, and he said the unit was going on leave. I thought, 'Good, then I can do it myself.' I told him to send my money back, but the fucker kept it, and he called me a couple days later and told me he killed Vlotsky. What kind of fucked-up job is that?"

"Then what?"

"A few days later, I got tipped off that there was a witness. I tried to get Kapasi on the line, but the Army had him in some kind of lockup. They were worried that Vlotsky's murder was Army-related. It cost me a fucking fortune in bribes to get him on the line. I told him that somebody saw him kill Lieutenant Vlotsky. He told me there was no way anybody saw him kill Vlotsky since he didn't kill him. Can you believe this asshole? I said, 'If you didn't kill him, who did?' He told me he gave the front money to his old cellmate from the Zoo to do the job. He was going to keep the second payment for himself. 'For the referral,' he said."

Mdoba asked for more water. He coughed most of it up before carrying on. "I about shit on the spot. He told me about Zorno. You already know about him since you killed him."

Holes were filling in lightning fast. My brain raced to keep up—Simba hired Mdoba to fix the board's vote; Mdoba hired Kapasi to whack Lieutenant Vlotsky; Kapasi subcontracted the job to lip-obsessed serial killer Ali Zorno. "Why'd you come here to Kapasi's house?"

"Kapasi went back on leave today. The Army decided he had nothing to do with Vlotsky's death, so they let him go. He called me, asking for the second half of his payment. I acted real nice and told him he did a great job, and I'd be there as soon as I could. I met him here and told him I wasn't going to pay him. You should have seen him getting all pissy about it. Why should I pay him for hitting Vlotsky when he didn't hit nobody?"

"What did you do to him?"

"I shot him. He had it coming to him. Then his dumb-fuck brother got all pathetic, crying and shit, so I burned a hole through his chest to put him out of his misery. I figure he's better off dead. His momma shoulda smothered him the minute she popped him out and saw he was a retard, am I right?"

Maggie was watching now. The repulsive torture scene not quite so repulsive anymore.

Mdoba rattled on. "Once I finished feeding the Kapasi brothers to the lizards, I was gonna open the cage and let the monitors loose. Let 'em shit the evidence all over Loja. Once I hosed that basement down there was no way it coulda gotten traced back to me."

After another dose of morphine, I asked, "What's Simba's relationship with Mayor Samir?"

"They're working together."

This final confirmation announced Paul's vulnerability in bright lights. "How so?"

"Simba approached Samir before the elections, asked him, 'Why split the power four ways when we can split it two?' You see what he meant? Bandur runs the drugs, gambling, loansharking, and prostitution in Koba. Chief Chang runs KOP. Mayor Samir runs the city government, and Simba runs his slavery operation. Get rid of Bandur and Chang, and you got only two left—Simba for the illegal shit and Mayor Samir for everything else."

The battle lines were finally clearly drawn—Simba, Nguyen,

and the mayor versus Paul, Bandur, and me. "How is the mayor planning to bring down Chief Chang?"

"I don't know that part. Simba never told me. All I know is they talk every day, so they can coordinate things."

"Who tipped you off about our witness?"

"Mayor Samir."

"Mayor Samir?"

"Yeah. He came to my boat to tell me."

"He was on your boat?"

"That's what I said. He told me that a cop—"

"Which cop?"

"Some guy named Kim. This Kim told the mayor that you guys had a witness, so the mayor came and told me about it."

"What exactly did he say?"

"I just told you."

"Tell me again."

Mdoba used a nursing-home voice—slow, loud, and deliberate. "He said that Kim from Homicide Division came and told him that there was a witness to the Vlotsky murder—some peeping-tom kid. He recited the kid's name and address for me, and then he left."

Make Yuan Kim our rat-fink cop.

Maggie stepped over and leaned into Mdoba's line of vision. "Do you have proof that the mayor came to your boat?"

"I have it on vid. I know how to cover my ass. He may be mayor, but he ain't half as smart as he thinks he is."

"Where's the vid?"

He was grinning now. "How 'bout lettin' me walk outta here?"

Sasaki said, "Tip, I think Juno could use your help."

Tipaldi moved in fast. He yanked one of Mdoba's hands toward the monitor who was hungry for seconds.

Mdoba shrieked. "STOP! STOP! I don't know where it is. STOP!"

Tipaldi stopped. "What do you mean you don't know?"

Mdoba panted, "I gave it to my girlfriend. I told her to hide it."

"Where'd she put it?"

The monitor was snapping at Mdoba's just-out-of-reach hand.

Mdoba said, "I don't know! I told her not to tell me where she put it. If you don't let me outta here, she'll have it destroyed. Call her. She'll tell you."

We needed that vid. It was our smoking gun. I turned to Sasaki. "What do you say?"

Sasaki fingered his lapels, shaking his head no.

"Paul needs this," I said with determined desperation. "You have to do this for him."

"Leaving a traitor alive is bad for business, Juno. We can't have people thinking it's okay to betray us."

"He's already lost most of his fingers. Tell people you let him live so that when people see his hands, it'll remind them of what happens to traitors."

Sasaki was thinking it over.

I said, "Paul won't survive without that vid, Matsuo."

Sasaki rubbed his face with a pinkyless hand and gave the smallest nod.

I called Mdoba's boat. Malis's buxom hologram dropped into the kitchen. I had it one-way conferenced—everybody could hear her side of the conversation, but she could only hear me.

"Have you ever met Mayor Samir?" I asked.

"Sure. He came to the boat to talk with Sanders."

"What about?"

"You want the vid, don't you?"

"How'd you know?"

"Sanders told me to hide it. He said that if he got in trouble, I should use the vid to get him out. Is he in trouble?"

"Yes, he is."

"How can I be sure?"

I let Mdoba's voice on the line. "Do what he says, babe. Everthing's gonna be okay if you just do what he says."

"Are they going to kill you?"

"Not if you do what Juno says. Okay?"

I cut Mdoba off then spoke to Malis. "I want you to bring the vid to me."

"I want money," she said. Mdoba tensed.

"I don't think you understand," I said. "If you don't bring me the vid, he'll die."

"I understand just fine. Go ahead and kill him, I don't care. How much can you pay?" Mdoba was fucked—sold out by his squeeze.

Mdoba turned wild at her betrayal. He was shouting and flailing his half-hands. The kitchen air crackled with lase-fire. Mdoba took three hits, the last to the head. Tipaldi kept his lase-pistol on target until Mdoba slumped over dead. Tipaldi put his piece back in his belt.

Maggie was stunned. I shrugged.

Malis and I settled on price. She told me she was already on her way back to Koba to retrieve the vid. She said to meet her at Club Dynasty on Bangkok at 2:00 AM.

I rang up Paul. His holo dropped into the Kapasi brothers' living room, setting off another round of hysterical lizard fits. "Paul, it's Juno."

"Yeah."

"We have confirmation that Mayor Samir and Carlos Simba are conspiring together. They're planning to take you and Bandur out."

Silence dragged on the other end. Paul said, "You're sure?"

"Yes."

"Do you have proof?"

"Mdoba's girlfriend is selling us a vid of the mayor telling Mdoba about our witness. We're meeting her at—" I almost said the name of the place, but I smartly held back. No telling who could be listening in. "We're meeting her in a couple hours."

"You want backup?"

"No," I said. Yuan Kim was a confirmed rat. C of D Banks was a likely rat. And it might not stop there. At this point, I didn't trust any cops not named Paul or Maggie. "We better do this alone."

"I understand. Bring it to my office as soon as you get it. We'll hash out how to go about getting the mayor neutralized."

"Got it. I'll see you there."

Paul sounded more exhausted than relieved. "Thanks, Juno."

I clicked off.

Maggie came up from behind and spoke in a quiet voice, not wanting Sasaki and Tipaldi to listen in from the kitchen. With all the lizard chatter coming from the cages, she didn't have to worry. "How long is this going to take?" she asked. "We have to get moving."

"It'll probably take Tip another ten or fifteen minutes to finish cleaning up. We'll hitch a ride back to Koba in Sasaki's flyer. We have plenty of time."

Maggie didn't look pleased about the idea of riding back with Sasaki and Tipaldi. "They didn't have to kill him."

"He was no use anymore."

Maggie shook her head disgustedly.

"What?" I said. "You really care what happens to a piece of trash like Mdoba?"

"It's you I'm worried about."

"What does that mean?"

"You act like this was no big deal. They fed a man's hands to a monitor for god's sake and you could care less."

"What do you think we did to that guy in Tenttown? And that bartender?"

"We didn't kill them."

"No. I just beat the shit out of them."

"I know," she said, and she covered her face with her hands. "That was wrong. I shouldn't have let you do it."

"If I hadn't done it, we'd still be wondering how our witness got killed right in front of us."

"This isn't why I became a cop, Juno. I wanted to do good."

"We are doing good, Maggie. We're going to stop a corrupt mayor."

She looked me in the eye. "But KOP is corrupt. You're corrupt. The chief's corrupt. And now I'm corrupt. What good does it do to stop a corrupt mayor when we're corrupt ourselves?"

"No. We're different from the mayor. The mayor's out for himself. He's conspiring with *slavers*."

"You and Chief Chang conspire with those animals in there. You really think you're better than the mayor?"

Her words cut right through me, the way the truth always did.

twenty-seven

IT was time to meet Malis. Maggie and I cruised through the city. I turned onto the Bangkok Street Strip. The street was still abuzz with late night action. Cars weaved helter-skelter with bikes zipping in between. Partiers rollicked in every direction, brandy glasses in hand. Signs interleaved so tightly over the narrow street that they created a neon ceiling. I parked at the end of the block rather than battle my way down the pedestrian-crowded street.

We stuck to the less crowded street center as we walked. Broken glass crunched under my shoes. Flashing neon stung my eyes. Doormen solicited offworld passersby with megaphone-amplified shouts of "First drink free" and "Live sex acts on-stage." My brain fizzed with overload.

The Club Dynasty doorwoman collected cover charges in full S&M regalia: monitor-hide skivvies and studded collar. She play-whipped customers through the door. I passed her a couple bills. She ran her whip up my thigh, stopping just short of my crotch. I ducked the hand she extended toward my temple. She moved for Maggie, touching the device attached to her fingertips to Maggie's temple, bombarding her brain with pornographic imagery. Maggie jerked away. I should've warned her.

Club Dynasty blared with eardrum-rattling dance beats. The dance floor was fogged over with O smoke. A small number of offworld men laid down dance moves with scads of Lagartan women who were wearing homemade miniskirts and cheap high heels. The women were battling for the affections of the offworld men. Hopes of finding an offworld suitor brought them out to the clubs with Cinderella dreams.

It didn't happen often, but it did happen. An offworld man would fall in love and take one of our women up to the orbiting castle in the sky. For her, it would be a dream come true. She'd never go hungry, and her life expectancy would be extended by a hundred years or more. But marrying an offworlder was rare. For most, the night would degenerate into a ruthless slut-off competition. The one who ground and teased the best would get to sleep with the offworlder, all but certain to be discarded the next morning.

We circled the dance floor, scoping tables for Malis. Discount perfume and opium smoke burned my throat. Maggie grabbed my elbow and pointed. Malis was in a wraparound booth surrounded by doped-up bar trash, passing an O pipe.

Maggie showed her shield to the group. Malis smiled and waved in drug-stupor stupidity. Higher-than-a-kite girlfriends cleared out and weaved to the dance floor. Maggie and I escorted Malis to the restrooms. There was a line at the women's. A steady stream of women was coming out with freshly poofed hair and water-doused shirts that clung to braless bods. We took her into the men's. The bathroom was empty except for two offworld men swapping stories at the sink. One modeled marbled skin that made him look like statue. The other was going with his everyday look—chiseled chin, sharp eyes, and a beguiling smile. A genetically enhanced ten. I badged them out.

Maggie seized Malis's bag.

Malis objected in a punch-drunk whine. "Heyyy, that'sss mmmine."

Maggie pulled the drawstring, reached in, and handed me the vid. I wrapped my hands around it like it was the Holy Grail. *The mayor's going down.*

"Youuu cccan't have that. It'sss mmmine."

I passed her the overstuffed money envelope.

Malis leaned into me, breasts first, looking for a new sugar daddy. "Hhhey, baby. You wwwant to ppparty? I'll show yyyou a good timmme."

Maggie pushed Malis away. "Let's go."

We moved back through the club. Maggie stopped. I looked over her shoulder. A badly dressed man had entered the club. I recognized him instantly—Carlos Simba. I grabbed hold of Maggie's elbow and led her across the dance floor. Gyrating bodies closed around us. We bumped our way through the sweaty mass to the other side and beelined for the back exit.

We dashed through the door. The alley dead-ended to the left. We sprinted right. An offworld car was parked at the end. I tried to stop and turn back. My ankle rolled over. I fell down hard. Maggie helped me up. The offworld car was emptying. Four figures were coming our way. We started trying doors— locked, locked, locked. Simba came out of the Club Dynasty door in front of two offworld heavies. I snatched the vid out of my shirt, scanned for a place to toss it out of their reach— nothing. Shit. Another door—locked! I clutched the vid to my chest. We were so close!

I kept my weight on the good ankle and faced the oncoming figures. They sashayed through ferns and alley trash with an offworld economy of movement. Maggie stayed next to me, putting a proud face over a terrified one.

There were seven of them all told. The offworld thugs didn't even bother to take our weapons. They knew how useless they'd be against offworld tech.

The seventh figure came face to face with me. Crime lord Carlos Simba said, "I'll take that."

My hands were viced onto the vid. *I should go for my gun. I might be able to kill Simba before they react. Or I could hostage him, use him to get us and the vid out of the alley.* Simba was staring me down, his hand held out for the vid. Offworlders surrounded us, clacking finger blades and flaunting brass knucks that emerged from under their skin. I calculated my chances—zero, zero, zero. I handed over the vid. I felt I was passing over KOP with it.

Simba tossed the vid over his shoulder. One of the thugs caught it and read the data with eye implants. "It's authentic," he said.

Simba stood in front of me—slicked hair, peaked forehead, and a poor-fitting store-cut suit that matched his man-of-the-people image. He was going to kill us. My legs went weak. I thought of Niki trying to go it alone and sank to my knees, my ankle wrenching uncomfortably under my weight.

Simba talked to Maggie. "Mayor Samir would like you to know that your deal is off. What good is an informant that chooses not to inform? He is very disappointed in you. You would be well advised to resign from the police. The mayor promises you nothing but shit duty as long as you stay. Consider yourself very lucky that we're not going to kill you."

Maggie didn't shrink from him. "Why not?"

"A dead cop with your family connections would complicate matters. There'd have to be an investigation, and that just doesn't fit into our plans at the moment."

Simba looked down at me.

I got to my feet, swallowing the ankle pain, summoning my emasculated self upright. *Kill me standing up.*

Simba roughly patted my cheek. It bordered on slapping. He didn't say a thing. He just turned around and walked down the alley, brushing through the ferns.

I yelled at his back. "Are you afraid to kill me yourself?"

His entourage of offworld goons turned to follow. They piled into the offworld vehicle and powered off, mysteriously leaving me alive.

twenty-eight

WE left the alley. I refused Maggie's help and limped. The ankle didn't feel broken, just a sprain. I tried calling Paul for the third time—no answer. I called his home. His wife, Pei, answered: no, she hadn't seen him; yes, he was still at the station; he must be in one of his meetings—that was why he wasn't answering.

Maggie said, "What do we do now?"

"We have to go see Paul. I have to talk to him." I started for the car.

"How did Simba know about the vid?"

I threw my hands up. How *did* he know?

Maggie grabbed my elbow. "Tipaldi."

I ran the possibility. The only people who knew about the particulars of the pickup were Sasaki, Tipaldi, Mdoba, Malis, and the two of us. Mdoba was dead, and Sasaki would never tell Simba. "You're right. It has to be Tipaldi." Unbelievable. Everything was going to shit. I half-stepped as fast as I could on the bad ankle. My heart raced dance beats as I hustled down the mossy sidewalk. "Tipaldi is the top strong-arm in the Bandur cartel. He has access to Bandur's books. If Simba flipped him, Bandur is going down—soon. I have to see Paul."

We covered the distance to the car in no time. We hopped in and raced to the station, not saying a single word on the way.

We left the car down the block and hurried into the station. Cops stopped what they were doing to watch as I half ran, half limped up the stairs. I felt a cop tug on my arm. "Not now," I said. I tore my arm loose from the grasp and my other arm was grabbed. Suddenly there were hands all over me. "What the fuck are you assholes doing? I have to talk to the chief!"

I heard Maggie protesting then I saw her on the floor, knocked down. I went berserk. I dug my feet into the floor. I couldn't feel the ankle pain. Cops reached for my legs, to pick them up. I kicked frantically, making contact with hands and shins until the first leg was seized, then the second.

I jerked violently against their hold as I looked back for Maggie and saw her at the end of the hall, some uniforms blocking her path. They took me into interrogation room two, threw me to the floor, and locked me in. I beat a chair on the floor until it came apart in my hands. Then a second one. I started on the table but ran out of steam before it broke. Three chairs left, I sat in one of the tall ones and waited.

This was it. The mayor had made his move. KOP was in his control. I wouldn't be stuck in here, detained by my fellow officers if it wasn't. I had to hope that Paul was still operating freely, finding a way to turn things around. The more I thought about it, the more sure I was that that was the case. Paul was one resourceful bastard. It would take a lot more than the fucking mayor to stop him. All I had to do was wait it out. Paul would spring me out of here, and Maggie and I would get back to work. We'd lost the vid, but we'd find other proof.

We made a good team, Maggie and I. She had a lot to learn, but she was sharp. She was right about there being little difference between Paul and the mayor, but it hadn't always been so. Paul *tried* to make a difference. It wasn't until he'd so clearly failed that he gave up and started looking out for himself. Who could blame him? How could anybody fix this place? The fact was he *did* try, which was more than I could say for myself. All I ever did was tag along.

Maggie was having a hard time picking the right side in this fight. I knew what side I was on. Paul was my friend.

The door opened—Gilkyson. He saw the broken chair and stepped out, coming back in a minute later with two well-built uniforms.

I turned on the smug. "What's wrong, Karl? You afraid of something?"

Gilkyson set a box on the table then sat in the short chair. What a dumb shit, sitting in that chair. When we'd grill somebody, we'd sit him in the short chair. It was a chair just like the others, but the legs were cut down by a few centimeters—made the suspect feel inferior having to look up at the interrogators.

He looked like a kid doing his homework at the kitchen table as he stretched uncomfortably to read a report he'd pulled out of his box. I draped my arms over the table, claiming its surface as my territory. Gilkyson was forced to stay back—out of my reach.

"Hello, Mr. Mozambe," he said.

"That's *Detective* Mozambe."

"Not anymore. You've been fired—effective immediately."

"On what grounds?"

"You've been fired for engaging in police corruption."

"You don't have the authority."

"You're right. I don't." He turned the report around for me. "Here is your termination report, signed by acting Chief of Police Banks. Paul Chang was removed from his position as chief of police. The mayor has appointed Diego Banks in his absence."

I told myself not to worry. Paul would figure out a way to get his job back. "You won't get away with this, Karl."

"We already have. He was escorted from the building a half hour ago.

Gilkyson pulled more goodies from his box. "Now Mr.

Mozambe, I have some propositions to discuss with you. I think you'll be interested in what I have to say."

I wanted to kick his self-righteous ass. "Talk."

"We've built a case against you. We know you take kick-backs from whorehouses and gambling dens."

"That's not true."

"I thought you might be resistant."

He started a vid. Holos of Bensaid and me at Bensaid's bar. Bensaid handed me a wad of money. We started arguing. Bensaid slammed his glass on the table. I walked out.

Next vid: Bensaid testifying against me.

Next vid: Me taking an envelope from a streetwalker in fishnets.

Next vid: Me taking a cut of the pool at a basement card game.

Next vid: Me shaking down a dope dealer, scoring some painkillers for Niki.

FUCK! FUCK! FUCK! "You can't do this!" I was up out of my chair, my finger in his face. The pair of uniforms lowered me into my seat.

Gilkyson talked over my head to the uniforms. "If he gets up again, cuff him." He lowered his gaze to me. "Please spare me your famous temper."

"What do you want?"

"I want your testimony."

"You expect me to testify against myself?"

"No. We want you to testify against Paul Chang."

This was why I was still alive. Simba let me live so they could use me to prosecute Paul. I wished he'd killed me. "No. I won't do it. I don't know anything."

"You were his partner twenty-five years ago. You're his best friend. You can't tell me you don't know anything about his activities."

"I don't know anything."

"You were there when he made his first big busts. In fact, you made them together. You know how he managed to rise so fast through KOP. You know all about his dealings with Ram Bandur and his son Ben. You know everything."

"I don't know what you're talking about. Paul Chang is a great cop."

"You'll tell us everything, or else . . ."

"I won't do it."

". . . we'll prosecute you. You'll go to jail. How long do cops survive in jail?"

"I can't testify against Paul. Do what you want to me. I'm no rat."

"Your misguided loyalty is almost touching, Mr. Mozambe. You leave us no option but to go after . . . let me see . . ." He checked his notes. "Natasha . . . is that her name? I understand she goes by Niki."

I couldn't speak.

"Her father was a drug dealer; right? She picked up some bad habits from him. I have a warrant here to search your home. Do you think we might find some illegal substances? If we find her in possession of anything illegal, it will carry a mandatory sentence, you know. Two to four years. How will she fare in prison?"

"The pills are mine. You've seen my hand. I need them for the pain."

"The warrant includes blood tests, Mr. Mozambe."

I lunged over the table. The cops responded with vice-grip holds on my arms. They had me back in my seat before I could touch him.

Gilkyson leaned back in his chair as he set a form in front of me, careful not to get too close. He marked an X. "This form is a testimony agreement. It states that you will testify against defendant Paul Chang in the case of the *People vs. Paul Chang*

on the charges of racketeering, corruption, conspiracy, and participating in a criminal enterprise."

FUCK! FUCK! FUCK!!! My body shook. *Paul's my friend. I
can't do it. I can't.* "You kicked him out of KOP. That's enough.
You don't need to prosecute him."

"I'm afraid we do."

"After all he's done for Lagarto, you're going to treat him
like this?"

"The man conspires with the most vile criminals in Lagartan history."

"I can't do it." My mouth was bone dry. I needed a drink.

"What's your answer, Mr. Mozambe?"

Sweat soaked my underarms. I felt sick. I had to piss. *I can't
sign.*

"Mr. Mozambe?"

We were so *close.* I held that vid in my hand. *What can I do,
Paul? I can't let Niki go to prison. I just can't.* I banged my head on
the table. . . .

I'm sorry, Paul. "W-what do I get for signing?"

"I always knew you were more reasonable than your reputa-
tion. I will bury the evidence against you. I will let you tear up
the warrant to search your home right now."

"You promise to leave me and Niki alone?"

"I promise. All we want is Paul Chang."

"I get my pension."

"That can be arranged. We'll let you retire instead of being
fired. How does that sound?"

What can I do, Paul? "Do you have a pen?"

Gilkyson had to hold my hand still while I moved my fingers
and signed by the X. He ran his scanner-hand over my signa-
ture, uploading it into the system.

⁜

They kept me locked up for another thirty minutes. I spent the time formulating a long-shot plan to save Paul. I had to redeem myself. They unlocked the door and ushered me out of the building before the silent stares of my former workmates. I was weaponless and badgeless. I wasn't a cop anymore.

I hit the street and was instantly drubbed by pouring rain. I called Paul. His holo materialized on the street, falling rain making his image blur. "Hold on, Juno." His holo froze on hold. Damn!

I made for the car, Paul's frozen holo floating alongside. I called Maggie. Her holo appeared on my other side, the three of us moving through the downpour. I blurted, "Where are you, Maggie?"

"I'm at the station. Where are you?"

"They just let me go. I'm on my way to the car."

"What happened? They wouldn't tell me anything. All I know is Chief Chang is out as chief, and C of D Banks is in charge. Nobody knows why."

"They're forcing me to testify against Paul."

"You agreed?"

"They have me dead to rights. They were going to arrest Niki."

"Niki? What for?"

"Never mind that. We can still pull this off, Maggie. I'm going to organize a raid of the spaceport."

"You're not a cop anymore, Juno."

"Paul and I still have loyal friends in KOP. They're not all rats. We'll find somebody to do it."

"What if it leaks back to Simba and the mayor?"

"We go anyway. We'll find something . . . we *have* to find something and find it fast, before the Bandur cartel crashes and the whole city comes under their control. Get all the paperwork together on the shipping orders. We'll need names, tracking numbers—anything related to Vanguard Supplies. I'll call you when we're ready to move."

We'd get proof of the slavery operation, proof of the mayor's involvement. Then they'd have to reinstate Paul. They'd let me recant my statement. I'd claim I signed it under duress.

I made it to the car and climbed inside. Holo-Paul passed through the passenger side door and took a seat. I waited impatiently until Holo-Paul finally unfroze. "Juno," he said.

"They're making me testify against you." I spat the words so fast that they were hardly intelligible.

"I heard."

"They were going to arrest Niki."

"I know, Juno. It's okay. You did what you had to do."

"I'm sorry, Paul. I didn't know what else to do."

"You had no choice. You're forgiven, okay?"

The knot in my gut began to loosen. "Thanks, Paul."

"Listen, Juno, you don't need to worry about this anymore. You're off the hook. Sasaki and I have it under control. We just made the decision to go to plan B while you were on hold."

"What's plan B?"

"We're going to take him out."

"What do you mean?"

"Mayor Samir. We're putting out a contract on him."

"Wait, Paul, there may be another way. Let Maggie and me raid the spaceport. We'll get you evidence of the slave trade."

"It's too late for that, Juno. We're going ahead and offing the bastard. He doesn't know who he's messing with." Holo-Paul smiled all chipper. I could picture Real-Paul's expression, closed fist, gritted teeth.

"Wait, let's talk about this first."

"The decision's already made, Juno."

"Dammit, Paul, let me handle this. I'll prove the mayor and Simba are running slaves. Once we get that proof, we'll be able to say that they trumped up the charges against you. We'll say we were probing into the slavery ring and the mayor fired you to kill the investigation. You'll come out smelling rosy."

"No. This way is better. You can't guarantee you'll get the evidence."

"Think it through, Paul. The mayor just fired you, and the next day the mayor shows up dead? Everybody will know you were behind it. You'll lose the public's support. Once that happens, you're finished."

Paul spoke with steely resolve. "He's taking KOP away from me, from *us*. I'm not going to let him get away with it."

"He already took it away. They're going to charge you with corruption. After you kill him, you think the new mayor's going to reappoint you?"

"If I lean on him hard enough, he will. I'll show him pics of his dead predecessor, and he'll learn to stay out of my way."

"You think you can intimidate the entire city?"

"If that's what it takes. We took over KOP, you and me. We can take over the mayor's office, too."

"You took over KOP because you wanted to make a difference. What do you want now?"

After an annoyed sigh, he said, "That was a long time ago. I was a fool to think I could change anything. Lagarto can't be helped, you know that."

I paused for a few seconds, arranging the words in my head. "You know what your problem is, Paul? You always think too big. Maybe saving the planet is beyond your reach, but you have it in your power to stop the slavery ring. As we speak, Simba's people are trolling Tenttown, buying up kids."

"What difference would it make if we did stop Simba? Another slavery ring would just take its place."

"Yeah, but until it did, think about all the kids that would've been saved. It would make a difference to *them*." I took a deep breath. "Listen to me, Paul, if you kill the mayor you won't get KOP back. Call off the hit, and we'll talk it out. Where are you?"

"I'm at Bandur's."

"I'm coming over." I started the car and steered for the Bandur place. "Tell me you won't do anything until we talk."

I felt encouraged when Paul didn't respond immediately. He was thinking it over. I was getting through. "You know I'm right," I said.

"Okay, Juno. We'll talk first."

"Is Tipaldi there?"

"Yeah, he's around here somewhere."

"Watch out for him, Paul. He's with Simba."

"You sure?"

"Hundred percent."

"Okay, Juno. I gotta go."

I gunned the gas.

twenty-nine

I SWUNG the car onto Bandur's street. I knew that if I could just keep Paul from killing the mayor, we could turn it all around. It wasn't too late.

I left the car running, jumped out into monsoon rain, and rushed up the walk past shrub animals that accused me, the mayor's turncoat witness, with still stares. Bandur's door swung open of its own accord. The home system's voice welcomed me and told me to go to the lounge. I skidded over the stone floor with wet shoes, my twisted ankle making me slide all the more. The lounge door moved aside for me.

The lounge was decorated with recessed lighting and space furniture. Tip Tipaldi came my way.

I met him nose to nose. "You're a traitor. You told Simba about the vid of the mayor."

Tipaldi thumped me in the stomach. I keeled over into a fetal ball, gulping for oxygen. I rolled on the lounge floor, Tipaldi's spit-shined shoes at eye level.

I gasped, "I have to talk to Paul."

A voice sounded from the far side of the room. "You're too late, Juno. You missed him."

I looked around, but couldn't see the source of the voice from my floored perspective. A pair of scuffed shoes with mismatched socks walked out from behind the bar—Simba. A second pair followed, imported leather—mayor. NO!

I looked up to see the two of them standing in front of me.

The smell of recent lase-fire registered in my nose. *Oh god, no.* It couldn't be. Paul was still alive. He would still pull through this one. He'd been down before, but he'd always wound up on top. He was too smart to let this happen. He was too damn smart.

The mayor spoke with a politician's rehearsed tone. "Sorry we can't talk. We're on our way out. We'll be placing our anonymous call in ten minutes, so you won't want to dillydally."

I watched the three of them leave, Tipaldi carrying a box brimming with tech equipment—Bandur's books.

I called out for Paul, knowing there'd be no response. "Paul!" My stomach felt like it had collapsed in on itself. I took deep breaths to keep from vomiting. I crawled on all fours, my arms and legs shaking. I made it to the bar and took a look behind. Matsuo Sasaki and Ben Bandur were lying on the tiled floor, one blackened hole in the back of each head. They'd been done from a kneeling position—execution style.

I grabbed a bar stool and pulled myself up. Music was playing—some kitschy lounge tune.

"Paul! Where are you? Paul?"

I saw him. I went to him, crossing the room on wobbly legs. I said to him, "I'm sorry." He didn't answer. He was sitting in an egg-shaped chair that floated over the floor, lase-pistol in his mouth, his brains slagged across the eggshell back of the chair.

I was home, on my sofa, watching the report for what must be the tenth time—Jessie Khalil on the street holding an umbrella, her hair sprinkled with just the perfect amount of rain. Her hair was wet enough to show how she was toughing it out in the elements to bring us the story, yet not so wet that her salon 'do lost shape.

"I am here at the home of Benazir Bandur, son of the deceased Ram Bandur reputed crime boss."

<A holo of Ram Bandur came to the foreground.>

"His son Benazir . . . "

<Father and son together. >

". . . has denied any involvement in criminal enterprises. A denial that is now proved unequivocally false."

<Cut back to Jessie Khalil. >

"It was early this morning that police were given an anonymous call stating that a shooting had occurred on these premises. It is believed that the call came from somebody on the house staff. When police arrived on the scene, they were confronted with a story so shocking that—"

Niki came out of the bedroom. She slept late this morning—pain-pill hangover. "Why didn't you come to bed?"

I didn't answer.

<Cut to Paul Chang in his formal uniform, addressing the graduating class from the academy.>

I made room for Niki on the couch.

Jessie Khalil reported on. ". . . Koba's honored police chief for the past ten years was removed from office by Mayor Samir. Last night, the mayor's office announced that it was going to file an indictment this morning formally charging Chief Chang with multiple counts of racketeering and conspiracy."

<Cut to Karl Gilkyson talking on the City Hall steps.>

"As you all know, Mayor Samir has made the elimination of corruption in the Koba Office of Police his highest priority since he was elected. We are prepared to take the first step in that direction by filing charges against former Chief of Police Paul Chang, who we allege is guilty of racketeering, corruption, conspiracy, and participating in a criminal enterprise. Former Chief Chang was relieved of his duties immediately when we secured our key piece of evidence, the testimony of police informant Juno Mozambe. Detective Mozambe and Chief Chang were partners many years ago, and Detective Mozambe is set to testify in court against his former boss."

Niki's hand slid over to hold mine.

<Cut back to Jessie Khalil.>

"In a bizarre twist, those charges will no longer need to be filed. Based on the initial findings of the Koba Office of Police, it appears that former Chief Chang came to the home of Benazir Bandur and killed both him and his associate, Matsuo Sasaki, before turning the weapon on himself."

Niki's fingernails dug into my palm.

Jessie Khalil rattled on. "Here's acting Chief of Police Diego Banks."

<Cut to Diego Banks.>

"Our initial findings indicate a murder/suicide. It has come as a total shock to me personally as well as to so many of our finest officers that Chief of Police Paul Chang was conspiring with Benazir Bandur, one of our city's most despicable criminals. It appears that Chief Chang was enraged upon learning of his impending indictment, and he took out his anger on the criminals who had led him down this path. He came to this residence and murdered both Benazir Bandur and Matsuo Sasaki. Uncertain of his imminent life in prison, he sadly took his own life."

<Cut back to Jessie Khalil.>

"The mayor is expected to make a statement later this morning, so be sure to stay with us. We will continue to bring you updates as soon as we have them. This is Jessie Khalil reporting for Lagarto Libre."

Niki rested her head on my shoulder. I ran my fingers through her hair. I felt her tears on my neck. For me, the tears wouldn't come. I squeezed a data chip in my hand and thought about the job I had to do.

thirty

I SAT on the roof of my house, watching the stars as lizards skittered around, soaking up the night sky with me. I took a hit of brandy straight from the bottle. The alcohol did a pretty good job of numbing me. I'd try to quit tomorrow; maybe I'd feel better.

I raised the bottle to Paul. Sorry, old friend. I should have known. Prosecuting Paul would have been ugly. He'd known too many people who could've created problems for Simba and the mayor. The corruption investigation was just a cover. They were planning to murder Paul all the while and sell it to the public as a suicide. They set me up. They used me to give their murder/suicide story credence. I was their tool, the pawn in a scheme to take over KOP and the Bandur organization. It played perfect in the news: Chief Chang had been angry and depressed; he'd just gotten fired; he'd been on his way to jail. The clincher: his old partner was going to squeal on him.

The stars glistened tonight, clear skies and a cool breeze. Tonight was the night. Maggie thought we should all be together. She'd invited Abdul, Niki, and me over to get a chance to see her new place. I'd told her no, not tonight. Tonight, I wanted to get drunk. Tomorrow, I'd be retired for good—just me and Niki from here on out. Nothing to do but sit back and watch the havoc I'd created these past months. . . .

I'd gone to Paul's house immediately after finding his body. I got a one-hour shoulder soak from Paul's wife when I broke the news to her. She was worried about their youngest son. "He's only a teenager; he needs a father." I stayed with her until her sisters arrived.

Before I left, I had Pei open Paul's safe. I took the data chip, Paul's copy of Bandur's books. It was part of the original deal struck between Paul and Ram Bandur. They had open access to each other's activities. It was the only way they thought they could trust each other. Nobody knew about the copy besides Paul, Bandur, Sasaki, and me. Now I was the only one left.

I paid out three months' worth of collection money for a hot computer system. I didn't want to rent time on the Orbital's systems because one of their surveillance worms could've sniffed out my activity. I bought the system off an old fence I used to collect from. The hump knew I'd lost my badge and jacked up the price on me. He gave me some shit about the shoe being on the other foot.

I spent three days scrolling through records, looking for anything that I could use against Simba, the mayor, or Nguyen. I wanted them all to pay for what they did to Paul . . . what they did to me.

Three days of brandy-swilling eyestrain passed before a name caught my eye—Manuel Hidalgo: trained engineer with a drug habit and gambling debts over six figures. I checked his background. He was once part of a public relations program instituted by one of the offworld shipping companies to employ Lagartans on their freighters. He flew for seven years before his O habit got out of hand, and he was cut loose.

I tailed Hidalgo for a week. He was turning tricks for five hundred a romp. He was being pimped by one of Bandur's people who now reported to Koba's new crime boss—Carlos Simba.

Hidalgo wasn't seeing any profit from his skin sales. Every peso went toward his gambling debt. According to the books, they were steadily raising his interest rate. After four years of back-alley blow jobs, he'd only reduced the debt by three percent. He'd be so old by the time he paid it off, he'd be gumming cock.

I thought he might be perfect for my plans. I evaluated his abilities: He couldn't afford to pay for O anymore, but instead of turning to glue huffing he'd kicked the habit—promising. He was overcharging his tricks and pocketing the difference, hiding the cash in the hollowed-out heels of his pumps—clever. He was taking a big risk by shorting a pimp. It was considered a capital offense—gutsy. One word summation: *potential.*

Niki, Abdul, Maggie, and I finished off the paella. I poured just half a glass of brandy for myself. I was getting to the point where I could half-glass my way through a bottle in no time. I wasn't the only one; Abdul was keeping pace. It was taking a two-drink minimum for either of us to forget feeling sorry for ourselves and get conversation turned to the good times we'd had with Paul. Maggie was the willing listener, our excuse to tell the stories one more time. "You ever heard about the time Paul . . . ?" Niki laughed at the right times, as if it were the first time she'd heard any of the stories.

Maggie turned the discussion serious. "I've been going through the missing persons files. I came up with seven more likely slaves. That makes thirty-six so far."

Abdul said, "You have to stop nosing around, Maggie. Somebody's going to notice."

"I can't just do nothing. They're running slaves and they're getting away with it. Doesn't that upset you?"

"Not as much as seeing you get killed."

"What else am I supposed to do? The mayor has it in for me. Chief Banks won't let me do any important work. Now he has me doing background checks on academy applicants. And that's in addition to the traffic violations work he's got me on. Their strategy to make me quit is becoming abundantly clear. They're loading me up with so much work that I can't possibly keep up, and then they're going to start filing dereliction-of-duty reprimands on me. I can't stand doing goddamned busy-work."

Maggie ran her hands through the hair behind her ears and talked directly to me. "When are you going to help me take over KOP?"

Niki's hand moved under the table to my knee and squeezed, signaling a tug of the leash. I was happy to comply. "It can't be done."

"Why not?"

"It just can't."

Maggie asked Abdul the same question. "Why not?"

Abdul looked at me. "Yeah, Juno. Why not?" The two of them were ganging up, applying the pressure.

My brandy was getting low. I added a dash to my glass. "First of all, you're a woman. KOP has never even had a woman captain much less a woman chief. Second, you're not ruthless enough. You have to be vicious. You don't have it in you."

"That's why I need you."

I couldn't say, "I'm not vicious anymore." Not with the scheme I was planning. If went through with it, I'd reach new heights of ruthlessness and viciousness. I couldn't let myself worry about the moral implications. I was on a mission—destroy the six of them: Mayor Samir, Chief Banks, Carlos Simba, Mai Nguyen, and double-crossers Tip Tipaldi and Yuan Kim. They had to pay for what they did to Paul. They had to pay for using me. They especially had to pay for underestimating me by leaving me alive. There was no time to help Maggie. She'd have to take care of herself.

I said, "If you're so bored at KOP, I have a job for you."

Maggie looked skeptical, "What's that?"

"I need financial workups on Simba, Nguyen, and Chief Banks."

"What for?"

"I don't want to say. Can you do it?"

Maggie tried to bargain with me. "You have to agree to help me first."

"You don't want me. You said you want to do it clean. You've got the wrong guy."

"I have the right guy. You can be rehabilitated." She said the last part with a smirk.

Abdul laughed aloud. Niki joined in. Abdul and Niki were right. There was no hope for me. I was a real bastard; that was all there was to it. There was no way I could ever redeem myself for the things I'd done. I couldn't get caught up in Maggie's dreams for a better Lagarto. I'd already tried to make Paul's dreams for Lagarto come true, and Lagarto was no better off. Once my scores were settled, I was going to try harder to make Niki's dreams of a normal life come true. There was still time with Niki.

"I can't do it, Maggie."

She relented. "What kind of financial information do you need?"

"I need to know the worth of their assets, cash flow—anything you can get your hands on."

While I waited for the financial workups, I had time to get one name crossed off my list.

I knocked back an entire bottle waiting outside Yuan Kim's place until the early AM. The house used to belong to his father, Chen. He'd passed it on to Kim when he'd retired from the force and moved out of the city. It was a middle-to-upper class neighborhood. Most yards were jungle-trimmed immaculate.

I watched his door through the prickly leaves of a shrub. I swatted mosquitoes to pass the time. I didn't wear bug spray. I didn't want some passerby picking up my scent. Bites covered my hands and neck. I must've lost a liter of blood. I drank brandy as an itch reducer, an orally ingested calamine lotion. No sign of Kim. He still hadn't come home—must've found somebody to service the snake tonight.

I needed to get moving before people started to wake up. I crawled out of the bushes and crept up to the house. Both doors were locked. I decided on a window entry. The basement window looked like the best bet—low to the ground, plenty of jungle cover.

I worked at the lock for a while. Fuck it, I just broke the glass. I used a broomstick handle that I'd brought with me to knock the glass out and beat away the sharp edges. I climbed through, dropping my hand into a lizard's nest. I got nipped, but luckily it didn't break the skin—didn't want to leave any blood evidence behind. I bumped around in the dark, sloshing through ankle-deep floodwater until I found the staircase and moved up into the bedroom.

I took the broomstick handle and taped it to my right arm. It was a perfect fit. I had prepped it by cutting it down to arm length. It was now attached to the outside of my arm, running from my shoulder to the back of my hand. I'd wrapped the tape extra tight around my hand, so it couldn't move—left just my fingers free, so they could grasp my piece's handle. I placed the gun in my hand. It held rock solid. I couldn't sight for shit—wouldn't matter. I'd take him at close range.

I sat on his bed, my hand tingling from the lack of circulation and mosquito bites. I heard keys jangling in the front lock. I got into position, standing in the door frame. When he rounded that corner, he'd just about run into me. I relaxed my body—just wait. I tuned into the sounds of Yuan Kim making

his way around the house. My entire body sizzled with anticipation. He was in the kitchen. That was the fridge opening and
closing. He'd be coming soon—keep breathing, nice and slow.

He came around the corner, unbuttoning his shirt. I took
care of business with two shots—the first in the chest to bring
him down, the second to the head. No "This is for Paul, you
cocksucker." No "Get on your knees and beg." None of that
bullshit. When you got a job to do, you do it—no room for ego.
Make it quick and simple—no complications.

I stripped the tape from my arm with a hair-ripping jerk.
Kim's glasses were on the floor. I pulled my shirtsleeve over my
hand, picked them up, and placed them on what was left of his
fried head. I stuck them to the peak of his nose, so they
wouldn't slide down.

The sun was up already. I sat back on the bed. It was too risky
to leave now. I'd have to wait five hours for nightfall. It was
Kim's day off; hopefully nobody would come looking for him.

The smell ripened fast. I rubbed a peppermint leaf paste onto
my upper lip. The menthol odor did a fair job of masking—
made it bearable. Lizards flocked up from the basement and
down from the attic. Flies gathered outside the windows, bumping the glass, probing for an opening.

The phone rang a few times, but nobody came. Generations
of flies hatched, fed, and swarmed around the house. The
lizards eventually moved on, heavy stomachs dragging on the
carpet. I raided his liquor cabinet, waited until the deep dark,
and then I stepped over his remains and left the same way I'd
come in.

Just like old times.

Time to get my other plans rolling.

The room had an hourly rate, but I'd gone ahead and paid
for the whole night. I lay sideways on the hotel bed with a

rolled up a towel as a headrest. I didn't want to touch the pillows. They were crawling with brown bugs. I didn't even know
what those things were. What a fucking hole this place was. It
was the kind of place you'd go when anonymity was more important than amenities.

I was staring at the ceiling, well aware of the phone that sat
within my reach. All I had to do was call.

A shiver of doubt ran through my mind. I was so sure a couple days ago. Killing Kim was easy. He deserved it. This was different. This involved innocents. Niki told me it was okay to go
through with it. I could stop the slavery ring. It would be for
the greater good. She was right, though I wasn't naïve enough
to believe that slavery would stop. But I could cripple the trade
for years, maybe decades.

I sat up. Four hits of brandy brought my nerve back. I
couldn't worry about the guilt. You either have guilt or you
don't. I already had it. It wasn't a cumulative thing. One more
destroyed soul wouldn't make a difference.

I made the call.

A holo of Manuel Hidalgo's pimp appeared in the hotel
room.

I asked for a male, straight hair, light complexion.

A half hour later, Hidalgo was at the door, secret-
compartment pumps strapped to clean-shaven legs, miniskirt
cut to skivvy-showing height, and at least two weeks of geo-
logical makeup applied layer over previous layer. He pranced
in and lisped. "You pay up front, five hundred pesos."

I pulled out forty thousand, set it out on the bed for him to
see. I let my right show in full shaking glory.

"Look who's the rich boy. Are you trying to impress me?"
His S's whistled.

I added another forty thousand to the pile.

"What's going on here? Who are you?"

"I'm your savior. Do you really talk like that?"

"No."

"Then cut it out. How much do you owe?"

"Who are y—"

I slugged him in the gut. The air burst out of his lungs. A kick took his legs out, and he thudded to the floor. His wig fell off, landing like a dead cat. He tried to roll away. I grabbed him by the hair and shoved the wig in his mouth.

"You listen to me, asshole! You work for me now. You will *never* ask me any questions, and when I ask you a question, I expect an answer. Do you understand?"

He was sucking air through his nose. I pinched it shut. "Do you understand?"

He nodded, his nose tugging at my wobbly hand.

I let go and yanked the wig out; saliva strands clung to the synthetic hair. "How much do you owe?"

"Hundred and ninety thousand." Lispless.

"I have eighty thousand on the bed there. It's yours."

He nodded again, confused.

"Here's what you're going to do. You will pay off your debts using that money as a first payment. You will not gamble with any of my money. You will quit prostitution, and you will absolutely *not* go back to doping. Do you understand?"

"Why?"

"No questions!" I slapped him hard. He yelped. I slapped him again. I said, "Do you understand?" He was guarding his face with his hands now, peeking at me through his fingers. "Do you understand?" My voice was insistent.

"No," he said with a whimper. "I don't understand, and that wasn't a question."

"You're right," I said with a leer. "That wasn't a question. What don't you understand?"

He spoke slowly, choosing his words carefully, trying to avoid any semblance of a question. "I don't understand what I'd have to do to earn that money."

"Here's what you have to do," I said. "You have to go to the spaceport tomorrow morning and apply for a job with a new company called Lagarto Lines. They have a freighter to crew and you will offer your services as an engineer. You can do that can't you?"

"I don't know. I guess so."

"Don't tell me you don't know. Tell me you understand. Tell me you *will* do it."

He was slow in answering. His eyes moved back and forth between me and the money. I saw the way he looked at the money. I had him. I just had to wait him out. He studied me. He studied the money. I kept waiting. Finally, he said, "I'll do it."

"If your bookie asks you where you got the money, you will tell him you stole it from one of your tricks."

"Okay."

I nodded. "You better be smart enough to realize that this is the best day of your life. You do as I say, and your debt will disappear."

"If I don't?"

I stomped on his hand. "No questions!"

He screamed. He held his damaged hand up in the air. One finger stood badly out of whack.

I whispered in his ear. "I'll be watching you." Then I walked out.

Maggie, Abdul, and I pored over the financials, an exhaustive workup on their assets and liabilities. Niki brought in tea every few hours. Spreadsheets and loan documents floated all over the room. Maggie ran computer analyses and hypotheticals on the numbers. Abdul hmmphed and uh-huhed through the

"Yes." He handed me a data chip. "I put the schematics you wanted in there, too."

"Excellent. Go now."

Hidalgo hung around like a puppy waiting for a pat on the head.

"Go," I said.

He skulked away, thoroughly dominated. I waited until he was out of sight then stalked down to the riverbank and unmoored a rented skiff. I steered for open water, the motor putt-putting along. One step closer to my vengeance. I couldn't erase the wicked smile on my face.

I gave the chip to Abdul and Maggie. They spent the next three weeks researching the nets, looking for optimal "camera" placements. When they returned the ship schematics to me, there were five red circles marking the spots. Their mood was somber. I had to keep reminding them—greater good.

Two more weeks passed before the time came to end my relationship with Manuel Hidalgo. I told him to come to Afrie's.

I waited for him at a table, sipping my brandy, working up the courage to take the last step. I watched Hidalgo come in and sit down at the bar. He was dressed proper, sporting new duds and a stylish hat—no more cast on his hand. He'd gone from screwing johns to squarejohn in no time. I got up from my table and brushed by him on my way to the bathroom. He joined me a minute later.

"You've done well, Hidalgo."

"Thank you."

"You've exceeded my expectations these past few months. I have good news for you. There is only one more thing for you to do. I have no doubt that you can handle it. When you've

performed this task, I will release you from our agreement—
all debts paid. How does that sound?"

He looked disappointed. He was so hooked on playing spy
that he was sad it was coming to a close.

"Take this bag. In it, you'll find five cameras and a blueprint
of the ship. The blueprint is marked to show you where I want
you to place the cameras. The placements I chose don't offer
the best vantage points, but they are in out of the way places,
so you should be able to escape detection. The cameras are already recording. All you have to do is put them in place and
then leave them alone."

"Do I need to retrieve them?"

"No, they'll beam a signal back on their own."

"Got it. I can do it; you'll see."

"I know you'll succeed. When I start receiving the feed, I'll
transfer the money into your account."

"Okay. Thanks." He looked like he had more to say.

"Spit it out."

"Can I ask a question?"

I nodded. He'd earned it.

"You work for the government, don't you?"

"I can't answer that, Manuel."

"You're going to expose the slave trade. I can help. I can testify."

"I won't let you testify. It would be too dangerous. You've done
enough for your people. Now take the bag and get out of here."

The instant he walked out my enforcer juices ran frigid. It
was done. Lagarto was about to begin its spiral into chaos.

I spent the rest of the night at the bar, trying to warm my
soul with a brandy bottle. . . .

From my rooftop, I watched the Orbital cross the sky. It passed
through constellations, drawing an arc across the heavens.

I peeked at my watch. Carlos Simba's solitary ship would be braking into our atmosphere in just a few minutes. I toasted Manuel Hidalgo again. Shit—bottle was empty. Niki padded across the roof. She'd set the alarm to wake her up in time to catch the show. She sat next to me, our feet touching.

"Do you think I did the right thing?" I asked.

Niki moved in close. "Does it matter?"

Not anymore it didn't. I'd had Abdul rig the cameras. He'd taken out the guts and replaced them with explosives, nothing too powerful, but enough to ignite the fuel tanks. He'd set the timers for reentry. Let friction burn up the evidence.

I wished there had been a way to save Hidalgo. He'd salvaged a good life for himself. I'd gone through it over and over, but just couldn't take the risk of him blabbing. He just wasn't stable. If I could flip him, so could somebody else. There couldn't be any ties back to me. I wasn't ready to risk my life or those of Niki, Maggie, and Abdul over him. Call me a coward if you want. I'd just add it to the list of my sins.

Greater good. It was a powerful argument, enough to convince Maggie and Abdul, but I knew it wasn't my main justification. They killed Paul. That was all the reason I needed.

I looked at my watch—started wearing it on my left.

Any second now . . .

There! A shooting star.

about the author

A former schoolteacher, Warren Hammond now works as an instructor in the computer industry. Over the past thirteen years, thousands of information-technology professionals have attended his classes. An avid traveler, he and his wife have trekked the Himalayas, hiked the Inca Trail, explored the Galapagos Islands, gone camping in the game reserves of Botswana, and toured the temples of Angkor Wat. In addition to writing *KOP*, he has also written *EX-KOP*, the second book of the series. Born and raised in upstate New York, he currently lives in Denver with his wife and two cats.